Praise for the novels of Wendy Francis

"Wendy Francis captures all the joy and pain of being an (almost) empty-nester in her latest novel. Picture a college graduation weekend on a lovely New England campus. Now mix in some booze, an ex or two, the in-laws, a trophy wife, and loads of secrets/scandals. Soon enough, no one is behaving at their best. A terrific summer read."

—Amy Poeppel, author of *Small Admissions*, on *Best Behavior*

"A delightful, smartly paced read… Francis writes with grace, depth and humor about complex family dynamics and the joy and heartache of watching young adults spread their wings and fly from the nest."

—Meg Mitchell Moore, author of *The Islanders*, on *Best Behavior*

"Wendy Francis's book thrilled me like a ride in a race car along the coast with the top down. It is everything a summer read should be."

—Elin Hilderbrand, *New York Times* bestselling author of *Summer of '69*, on *The Summer of Good Intentions*

"Francis illustrates with charm and insight the drama and love of friendship and sisterhood, realistically portrayed through relatable and likable characters. A great summer read for fans of Jennifer Weiner and Emily Giffin."

—*Library Journal* on *The Summer Sail*

"*The Summer of Good Intentions* is a tender and vivid portrait of a family by the sea, of three unforgettable sisters and the tidal pull of their love and secrets. Wendy Francis is a wonderful writer. She made me feel the salt air."

—Luanne Rice, *New York Times* bestselling author

"The setting of this enjoyable novel is enticing, and the tone is breezy. A sure bet for your summer beach-reads list. Recommend this one to fans of Elin Hilderbrand and Anne Rivers Siddons."

—*Booklist* on *The Summer Sail*

"Filled with the sweet briny air of Cape Cod, this extraordinary tale shows that, together, we can weather all the seasons of life."

—Patti Callahan Henry, *New York Times* bestselling author, on *The Summer of Good Intentions*

Also by Wendy Francis

Three Good Things
The Summer of Good Intentions
The Summer Sail

BEST BEHAVIOR

WENDY FRANCIS

GRAYDON
HOUSE

GRAYDON
HOUSE®

Recycling programs
for this product may
not exist in your area.

ISBN-13: 978-1-525-80462-5

Best Behavior

Copyright © 2020 by Wendy Francis

Quote from "Parents Are The Real Graduates" by Erma Bombeck printed with permission
from the estate of Erma Bombeck.

This edition published by arrangement with Harlequin Books S.A.

Graydon House
22 Adelaide St. West, 40th Floor
Toronto, Ontario M5H 4E3, Canada
www.GraydonHouseBooks.com
www.BookClubbish.com

Printed in U.S.A.

For Eva Kay

"Graduation day is tough for adults. They go to the ceremony as parents. They come home as contemporaries. After twenty-two years of child-raising, they are unemployed."

—Erma Bombeck

ONE

On Thursday morning, the temperature outside is seventy-one degrees and climbing while Meredith Parker considers which of a thousand recommended places she would like to visit before she dies. Not that she's anticipating dying anytime soon, but she needs a distraction. She figures she has already seen at least a handful—Yosemite (breathtaking, as advertised), Niagara Falls (overrated, in her opinion—and *cold*), and San Francisco (lovely, with a charming, hippie vibe). It's the exotic locales that have eluded her over the past forty-six years, places like Tahiti or Rome or the Swiss Alps. Although, come to think of it, Meredith doesn't really care for skiing, so she can probably cross the Alps right off her list. But Rome would be nice—all that history and pasta—and wine! A cheap fare must be available on one of those best-deal websites, if she searches long enough. Yes, she's fairly certain she can persuade her husband, Joel, that Rome should be their first-ever international destination, the new green pin on their *Where Have You Been?* map that hangs on the wall in the den. That is, of course, once the kids have settled into their new homes.

And with the thought of her children's imminent departure, Meredith's throat tightens. *What's the use?* she thinks. No number of mental hijinks will make her forget the real purpose of today's trip. She, Joel, and her mother, Carol, are tracing the familiar route up from New Haven to Boston, as they have dozens of times before, the trees beyond the window zipping by in a curtain of emerald green.

But this weekend will be different.

Because this weekend marks the twins' college graduation, an event that seemed impossibly far away only a few years ago, even a few months ago. Tomorrow her babies, the ones she used to cradle in each arm, will accept their hard-earned diplomas and officially step out into the great wide beyond, otherwise known as Adult Life.

Last night, when she'd gone to her neighborhood book club, the room had been abuzz with excitement over the upcoming weekend. "You must be bursting with pride!" her friend Lauren exclaimed. "I can't believe that Cody and Dawn are already graduating. It's so exciting." And Meredith had nodded, as if she, too, were in a state of shock over this improbable fact.

It's true that she couldn't be prouder of the twins, but the moment is bittersweet. Soon, Cody will be off to Bismarck, North Dakota, to teach high school history, and Dawn is headed to Chicago to work at an advertising firm. Her kids will be so far away, they might as well be moving to Bangkok. Even though she knows it's irrational, Meredith is racked by the feeling that after this summer she might never see her children again.

Admittedly, she is at a corner, or more specifically, at a crossroads in her life. Images of a two-year-old, chubby Cody racing into her arms or of a young Dawn asking for "one more good-night tuck-in" swim through her mind. She can still feel those small arms wrapped tightly around her, the love so palpable she used to think her heart would leap from her chest to theirs. How is it possible that her babies are graduating from college this weekend?

With Lauren's comment, Meredith had cast her gaze around the book group (who, truth be told, rarely ever discussed the book at hand) and realized with a start that the difference between her own life and that of her friends suddenly stretched before her like a giant yawning chasm: Meredith was about to say goodbye to her kids once and for all, while her neighbors still had years of child-raising ahead of them.

Lauren had offered her an affectionate pat on the shoulder, as if she could read Meredith's thoughts, and handed over a generous pour of chardonnay, which Meredith accepted gratefully. Maybe, she allowed herself to consider, Lauren was right. Maybe the graduation weekend *would* be exciting, as pleasing as a perfectly folded fitted sheet. Tuck this person into that corner, that person over there, *smooth it, smooth it*, and everyone would get along swimmingly.

Given her patched-together, hybrid family, though, Meredith sincerely doubts it. Her ex-husband, Roger, will be bringing Lily, his new wife of six months. And as fine as Meredith is with *the idea* of Roger's remarrying after all these years, his new marriage somehow feels forced, as if he has just purchased a new set of golf clubs that he's eager to show off to the rest of the family.

"I know. It's crazy, right?" Meredith had managed to get out after swallowing her wine. "The twins are officially all grown up."

Lauren, a corporate attorney, has two young girls, six and eight, whom Meredith adores and dreams of kidnapping one day. (She tells herself it wouldn't really be kidnapping, though, since they're all neighbors, and obviously she would do Lauren the courtesy of asking before moving the girls into her own home.) As it is, she helps out with the girls whenever she can, usually after school when Lauren works late and Meredith is already back from her shift in the NICU. The girls have her pegged for a softy and know full well that she will buy them ice cream, bake chocolate chip cookies on a whim, and watch every terrible mermaid movie that's available for streaming. They call her "Auntie," which makes her heart swell and break simultaneously.

Some days she wishes she and Joel had tried for their own children way back when, even though the timing was off—they didn't meet till Meredith was in her late thirties—and there would have been a considerable age gap, more than a decade, between a new baby and the twins. But at least she would still hear young voices in the house, would have someone to ferry to ballet practice or help with a book report. As exhausting as it could be some days (that Taj Mahal built out of marshmallows for fifth grade nearly killed her), she misses the maternal responsibilities she was once counted on for, feels the lack like an unfamiliar brittleness settling into her bones.

Theoretically, she understands that the twins flew the coop four years ago when they left for college. But that was different. The kids continued to call every Sunday night, and she and Joel could drop by on the odd weekend. Luckily, both children had decided on the same college in Boston, making spur-of-the-moment visits ridiculously convenient. But traveling so far away for jobs where she might see them only once or twice a year for Thanksgiving and Christmas? She honestly doesn't know how—or if—she can handle it.

Thankfully, no matter what faults she and her ex-husband, Roger, might have had as a couple, their kids have turned out all right—better than all right—and Meredith lets herself relax slightly with this thought now. Dawn, hands down her most difficult child during the teenage years, has blossomed into a bright young woman. Gone are the days when Meredith's every comment would prompt an eye roll from her daughter. And despite an unfortunate hiccup with the Administrative Board last year, Dawn has managed to pull off graduating with honors. Meanwhile, Cody (Meredith's lips part into a smile when she imagines him striding across the stage in his gown) is graduating Phi Beta Kappa. Not only that, but he set the school record for all-time rushing yards this fall, leading his football team to their best season in fifteen years. Cody has become a rock star on his small New England campus, and as his mother, Meredith can't help but feel a bit smug. After all, she was the one who whipped up protein shake after protein shake and lugged him to hundreds of high school practices. She was the one who allowed her lovely den to be transformed into a weight room filled with smelly sneakers and barbells for four years.

If she knows one thing deep in her bones, it's that she is a good mom, one who has raised hardworking, resilient children. She imagines holding her breath as they parade across Bolton's commencement stage, much as she did when they took their first ungainly steps across the kitchen floor, Cody wheeling ahead in wide, determined strides and Dawn following a few paces behind, her tongue twisted into a tight coil of determination. Meredith is enormously proud of them, and, quite honestly, of herself. She didn't abandon her kids like Roger did, when he'd seen fit to put his penis where it didn't belong. But that was nearly ten years ago, water under the bridge—more of a tepid stream wandering through her mind these days than a charging river.

She drums her fingers on the armrest as the car hurtles forward. How many times have she and Joel driven up to school for the kids' sporting events or to treat them to dinner? Certainly more than she can count. On the rare occasion, her mother, Carol, will also pack herself into the car to say hello to her grandchildren. Now her mom sits in the back seat, her hands wrapped tightly around a beaded purse, which Meredith knows carries two envelopes thick with cash. Graduation gifts. In the trunk are their suitcases, some extra packing boxes and tape (just in case), and the twins' graduation presents.

Meredith has checked her weather app only about a hundred times this week, and each time the forecast is for bright sunshine, accompanied by unseasonably warm temperatures for mid-May. If the meteorologists are correct, tomorrow—graduation day—will bring the humidity index to 90 percent. *Rain without actual raindrops*, she thinks. At the moment, though, she would never guess it—the pillowed blue sky stretches before them like a big fluffy blanket.

"Thank goodness there's no rain forecast for the weekend." She turns toward Joel, his hands resting at a steady two and ten on the wheel. "It could be worse."

"Yes." He grins. "My little optimist. Although, I imagine there'll be a few pop-up storms, if you know what I mean."

Her hand swats at his arm, a big, bulky bicep that looks custom-made for comforting. "Stop it. You're not funny."

She knows what he's referring to, of course. From Friday to Sunday afternoon, they will share the weekend not only with the kids but also with Roger, Lily, and Roger's extended family. Plenty of opportunities for metaphorical thunderstorms and lightning bolts. Meredith has made Joel promise to be cordial for the entire weekend, no matter how obnoxious Roger might become after a few cocktails or what revealing outfit Lily might wear.

And Meredith, herself, has resolved to take the high road. Lily is fine, of course, in that way that any second wife who is twenty years younger than your ex-husband is fine. She has long jet-black hair, a pert ski-slope nose, and an ass that refuses to jiggle. Looking at Lily reminds Meredith of staring into a bright light, one that she has to shield her eyes from but can't resist peering at, anyway. In fact, Lily's breasts are so perfect that when Meredith was first introduced to her, she found herself longing to reach across the kitchen island to squeeze one, just to confirm they were phony, imposters.

So, when Roger announced six months ago that he and Lily had eloped, Meredith was surprised. Stunned, actually. She'd always assumed that Lily was one more link in the long chain of women who'd sauntered through her ex-husband's life since they'd divorced ten years ago. She didn't expect Roger to settle down ever again. In fact, she'd told herself that was the reason they'd gone their separate ways in the first place: Roger simply wasn't cut out to be committed to another human being, much less to a family. Apparently, she'd been mistaken.

She gives his new marriage two years tops.

"Relax. It all will be fine," Joel says now, as if reading her mind. She wonders if he's referring to the kids' graduation specifically or to the four days ahead more generally. The long weekend looms ahead like a head cold—one that should resolve itself quickly but could just as easily turn into something more dire, like a nasty sinus infection, bronchitis, tonsillitis even, if not properly tended to.

She chases the thought away, smooths her skirt (a summery pink A-line that she snagged off the sales rack at Nordstrom last week), and silently recites her goals for the weekend, goals which she outlined in bed last night. 1) She will refrain from overwhelming the kids with affection or gushing about how proud she is. No point in embarrassing them in front of their friends. 2) She will limit herself to two (three at the most!) cocktails each night to avoid any snide comments about Roger and/or Lily. And 3) She will be the personification of grace under pressure. Yes, Meredith intends to be the Jacqueline Onassis of graduations.

It's all about the kids, she reminds herself, no matter what might happen, might go wrong. Because surely *something* is bound to go wrong. No matter how many times she envisions Dawn and Cody striding across the stage, her thoughts are interrupted by how exhausting the weekend will be.

Seventy-two hours of good behavior.

At least tonight it will only be her and Joel and the kids. Roger and Lily are busy preparing their home for the party on Saturday, which, from her ex-husband's intermittent texts, is beginning to sound a lot like the presidential inauguration. Roger has promised the twins a "killer" celebration and appears to be more than living up to his end of the bargain. There will be swimming in the backyard pool, unlimited barbecued wings and ribs, and a DJ with dancing just steps from the ocean. Meredith prays the party will be memorable for the right reasons.

As soon as the ink was signed on the divorce papers, Roger moved up to Boston and into a mini-mansion, leaving Meredith to wonder if he'd been hiding money under their mattress all those years. She has visited the new house occasionally, usually when dropping off the kids for a month's vacation over the summers, but once the twins got their drivers' licenses, they were free to drive up to Boston on their own, trimming Meredith's interactions with Roger to a handful a year. Then both kids decided to apply to colleges only in the Boston area—Northeastern, BC, Harvard, Babson, Bolton—and she couldn't help but feel that they'd chosen their father over her. Why didn't they want to stay closer to home, *her* home, she wondered? The distance, the choice, stung. But when ultimately they both settled on Bolton, a quaint little campus on a hillside outside Cambridge (which also happens to be Meredith's alma mater), she was pleased.

Meredith, of course, could hardly pick up and move after the divorce. At the time, the twins were twelve and had launched themselves into the hormone-addled world of middle school. She thought it important for them to keep the same circle of friends, especially since their own family had recently imploded into a thousand tiny bits. As ever, Roger's timing had been impeccable. Just when she was getting back on her feet, having taken a job in the NICU at New Haven Children's Hospital, Roger announced that he'd fallen in love. With someone else. Meredith can still conjure up the smell of pancakes from that morning, the sound of the television blaring Saturday morning cartoons from the family room.

In the wee hours of the night, while she tended to tiny premature babies at the hospital and her mom slept over with the kids, she would counsel herself that there were worse things than a husband's leaving you. Like being swallowed up by a sinkhole. Or contracting the Ebola virus. How many nights had she promised herself that she'd sworn off men, for good?

But then, at a fund-raising event for the hospital, she bumped into Joel, standing in front of the same silent auction item as she (tickets to see a show at the Shubert), and before she knew it, he was switching out his place card so that he could join her table. A few hours of conversation in and she'd thought, *Oh*, with a glint of surprise. *I get it. Here's the man I was supposed to marry.*

She glances at Joel again, his soft, kind eyes trained on the road. Unlike her ex-husband, Joel falls squarely into the realm of good, trustworthy men, a guy who recycles (without being overly zealous about it) and who works as a counselor for troubled youth at a small high school outside New Haven. He comes so well versed in adolescent angst that sometimes Meredith thinks she must have looked him up in a catalog and special-ordered him for her kids. Joel understands teenagers' dark sides in a way that eludes her, so much so that she calls him the Teenager Whisperer. Dawn liked Joel almost immediately, and even Cody (ever protective of his dad) eventually warmed to his stepdad's goofy humor and bear hugs. Joel has cheered just as loudly as all the other dads on the sidelines of Cody's football games and Dawn's cross-country meets. In her second husband,

Meredith has finally gotten what she deserves—a marriage that provides solace, like a pair of comfy, thick socks on a cold winter night.

From her pocketbook, she pulls out the creased agenda for graduation weekend, which she printed out at home earlier this morning. When she opens the folded-over page, Roger and Lily's formal invitation for Saturday's party falls into her lap, and she stuffs the shimmery gold-trimmed card back into her bag before reading from the graduation schedule:

> *Please join us for cocktails and a buffet dinner at*
> *your Graduate's dorm.*
> *Thursday Evening, 5:30–9:00 p.m.*
> *Dressy casual attire*

She had been puzzled by the request for "dressy casual." What did it mean, exactly? Certainly not formal wear, but what then? A summer dress? A linen suit? Or was that too matronly? She wondered if all the other moms would be wearing skinny jeans with a flowy top. She texted Dawn for advice, but her daughter had been of little help. Wear whatever you're comfortable in! I'm wearing a sundress. So Meredith settled on the pencil skirt, pale pink, and a summery white blouse. She hopes it suggests elegance with a hint of youthfulness.

At least tonight, she doesn't have to worry about being upstaged by Lily.

When she had lunch with her friend Steph the other day at the mall, Steph had laughed at her fashion deliberations. "You'll be fine. Whatever you wear, you'll be Cody and Dawn's beaming mother." Steph leaned back in her seat and grinned. "Can you believe our kids are actually graduating? Finally." She has a son the same age, about to graduate from Brown. "Now we'll be free!" She clinked her wineglass to Meredith's, then leaned in and whispered, "Tell me the truth. Aren't you elated? I'm so happy they're done, I could do a little dance." And, in fact, she stood up right there, in California Pizza Kitchen, and spun herself around in a circle. Meredith had laughed along with her.

Yes, she is pleased that the kids have made it through. But *elated*? No, *elated* isn't the word she would choose. Happy, definitely proud, relieved maybe. And a little sad. Because commencement is such a funny word, isn't it, when what they're really celebrating is an end, a closing of the door on her kids' adolescence? An acknowledgment that her work as a mom is more or less finished. She spent so many years worrying that the divorce had screwed up the twins permanently, but Dawn and Cody had proved her wrong. They'd braided together, shucked off their therapy sessions like an old, heavy overcoat, and helped each other through instead. *A twin thing*, Dawn had explained, sounding both impossibly young and wise at twelve. *You don't have to pay for some strange doctor to listen to us. Cody and I have each other for that.* And for once, Meredith had listened, grateful that her kids had each other.

When they were young, she used to fantasize about lazy days when she'd no longer be needed for a carpool, wouldn't have to wheedle them into doing their chores or their homework. Grandmothers at the supermarket would tell her to "enjoy every minute" because childhood zooms by so quickly, but their admonishments only made her skin prickle with irritation. "Before you know it, you'll be an empty nester," they'd say, a knowing gleam in their eye, and Meredith would think, *You've got to be kidding me. That's decades away! I'm so tired! What I would give for an empty nest for only a few hours.*

Except here she is now, her birds hovering on the edge. And all she can seem to focus on is how far away the ground is. For her babies and herself.

She slips the agenda back into her bag and switches on the radio to a jazz station, a Dizzy Gillespie trumpet extravaganza, and drums her fingers to the beat. *Commencement,* she thinks again. A new beginning. A fresh start for them all. Is it too much to hope for? *Probably. But it's worth a shot.* Considered in the right light, this graduation is practically a baptism—a sweeping away of sins past. Meredith will try her level best to see beyond them and, at least for the weekend, anticipate all that might be. In a good way.

And if she has to wring a particular swan's neck to keep things on course?

Well, so be it.

As he guides their beat-up Subaru toward Boston, Joel watches his wife from the corner of his eye when she removes the weekend's agenda from her purse, puts it back, then takes it out again. Joel is in love with Meredith, but that doesn't mean that everything she asks him to do comes easily. Of course, he wants to be there for the kids this weekend—he loves them like his own, thinks of them as his own ever since he married Meredith seven years ago. Watching their faces light up on stage when they get their diplomas? He wouldn't miss it for the world. But he also understands that along with the celebration comes a tangle of emotions for his wife, which she is clearly still sifting through.

If you ask him, Meredith is a bit of a wreck.

Joel so wants to guide her through the next few days, but

the truth is that he's averse to large social gatherings of the hoity-toity type (he's much better with a suicidal teen one-on-one). The thought of an extended weekend of events where he has to make small talk with strangers was enough to send him out the door at six this morning to pump out three miles and shake off the jitters (no easy feat for his two-hundred-pound frame). Last night, Meredith even promised him that there would be pockets of time when they could slip away from the planned activities on campus and sneak back to the hotel to lounge by the pool. Where they could gossip about everyone to their hearts' content. When she'd shared her goals for the weekend, Joel joked, *You're such a planner, you'd probably jot down a to-do list right before a tornado hit.* But what he didn't tell her was that he'd fashioned his own refrain for the weekend for whoever might be listening: *please grant me strength. Grant me patience. Above all, grant me a sense of humor.*

Because he wants everyone to have a fantastic weekend. The stuff of memory books. All the family, the whole lot of them, will be together, and Joel can't recall the last time that happened. Maybe at the twins' high school graduation four years ago? This weekend, Roger's brother, Georgie, will be flying in from London. And Roger's parents—dad, Harry, and mom, Edith—are driving down from Maine. Edith is a female facsimile of her son—thin, uptight, with an air about her that jangles with old money. And Harry always looks as if he'd rather be anywhere else than at another family event. Joel and Meredith have laughed about it. Are they really so difficult to endure? Maybe it's Harry's own son, Roger, who drives him nuts.

Since he and Meredith are only children themselves, they will be supplying no aunts or uncles for the occasion. And with Meredith's dad gone and Joel's parents in an assisted living facility down in Florida, the gathering will be decidedly lopsided. He and Meredith will be the odd couple out along with Meredith's mom, Carol, as their sidekick. Joel feels a small chuckle escape from somewhere deep inside his throat. *The Odd Couple* sounds about right. Joel can play Felix to Meredith's Oscar while Carol provides commentary from the peanut gallery.

"What's so funny?" Meredith asks, her eyebrows knitting into tiny boomerangs.

He shakes his head, reaches over to squeeze her hand. "Nothing."

"The weekend is going to be great. Just like you said."

"Of course it is." Joel doesn't dare look her way, in case she calls him out on the fact that he said this yesterday with a scissor of sarcasm. He understands that their family embodies the "new" American household, which is to say, they are a stepfamily or a blended family—a constellation so common these days, yet it still takes him by surprise that he has ended up a part of one, as if he deplaned in the wrong city and should be hurrying along to the next gate. By no means did he instigate the "stepness" of his family (thanks to good old Roger for that), but Joel has placed his foot firmly in the center of this particular constellation, rearranging a few stars so that he, too, might fit.

He was surprised when Meredith appeared interested in him at the fund-raiser, even more shocked when, a few months later, she told him that she thought she was falling in love. Women like Meredith didn't typically fall for beefy guys like Joel, at least not back in college. But she explained that the honeymoon of lusting after "bad boys" ended once you'd been married to one for fifteen years. Joel understands that the traits that once made him trusty "friend" material in college now count as admirable husband qualities, things like integrity, good listening skills, and a certain physical heft that a surprising number of women seem to find reassuring.

"I'm done with guys like Roger," Meredith explained on their first real date at a small neighborhood Italian restaurant, two bowls of linguine steaming in front of them. "I want steady and true in a man." She shrugged. "You know, like a pickup truck. No more Ferraris for me."

Joel had laughed, uncertain if he'd just been complimented or insulted. Joel is no Ferrari, for sure, but having gotten to know Roger over the years, he's not sure Meredith's ex is, either. Flashy and quick, yes, but Roger strikes him as all paint and gloss, without much substance under the hood.

"Geez!" A navy blue Mercedes suddenly veers into their lane, and Joel lays on the horn. "Why is it that the closer we get to Boston, the crazier the drivers get?"

Meredith makes a *pfft* sound. "You say that like you're surprised."

"Not surprised. Annoyed."

Joel loathes Boston drivers, all of whom drive as if passing their drivers' tests merely required signing in on exam day. If it weren't for the kids, he would avoid the city altogether. For Joel, the cozy enclaves of New Haven move at about the right speed. But that's what kids are for, right? To make you push your boundaries, try new things.

Joel thinks back to when he first met Dawn and Cody, right around the same time he'd abandoned the thought of ever becoming a husband or a dad (love hadn't really knocked on his door since high school, despite various ill-advised ventures into online dating). But suddenly, there were two kids peering up at him with huge, expectant eyes. Cody especially. One morning when Joel was trying to sneak out of the house before the kids woke, twelve-year-old Cody stepped out of the bathroom. He eyed Joel up and down, as if trying to decide if he were an intruder or a handyman there to fix the faucet.

"Hey, buddy." Joel feigned nonchalance. "Whatcha doing?"

"Peeing. Did you sleep over in my mom's bed?"

Kids were nothing if not direct. Joel weighed how best to answer, but he'd found that telling the truth was usually the best tack with kids. "Yeah, I was just heading out."

"Why don't you stay for breakfast?" Cody asked. "I'm really good at making French toast." And with that simple invitation, Joel had slipped into their mornings, a big, happy mutt who had padded under their kitchen table and never left.

Kids are Joel's soft spot, always have been. All those insecurities they try to hide, the walls they put up, when really adults are as scared as they are, maybe about different things, but still scared. Grown-ups just don't let on. Getting a kid to open up makes Joel's heart pump like nothing else. He enjoys helping his students slay their dragons, talking them through their lairs, one careful step at a time.

Over the years, he has gotten to do a little of this for Dawn and Cody, even though their dragons constitute more of the garden-variety: stress over tests or a grade-A bastard boyfriend who jilted Dawn at prom; Cody getting caught downing beers in the back of the school during a basket-ball game (a serious enough infraction to warrant a three-game suspension from the football team next season, but pretty typical stuff in Joel's estimation). Yep, Joel has witnessed plenty worse—kids sky-high on heroin; teens beaten at home, who try to hide their bruises under sweatshirts or makeup; the girls who starve themselves down to ninety pounds and still call themselves fat. He has had the bad luck of counseling a few suicidal kids in his fifteen years as guidance counselor at Washington High, and it has added a couple of layers of extra skin to his bulk, for sure.

But even though he can handle the occasional wayward teenager, no one prepared him for the fact that becoming a stepdad also meant showing up for a whole host of gatherings with the ex's family. Events like first communions, Christmas, Thanksgiving, confirmations, birthday parties, graduations and, he supposes one day, weddings. Sure, the divorce agreement stipulates division of time over the holidays and summers, but it hardly offers a blueprint for stress-free gatherings on the less formal occasions.

Joel thinks someone should write a how-to manual, complete with instructional dialogue, along the lines of, "Good to see you, Roger. How's work going?" or "Gosh, this shrimp cocktail is tasty, isn't it?" Blasé comments to skate by potential confrontation while also throwing open a conversational window. Talk to sidestep an awkward missed child support payment or a previously terse email exchange. Maybe in his retirement years, Joel will get around to writing it, *A Guide to Celebrations for Step and Blended Families.* Nah, that sounds too bland, too technical. Maybe *I Wish I Didn't Have to Be Here.*

Splitting parenting duties with Roger over the years has been like playing an involved Jenga game, one whereby you have to determine which block can be removed without upending the whole order. Such as who would white-knuckle the dashboard when the kids practiced for their drivers' licenses (Joel and Meredith), or which parent could get a better deal on a car for the kids (Joel was happy to cede that one to Roger, who'd bought Cody and Dawn *separate* rides, used Honda Civics), or who should be in charge of touring colleges with the kids (they'd split that one more or less evenly with Roger, based mainly on geography). And then there was The Year That Shall Not Be Mentioned, the kids' junior year in high school, when the twins (really, Dawn) had decided they wanted to try living with their dad full time up in Boston. It lasted only ten months, but it almost killed Meredith.

Although he has tried to erase from memory that painful year when his wife morphed into a different person, it won't quite go away. Meredith would come home from the NICU, change into her sweats and pour herself a cocktail before bingeing on reality TV, as if to remind herself that other people were enduring much worse. On the weekends, she'd drive up to Boston for casual "check-ins" on the kids, though they struck Joel more as adventures in stalking. About half an hour before arriving, she'd phone the twins to say she was in the area and ask if she could drop something by the house. *A pair of Dawn's sandals that she might want? A tin of Cody's favorite peanut butter cookies?*

Her transparent attempts to wedge herself back into the kids' lives while they lived with Roger had been heartbreaking to watch, and so when the twins decided to return home to New Haven the following summer, Joel had breathed a sigh of relief. Dawn proclaimed she was "so done with those snobby girls" at the private school Roger had enrolled them in, and Cody agreed it was "lame." As glad as Joel was to have them back home for their senior year, part of him wanted to pull them aside and shake them, ask if they had the faintest idea of the hell they'd put their mother through.

Yeah, no playbook for that year, either. Joel knows it's harder for Meredith to deal with her ex than it is for him. *Keep things civil. Swallow your pride. Remember, it's all about Dawn and Cody,* he tells himself. Once, Joel went so far as to suggest he adopt Dawn and Cody to make it official, but apparently this isn't possible so long as their dad is around. Joel doesn't mind being a stepdad—it's a lot like being the cool uncle. One who gets to impart his wisdom without provoking an instant knee-jerk reaction, which is how Dawn, at least, usually responded to her mom in high school.

Over the years, Joel has stepped into the role of the funny guy, the one who lightens the mood around the dinner table. So different from all those years when he used to come home to his bachelor pad and crack open a Pabst Blue Ribbon on the couch, the apartment so quiet he could hear his own breathing till he switched on the TV. He knows he's lucky, becoming a part of his family and escaping permanent bachelorhood, a fact he'd grudgingly resigned himself to before meeting Meredith.

For all their sakes, though, he hopes like hell this weekend will unwind smoothly. Herding together families and stepfamilies and grandparents and friends' parents, all probably several sheets to the wind by Sunday, however, sounds like a recipe for a human Molotov cocktail. Give it a little shake, and the contents could easily turn combustible.

"Did you get some?" Dawn's dark hair hangs in a curtain across her shoulder. Her mom has been on her case to cut it, or at least get it trimmed before graduation, but Dawn likes it long. She thinks it lends her an air of mystery, a shade to hide behind, and besides, Matt makes a purring noise whenever he runs his hands through it. With long hair, she can pretend she's voluptuous when there's nothing else remotely voluptuous about her. Her body is all skin and bones, a remnant from her days as a ballerina, when her childhood and teenage years were marked by four-hour-a-day practices. Dawn still has nightmares about her instructor shouting, "Posture! Posture," her hand pressing against Dawn's backbone, her fingers pinching hard at Dawn's midsection, where there was only skin to pinch. Grueling and mostly miserable is how Dawn remembers those days. But her instructors insisted she possessed a natural talent coupled with a ballerina's body, such that it might put her in the running for the conservatory one day.

She endured the endless practices, the pulled muscles and broken toenails (and toes), the millions of leaps and pliés and spins, the pressures of performances, until her freshman year in high school. Until, that is, it all became too much. She remembers the overwhelming sense of relief she felt when, at fifteen, she confided to her mom that she wanted to quit. How she'd feared Meredith would explode—*all that money spent! All those hours wasted!* But the news landed easily, as lightly as a butterfly, as if her mom had been expecting it all along. Maybe the sport had worn her mother down, too. The constant complaining, the complicated carpooling schedules taped to the refrigerator door. The exorbitant expense of hideous costumes and the endless pairs of pointe shoes. Maybe her mother was as sick of ballet as she was. In any case, when Meredith met her gaze in the rearview mirror, all she said was "Why?"

Dawn remembers scrambling to put her misery into words, blinking back tears.

"Too much pressure?" her mom gently suggested.

"Too much everything," Dawn replied. Mostly (though she didn't say it) she didn't think she could stomach the sound of her friends making themselves sick in the bathroom anymore, the constant *click, click* of the scale weights when a dancer stepped on, the brutal competition of it all. The audition for prima ballerina in *Swan Lake* was what truly broke her, though—the ugly backstabbing and behind-the-scenes gossip among dancers whom she'd assumed were her friends. At first, Dawn was devastated when she didn't get the lead, but then, the more she thought about it, the more outrageous it seemed. Because, really, they were fighting over a *swan*. A stupid, obnoxious bird in a tutu. Dawn's mother didn't pressure her to stick with dance or give her some lame lecture about the importance of not giving up when things got tough. Instead, she'd said, "Okay. When would you like your final lesson to be?" To which Dawn replied, "How about tonight?" And that was the last time she'd slipped her feet into pointe shoes for lessons, even though occasionally she'll still twirl around her bedroom.

"Yeah," Matt says now, as he lets himself into the room and collapses on the couch. "Just a pinch, but enough, you know?"

Dawn breaks from her reverie and nods. She doesn't know what he's talking about but pretends that she does. That she hasn't tried weed until now, this in a state where you can legally smoke it or even devour it in a chocolate lollipop (though technically, marijuana still counts as an infraction on campus) is embarrassing, verging on humiliating. Matt has smoked plenty of joints with his roommates, so he knows who sells and who doesn't. Not that she'd call her boyfriend a stoner, but at least he can inhale without coughing up a lung, which is precisely what Dawn does after taking a puff on the joint he has rolled. Her vision goes blurry for a few seconds and she swipes at her eyes. Matt grins at her, wickedly.

"Went down a little rough, huh?"

She clears her throat and squints in his direction. "I don't feel anything, do you?" After a minute, she adds, "*Ew*. That aftertaste is gross."

Matt studies her with hooded eyes. "It'll pass. Chill, babe." He takes another hit while she stumbles to the bathroom sink to cup cold water into her hands, swallowing greedily. The water cools her tongue, and she brushes her teeth for good measure, her reflection staring back at her in the mirror. *Nope, still nothing.* She feels completely normal. When she returns to the couch, Matt lays stretched out on his back, his hands resting on his chest like a mummy. Dawn curls up next to him, her body a lanky S. "I don't know how you smoke that stuff. It tastes awful. And I don't feel anything, anyway."

"Give it time, babe." Matt strokes her hair with his fingers. In the corner of the room, a soap opera plays on the small, beat-up television that Dawn rescued from a Dumpster during her freshman year, some senior's discard. Soon it will be heading back to the dump, when Dawn clears out all her stuff after graduation. She watches the daytime drama without really watching. Even if her first toke has been a bust, she doesn't care. So long as she and Matt get to hang out together before their families arrive, before they have to be disgustingly polite and upbeat, she'll be happy.

Everyone assumes that Dawn is excited to finally be graduating. And, yes, there had been some question about whether she actually *would* graduate, having to face the

Admin Board last year for charges of cheating on a final. But all that got resolved (even though she's not sure her parents ever entirely believed her explanation). She and her friend Beth were accused of having suspiciously similar essay answers on an anthropology test—but that was because they'd studied together! In advance of the final, their professor had handed out a list of possible questions, and Beth and Dawn had discussed potential answers. No surprise their essays were similar. It wasn't as if they'd copied from each other's exam books.

In the end, all that really mattered was that the Admin Board gave them a slap on the wrist and ended the common practice of professors handing out questions before an exam. Even though Dawn knows she should be pleased with the end result, there's a lingering piece of her that still resents having to defend herself to her parents that awful day. Surely, they would have come to golden child Cody's rescue immediately, convinced of their son's innocence. But with Dawn, for some reason, those convictions were murkier, quicker to evaporate through the tiniest crack until the Admin Board itself had exonerated her.

So, yes, even though she is gratified to be graduating, today all she feels like doing is throwing up. Because on Sunday she heads back to New Haven for the summer to work as a lifeguard at the YMCA. Unless Matt plans to fly out from Chicago for a surprise visit, she won't see him until September, when she starts her job in the Windy City.

At least we'll be together in the fall, she tells herself. They planned it that way. In the mornings, they'll take the Metra into Chicago, then transfer to the ferry that will deliver them across town, Matt to his job at a real estate firm and Dawn to her advertising company. Dawn can hardly wait to play grown-up, to pretend that she and Matt are off to work like any normal couple. But that's a long three months away.

She pulls her cell off the table and glances at the screen. No text back from Cody yet—what's taking him so long? They need to talk. It's one thirty. Still, plenty of time before she has to shower and get ready, before she has to chase Matt out and spray down the room. Not that her mom would even recognize the scent of marijuana, but it can't hurt to be safe. (Her stepdad, if he notices, would probably be too cool to mention it.) Dawn rolls over on top of Matt and snuggles in closer.

That her stepdad will be around this weekend to run interference comes as a relief. Joel reminds Dawn of a giant, easygoing seal basking in the sun, one who reacts only if provoked. Most important, he can steady her mom, who has the ability to whip even the smallest nonevent into a tornado. With Joel, what you see is what you get, no frills. Dawn's real dad, on the other hand, embodies the polar opposite, always buying her gifts and trying to woo Cody and her so that they'll stick around Boston after college. Cody says it's Roger's way of making up for his guilt over abandoning them as kids (Cody's minor is psychology). To which Dawn replies, *Yeah, right.* Let their dad grease the grooves of his guilt however he wants. As far as she's concerned, he went AWOL for most of their childhood, ripping up the memo that forbids parents from being selfish and capricious. That's territory typically reserved for kids, and Dawn and her brother have been robbed of it.

She blinks her eyes hard as her head begins to spin, the light cutting in through the window blind slats and casting miniature rectangles along the wall. A battered Imagine Dragons poster hangs in the patch of light. Come Sunday, it will get chucked along with the rest of her artwork, if you can call a few more band posters art. Her dad has promised to drop by on Sunday to help move her stuff, even though it's not necessary. Matt can help, and her mom and Joel (and her nana) will be here, too. But apparently, her father considers it some kind of weird dad duty, moving his kids out of their college dorm rooms.

"Wanna take another hit?" Matt asks.

She shakes her head, then burrows it between his neck and shoulder and inhales his scent, which smells like fresh cut grass and vanilla. Dawn sincerely hopes her dad doesn't make an ass of himself this weekend. Of course, there are no guarantees, not with Lily in the picture. As if it weren't awful enough that Dawn's new stepmom is young enough to be her sister—there's not even a decade between them! Dawn does her best to ignore Lily whenever the family gets together, and, thank goodness, Lily finally seems to be taking the hint.

A few weeks ago, she'd tried befriending Dawn, inviting her out for lunch at Trident Booksellers on Newbury Street, followed by pedicures. Dawn endured it like the one root canal she'd had in her life, which is to say with as few words as possible and a silent prayer that her misery would end quickly. When Lily paid with Roger's credit card and signed her name, Mrs. Roger Landau, in round, loopy letters, Dawn half expected her to turn the *U* into a smiley face. She'd sat on her hands, willing herself to shut up. But really, if someone was going to waste her dad's money, then Dawn preferred it to be herself.

"Did I mention it would be really stupid to get caught with this stuff the day before graduation?" She slips a leg between Matt's. Even as a blanket of tiredness settles over her, she feels jittery. Why did she think getting stoned before her family arrived was a good idea? *Oh, right*. Matt dared her, told her she wasn't allowed to graduate without having smoked a bud at least once in her life. *No big deal*, she said. *Bring it on*. But she didn't expect the experiment to fail, with her lying on the couch sober and Matt fading off into never-never land.

"Shh," Matt whispers into her ear. "You worry too much. No one's around. Besides, Jerry doesn't want to catch us. Can you imagine how bad he'd feel if he had to shut us out of graduation?" Jerry, a graduate student in the veterinarian program, is their dorm proctor. Over the years, he has overlooked numerous student transgressions, sometimes even being the source of them.

"I guess you have a point." Matt rolls over to realign his body on top of hers and sets down the joint on an abandoned soda can. Gently, he lifts the edge of her shirt, circling her belly button with small kisses that feel like butterfly wings stroking her skin. Dawn pulls off his T-shirt, then hers, prompting a moan from Matt when he sees that she isn't wearing a bra. His tongue slowly traces an imaginary line from her belly button up to her breasts while he unzips her jeans.

"When's Claire coming back?" he asks, tugging at her jeans.

"Not till dinnertime. She's working at the café." Dawn wiggles out of her pants and tosses them on the floor. Claire is Dawn's roommate, and though they didn't become instant best friends like some roommates she knows, they'd been compatible roommates for four years. At least Claire doesn't do crazy things like light her hair on fire, a trick one girl tried sophomore year on a dare.

"Awesome," Matt says. Dawn's head feels fuzzy, and her heart boomerangs around in her chest. Maybe the weed is beginning to work after all? She promised Matt they would have the entire afternoon to hang out together, but Cody still hasn't gotten back to her. She needs to talk to her brother before her mom and Joel get here. There's a photo he must see, something that's potentially stomach-turning, but she doesn't dare text it to him because what if, somehow, it ends up in the wrong hands? What if it's already in the wrong hands? The sender's cell number is blocked.

Dawn knows she should be the one to show the photo to her brother. It's the kind of thing that could make a guy keep looking over his shoulder, up until the very minute his diploma rests securely in his hand.

Lily stares into the fridge, creating a mental checklist of the plates chilling on the shelves. The caterers have dropped off a few items early to ensure that Saturday's party goes smoothly. *Cheese plates—check. Juices and sparkling water— check. Miniature quiches—check. Wings and ribs marinating— check.* She shuts the fridge door and strolls over to the wall of windows, where she can see Donna, the party coordinator, chatting with the grounds crew. At the moment, they are struggling to set up an enormous white tent on the back lawn. A few guys lug stakes and heavy hammers to secure the tent, while a young woman works to untangle a string of white lights about a mile long. Along the yard's perimeter, the purple hydrangeas have burst into full bloom, as if they've been waiting all month to pop at exactly the right moment, an orchestrated event for graduation. Farther out, half a football field away, the lawn gives way to a pebbled beach, where ocean waves kick up white spray. It's a gorgeous venue for a graduation. *Do the kids even realize how lucky they are?* Lily wonders. Or maybe when people grow up with such largesse, they forget to appreciate it.

Secretly, Lily is glad that she fell in love with Roger before getting a peek at this house. Most nights, when they were first dating, they would party in the city and then wander home to her small apartment in Beacon Hill. Roger always said he preferred to stay at Lily's rather than make the forty-minute trek back home. But after dating a few weeks (and when Lily was pretty certain that Roger was the One), he'd invited her out to his house in Manchester-by-the-Sea for dinner. He'd picked her up dressed in a sharp seersucker blazer, a white shirt and khaki pants, suede loafers without socks, little tan lines snaking around his pale ankles. Lily remembers it as if it were yesterday, when she hopped in the convertible and pretended she was being whisked away in her own fairy tale.

Which, it turned out, she kind of was.

When they pulled up to the house, it didn't seem possible that he lived there all by himself—that is, he and his hulk of a Saint Bernard, Moses. Somewhere in the back of her mind she'd understood that Roger was wealthy—after all, the man drove a BMW convertible and was able to secure sought-after tickets to a Patriots game within minutes. She understood that some of his clients were Boston sports icons. But she hadn't been expecting a sprawling clapboard house by the sea with floor-to-ceiling windows that peered out on a neatly manicured lawn, a crystalline pool, and the ocean just steps beyond.

That night, he boiled lobsters in the chef's kitchen, covering her ears when the beady-eyed creatures screamed and tried to escape the pot, Moses barking wildly. Out on the veranda, a white-draped table awaited with a bouquet of wild roses, their vibrant pink hue reminiscent of the color of the inside of a grapefruit. Moses settled heavily at Roger's feet, and then they'd proceeded to talk into the night, Roger refilling her glass with prosecco while the sun tumbled casually into the ocean. If she hadn't fallen for him before that night, she would have always wondered: Did she love him or did she love the lifestyle a future with Roger promised?

A soft breeze plays with the linen curtains, and Lily sweeps them aside. Being so close to the ocean helps to cool the house, but already the humidity of the day is starting to creep in. Friday and Saturday are forecasted to be the hottest days of the month yet, which is why she persuaded Roger last minute that they should rent a tent. It required calling in a favor (an old boyfriend of Lily's runs a local wedding company), but it was well worth the price. No one can expect Roger's parents or Meredith's mom to cool off in the pool like the kids. Plenty of shade and cold drinks, preferably with copious amounts of alcohol, will be necessary.

She watches while two young men roll a steel fire pit across the lawn out to the private beach. Roger insisted they have a bonfire, a family tradition, after the day's festivities. But when Lily went out to the garage to dust off the old fire pit a few weeks ago, it looked as if one strike of a match would set the entire house ablaze. She'd found a suitable replacement online and stocked the pantry with graham crackers, chocolate bars, and marshmallows. A pile of tinder wood sits next to the garage, at the ready.

She cranes her neck from side to side and hears a sharp crack. It feels as if she has been planning this party for weeks. In fact, the whole graduation celebration is beginning to feel a lot like a wedding. Which strikes her as hugely ironic because for their *own* wedding, Roger insisted on eloping to Vegas. Lily isn't sure why she cares so much that everything goes well on Saturday. Maybe because she wants to impress Roger? Dazzle Meredith with her good taste and flair for parties? Make the kids happy? Ha! Dawn and Cody can barely stand her. But that won't stop Lily from trying. They can't hate her forever, can they?

Well, maybe Dawn can.

When she'd treated her stepdaughter to lunch the other week, Dawn had acted put out, as if spending time with Lily was a colossal inconvenience. Lily thought they were past the awkward stage of taking the measure of each other (she'd gotten to know the kids a little on the odd weekend when they'd come home to do their laundry or grab a home-cooked meal). They'd had pleasant enough chats at the kitchen island over plates of microwaved nachos, or so Lily thought. By now, she'd assumed everyone would be inching their way closer to feeling like a family. But then, at lunch, she'd found herself backpedaling, struggling to make conversation while Dawn kept checking her cell phone that was blowing up with texts.

"Can you at least turn the ringer off?" Lily had implored.

"Sure." Dawn shrugged. But it didn't stop her from texting, even while she nibbled at her salad. Any visions Lily might have been harboring of the two of them shopping arm in arm like best friends had gone up in smoke.

No, Dawn isn't interested in hanging out with her. And Cody, while nice enough, seems to assume Lily is just another one of his dad's temporary diversions, despite the gleaming ring on her finger. Maybe, Lily allows, everyone simply needs some more time to get used to each other. After all, six months is but a blink in a family's lifetime.

She glances at her watch, relieved to see there are only fifteen more minutes to go before she can take another pill. This morning she woke up with a throbbing headache (no doubt stress related), and the first Tylenol of the day has done little to dull the daggers shooting through her head. Happily, the medicine cabinet is well stocked with painkillers, ever since Roger broke his hand a few months ago—thanks to Meredith, who had the audacity to run him over with her car. Well, "run over" might be a bit of an exaggeration, but Meredith *did* hit him with the front bumper of her trusty Subaru in Roger's own driveway. *I stepped on the gas pedal instead of the brake!* she'd explained, as if the whole incident were incredibly funny.

Sure thing, thinks Lily.

On bad days, she suspects that Meredith's run-in was less of an accident and more of a comeuppance. A little wedding present for Roger only a few months after he'd married Lily. But Roger insists it was an accident, as well—he was looking down at his cell phone when Meredith was inching along the driveway and had practically walked into the car himself. Next thing he knew, he was flying across the front lawn. He and Meredith *laugh* about it now, as if it's their own private joke. Lily doesn't get it. If she were Roger, she would have been pissed. But as her friend Alison likes to remind her, if Lily invests too much time analyzing every interaction between Roger and his ex-wife, she'll drive herself crazy.

And she has zero interest in doing that.

Though why Meredith seems to dislike her so much baffles Lily. Meredith and Roger have been divorced for almost ten years. Ten years! Ten years is sufficient time for the country to conduct a new census, for goodness sake. And Meredith seems happily married to Joel, who strikes

Lily as a sweetheart. Lily's friends say Meredith can't contain her jealousy, that she's envious Roger married someone so much younger. But Lily considers that naive. She and Roger love each other, and when you love someone, age doesn't matter a whit. And if Meredith truly loves Joel, why should she care if Roger found someone else?

Her thoughts are interrupted by the sound of Moses barking downstairs, probably another delivery that Donna can handle. Lily should really take the dog for a walk before she heads off to yoga. She searches for a pair of yoga pants, discovers them balled up in her bottom dresser drawer, and throws them on along with a fresh T-shirt. Once she finds a brand of clothing she likes, she tends to stockpile it, and these Cut Loose shirts fit in all the right places without being the chintzy, see-through material of some of the chain store T-shirts. About a dozen T-shirts, all in different pastel shades, sit rolled into tight cylinders in her drawer like so many burritos. She snaps a quick photo and posts it on Instagram for today's "enhancer."

Even though Lily would never call herself a social media influencer—she doesn't have nearly enough followers to warrant that title—a suitable number of companies send her free samples to chat up online and, as a result, she now has close to fifty thousand followers. It's not a job exactly, but with the amount of free clothing and products she gets to play up on Instagram, she's saving Roger a bundle—and it's a far cry from her waitressing days. Companies like prAna, Fresh Produce, and Athleta reach out to her whenever a product needs a little extra nudge, usually after it's been available for a while or might be going stale. Like the understudy to a Broadway musical, Lily shows up when reinforcements are needed, and she's made a bit of a name for herself as a fashion maven, albeit with eclectic, slightly bohemian tastes.

She adds a hashtag of #cutloose #comfiestshirtsever to the photo. That'll do for today.

She's looking forward to her class and stretching out her back muscles that feel as tight as a stitch. Even at thirty, her body is already starting to show troubling signs of middle age, with saggy bits and niggling lower back pain. Once graduation weekend is over, though, she can finally relax. She's simply trying to approach the weekend with as much grace as possible, with as much grace as Roger will expect from her.

A knock on the bedroom door interrupts her thoughts. "Mrs. Landau?"

"Yes?" An awkward jolt runs through her whenever she hears her name attached to Roger's. In her mind, she is still Lily Sullivan. The party coordinator pokes her head into the room.

"We need your okay on the floral arrangements in the dining room. Would you mind taking a look?"

"Of course, I'll be right there. Thank you, Donna."

Lily dots her lips with a faint gloss, pulls her hair up in a ponytail, and goes into the bathroom to grab a tiny pill from the bottle. With a long drink of water, the tablet winds its way down her throat like a smooth pebble. Then she heads downstairs to approve the centerpieces and take Moses for that walk.

TWO

When they pull up to join the jagged line of cars in front of the Boston Harbor Hotel, Joel jokes, "Check it out, honey. Our Subaru fits right in." There's a Lexus, a Jaguar, a Porsche, and a Range Rover—they might as well be attending the Emmys in Los Angeles.

Meredith nods absently, unamused—she's watching a cluster of millennials striding by on their lunch hour, their navy blazers slung over their shoulders in the afternoon sun. To Joel, they look about fifteen years old. Mixed in with the young businessmen are the easy-to-spot tourist families, their fanny packs looped around their bellies, cameras slung about their necks. One dad lugs a toddler's car seat with him. *God bless him*, thinks Joel. He would have never been willing to do that with the kids when they were little. Safety be damned—he'd have strapped the twins into a cab on his lap with his own seat belt and called it a day.

When they reach the head of the valet line, a gray-suited man in a top hat steps forward to claim Joel's keys. *Not exactly a Motel 6*, Joel thinks. *I could get used to this.* He climbs out of the front seat, hands the guy a few bucks, and trots over to the curb to join his wife and mother-in-law. Laid out before them is Boston's sprawling financial district, an appealing jumble of stately historical buildings and sleek modern architecture. Skyscrapers, seemingly conjured from nothing but air and glass, stretch above them, and Joel feels a bit like the country mouse come to visit the big city.

Zipping up the middle of Atlantic Street is the Rose Kennedy Greenway, a welcome bit of nature in the heart of capitalism. Flowering trees and random sculptures dot the park, where couples lounge on blankets. A few kids toss a Frisbee back and forth. Others are enjoying a quick sandwich on one of several artfully painted benches. It's as if a coquettish maiden has come to town to remind the captains of industry what it's like to have fun. Joel recalls some grumblings a while back about the accumulating years and exorbitant costs of moving the city's highway system underground, but, boy, is the park ever inviting today.

"Well, isn't this wonderful?" Meredith says, as if reading his thoughts.

"Lovely," agrees Carol.

The fact that his wife has chosen one of the swankest hotels for their stay—and not some dorm room on campus offered to parents at a reduced rate, but that is surely up four flights of stairs with no air-conditioning—buoys Joel's mood even further. Typically, they would be among the first to reserve a dorm room, but Meredith insisted they splurge for this weekend. For a brief moment, he's seized by the urge to grab her hand and toss down a blanket on the Greenway, where they can enjoy a romantic picnic. They haven't done anything spontaneous or fun in what feels like forever.

"Well, I suppose we should check in?" Carol says.

Joel sighs at his mother-in-law's unintended buzzkill, *but yes*, he supposes, *they should*. They stroll through a massive archway that opens onto a pavilion with striking views of the harbor. Joel doesn't know much about architecture, but even he can tell that this place, with its lofty rotunda and intricate masonry, is a piece of art disguised as a hotel. He can't stop grinning. Just as Meredith promised when she booked the rooms, "It should feel like a *vacation*, not a goodbye."

He gets it now. She's processing a lot. This place will most definitely help alleviate the sting of the kids' graduation.

"Maybe after we check in," he suggests, "we can grab lunch outside on the patio?" Already, a number of hotel guests sun themselves while nursing glasses of wine over salads.

"Good idea." Meredith consults her watch. "Only one o'clock. We've got plenty of time—the kids aren't expecting us till five."

They file through a revolving door, depositing them inside the hotel's marbled lobby. At the center is an enormous mahogany table flecked with long-stemmed vases, each one filled with a white iris that stretches like a swan's neck. Men in white oxford shirts and women dressed in boldly colored summer dresses mill about the lobby, as if they might be here for a Lilly Pulitzer trunk show. Joel feels distinctly out of place in his khaki shorts and Life Is Good T-shirt, but the front desk lady gladly accepts his credit card at check-in nevertheless.

An elevator swoops them up to the tenth floor, where at

the end of a winding hallway, their rooms await. And Joel, as much as he likes his mother-in-law, is pleased to see that Carol's room sits a comfortable few doors down from theirs.

"We'll meet you in the lobby in fifteen, okay, Mom?" Meredith calls out, but Carol has already disappeared into her room.

Meredith shrugs and slides the electronic key into the lock, allowing their door to open onto a room with a king-size bed covered in a fluffy white down comforter and a gazillion pillows. Against the wall rests a cherry armoire, a giant television, and a mirror that can accommodate even Joel's generous frame. At the edge of the room, two wing-back chairs abut sliding doors that open onto a small patio with views of the harbor.

"This," Meredith says, flinging herself onto the bed, her arms outstretched as if she's backstroking across it, "is how the other half lives."

He chuckles. "Well, honey, you're in luck. Because today you *are* the other half. In fact, this whole weekend, you're the other half." Which is when it hits him.

They've often joked that once the kids graduate, they'll be able to travel to Turkey or Budapest or Tanzania—wherever they can dream of on a moment's notice. *Just think*, they would say on lazy Sunday mornings over coffee. *All that tuition money channeled into travel, a new deck, a fancy car.* Crazy to think that the moment is almost upon them. Not two years out, not four months, or even three days. As of tomorrow, no more tuition bills will be arriving in his in-box. Now the only fiduciary debt left for the twins' education is their nominal federal loans, for which interest hovers around 2 percent (and which, he's made quite clear, will be the twins' sole responsibility). It's enough to send Joel humming as he pokes his head into the bathroom to investigate further—more white marble, a glass-encased shower with a rain showerhead and, he notes, interestingly, a bench.

"Are you *humming*?" Meredith calls out.

"So what if I am?"

"Nothing. I could have sworn it sounded like 'Zip-a-Dee-Doo-Dah,' which I haven't heard a soul hum since Cody walked into Toys 'R' Us when he was four years old."

"Can't a man be glad that he gets to spend a long weekend with his lovely wife in a luxurious hotel?" Meredith is standing at the patio slider now, and he comes up behind her, wraps his arms around her. Her hair smells like lemons, the scent of her shampoo.

"Of course he can. I guess I was a little worried that this weekend might be tough for you," she says.

"Tough?"

Meredith leans back against him. "Yeah, you know, what with Roger and Lily and the whole family descending."

Joel pauses a millisecond before responding. Should he admit the truth? That as much as he doesn't look forward to seeing Roger and his crew, Meredith is really where his concerns lie for the weekend. He just wants her to survive this rite of passage for the kids.

"Don't worry about me," he says, watching the flotilla of sailboats dipping and climbing on the water below. "I'm perfectly content." A ferry churns its way across the harbor, and farther out to sea, an old-fashioned galleon with massive white sails glides by, as if straight out of a movie. "Wow, isn't that a sight?" he says and squeezes her tightly.

"Amazing." She gives him a quick kiss before heading over to the bed to unpack, and Joel collapses in one of the chairs to watch her pull out sundresses, multiple skirts and jackets, and even more shoes from her suitcase, scattering everything across the bed. It looks as if a small but mighty hurricane has swept through their suite.

"Are you really going to wear all those outfits this weekend?" The two pairs of slacks, a couple of shirts, and the navy blazer he has packed for himself swim through his mind.

Meredith pretends not to hear him while she stares into the closet—or maybe she genuinely doesn't hear him because she's lost in thought. "Why is it," she asks, "that hotels, even the fancy ones, never give you enough hangers?"

"It's a conspiracy. Meant to drive you insane."

"Ha," she says, as if she suspects this might be possible, even true. "You know, now that the kids are out of college…" Her voice trails off while she works to slip a purple sundress onto a hanger. "We can live a bit more extravagantly."

"Funny. I was just thinking the same thing."

"Does that make us selfish?" Joel ponders her question, and decides that, if it does, then he much prefers selfish Meredith to bereft Meredith, which is how she's been acting these last few weeks, as if the kids are moving to another planet, not halfway across the country. Though it's not as bad as The Year That Shall Not Be Mentioned, Meredith has retreated into her own private world of late. As if she's made a silent pact to refuse herself anything that might afford her pleasure. He'd been so glad when she announced she was going to book club last night, but then she'd come home upset because all anyone could talk about was Dawn and Cody's graduation. "I went so that I could discuss *the book*," she complained. "Not to be reminded that my kids are leaving me for good."

Joel has debated suggesting some kind of therapy but worries that Meredith will only scoff at him—it's not her style.

And the thought of having to *pay* someone to listen to her empty-nest troubles will, he knows, smack of self-indulgence to her. "That sounds like something Roger's new wife probably does. After she's done with her morning yoga and massage and shares a chai latte with her friends, she heads off to her therapist to confess all her worries—though what those could possibly be, I can't imagine." This had been Meredith's pointed retort when he casually floated the idea of therapy for a friend across the dinner table one night, to see if his wife might be open to counseling in general.

Not so much.

But selfish Meredith? That he could get used to. Selfish Meredith possesses a joie de vivre that reminds him of the woman he fell in love with. One who is a bit of a dreamer, who's happy to shuck her responsibilities at least for a few hours. Maybe selfish Meredith will want to visit Ireland with him and kiss the Blarney Stone. Maybe selfish Meredith won't worry about the kids quite so much and will accept that the future that's about to unfold could quite possibly, actually, be wonderful.

"If it does, then I think I like selfish," he says finally, getting up to grab the remote from the bedside table and flopping down on the wedge of bed free of clothing. ESPN comes on, but it's a random college lacrosse game, which Joel enjoys about as much as watching grannies bowl. He lets his mind wander as he anticipates tonight and how much glad-handing will be required of him at the banquet, indeed for the entire weekend. He's pretty sure that most of the other dads will be hedge fund managers or otherwise involved in the financial industry. *Money-printers,* Joel's dad used to call them disparagingly.

He braces himself for the vacant, slightly condescending

gazes the other fathers will fix on him when he describes his job as a guidance counselor at a high school. He's been there before, standing across from some dude in his Vineyard Vines jacket staring blankly over his head. Typically, Joel's job talk will prompt a hearty clap on the shoulder and a pronouncement that he should "keep up the good work," or an insult masquerading as a compliment, such as, "Glad someone's doing work that matters."

He can see it in their steely eyes, their look that says he doesn't quite measure up. He reminds himself that these are the same guys who've probably missed dozens of their kids' sporting events and school plays, who rarely made it home for story time and a good-night hug. He wonders if a piece of them ever regrets it, or if they're too wrapped up in themselves to even realize what they've missed. Still, it's a gauntlet Joel would prefer not to walk, a self-assessment that's better done with a few beers on their back porch at home.

"Is it just me?" Meredith asks, "Or, as much as I'm excited for this weekend, am I the only one who will also be relieved when it's over?"

He rolls onto his side to face her. "What's this? You mean you're not looking forward to spending the next seventy-two hours with your ex-husband's family? Not that anyone's counting the hours, of course." That gets a little smile. "And how about Harry and Edith? They're always such a delight." He hops off the bed and feigns as if he's Roger's dad giving him the hairy eyeball. "Joel," he intones in Harry's curmudgeonly voice, "you seem to have put on a few pounds since I last saw you. What's your secret? *Har, har.*"

Meredith laughs again. "Oh, God, he's awful, isn't he?

Ugh, I can't believe we have to hang out with them all weekend."

"Technically, we only have to talk to them at Roger's party on Saturday."

"Don't forget about dinner tomorrow night."

"Oh, and that. But besides those two highly awkward events, we should be scot-free." He falls back onto the bed. "Let's make a plan right now that we'll converse only with other bereft-looking parents this weekend."

Meredith pauses, a hanger in hand, and smiles. "What would I do without you?"

He shrugs. "Probably die of boredom." Somewhere behind the standoffish exterior she's been flaunting the last few weeks is the woman he knows and loves. Meredith admitted it herself: she just needs to get through this weekend.

"I'm not sure about that," she says, placing another dress in the closet.

"Oh, I am," he disagrees. "Now why don't you come over here and relax for a minute." His hand reaches out for her. And for a few sweet minutes, Meredith relents, allowing herself to settle into his arms while he holds her tightly, even though, for Joel, it's never long enough.

It used to drive Meredith bananas, the amount of time it took her husband to order a proper beer. Typically, Joel would make some poor waitress rattle off a long list while he considered each lager before deciding, and then ultimately, changing his mind. It was like watching the man try to broker an arms deal with the Saudis. But over the years, she has come to consider it an endearing trait, which is, she supposes, one of the secrets to a good marriage. When you can view your spouse's peccadillos as charming mannerisms, you know you're in it to stay. Plus, how can she not love a man who puts such exhausting thought into his beer selection? Imagine the brain power he must devote to more important things, like their taxes or their 401(k)s!

She fixes him with a look when he finally announces he'll have "the Sam Adams Summer Lager," and then adds, "On second thought, how about an IPA? That sounds good."

"So, you'll have the IPA?" their waiter demands, crossing out "Sam Adams" in little blue strips on his notepad.

"Yes. Please." Joel closes the drinks menu as their waiter hurries away. "What?" His eyebrows shoot up on his forehead.

"You know what." Meredith wriggles her lips into a smirk. Still, she can't bring herself to reprimand him on such a beautiful day.

"So, tell me more about this party that Roger is hosting," Carol says, lobbing a conversational brick onto the table. "It sounds like typical Roger—spending tons of money to win his children's affection." Joel snorts. Meredith picks up her cloth napkin, which is twisted into some sort of bird— a swan, perhaps?—while her eyes dart back and forth between her mom and Joel. Are they really going to do this now? She undoes the bird's wings and smooths the napkin on her lap. As much as she loves her mother, is indebted to her for all that she has done for her and the kids over the years—especially those first years when Roger left—Carol still enjoys disparaging Roger whenever she gets a chance. It makes Meredith feel both exasperated and, somehow, oddly defensive.

It's strange, she thinks now, how a person can go from loving someone, to loathing him, to simply not wanting to be around him. That pretty much sums up her feelings for Roger. She tolerates him because he is her children's father.

She once joked that her relationship with Roger was like her love affair with tuna salad: it began as adoration, then morphed into repulsion (when she was pregnant), and finally settled on something like grudging acceptance. Now, while she can bear to be around it, she would never, ever choose tuna (or Roger) off the menu again for herself.

But Carol's constant harping on her ex-husband won't make the weekend any easier. When they married, Meredith was young, naive, easily enchanted—all traits that made her the perfect target for Roger's charm. And while her fury over his betrayal years ago has abated, her mother seems incapable of letting go. Instead, Carol stokes a furious little ember inside of her, one that waits to burst into flame at the slightest provocation.

"Not that I'm complaining," Carol quickly adds as their waiter returns and sets down their drinks. "My grandchildren deserve every good thing."

Meredith twirls the olives in her martini, glides one off a toothpick, and considers how best to respond while the sharp tang of pimento nips at her tongue. "I'm not really sure what he's got in store," she says finally. "Sounds like a barbecue, some swimming, a chance for the kids to hang out with their friends."

"And is that Lily woman going to be parading around in her bikini, I suppose?"

Joel nearly spits out his beer but manages to recover, rubbing the back of his hand across his mouth.

"Mom!" Meredith exclaims. "It's not like she's an evil stepmom. I'm sure Lily will show more class than that at the party." But, honestly, she doesn't know what to expect this weekend from Roger's new wife—Meredith's replacement, for that's who she really is. Will Lily retreat to the sidelines like the marginal player she has been in the twins' lives thus far, or will she insist on being the star, which appears to be her default mode the few times Meredith has been in her presence? She imagines gorgeous Lily fawning over her guests, changing into multiple outfits over the course of the day, each one more marvelous than the last. Meredith sincerely hopes the woman will have the decency to cede the limelight to the kids this weekend. The last thing she needs is Cody's friends ogling his stepmother in a bikini. *Ugh.* It seems so unfair that she might have to deal with such unseemliness on a weekend that should be filled with only pride and joy.

They consume their Cobb salads in silence, and Meredith gazes out at the harbor that sparkles as if on fire in the midday sun. Is this how the weekend will go then, she wonders? Will the mere thought of Lily usurp every happy moment she might have? *Absolutely not,* she decides then and there. She has *earned* this weekend and not even the stunning Lily can rob her of that. Joel reaches across the table to take her hand and rubs his thumb reassuringly across her silver rings. But Meredith leans back in her chair and smiles. *It's okay,* she attempts to signal through marital telepathy. *Everything is fine.*

She thinks back to when the kids were young and so much of her time was devoted to shuttling them to sports, how the twins had needed her then in tangible ways. The countless hours Dawn spent rehearsing in the ballet studio! Meredith secretly thought her little girl might be destined for a professional ballet troupe, the way her lithe body seemed to absorb Tchaikovsky's music as she pirouetted across the floor. Nothing else in Dawn's life has benefited from such attention, such dedication as her dance. In fact, the only place Meredith can recall her daughter's taking direction, the only place she has ever been remotely pliable, is on the dance floor. Dawn has always been her stubborn child who, like an irascible swan, can attack without warning.

But Dawn is also the twin who feels the most deeply, who cries at the end of terrible, not-so-sad movies. She even teared up watching *Despicable Me* while all her girl-friends were bent over in laughter. *Despicable Me!* And once, she'd invited a girl—whom Meredith hadn't even realized was in Dawn's kindergarten class—to her birthday party last minute so that she wouldn't feel left out. Meredith knows, too, that Dawn would do anything for her brother, including taking the blame for him, that she loves him no end.

Cody, on the other hand, has always been her rock-solid child, the one to remind her in those first months after the divorce to grab her car keys or an umbrella, the child who would stop off at the corner store for milk, if needed, on the way home from school. That they are graduating to-morrow seems impossible.

"Well," Carol announces, her drink drained and her salad picked over, "I think I'll sneak in a short nap before to-night's festivities." Meredith looks down at her own salad and is surprised to see that she has devoured it.

"Good idea," Joel says amiably and checks his watch. "I might do the same. Only two thirty. We should probably leave a little after four to allow for traffic?" It's a question, and Meredith nods.

"Yes, let's meet in the lobby at 4:15."

"Okeydoke. See you then." Carol excuses herself with a tidy wave of a hand over her shoulder before heading into the hotel.

★ ★ ★

When they get back to their room, Joel unzips Meredith's skirt and attempts to maneuver her gracefully onto the bed. She desperately wants to lose herself in the moment and forget about the potential stresses of the weekend. When will they ever get to stay in such a nice place again? This hotel is like the Sultan's Palace. And when, she wonders, was the last time they had sex? Last week maybe? The week before that? It's awful that she can't remember, but life has been hectic, her hours at the hospital crazy lately. She tugs off Joel's T-shirt, and he kisses her, soft kisses that taste like beer. Soon, both his jeans and her clothes are on the floor, and his finger traces the line of her arm, the swell of her breasts, and then farther south, until, in one swift motion, all her worries abruptly glide off her, her toes curling into tight little commas.

"Oh. My. God," she says, and minutes later, Joel collapses on top of her, letting out a satisfied grunt.

"*Phew.* I think someone needed that," he says.

"Speak for yourself," Meredith teases, though she knows he's right. Things have been, if not tense between them these past few days, a bit too civil. Like his heading out for a run this morning with no explanation. Or the fact that, the last couple of nights, he has rolled away from her in bed and fallen asleep within minutes. Whenever there's an impending family event involving Roger, Joel seems to retreat a touch. Her ex-husband is harmless, but she supposes Joel might not see it that way. After years of hating him, she now thinks of Roger more as an annoying uncle who won't shut up at Thanksgiving dinner but who is, nevertheless, tolerable in small doses.

Her friend Barb calls such people "dosey," which Meredith finds both hilarious and brilliantly on-the-mark. It describes a handful of acquaintances in her life whom she can stand to be around, sometimes even enjoy hanging out with, but only for discrete periods of time. In Joel's case, though, Meredith chalks up his unease to some strange alchemy of male machismo, where husbands and ex-husbands don't mix. If things were reversed—if Joel, say, had been married before—Meredith suspects she'd be insufferable, maybe even refusing to attend family events that included an ex-wife. She understands that she has to be careful not to push too hard.

She climbs out of bed to shower, and before long the massaging thrum of hot water on her back lulls her into a kind of trance. The hotel has provided complimentary body wash that foams up across her stomach, and the bubbles pop with a delicious eucalyptus scent. After she steps out and dries off with an oversize plush towel, she spies Joel stretched out across the bed, his eyes trained on a golf tournament on TV. The man has never played golf a day in his life, and yet for some reason he can watch it for hours. "It's relaxing," he offers by way of explanation. "Same reason you watch those flip-it-or-leave-it shows."

"If you mean golf puts you to sleep, then I agree."

He's mistaken about her home improvement shows, however, which provide so much more than just the nuts and bolts of do-it-yourself projects. It's easy for Meredith to see beyond a house's warped doors and cracked beams and imagine what *could be*. Not just a new floor plan but the satisfaction once the project is completed. She understands the appeal of a fresh coat of paint, a transformed kitchen, a new view out a bay window. In fact, when the kids first left for college, she'd spent hours fantasizing about reconfiguring their bedrooms into a craft room or a home office or even a massage room. Here they are, though, about to graduate and Cody's dusty trophies still line his bedroom shelves. Dawn's ballet slippers still hang from pink satin ribbons across her closet door.

While Meredith can't say exactly why nothing has changed, it didn't feel natural to take over the kids' rooms right then. It was as if, by wiping their rooms clean, she would be sweeping away all her dearest memories—how every night she would build a nest of pillows around little Dawn to help her fall asleep or when young Cody would challenge her to a hoops game on the Nerf basketball net hanging over his door. The thought of trying to enjoy a massage in her new massage room, knowing she'd donated her children's keepsakes to Goodwill provided another deterrent. But maybe after this summer, she'll actually *do* something with the bedrooms. Convert them into a pottery room or a dark room, even though she neither throws pots nor takes photos.

But she can learn.

Joel heads for the shower, and when she drops her towel, Meredith catches a glimpse of herself in the hotel mirror, prompting a heavy sigh. Lately, she's been feeling as if a Mack truck has run her over. Every afternoon, around two o'clock, a wave of tiredness crashes over her body, making her long to curl up and nap alongside the babies in the NICU. Is it the big changes in her life that fan such exhaustion, she wonders, or something more dire, like early onset menopause? Although as her friend Diane unhelpfully pointed out, it wouldn't be considered "early onset" in Meredith's case since she now actually hovers around "that" age.

As much as Meredith hates to scrutinize her body under

any light, the quick glimpse in the mirror turns into an inevitable examination. Her breasts, it seems, have held up well enough, despite having nursed the twins, but the rest of her—like her stomach (*still* ample inches to squeeze despite cutting out carbs the last few weeks!) and her dimpled thighs—screams middle age. She needs an intervention, wishes those fellows from *Queer Eye* could waltz in here, snap their fingers, and work their instant magic.

Short of that, she opts for the control-top Spanx she packed "just in case," because there's no use pretending she can hold in her stomach for the next several hours (unlike her breasts, her stomach has never recovered from being stretched to the size of a punching balloon). If this is what perimenopause is like, she thinks, then Meredith wants no part of it. It hasn't just slowed her metabolism to a crawl—it has murdered it! Buried it in a ditch somewhere under a sketchy highway, never to be found again.

Even though she wasn't planning on changing out of her pink skirt and top from this morning, when she tries on the sundress with purple flowers, it's clearly the better choice. It makes her appear less matronly, the dress highlighting the subtle tan she got last weekend when they took a quick trip to West Haven Beach. Maybe it will give her the extra shot of confidence she sorely needs right now. Of course, tonight's affair is a low-key buffet, but she suspects the evening will set the tenor for the entire weekend. The dress, cut low enough to reveal a bit of cleavage, fits her to a T. Meredith thinks she looks not half-bad, which is the high bar she sets for herself these days.

Blame it on vanity, but she does not want to become one of those middle-aged moms who post slightly-out-of-focus, above-the-shoulder photos on social media. Which reminds her—she grabs her cell from the bedside table and checks Instagram one last time to see if the kids have posted anything, a bad habit of hers that has recently become more like an obsession. But there's nothing. Only a long stream of photos from the celebrities she follows: Hoda Kotb, Seth Meyers, The Pioneer Woman, and so forth. As she does a final scroll through, her finger pauses on a photo of a giant white tent. Lily has posted it in the last half hour (yes, Meredith grudgingly follows Lily because Lily posts *all the time*, so Meredith feels pressured to check, particularly on this weekend when their lives are bound to intersect). At times, Meredith feels like a jealous teenager stalking the popular girl in high school, but this feeling does nothing to deter her. Lily has somehow managed to accrue 48,342 followers, which blows Meredith's mind.

Underneath Lily's post is the caption, "Getting ready for graduation day!" #celly #soproud #dawnandcody. Meredith feels an instant tug in her chest. Is it jealousy? Sadness? Anger? Shouldn't she be the one posting photos of a graduation tent on a lawn so green it could double as the golf course for the PGA tournament? With a small stab of envy, she notes that both Dawn and Cody have already "liked" the photo.

Meredith takes a selfie in her floral dress and considers posting it online with the heading, "Can't believe graduation day is almost here!" with hashtags of #lovemykids #feelingfabulous #soproud, but then stops. Lily will surely see it (Meredith knows Lily follows her because Lily "likes" her posts on occasion). And when Lily sees the post, she will instantly chalk it up to Meredith's feeble attempt to outshine her in a field where Lily clearly excels (Meredith has exactly fifty-seven followers).

Instead, she toggles over to the app that the college has conveniently provided for graduation weekend and that Dawn forwarded to her this afternoon. It lists all the pertinent events with times and locations, and Meredith suspects it will soon fall into her can't-live-without category for the weekend, much like Tylenol and booze.

"Wow, you look amazing." Joel has stepped out of the bathroom, a towel wrapped around his waist. Small beads of water cling to his shoulders.

"Don't sound so surprised." Meredith performs a coquettish twirl, her dress spinning out around her. How immature, she thinks now, and slides lip gloss and a powder compact into her purse. Trying to compete with Lily on social media! She reminds herself of the advice she gives the kids: social media isn't real life. It reveals only what people *want* you to see. Meredith is Dawn and Cody's mom, not Lily, who has been a stepmom for all of six paltry months. If anyone gets credit for shepherding her children to graduation day, it's Meredith. Well, Meredith and Joel. Save for writing an occasional check, Roger did precious little for the children after he left, and even less, if it's possible, before that. No, Meredith will not engage in a self-imposed war of jealousy with some sexy tart who's almost the same age as her kids, for goodness sake! She has plenty of other things to think about, to be excited about.

And so, apparently, does Joel, whose towel has just dropped from his waist.

THREE

Down in the lobby Carol is already waiting for them, dressed in a cardinal red dress and her signature strand of pearls. Around her lingers the unmistakable cloud of Lancôme Poême perfume. Neither her mother's nap nor the humidity has dampened Carol's gray bob one bit, and her thick, straight hair bounces with authority as she turns to greet them.

"There you are! I've already asked them to pull up the car," she says. "You look darling, darling," she tells Meredith. "You, too, Muffins."

"Muffins" is her mother's improbable nickname for Joel, who, when he first met Carol over brunch, managed to devour three blueberry muffins. Ever since then, Joel has been Muffins to her mom. Meredith thinks it's sweet, a term of endearment. Though after Roger, she supposes her mother would have considered any other man to be a cupcake, a scone, a dreamy biscuit. The name seems to have grown on Joel over the years, too, because he signs Carol's birthday cards, "Love, Muffins."

"Thanks, Mom. You look fantastic yourself."

"Flattery will get you everywhere," she says as the valet pulls up in their dusty Subaru. The three of them climb in, and Meredith shoots the kids a quick text to let them know they're on their way. According to her app, they should be at the school in twenty-three minutes. Meet you out front of the dorm, she texts. OK! Dawn texts back within seconds.

Joel navigates the complicated maze of tunnels leading out of the city, across the Zakim Bridge and past the TD Garden, the blue-green ribbon of the Charles River unspooling below. They almost take the wrong exit, but Joel corrects their route, making a last-minute swerve into the right lane and prompting a string of irate horn blares. Old factories, three-decker houses, and billboards promoting everything from new waterfront condominiums to car insurance sprout up like weeds along the highway. Before long, they exit off the freeway and wind their way through back streets toward the school, where the landscape eventually begins to breathe more easily.

Just a few weeks ago, Meredith drove up to say hello to the kids, and every time she sets foot in the old neighborhood, a sense of déjà vu descends, as if she might still be a student here, dressed in her Levi's, a baggy sweater, and clogs. That was nearly thirty years ago, but things haven't changed all that markedly. The neon sign for Redbone's barbecue still beckons down a side street, as does the sign for the Somerville Theater. Sadly, Johnny D's, where she spent countless nights drinking cheap beer and kissing boys she probably shouldn't have, has shut down.

They travel along the main street, appropriately nick-
named the Avenue of the Churches, and while several stee-
pled buildings remain, the street appears to have evolved
into something slightly grander over the years, as if a big
sister has come to dress it up and offer pointers on etiquette.
The ramshackle Victorian houses, once off-campus housing, have been bought up by young professionals, evident
from the tidy herb gardens that now front expansive porches
painted in tasteful shades of purple and green. BMWs line
the freshly paved driveways.

As they draw near campus, it's obvious that it's Bolton's
graduation weekend with the rolled-up carpets, abandoned
mini-fridges, and crushed packing boxes littering the curb.
Meredith swallows hard when she considers the moving job,
times two, still ahead of them this weekend. She hopes the
kids have at least started packing—she has only reminded
them a million times, even going so far as to drop off boxes
for this very purpose the other weekend. Beyond the car
window, a handful of families strolls toward the main quad,
dressed for the various dinners hosted in the dorms tonight.
Most parents appear to have shucked formality for comfort
on an evening that is growing increasingly warm. A few
senior girls in blush-colored dresses wobble in their high
heels. *Flamingos in shoes*, Meredith thinks. Every one of them
wears her hair down—long and straightened. How they can
stand to leave it down in the heat is beyond her. She would
melt into a puddle.

The parking lot is already full when they pull in, cars
wedged in at odd angles in what can only be described as
creative parking.

"Over there," Carol calls from the back seat, her bony
finger pointing up ahead and to the right.

"Good eye, Mom." After a few tries, Joel manages to squeeze the car in between two behemoth SUVs, and Meredith hops out to open the back door for Carol, careful not to nick the Lexus next to them.

When Joel comes around the other side, his sport coat looking a little snug, Meredith can't resist reaching over to unbutton it. If he had a pipe, he might well be mistaken for a professor on campus. Typically, her husband dresses up only for weddings and funerals (khakis and a blue oxford shirt are his work uniform at school), and she appreciates the fact that he has purchased a new blazer for this weekend. If he'd asked her to go along shopping, however, she might have gently encouraged him to buy one size up.

"It's too hot," she says now, as if undoing one button will make all the difference between his sweltering and being comfortable tonight. "Shall we head over? I'm sure Dawn and Cody are waiting for us."

The truth is, Meredith isn't at all certain that the twins are waiting for them. While Dawn has answered her texts, Cody has responded with only radio silence. She hopes it's because he's busy packing. Maybe he packed his phone by mistake, and it's buzzing in the bottom of a box somewhere? But even she recognizes this thinking for the fallacy that it is. Cody is never without his phone, which might as well be his third hand.

When the kids were younger, she knew their schedules by heart, not just their after-school activities but during school, as well. Snack time was at ten thirty, gym on Mondays, music on alternate Tuesdays, and chorus on Thursdays. Roger was incredulous that she could name everyone in the twins' classes and also describe their little personalities, as rich and varied as a Ben and Jerry's ice cream list. But Meredith had thought, *How could I not know?* She'd volunteered enough times to recognize which kids needed coaxing to come out of their shells and which ones would be the first to dart their hands into the air to answer a question. Even though she has had to cede control of the twins' (and their friends'!) schedules long ago, she still misses the comfort that comes from having a firm grasp on their whereabouts.

Of course, she trusts her son, and up until this year, if she had to place a bet on which child was most likely to graduate with honors, it would have been Cody, hands down. But recently, Dawn has pulled herself together, scoring good grades and surrounding herself with a nice group of friends from her cross-country team. Most surprising of all, she got a job offer before Cody. Halfway across the country in Chicago, but an offer nonetheless, at a crack advertising firm. Cody, on the other hand, has sounded oddly distant over the phone these past few weeks. Meredith wonders if maybe he's having second thoughts about moving thousands of miles away to North Dakota. Perhaps, she speculates, the dreamy appeal of life-after-college is starting to feel a bit more real.

Joel grips her hand as they walk up the stone-paved path that meanders past the campus's administrative buildings, their walls blanketed in ivy that's the color of a ripe avocado. Up ahead, off to the left, sits the cluster of dorms where tonight's banquets will take place. As if to prove she can, Meredith's mom leads the charge up the hill, and neither Meredith nor Joel says anything to stop her. Meredith can feel a familiar tug in her calves. No wonder she was in such great shape in college! She must have walked ten miles a day across the rolling hills of this campus.

When they reach Pratt Hall, a group of guys is tossing a

football around out front. No sign of Dawn or Cody anywhere. Meredith feels her spirits dip a tad—did she really
expect the kids to be waiting out front for them? She reminds herself to keep her expectations in check. Just because
she has pictured this weekend so many times in her head
doesn't mean it will play out exactly that way.

"I'll text Dawn," she says and flops down on a paint-
chipped bench in front of the dorm that looks as if it has
seen better days. "Tell her we're here."

"Great." Joel claps his hands together as he steps away.
"Hey, buddy, over here!" he calls out to one of the boys
with the football. And before she can stop him, her husband
has shrugged off his sport coat and is cavorting about in a
game of tag football. *He's lost his mind*, she thinks, because
within minutes he'll be sheeted in sweat. But she also realizes there's no stopping boys from being boys. Of which
her husband is decidedly still one.

Carol, seemingly reaching the same conclusion, drops
onto the bench beside her. "Not much longer now," she
says and tenderly pats Meredith's knee. Meredith isn't sure if
she's referring to seeing the kids, or graduation day, or something else entirely, but she agrees, "No, not much longer."

Just then her phone pings with a text from Dawn, and
her stomach flutters. "They're headed down," she says, and
her mom shoots her a smile, as if she understands all too
well what lies ahead for her daughter in the next few days.
Meredith smiles back and waits for her beautiful children
to push through the door.

FOUR

Earlier, Thursday afternoon

Dawn is freaking out. Or, was freaking out. When Cody didn't show up to look at the photo earlier this afternoon, she bit her thumbnail down so far that it began sprouting bright red droplets of blood. Which is why her thumb now sports a Buzz Lightyear Band-Aid (the only kind she could find in their medicine cabinet). Even the weed did little to soothe her nerves. Finally, when she couldn't take Cody's silence anymore, she typed, YOU BETTER MEET ME RIGHT NOW IF YOU DON'T WANT YOUR BUTT KICKED OUT OF SCHOOL. That got his attention. The photo is of Cody, himself, handing over a paper to a junior who's notorious for dealing drugs on campus. The photo reveals a date from last week. "Does your brother know it's not smart to sell papers for drugs? In fact, some would say it's illegal. Hope no one finds out before graduation."

Who would have it out for her brother? Or is it Dawn

they intend to humiliate? Why didn't they send it directly to Cody? When Cody finally texted back around four thirty, I'm in my room. Why don't you come over here? Dawn had marched over in exasperation.

Now when she lets herself in, her brother lies sprawled out on the couch, his fingers wound around a controller aimed at a TV screen blaring with gunshots. Dawn despises Call of Duty, a game that she thinks explains a lot about male behavior in the current culture. She even wrote a paper about it for her sociology class. Her eyes skirt across the detritus of Cody's room, which currently resembles a garbage pit—pizza boxes everywhere, empty beer cans, packing boxes that have yet to be packed. That her parents think her brother is a model child strikes her as slightly hilarious. A snapshot of his dorm room would lead anyone to conclude that it's the bedroom of a slacker teenager at best, maybe even a serial killer, but definitely not a guy about to graduate Phi Beta Kappa. Sometimes she wonders if Cody really *is* so smart or if maybe he's paying someone to write his papers, slip him an early exam. She's heard of worse offenses to keep the high-octane athletes in school, special "tutors" to boost failing grades. Rumor has it the tutors do all the work.

Dawn thinks back to when they were in high school together, often in the same classes, and Cody would pull in the highest test score. It used to irk her—his scores were usually only a few points higher than hers, but Cody would inevitably throw the curve for the rest of the class. The possibility that he actually is brilliant, just lazy, seems more likely. Maybe he's an idiot savant, she thinks, as she steps over a pilled brown blanket lying on the floor. Cody finally glances up and says, "Hey." His seersucker jacket dangles from a hanger on a doorjamb. Apparently, his roommates, Brad and Toby, have already cleared out for the banquet.

"What are you doing?" Dawn plops down in a worn recliner, a remarkably ugly brown-and-gold striped chair that's about a hundred years old. She remembers Cody dragging it from his bedroom at home freshman year and how ecstatic her mom was to finally be rid of it. "Aren't you a little bit curious about what I have to show you?" she asks, desperate for some kind of reaction from her brother.

She's growing more frustrated by the minute, especially now that she understands she left Matt behind for *this*. Dawn is not about to rescue the golden child today. She deserves this graduation weekend and the accolades just as much as, maybe even more so, than her brother after the year of hard work she's put in. Too many all-nighters fleck her distant memory. Her mom always assumes that Dawn is the difficult child, stubborn and unyielding, but what she doesn't know is that Dawn has pulled her brother out of plenty of jams, too. Like that time he almost got caught at an off-campus bender that the cops busted up. Dawn whisked Cody right out of there.

"Yeah, what's up?" he asks, his eyes still locked on the television.

She unlocks her phone, pushes up out of the chair, and waves the photo in front of him, a gesture that at least gets him to press Pause on the stupid game. Dawn can only glimpse her brother's profile when he sees the photo and caption, but she's pretty sure she detects a flicker of surprise ride across his face.

"So?" he says after a few seconds and unfreezes the game, the sound of gunshots piercing the air again. "It's from last week. We were at the gym. What's the big deal?" Dawn takes the phone back, stares at the photo.

"That's it?" She's glaring at him, not that he would notice. "I've been worried sick all day about this, and that's all you have to say? *No big deal?*" An oscillating fan stands in the corner, and every so often it sends Cody's floppy hair flying so that it stands up like a tuft of chicken feathers.

"Look, chill out. Eddie asked me to look over his final paper for psych. I guess he was on the verge of flunking the class, so he wanted my help. I told him I'd do it, no strings attached. So, that's what I did. I edited his paper for him." Cody glances up from his game for a moment. "You know, it wasn't even half-bad."

Dawn vacillates between desperately wanting to believe her brother and calling him out on the crock of BS he very well could be feeding her. His explanation, detailed enough to be credible, warrants some consideration. She's known Cody all her life, and it's not like him to be involved in drugs. Surely, she would have seen signs of it before this? Just a hair away from accepting his explanation, she remembers the backpack. "If that's the case," she presses, "what's in the backpack that he's handing you?" Cody pauses the game again, grabs the phone out of her hand, and takes another look. But instead of offering up an excuse, he shrugs. "How am I supposed to know?"

She is so taken aback by this nonexplanation that she's momentarily speechless. While it's true that Eddie holds the backpack, anyone looking at the photo would argue he's about to hand the bag to Cody. Without a doubt, it's an exchange of some type. But is it drugs? Just because that's the reputation that precedes Eddie on campus doesn't necessarily mean her brother is getting drugs in return for an "edited" paper. Of course, Dawn doesn't buy the edited paper story one bit. She's pretty sure that paper was written by Cody. For Eddie. Like 95 percent.

"You don't *know*? Really, Cody?" she demands. "You expect me to believe that? Aren't you even a little bit worried about the caption under the photo that accuses you of trading a paper for drugs?"

He flips off Call of Duty, tosses the controller on the table, and jumps up from the couch. He grabs the phone from her and studies the picture one last time before shoving it back into her hand. "Regardless of what you might think, that picture proves squat about squat." He pulls out a cigarette from a random pack of Lucky Strikes lying on the table, lights up. "Besides, who the hell would take it? It's twisted."

At least that's one thing they can agree on: it *is* twisted in a *Cape Fear* kind of way. "I don't know. You tell me. Does someone have it out for you? Why would someone try to frame you? Were you screwing around on Melissa?" It's the first thing that springs to mind, and Dawn instantly regrets saying it. Melissa has been Cody's on-again, off-again girlfriend for the last four years.

"No f'ing way. I'm not like that." His cheeks flare with color, a reaction so uncharacteristic that Dawn takes a quick step back. "I don't sleep around. Besides, we broke up."

"Wait, what?" Dawn falls back into the ugly recliner and hugs a pillow to her chest. "You're kidding, right? Since when?"

"Since this afternoon." He blows smoke out the window, uncharacteristically pensive. "It wouldn't have lasted anyway. I'll be in New Haven all summer, and she's flying back to LA. Then it's, see ya, world, I'm off to North Dakota."

Because she can't think of a better way to signal her disappointment at the moment, Dawn whips the pillow at him, which he fake-blocks with an elbow. "That seems like a really stupid reason to break up with someone you care about. I mean, it's not like Melissa even has a plan for next year. Maybe she'll want to move out to North Dakota with you."

Cody snorts. "Yeah, right. And do what?"

She shrugs, considering. "I don't know. Open a jewelry store? Work at your school?" She gets up to stand closer to the fan and lifts her hair. The breeze feels good on the back of her neck that's already perspiring.

"Anyway, it was never that serious," he adds and collapses into the chair next to the window, as if the last four years have meant nothing. The unfortunate fact is that Dawn actually *likes* Melissa. Breaking up with her is one of the dumber things her brother could do. Melissa is beautiful and nice and graduating with a degree in biology. Surely, there are creatures she could study in North Dakota? Maybe get her master's degree? Also worth noting: Melissa is one of the few girls who can tease Cody without his flying into a total rage. That Cody has suddenly dumped her just further confirms that her brother is strangely determined to see how much he can screw up his life before receiving his diploma tomorrow.

"Well, I think it's safe to assume someone's unhappy with you." Dawn slips her phone back into the little embroidered purse she bought for tonight. "Look, I don't want you to get in trouble, especially not now, with graduation tomorrow."

He runs a hand through his hair, a languid trail of smoke lisping into the air. "Don't worry about it. So what if I edited Eddie's paper? Big deal. You can't even tell that it's a paper. It could have been my picks for fantasy football or something."

"In May?"

Cody shrugs. "You know what I mean."

Dawn studies him by the window with his cigarette, another recent habit at odds with her brother's clean-cut football star image. She's already texted him articles about how his lungs turn blacker with each passing cigarette, articles that she's pretty sure he deletes without reading. Probably a passing phase, she tells herself—her brother trying out the wilder side of college life before it's too late. Well, he has roughly twenty-four hours to go.

She considers what Cody has just told her. The photo has been in her possession since ten o'clock this morning, almost seven hours now, and nothing has happened. No more texts, no requests for payoffs or anything remotely resembling blackmail. Maybe Cody is right. Maybe the photo means nothing, just some idiot pulling a pre-graduation prank. One of his football buddies will probably text him later tonight, asking him if he freaked out when Dawn showed him the picture. They probably assumed that his sister, the worry-wart, would give it to him right away.

She pulls her long hair out in front of her face and begins twisting three strands into a loose braid, saying nothing. She misses the days when she and Cody used to confide in each other, when they were each other's trusty sounding boards. No sin was too big or too small to seek out advice on. Once when Cody was ten and crashed their mom's rearview mirror while hitting a tennis ball around in the driveway, he'd run into the house to ask Dawn what to do. She knew her mom would figure it out eventually and said to tell the truth. It turned out to be the right decision

since Meredith had watched the whole incident unfold beyond the living room window, anyway. Cody has helped
Dawn, too—for instance, last year when she went before the
Administration Board to defend herself as the innocent student that she was. It was Cody who coached her on what
to say to the intimidating panel of professors who sat across
from her, their thick gray eyebrows knitted in judgment.
Cody (not her parents), who told her to act confident, that
she'd done nothing wrong, only prepared in advance for
her final.

"So, who do you think will be weirder this weekend?
Mom or Dad?" he asks now in a not-so-transparent attempt
to change the subject.

And Dawn's willing to play along, to drop the subject
for the moment. If Cody's not concerned, why should she
be? She weighs his question. "Well, Mom seemed pretty
emotional when I talked to her last night. I think it's going
to be hardest for her. But you know Dad. Always has to be
the life of the party. He's the wild card."

"And, of course, we haven't mentioned the lovely Lily."

"Eww, stop calling her that. She's not even close to
lovely."

Cody shrugs. "Dad seems to think so. C'mon, she's his
midlife crisis, his trophy wife."

"Okay, please stop." Dawn hugs herself. "Let's not turn
Dad into a total cliché." Although she hates to admit it, she
also suspects this might be the case. "You seriously think
she's hot?" Dawn doesn't know what to think of Lily, who
is pretty, she supposes, if you like big boobs, small waists,
and long hair. To her eye, her stepmom looks manufac-
tured, not quite real. Though she realizes asking her brother
about their stepmom's appearance qualifies as almost gross,

she's eager for an objective opinion, a male opinion other than her dad's.

"She's definitely an eight. Maybe even an eight and a half."

"Eww," Dawn repeats.

Cody shrugs. "You asked." Her phone pings with a text. "Come on," he says, pushing back his chair from the window and rising to his feet. "I can see Mom and Joel and Nana. They're out front."

Lily concedes that she might feel a tiny bit dejected on this, the night before graduation, an evening that she and Roger were supposed to spend together reviewing any last details for Saturday's party. There are two steak filets marinating in the fridge, waiting to be grilled for dinner, and a short list of to-do items left on her trusty legal pad. Things that only Roger can tend to, such as signing the kids' graduation cards and finalizing the order of the photos in the slideshow that Lily has spent the last few weeks pulling together.

There are adorable photos of Dawn and Cody when they were maybe three years old, apple picking in New Hampshire. Cody's face reflects that delicious toddler chubbiness, his hair spiraling in luscious curls the color of corn silk. And in young Dawn, Lily can glimpse the beginnings of the beauty she will become, her rosebud lips perfect even as she pouts over an apple. Then there's Cody at his first T-ball game, his expression so intent and serious, and another of Dawn curtsying in a pink tutu, her dark hair coiled into a fat bun. A handful of family photos at milestone events—birthdays, Thanksgivings, Christmases—showcases Roger and Meredith looking on, the proud parents in the background. Lily has included these photos in a gracious nod to Meredith, though Roger never inquired if they might make Lily uncomfortable. She knows that in his mind, they are all one big happy family for the weekend, coming together to celebrate the kids.

And Lily is willing to go along with that reasoning, mostly because she doesn't wish to begrudge Dawn or Cody any happiness. She's excited for them, even proud, though she knows she deserves none of the credit for their success. Having officially joined the family during the twins' senior year in college leaves her feeling somewhat like a distant aunt, one who might send books or a new video game at Christmastime. Her involvement in their lives has been at best tangential, afforded in small random moments such as when they drop by the house on the odd weekend. Lily has always been welcoming, she thinks. If anything, the twins remind her of what it felt like to be young—the insecurities, the phobias, the worrying that nothing will ever go right.

But roughly one hour ago, Roger called to say that he was heading over to the kids' Thursday night banquet after all. The sound of heavy traffic poured through his Bluetooth speakers while she listened to him exult over the fact that he'd managed to leave work early. "Told the client my kids were graduating this weekend, and he asked me what the hell I was doing talking to him." Roger laughed on the other end, delighted to be set free.

"That's great," Lily said, not pointing out the obvious, which was that he was effectively canceling their dinner date. But it's graduation weekend! If his client can excuse Roger from work, surely Lily can wave off a silly little planning dinner.

So now she sits alone, drifting on a large blue raft in the

pool while nursing a glass of wine and waiting for her friend Alison to arrive, whom she invited over approximately half an hour after Roger called. Moses, whom Lily has come to adore over the last year and a half, lies in a shaded patch on the patio, keeping her company. Since the buffet is such a casual affair (and Roger hadn't planned on attending in the first place), there is no need for Lily to show up tonight. He wouldn't expect her to come on such short notice anyway, he explained. Plus, she'd seemed a little "stressy" this morning. *Is everything okay?*

Stressy? *Why thank you for noticing*, she thinks now. Although she's secretly relieved that her attendance will not be required at tonight's buffet (who wants *that* added pressure?), she's irked that Roger has seen fit to make this sudden change of plans while deleting her from an event so easily, as if it's no big deal. As if she's not really part of the family.

It's not that she's concerned an old flame might be stoked between him and Meredith—that fire went out long ago, as Roger has reassured her plenty of times. Sometimes, if she squints, Lily thinks she can see a faint resemblance to Melissa Gilbert from *Little House on the Prairie*, whom apparently, Meredith would get mistaken for when she and Roger first dated. But now Meredith strikes her as one of those women who used to be attractive until middle age added a good thirty pounds. Lily can point to several such women who talk nonstop about their successful children, as if to say, "See! I've let myself go for the sake of my children! Everything I do is for them."

No, she's not threatened by Meredith in the least. It's just that lately she's been feeling like a bridesmaid at her own wedding, tasked with getting every detail right for the party and with little thanks. As she has reminded herself a million times, this weekend is but one in a long string of weekends ahead for her and Roger. Surely, she can be pleasant and easygoing for seventy-two hours. Surely, she can bite her tongue when her instinct is to cry out, *A simple thank-you would be nice!*

Besides, Lily is accustomed to not getting her way—she just thought that things would be different after she married Roger. That Roger, so romantic when they were first dating, would want to share dinner out on the deck every night before they climbed upstairs to make love. And while it's true that they'll still occasionally head out for a romantic evening, an encroaching loneliness has begun to permeate her days. Roger seems even busier at the office now than when they were first dating. Lily gets it—her husband works hard for all the advantages they have (look at this amazing house! This pool! The ocean views!)—but she never imagined marriage could be so, well, isolating.

She spins herself around on the raft and marvels at the rosy orange streaks that light up the sky in broad swaths of color. It's a gorgeous summer night, the kind that's ideal for backyard barbecuing and skinny-dipping to escape the heat. It dawns on her that she hasn't spent much time out here yet, even though they filled the pool in early May. The weather has been nice enough, but Lily, somewhat to her own consternation, has become slightly obsessed with daytime TV. Not the soap operas which strike her as pure fluff (she does have *some* standards), but the talk shows. *Ellen* is her favorite, though Lily will watch pretty much anything that features real-life drama. In the past month, a particular stable of shows has become her daily fix to fill the hours while Roger works. Because, let's face it, there is only so much Instagramming she can do before Lily, let alone her followers, gets sick of herself.

Admittedly, with a constant crew descending on the house to prepare for Saturday's gala, it's a craving that has been harder to feed these last few days. The coordinator, Donna, seems perfectly competent, and so Lily has given her the green light to make any further decisions regarding the details. Since she can no longer lounge in the family room with the fifty-inch wall-mounted screen, she and Moses now hide out in the bedroom on her gigantic king bed, following the troubled lives of folks who, she knows, could just as easily be her.

She can't stop thinking about today's episode, a repeat from years ago. There is a particular talk show host who prides himself on digging up the most egregious stories, and even though Lily sometimes feels uncomfortable, like a voyeur, she still watches, mesmerized. Today's show focused on a couple fighting over paternity. The boyfriend insisted he wasn't the father of the child while his ex-girlfriend maintained he was. The mom stabbed her finger at a photo of the baby on the screen behind her and yelled, *Look at those eyes. She and her daddy have the same eyes!* The audience seemed to agree. When the host pulled the DNA results from the envelope (*not* the father), the audience gasped, and the poor woman rushed offstage. The story is so tangled and tragic, it's enough to make Lily wonder if perhaps they were paid actors.

The fact that she has become a stay-at-home wife who watches daytime TV both thrills and embarrasses her. For all her life, she has had to pull her own financial weight, even if only as a waitress, and now she no longer needs to worry about from where next month's rent check will come.

The sensation is unfamiliar, like a newly capped tooth that she can't stop running her tongue over to reassure herself it's still there. But she also can't stop watching the shows—maybe it's the nagging sense of what-her-life-could-have-been that gives them such a gravitational pull.

Before she met Roger, and long before she escaped Kentucky, Lily grew up in what can only be described as less-than-ideal circumstances. Shelia, her mom, prided herself on the number of beers she could drink while still walking a straight line. Her daddy was but a fluff of tumbleweed that rolled in and out of their lives, but mostly out. Her girlfriends always told her she was too smart, too pretty to stay in their Podunk town, making straight As in high school. But there was no money for college, certainly no graduation celebration like this.

Lily has a vague recollection of, on the eve of her graduation, staying up with Shelia to watch *Terms of Endearment*, her mom's favorite. They made root beer floats and put their fuzzy-slippered feet up on the ottoman. But when Lily woke the next morning, pulled on her new linen dress, and went into the kitchen to say good morning, she spied the empty bottle of gin lying on its side in the kitchen sink. When she stepped into Shelia's bedroom, her mom lay passed out on her waterbed, snoring to wake the dead. Lily didn't even try to rouse her. She was the class salutatorian, but it didn't matter. No one from her family was there to congratulate her.

If only her mom could see her now! She wouldn't believe where Lily has landed. And maybe, Lily thinks, her mom *is* watching over her from somewhere, somehow. It's possible. Lily has never been big on religion, but she'd like to think there's something more to her mother's life than being buried several feet underground in a Kentucky cemetery. That she's a presence hovering above, probably with a gin and tonic in her hand. The thought almost makes Lily smile. "Well, isn't this something?" her mother might say and nod her head. "I always knew my little girl would go far." To which Lily would reply, "I've earned it, don't you think, Mama? I've worked hard to get here."

Lily doesn't intend to fine-tune her pity violin this weekend, but the contrast between her graduation day and the twins' couldn't be more vivid. In fact, it borders on the comical. Even if they wanted to, the kids can't escape commencement day. A gazillion dollars have been spent to ensure that there will be ample celebrating, endless merriment. Tomorrow Roger's brother, Georgie, arrives from London in time to catch the ceremony at one o'clock. And the original Mr. and Mrs. Landau, mirthless Harry and his formidable wife, Edith, will soon enough be marching around, as well. Thankfully, they've opted to stay at the Marriott a few miles from the house. (Lily has met Roger's parents only once, when she got the distinct impression that neither of them approved of her nor the marriage.)

Round and round the merry-go-round we go, she thinks as she dips her hand in the pool water, sending the raft spinning. Just one little weekend. *Easy-peasy.* The extra pill she popped following Roger's call is starting to chip away at the jagged edges of her thoughts, that warm, buzzy feeling stretching down to her toes. She's beginning to feel optimistic about the weekend again—it can't be *all* bad, can it?—when her phone pings with a text from Alison: she's out front.

Perfect timing, Lily thinks.

FIVE

Thursday evening

Dawn, in her yellow dress, is a virtual splash of sunshine. Of course, Meredith could never say this to her—it would only prompt an eye roll.

"You look beautiful, honey," she says instead, pulling her daughter into a hug that's more or less reciprocated.

"Thanks, Mom. So do you. I like your hair." Meredith self-consciously tucks a strand behind her ear, pleased that someone has noticed her recent caramel highlights.

"And Cody." She rests a hand on the sleeve of his seer-sucker jacket. "You look so handsome, you could be James Bond." This last comment definitely begets an eye roll from them both.

"Last time I checked, Bond was swarthy, Mom. With brown hair," he points out.

"No, no, not Pierce Brosnan. The other guy. You know who I mean." Meredith involuntarily glances to Joel for help, but he's holding an ice bag on the back of his head, where a football conked him only minutes ago. Thanks to a quick-thinking senior who grabbed the ice, the goose egg doesn't appear to be too awful. Meredith reassures him that he'll most definitely live, but she can't help but feel it serves her husband right—what was he even thinking, playing football with those boys? "Oh, what's his name? Daniel something. Anyway, it's so good to see you two! I can't believe my babies are graduating."

"Mom. Stop." It's a two-word command, as if Dawn can already anticipate the torrent of emotion that will spill from her mother this weekend unless great strides are taken to prevent it. The master of the deflective move, she turns to hug her grandmother. "Thanks for coming, Nana."

Carol's bony hand grasps hers as they pull apart. "I wouldn't miss it for the world, honeybunch."

"Hey, are you going to be okay? Like seriously?" Dawn eyes her stepdad warily.

"What? This?" Joel points to his mop of hair, soaked through with sweat or water, Meredith can't be certain. "It's nothing. Just a little bump. You look amazing, by the way. And, Cody, my man," Joel continues, "Who knew you could clean up so well? Looking sharp."

Dawn grins, while Cody, hands in his pockets, digs the toe of his suede Buck into the dirt as if extinguishing a cigarette. "Thanks, man."

Her children are playing it so cool, Meredith wants to scream! Once again, she finds herself wishing she could rewind to the days when they desperately needed her. Such as the time when Cody chipped his front tooth on a slide and only Meredith could calm his cries. How she let him pinch her hand as hard as he wanted when the dentist slid the Novocain needle into his gums, prompting a wave of tears. Or, the day when Dawn got cut from first line in *The Nutcracker*, the way it stung and how she turned to her mom for comfort and reassurance. Meredith recognizes that, like everything else in life, the twins' growing up has been a process, baby steps that have led them further and further away from her to this day. It doesn't preclude her, though, from brushing Cody's shaggy bangs out of his eyes now.

"C'mon," Dawn coaxes, probably sensing her mother is on the verge of having a moment. "We're already late to the party."

They head around back to where a massive white tent is hiding (or more like grandstanding). Joel hikes his ice bag into a trash bin, and Carol grips Meredith's arm as they navigate the grassy lawn in their heels. When they step inside the tent, Meredith has to blink against the relative darkness. Hundreds of tiny white lights dangle from over-head, and bouquets of blue-and-white balloons drift languidly above the tables.

"Goodness, it's like a pep rally and a wedding reception combined," she whispers and counts approximately ten long rows of tables draped in white. In one corner sits the buffet, covered in trays of steaming food—a regrettable choice, Meredith can't help but think, for such unseasonably warm weather. In another corner a band with Rastafarian dreadlocks and tie-dyed shirts warms up on the bongo drums and guitars. Off to the left, she spies the makeshift bar and feels nearly as gratified to see an industrial-sized floor fan nearby. Already, little beads of sweat are forming beneath her Spanx girdle.

"Mom, can I get you a cocktail?"

"Whatever you're having, dear," says Carol. "Think I'll head to the buffet before all the good food gets taken."

"Me, too," says Dawn, then Cody.

"Me, three," chimes in Joel. "Grab me a beer, would you, honey?"

When Meredith arrives at the drinks table, the huge fan sends a rush of muggy air her way, and she wallows in the tepid breeze, taking a moment to scan the room. Already, graduates and their assorted families crowd the tent. Her mother will be pleased by the robust showing of grandparents here. Parents, grandparents, uncles and aunts—everyone grins and shakes hands as they circulate about. Some of the dads could be former college football players, big-shouldered guys who confidently stroll around with a drink in hand, and several mothers parade by in sleek, bare-backed dresses, revealing early summer tans. Is it just Meredith, or do these women look as if they're trying too hard to appear ten years younger?

Then there's another group, an occasional gray streak in their hair, who've clearly checked the *I Don't Care: I'm A Mom* box, and who circulate in flowy summer skirts with elasticized waistbands. Meredith, in her heels, covetously eyes their sandals with comfortable, squishy soles.

Somewhere in between these two groups is where she hopes to fall tonight. Despite being on the Keto diet for the last few weeks, it dawns on her that the five pounds recently shed from her frame makes precious little difference in the scheme of things. Back at the hotel, after she'd changed into her dress, she'd been feeling confident, almost pretty, but now she realizes she's just another invisible mom, come to watch her children graduate. Maybe when she gets back home she'll reconsider Botox, something to hoist her back onto the plane of visibility. Her friend Donna tried it and now resembles a twenty-year-old. A twenty-year-old with overly plumped lips and a frozen forehead, but still.

When it's Meredith's turn in line, a young man who bears a striking resemblance to Tom Cruise fetches her two glasses of merlot, and she happily slides a five-dollar bill into his tip jar. Poor Joel will have to fend for himself—two glasses are the most she can carry without spilling all over herself. It's on the way back to her table when she spots the woman: a few feet away stands a tall blonde wearing the *exact* same sundress as Meredith, except hers is probably a size two and has a deep slit running up one side. *Is* it the same dress? Did the woman cut the slit herself to better show off her toned calves? Meredith wonders. She quickly ducks her head, hoping to sneak away unnoticed...

But it's too late.

"Hello, excuse me!" the blonde calls out, and when Meredith glances up, the woman's elongated fingers flutter in her direction. Before she knows it, the stranger, who might be in her late thirties, early forties at the most (only a few crow's-feet), is standing beside her. "I'm sorry, but I couldn't resist coming over. What are the odds that two of us are wearing the *same* dress tonight? Did you get yours at Saks, too? Honey, come here!" She gestures toward a dark-haired man, equally exquisite and apparently her husband. "Come take our picture. This is unbelievable!"

"I know, so funny, right?" Meredith tries to play along, but it's evident that if their photos were posted side by side in *People*'s "Who Wore It Best?" competition, Meredith would get maybe 2 percent of the votes. She smiles halfheartedly into the bright flash of the husband's cell phone. A quick round of introductions and Meredith discovers that the woman's name is Penelope, "like Cruz," she clarifies, and her son, James, will graduate tomorrow.

Meredith can't resist a little name-dropping herself. "So nice to meet you. I'm Meredith Parker. Cody's mom, you know, Bolton's running back?" This prompts more excited squeals from Penelope.

"Honey, this is Cody Landau's mother! Can you believe it? I'm wearing the same dress as Cody Landau's mom! How cool is that?" A bit of Penelope's iced margarita splashes onto her dress. "Oopsies! Good thing my dress, I mean, *our* dress, is purple!" A few more cocktails and Meredith would be willing to bet that Penelope will be tucked into bed in another hour or so. She works to free herself from the woman's grasp as politely as she can. "Very nice meeting you. See you tomorrow, I hope."

"Hope we're not wearing the same dress at graduation!" Penelope chirps, as if they're new best friends. *Definitely a GAT mom*, Meredith thinks, the moniker she and her friends used to ascribe to the handful of moms who dressed up for school pickups and drop-offs, their hair and makeup flawless at seven thirty in the morning. Glamorous All the Time.

When she finds her way back to her family, it appears to include only Joel and her mom.

"What happened to you?" he asks. "I was worried you'd gotten lost."

"Drinks line took forever. Where'd everyone else go?"

Joel's head tilts to the left. "Over there. As soon as we got some food, the kids hightailed it to sit with their friends."

Meredith frowns. "Is that allowed?" Separating from the family seems to break some unspoken rule of graduation etiquette. "I thought they were supposed to eat with us."

"C'mon, honey. Relax. They're going to be with us all

weekend. They want some time to hang with their friends."
He leads her to a table with a handful of empty seats, and
Carol follows a few steps behind them.

"M'ladies." He sets down a plate he's prepared in advance
for her. The evening's theme appears to be surf and turf:
steak, swordfish, julienne carrots in herb sauce, a roll with
a thick slab of butter. It counts as a small godsend because,
even though Meredith didn't ask for a plate, she can by-
pass the buffet line, which currently snakes all the way to
the back of the tent, and she digs in eagerly. The steak is a
little tough, but it doesn't prevent her from trying to trim
off the fatty parts with the plastic knife provided. Until it
snaps in two. Joel laughs.

"Honestly, you'd think we've spent enough money on tuition to afford real knives at our kids' graduation, wouldn't
you?" he asks.

"You'd think," she says. The swordfish, on the other
hand, breaks apart easily into succulent, flaky bits, and the
marinade—lime and something else she can't quite put her
finger on, coriander, maybe?—makes for pure ambrosia.
"Oh! I almost forgot," she says between mouthfuls. "Sorry
I couldn't manage a beer for you—my hands were full. I
can go back—"

"No worries," he says, "I've got one right here," and
Meredith sees that, indeed, her husband has already flagged
down a waiter who's conveniently pushing a beer cart their
way.

"Isn't it kind of strange?" she muses. "I know it's not a
college reunion, but somehow it feels like one. These people are roughly the same age as we are. Heck, some of them
were probably in my class at Bolton. Do you know what I
mean?" she continues, trying to make Joel understand, but

maybe it's a girl thing. Maybe men don't get caught up in such silly games. "It's like there's this silent judging going on about whose parents have held up the best." The whole dress incident has unnerved her. *This ridiculous self-judging has got to stop, she thinks. Lily isn't even here!*

"I guess so," he offers now. "Hadn't really thought about it."

Meredith shrugs at his nonresponse and resumes people-watching. There are fancy folks who strut around as if they're the school's biggest donors and others who have already found their way to the dance floor and sway tipsily. She watches parents and soon-to-be graduates filing past the buffet and is struck by how many girls have forgotten—neglected?—to wear slips with their very short, in some cases miniscule, dresses. In the right light, she can spy not only the outline of their underwear but also the strips of their skinny, hardly there thongs. (And if she can see the inverted little V that travels up the girls' backsides, then she's fairly certain all the senior boys can detect it, too.) *Please, God*, she prays, *let Dawn have had enough sense to wear a proper slip.*

"Well, color me teal," her mother says suddenly, interrupting Meredith's thoughts. Her eyes follow a woman emerging from the buffet line in a turquoise dress and scarf with matching shoes, headband, and bag.

"Mom, behave yourself." Nevertheless, a tiny laugh escapes her. Meredith may have just lectured Joel on the foibles of comparison minutes ago, but this woman *is* a virtual sea of teal, head to shoe. It's impossible not to notice.

"I mean, there's just so much of it," her mom insists. "And the color isn't doing her complexion any favors. That's for sure."

"This coming from a woman who judges people by the books they post on Goodreads," Meredith points out. From time to time, her mother will look up what people in her church group or book club are reading. But Meredith knows as well as Carol that her mom relies on the site as a kind of background check, her own personal Rorschach test. If someone loves the same books that she does, like Elinor Lipman's *Isabel's Bed*, for instance, then they can be instant friends. If, however, they're inveterate readers of military history, her mother will harbor her doubts until the person rates a book she approves of.

Carol sniffs, fanning herself with the accordion-like fan she's fashioned out of a napkin. "You may not be able to judge a book by its cover, but you can most certainly judge a *person* by their book covers." It's a mantra so familiar coming from her mom that it might as well be painted on a wooden sign from HomeGoods and posted above her front door. Sometimes Meredith thinks her mom might be on to something, though: maybe a person *is* more likely to find his or her match on Goodreads than on any of those dating websites.

"Could be true," she offers now. "I mean, what if Goodreads were to dig a bit deeper, ask something like, 'Do you like horror fiction? If your answer is *no*, then please proceed to the next question about historical fiction.' And so forth, until your profile gets paired with someone who shares similar reading tastes. Imagine the money you could save on books alone?"

"Now you're thinking." Carol winks wickedly. "I wonder if any studies have been done on the staying power of relationships when spouses have similar tastes in books. I'll bet you it's a bond as strong as love. Maybe even stronger."

Meredith laughs and turns to get Joel's opinion, only to notice that her husband's face has turned an alarming shade of red. "Are you all right?" He's rolling a frosty beer bottle across his forehead. She lays a hand on his other arm, which is warm and tacky to the touch. "Is your head bothering you?"

"Couldn't be better. Just a little warm."

"You look a little—" she pauses "—flushed. Why don't you go out and get some air before the awards ceremony?"

He shoves the last piece of medium rare steak into his mouth, then says, "Good idea," and dabs his face with a "Class of 2020" napkin before standing. "It *is* getting a little toasty in here, isn't it? Back in a few."

Minutes later, Dawn materializes at their table with a friend, and Meredith remembers now that Dawn's yellow dress has a built-in slip already. *Thank goodness.*

"Nice to see you again, Shauna," Meredith says. Shauna resembles so many of the other girls here with her long straight hair, lean runner's legs, and eyelashes so thick they look as if they've been glued on—which, according to Dawn, some girls actually pay a small fortune to do these days. Shauna's white dress hits at midthigh, reminding Meredith of a nightie she wore on her honeymoon. *Really?* she thinks. *This is what passes for graduation attire these days?*

"Hi, Mrs. Parker."

"You both look beautiful. Where's your brother, honey?"

Dawn glances at Shauna, as if they might be complicit in Cody's whereabouts, then shrugs. "He's probably off with Brad and Toby somewhere."

"And what about Matt? And Melissa? I haven't seen either of them around."

"They're both at their own dorm dinner," Dawn explains.

"We'll see them later. Well, at least, Matt. Not sure about Melissa. You'd have to ask Cody."

"Oh, right. That makes sense." Meredith gets the funny feeling that her daughter is revealing only half-truths at the moment, but she doesn't dare press, not in front of Shauna in her nightie.

Soon there's a clinking of silverware against glass, prompting heads to swivel to the front of the tent. "Please, if I can get your attention," calls Dean Tillman, the dorm's headmaster. "Please, everyone, back to your seats," he urges. "We're going to start the awards ceremony as soon as everyone gets settled with their families." Dawn tells Meredith she'll be right back; she's walking Shauna to her table. Now if they can just find Cody to join them, Meredith thinks, everything will be perfect.

She searches the room for the familiar head of corn-silk hair, the easygoing stance that her son seems to inhabit so naturally. Surely, he'll seek them out now that the dean has asked the graduates to join their families. Near the tent's entrance, clusters of people are beginning to scatter, returning to their tables. And that's when she spots him, her stomach performing a somersault. *Roger.*

Her ex-husband has come to crash this party, after all.

Well, I'll be damned, she thinks. Roger is the last person she expected to see tonight. Not that he shouldn't be here— *he should.* But he'd already apologized to her and the kids, saying there was no way he could possibly make it tonight, some big client closing on a huge deal, and so on and so forth. Typical Roger excuses that used to drive her batty back when they were married. These days his excuses skate by her, but she'd worried about how the kids would perceive his absence tonight. Maybe Roger has had a change of heart, Meredith thinks. Maybe he realized that you only get to celebrate your children's graduation once and you'd best take advantage of it. She hopes that's the case. Maybe Lily urged him to come, but she doesn't even see Lily. It's only Roger, looking slightly adrift, as if waiting for someone to rescue him.

Well, it won't be Meredith, that's for sure.

After they settle in their seats, Joel spies her over at the drinks table before she notices him. Thankfully. It gives him a moment to collect himself, get his bearings, and make certain it really *is* her. A profound sense of déjà vu sweeps over him. There's the familiar hue of her hair, auburn with a touch of gray, and that intense focus, which, at the moment, centers on the man in front of her. Kat angles her head to one side as if considering something her companion has said, then laughs. Even from afar, it's the same laugh Joel remembers from high school, husky, earthy. She might have put on a few pounds (*welcome to the club*, he thinks), but otherwise, she could be the same girl sauntering down the hall of Grafton High toward his locker after fifth period, coming to ask if he wants to grab a milkshake at the Dairy Queen, and making his heart beat a thousand beats per minute.

He shakes his head, as if to chase away a foggy dream, and digs into his swordfish. Will Kat even remember him? Of the two of them, he has changed the most—less hair, sagging middle, wrinkles around the eyes, a salt-and-pepper beard. Back in the day, he and Kat had been what they called "an item." For almost two years. She was "his first" in every meaning of the word, first crush, first love, first girl he went all the way with, first girl to break his heart.

Joel considers now, in some ways, she was also the *last* girl to break his heart since technically he didn't fall in love again until he met Meredith. *How pathetic is that?* he thinks. This graduation isn't meant to be an exercise in self-evaluation, but damned if he doesn't feel a tad inferior himself at the moment. All through college and graduate school, he'd flirted around, dating girls for a few months at a time, but nothing serious. Not because he never got over Kat—no, he won't give her that much credit—but because he never clicked with anyone else completely. Until Meredith. And with Meredith, it wasn't even about clicking, because his heart had locked instantly and completely onto hers. One hundred percent.

Still, he wouldn't be honest if he didn't admit that Kat has stayed with him all these years, somewhere in the deep recesses of his mind. That's probably not unusual for a first crush, but they were more than that—at least he'd like to think so. True friends till their friendship fizzled out as suddenly as a white dwarf planet dwindles in intensity. On a frigid winter night when Kat had called from Berkeley to tell him she'd met someone else. *Wow!* Joel hasn't thought of that phone call in years. Decades.

He flags down the guy with a beer cart, helps himself to a frosty Sam Adams, and rolls the bottle across his forehead before taking a sip. Maybe it'll freeze the pores in his skin that seem to be leaking sweat. *Damn, it's hot.* The muggy, sticky air reminds him of a summer he spent out in Minnesota as a camp counselor, the nights as scorching as the days, the mosquitoes as big as horseflies. Between the heat and Kat, he's not sure how long he's going to last here. Meredith is saying something about how this feels like a college reunion, but Joel can't really connect the dots. Everyone's dressed up for sure, but aren't they all here to celebrate their kids?

He leans over and asks, "How long is this thing supposed to last?"

"The invitation said five thirty to nine o'clock. I doubt it will run that long, though. Why, eager to get going already?" she teases. The band has kicked it up a notch, and "Don't Worry, Be Happy" floats across the steamy air.

Now he wonders why they possibly thought it was a good idea to arrive on time—wouldn't six o'clock have been preferable?—but he promised himself he'd be cordial the entire weekend, not the annoying plus-one on Meredith's ticket. And he intends to stick to his word, bump or no bump on the head, Kat or no Kat. As casually as possible, he twists around in his seat to determine if Kat still lingers somewhere near the bar. But the drinks line—more like a mob now—has multiplied exponentially, and the odds of finding anyone in it are about as good as his locating his recently discarded beer cap.

Maybe, he thinks, Kat won't be able to pick him out of this crowd anyway, a thought that both relieves and pains him. It would be nice to catch up, find out what she's been up to. He's tried searching for her on Facebook and Twitter a few times but has come up empty. And now here she is at the same graduation awards ceremony as he. It suddenly dawns on him that one of these graduates milling about must belong to her. Remarkable. A son? A daughter? Twins? Somehow a son seems more likely, though he can't rightly say why.

"Are you all right?" Meredith asks. Her eyebrows are scrunched together the way they get whenever she's worried, and she rests a gentle hand on his arm.

"Couldn't be better." He smiles. "Just a little warm."

"You look a little…flushed," she finally settles on. "Why don't you go out and get some air before the awards ceremony?"

As soon as she suggests it, Joel realizes that's exactly what he needs. Some fresh air would do him good. A few minutes to regain his composure. He excuses himself, grabs his beer, and hurries outside.

Thanks to the lightest of breezes, even the thick, humid air outside feels invigorating. Joel's not typically a claustrophobic guy, but it sure felt like that tent was closing in on him. The sky is beginning to purple, and he unbuttons his top two shirt buttons, his jacket shed long ago. Beyond the tent, near a plot of dreary-looking hydrangeas, students clump together in small groups, the tangerine glow of a cigarette flickering like a firefly as they pass it among themselves. Several kids sit scattered across the back steps of Pratt Hall, and Joel eavesdrops on their conversation, of which he can discern only the hazy parameters. Something about a guy named Tommy, a car, and the dean of students. Whatever the story, it seems to have ended well enough, and the group breaks out in riotous laughter.

Was I ever this young? Was I ever so carefree? It seems impossible to Joel. He vaguely remembers graduation day from his local college in Vermont, just a stone's throw from where he grew up. Can recall the celebration afterward when he and his parents and a cousin went out to dinner at Applebee's (Kat had celebrated with her own family). He even remembers their waitress, a young girl who'd graduated a few years ahead of him in high school. Her name eludes him now but her face still lingers, a girl who'd been in all honors classes and yet had never made it to college, standing beside his table and taking his order. Back then, he'd felt sorry for her, stuck in their hometown, no aspirations to speak of. But now, seeing himself next to these soon-to-be graduates, his own graduation celebration at an Applebee's strikes him as marginally pathetic.

The thought of a cigarette, though he hasn't smoked in years, appeals to him, just like every now and then he'll crave a shot of whiskey to steer him through the night after a particularly rough day at school. He's thinking about how he might try to bum a cigarette off one of the kids when he recalls an elaborate report Cody wrote in sixth grade about the effects of smoking. Cody was such a gifted kid. It was evident early on, and though his teachers had advised them to transfer Cody to a gifted and talented charter school, Meredith had resisted, reluctant to split up the twins.

Joel still considers it the right decision. Because Dawn was clever, too, her head usually buried in a book. In fact, one of the few disagreements he'd had with Meredith was over whether Dawn should be allowed to read at the dinner table—Joel had argued against it, declaring dinnertime family time. (It was one of the few truisms that had stuck with him from his graduate studies: family dinners were supposedly an important predictor of a child's future success.) Meredith had been surprised that Joel, typically reticent when it came to disciplining the kids, felt so strongly about it.

A gentle hand rests on his arm. "Joel?"

He startles, still stuck in the memory.

"I thought that was you," Kat says, smiling. "How are you?"

Is this the real Kat or just an illusion of the Kat he thought he saw earlier? Joel struggles to reorient himself as he peers at a slightly older version of the girl he once dated, once cared for deeply.

"Kat," he says. "My goodness! Hello!" His voice sounds overly jubilant, as if he's trying too hard, and he feels himself wince. "What a surprise. You look great!" When he pulls her into a hug, her drink splashes onto his arm, prompting an awkward laugh from them both.

"What are you doing here?" For a brief moment, he gives her an appraising look and concludes she's more or less the same, maybe a few more lines etching the corners of her eyes. Still beautiful. "Don't tell me we're both old enough to have graduates here."

"Well, you are, but I'm not." She winks. "I haven't aged since high school." A passing waiter offers him a napkin, and Joel takes it gratefully, blotting his arm that now smells faintly of vodka. Kat swirls the remainder of her drink with a swizzle stick and gazes up at him thoughtfully. "I'm afraid I do have a college graduate, though."

Joel shakes his head. "Impossible. The girl I used to date was never going to get married, never going to have a family." He wishes he'd thought to grab another beer as his current bottle, he now notices, is emptying fast.

Kat tilts her head to one side, her eyes narrowing. "Did I say that? Huh, I don't remember."

Her admission, as truthful as it sounds, takes him by surprise. The Kat he remembers was adamant about earning a doctorate in psychology, even if it meant at the expense of a family one day. Occasionally, when they hung out in the parking lot after practices (swim for her, wrestling for him), she would mention graduate school, dreamily describing her life to come, as if she knew something he didn't, the exotic outlines of her future evident only to her. Joel didn't pretend to really understand, but if anyone could envision a future for herself, it was Kat, who walked around school cloaked in a wisdom that made her seem years older than the rest of them. Which probably had a lot to do with why he fell for her in the first place.

"Her name's Cassie. Short for Cassandra," continues Kat. "You'd like her. She's supersmart, but, of course, she wants to be a teacher."

"Reeally?" Joel draws out the word, pondering all the information that's just been revealed, such as that Kat has a daughter, most likely a husband, and that she still thinks teaching is a subpar profession, implied by the "but" in her description.

"That's fantastic—I mean, that you have a daughter. I take it you're still against teachers, then?" Joel had considered going into the classroom before he got his degree in counseling, but soon discovered he was a better listener than teacher. Kat thought if you were going to go into the business of psychology you might as well use it to help as many people as possible. She fantasized about opening her own private practice one day.

She clucks her tongue. "I was never *against* it. It's just that most teachers are still grossly underpaid. And Cassie is so smart, she really could make a difference in the world, you know? And make some money doing it. That's all I'm saying."

"Point taken." He smiles. She's the same old opinionated Kat after all.

"Oh, and I got married, which you probably figured out by now." Joel takes another swig of beer. "For a few years. But he turned out to be a real bastard, as you might imagine." (Joel is trying to imagine.) "So, I remarried, and this time I think I got it right." Joel continues to nod, agreeing with everything Kat says. "Her name is Ruby. She works in finance. I think you'd like her."

His eyes widen at this pronouncement. "Oh," he says, unable to respond with anything more. "Wow, that's terrific." He nods his head and can feel Kat scrutinizing him for a reaction. He's walking a thin line here. He doesn't want to disappoint her, either by overplaying the news or by appearing too nonchalant.

"Yep," she says now, as if he's asked her to confirm it. "Turns out I prefer women to men."

A grin spreads across his face. Somehow, it's comforting to hear these words coming from Kat, the girlfriend who once wielded such power over his heart. "Funny, me, too," he offers finally, and Kat laughs.

"What about you? Married? You must have kids."

"Yes and yes," Joel responds. "Married for seven years now. Two stepkids, Dawn and Cody, both of whom are graduating tomorrow."

She takes a step back. "No kidding? I never pegged you for a father of twins."

"I know, right? Of course, no one ever thinks of himself as becoming a parent of twins. You kind of fall into it. Anyway, they're super kids. Dawn ran cross-country, and she's off to Chicago to work at an advertising firm, and Cody, like your daughter, has decided to teach." He's talking too fast, saying too much, but he can't stop. "In fact, he's working out at a reservation in North Dakota this fall, teaching Native American high school kids."

A passing waiter whisks away Kat's empty cup, and Joel happily trades in his empty for a fresh Sam Adams. She smooths her dress across her stomach, one of those long maxi dresses that hovers above the ankle. "Wow, that's

amazing. Good for him. And good for you. I'm happy for
you. You always wanted a family." He smiles, unsure of the
direction this meandering conversation should take next.
Does he want to delve into the complicated web that represents his entire extended family, including Meredith's
ex-husband and former in-laws, who will be around later
this weekend? Somewhere from the back of his mind, the
answer catapults forward: *no.* The whole weekend stretches
ahead of them—there will be plenty of time for further introductions, should they be needed, in the unlikely event
he bumps into Kat again. And with over a thousand graduates, it seems pretty damn unlikely.

"You never made it back to any of the Grafton High
reunions, huh?"

"Nah." Joel shakes his head. "Reunions aren't really my
style."

She plows ahead. "And your parents? How are they
doing? I always loved your dad. He was a funny bastard."

A small chuckle escapes from Joel. It's true—his dad,
a janitor at the high school, was opinionated about many
things, including whether or not Grafton High would win
the championship football game any given year. "They're
okay. Both at an assisted living place down in Florida now.
It's pretty tough for them to get around these days."

"Oh, I'm sorry to hear that." Kat's face pinches into something like concern. "Well, tell them I say 'hello.'" The various groups outside are beginning to thin out as people head
back into the tent for the awards ceremony. "It's funny,"
she says, as if a memory has snuck up on her. "To this day,
whenever I think of you, I think of pistachios."

"Pistachios?" He has no idea what she's talking about.

"You don't remember?" Her eyes flash, a mixture of daring and mischief. "Pistachios and lobsters?"

Oh. One weekend they'd gorged themselves on a giant bag of pistachios that Kat's mom had bought at one of those supersaver stores. With a million discarded shells lying at their feet, Kat compared pistachios to lobsters. "They have a lot in common, you know." Joel had given her a hard time because he couldn't fathom how the two were remotely similar. *Lobsters and pistachios? How do you mean? When you get a bad one, you have to toss it out?* Kat shrugged. *Isn't it obvious?* she explained. *You put in all this effort for little return. One tiny nut, only a morsel of lobster meat.* She squeezed her finger and thumb together, as if to demonstrate exactly how little. An analogy that had struck him as both crazy and incredibly insightful at the time. Now, in retrospect, the memory swoops over him for what it was: two friends enjoying each other's company. Probably a few beers were involved, as well.

He grins, feeling himself sliding into their old rapport. "That's right. I forgot. Too much work for too insignificant a return, right?"

"Something like that." This larger metaphor suddenly seizes him with a sickening feeling. Is this what Kat had concluded about him during her freshman year at Berkeley? That Joel was too much work with too little in the way of return? But, no, that's ludicrous. She'd met someone else. The long-distance relationship thing was hard, impossible. From the sounds of it, Kat didn't want to sign up for a serious boyfriend in the first place.

"Well, it was really nice bumping into you." She's smiling at him. "Guess I should get back. See you around this weekend?"

"Yeah, sure thing," he says. "That would be great." He knows he should head back to his own family, but he doesn't want to follow too closely behind, lest Kat thinks he's stalking her. He waits until she rounds the entrance to the tent and wonders if her daughter, Cassie, knows Dawn. Or Cody. He doesn't recall either twin's mentioning a Cassandra or a Cassie, but then, what teenager tells their parents every detail of college life?

He's not sure how well he'll handle meeting Cassie, if it comes to that. Will he be struck by the thought that she could be the daughter he and Kat might have had together instead of Kat and the bloke she apparently married? He hopes not. To be honest, he's not sure how adeptly he'll handle *any* of this weekend. Wistfully, he thinks again of his guidebook for stepparents. If only there were a chapter he could turn to about bumping into an old girlfriend, your first true love. Who is now married to a woman. And then having to return to your family as if nothing has happened.

Well, can things get any stranger? He sure as hell hopes not. After draining the rest of his beer, he tosses it into an overflowing recycling bin and steps back into the tent, bracing himself for whatever might come next.

And that's when he spots Roger, sitting at their table, his gaze resting squarely on Meredith.

SIX

Dawn can hardly believe her dad actually showed up. Roger isn't supposed to be here tonight because of work, but it's nice to see him. She'd like to think he came because, in the end, it was too difficult to stay away—he wanted to see his kids on the night before they graduate, before they take flight from the proverbial nest. Unfortunately, though, a part of her assumes he has come only because of how it would look if he *didn't*. Bad publicity.

So much of what her dad does these days seems to hinge on how it will play for business purposes, which is, of course, totally annoying. Will he be photographed in the society pages of *The Boston Globe* or *Boston Magazine*? Her dad is "a man about town," gracing various charity functions, usually with his arm wrapped around Lily's slim waist. With every photo that runs in the paper or online, Dawn thinks her mother must die a slow death. Not because Meredith still has feelings for Roger, but because it's as if he's rubbing his good fortune in her face. *Look at the hot tamale I ended up with! Not too shabby, right?* Sometimes, if Dawn spies a particularly fetching photo of Lily and her dad online, she'll text her mom to tell her to avoid social media for a few days.

Meredith always waves it off, as if she couldn't care less, but Dawn knows she follows Lily on Twitter. What must she think when she sees Lily, who's only slightly older than her own daughter, posed at her ex-husband's side? If it were Dawn, she'd totally flip. She gets that her mom and Joel are meant for each other (if you ask her, her mom should have married Joel in the first place), but that can't make it any easier to watch her dad parading about town with an attractive younger woman on his arm.

And now here he is, front and center. She watches him search the room, maybe looking for her or Cody, or, quite possibly, the paparazzi. Lily, strangely, is nowhere to be seen.

"Lookee who's here." Cody nudges her. "Glad he could take time out of his busy schedule for us."

Cody, once their dad's eternal defender, has been on a kick lately to criticize him at every turn. But Dawn would like to give their father credit where credit is due. "I know. I already saw him." She pushes a cluster of bracelets up on her forearm, sending them jingling against one another. "I'm glad he's here."

"Yeah, right," snaps Cody and turns back to his posse of friends.

"Your brother doesn't sound too impressed," says Shauna, who, Dawn knows, harbors an unhealthy crush on Cody, even though her brother has (or is it *had* now?) a serious girlfriend.

"Not my problem." Dawn waves at her dad, her bracelets

clinking, but he doesn't see her. Without Lily by his side, he looks a little lost, as if he's wandered into a parking lot at IKEA and can't recall where he left his car. She pulls her hand back and starts in on her thumbnail again, gnawing at it like tiny fire ants. "Uh-oh," she murmurs.

"What?" asks Shauna.

"My dad. He's going over to my mom's table."

"So? What's the big deal? Where else would he sit?"

Dawn rolls her eyes. "Um, *they're divorced*, Shauna. You know that." But her friend shrugs as if she still can't fathom why her mom and dad sitting together could spell a disaster of epic proportions. Dawn avoids explaining the weird dynamics of her family, such as that her mom will probably be all right, so long as Lily, wherever she is, keeps her distance. But her nana, who still harbors a grudge, might very well try to throw her dad out of the party.

Dawn sighs. Shauna does have a point, though. It's not as if this is a company party, where her father can glad-hand everyone—eventually he'll need to sit *somewhere*. And she concedes that it makes the most sense that he sits with the entire family. If only everyone will be on their best behavior.

"Sorry, Shauna, but I've gotta go." Dawn makes a beeline for her mom's table, not bothering to ask Cody if he's coming. As far as she's concerned, her brother has declared his allegiances for the night, which rest squarely on himself. He'll be of little help when it comes to nursing the family flame of togetherness this evening. Plus, ever since she showed him the photo, he's acting weird, like more of a cocky jerk than usual. Dawn needs to get away from him and his friends, who are all jacked up on Red Bull and probably something else. For days, Cody and his football pals have been planning a senior prank for graduation (a Bolton tradition). Dawn could give a sweet whatever—she has better things to do with her time than get in trouble for a stupid prank, but each time she points this out to her brother, he accuses her of being a killjoy.

At the table, she nearly collides with her dad, who clicks his tongue and pulls her into a hug. "Look at you, Squiget!" he exclaims, invoking her childhood nickname, a mix of *squiggly* and *fidget*. "You're stunning." An unmistakable whiff of cologne rides over her as her face presses into his shirt collar.

"Thanks, Daddy," she says, when he releases her. "You didn't see me but I was waving to you. I'm so glad you could come." It's her feeble attempt at making him feel welcome, and he grins. He's dressed in a lavender golf shirt and khaki pants, and his dark hair has gone wavy in the heat, like it used to do when they'd travel to Florida for spring break. Two thin gold chains loop around his tanned neck. From one dangles the initials *R* and *L*, a wedding gift from Lily. It's so tacky, Dawn thinks, it almost counts as cool. Roger turns to greet her mom.

"Roger, what a nice surprise." Meredith stands and leans in for cheek kisses, a weird thing her parents do whenever they see each other now. It's as if they've agreed that, in lieu of physical contact, they will exchange pretend kisses for civility's sake. Her mom's acting prowess, however, could persuade even Dawn that she's truly pleased to have Roger here tonight. Her dad offers some explanation about sneaking out of work early and sends a nod in Carol's direction, who acknowledges him with a cool nod of her own.

An awkward moment ensues when her father casts around for a seat, and as he's about to lower himself into a chair,

Meredith stops him. "Oh, no, sorry. That won't work. Joel's sitting there. He just stepped outside for a minute." A confused, almost pained, expression falls over her father's face.

"Dawn, honey, where are you sitting?"

Dawn doesn't have the heart to say aloud that she'd prefer to sit with her friends rather than her own family and so she hasn't joined this particular table yet herself.

"I don't know." She giggles as if it's funny that they all suddenly find themselves in this predicament, an imaginary game of musical chairs.

"Well, we'll have to find some seats then, won't we?" He shoots her his customary I-can-fix-this wink and grabs a few empty chairs from an adjacent table, lugging them back to the table. Dawn wedges herself into a vacant seat between her mom and dad, and her mom reaches over to pat her knee, as if to say, *Don't worry. The nuclear bomb that you think is about to go off in our family at any moment? Well, it's never going to see the light of day because I've got the detonator hidden in my purse.*

Not that the thought exactly comforts Dawn because her mom is probably the least emotionally stable person here tonight. She's counting on her stepdad to steady Meredith, and at the thought, she searches in vain for Joel as Dean Tillman steps up to the podium to begin his opening remarks. Dawn's loyalties are madly ping-ponging back and forth between her parents. *Her poor dad.* Typically, Roger owns every room he walks into, but to see him now, perched uncomfortably in his folding chair, she'd think he was at the wrong party. *And her poor mom!* Meredith has been completely and unfairly ambushed, as if her ex-husband has just photobombed her own wedding. Not that Meredith and Roger can't be cordial, but now her mom will have to present a cheery face the entire night when she probably assumed she and Joel could enjoy some alone time with the kids.

Well, it's only a hiccup, thinks Dawn. And, unlike her brother, she's truly pleased that her dad has made the effort. Maybe Lily's absence will help ease the sting of the surprise, make the night somehow bearable, even pleasant. Which leads Dawn to wonder where, precisely, *is* Lily tonight? Sick? At home in protest? No one has dared to ask. Are Lily and her dad fighting? The thought sends a small smile skating across Dawn's lips.

When Joel finally returns to the table, he slides into his chair, mouths *Sorry* to Meredith, and reaches over to shake Roger's hand, a small token for which Dawn is grateful. Her stepdad has always been nothing but gracious toward Roger, and it seems this will remain true for graduation weekend. Meanwhile, her dad, apparently weary of Tillman's remarks, leans over to ask her about finals and her latest report card. "How did you do, Squiget?"

"Straight As. One A minus."

"Atta girl." Just as he used to do when she was little, he swings an arm around her shoulder and squeezes tight. Her chest constricts with this long-ago, familiar gesture of her father's affection, like a secret handshake. She'd almost forgotten.

What Dawn has told no one is that she secretly hopes her name will be announced at tonight's awards ceremony. There are a host of awards being handed out, some with an appealing sack of money tied to them, including Athlete of the Year, the School Spirit Award, and a Senior Scholar Award. Last year she would have laughed if anyone asked if she were eligible for such a prize, but this year Dawn's grades have been exceptional. And, by a stroke of luck, the award takes into account only grades for senior year. Everyone else she knows, her brother included, has let their grades free-fall during this last semester.

Everyone except Dawn.

For once, it seems possible that *she* might be the twin who gets recognized instead of her superstar brother. It would be so gratifying, especially after last year's fiasco with the Admin Board. If she wins this prize, it will be a complete and total vindication. A middle finger to the administration for putting her through that private hell. She's so nervous that she's gnawing on her cuticle again, but she doesn't even notice till her mom playfully pulls her hand away, just as she used to do when Dawn was younger.

Next thing she knows, Cody is scooting a chair over to their table and plops down beside Joel. Dawn watches him settle in for what will likely be one more glorious moment in the storied life of Cody Landau. Who else other than her brother, star running back of the football team, could possibly clinch the Athlete of the Year award? He squirms out of his blazer, flings it over the back of his chair, and proceeds to drain an entire glass of ice water. Turning back to face the podium, he crosses his arms and awaits the gods to crown him with his newest laurel.

They are six awards in when Mr. Tillman announces that the next prize will go to Athlete of the Year. He teases the audience, a bandmaster leading his charges, and offers up a vague hint at the winner. Dawn watches Cody bend forward in his seat, bouncing on the balls of his feet, ready to sprint to the podium. Already beaming, her dad winks at her mom, and Cody's pals shout, "Cody! Cody!"

"And the recipient is—" Mr. Tillman pauses for effect. "Garett Henley!" There's a millisecond of hushed, stunned silence followed by thunderous applause for the Bullfrogs' quarterback. "Garett? Where are you, son?"

Garett, along with his entire family, rises to his feet and high-fives his brothers before trotting up to the front. Dawn almost guffaws out loud. A *swoosh* of self-satisfaction overtakes her. She can't help it because, well, everything always comes *so easily* for her brother. Being his twin can be demoralizing sometimes, so seldom does her brother fail. Her dad leans over to whisper something into his ear, but Cody just shrugs. By the time Garett reaches the podium, the entire tent is up on its feet, applauding. "Garett, Garett," they chant, and her brother good-naturedly plays along, fist-pumping the air.

Well-done, Garett, thinks Dawn. Her relief that, for once, her brother has been skipped in the congratulatory lineup mixes with incredulity and for a brief moment, she feels selfish, guilty. Has her hoping for her own award in some oddly karmic way denied Cody his? She knows it's crazy, but guilt stirs in her nonetheless.

After Garett collects his trophy, Mr. Tillman continues down the list of award recipients. Dawn counts three more until Scholar of the Year. It's such a silly, trumped-up title that it's almost embarrassing. Why couldn't they call it something less pretentious, maybe Best Student of the Year? *Scholar* sounds far-fetched, something out of *Downton Abbey*. She glances at her mom, then her dad, and tries to crystallize the moment in her head—the moment before winning her first-ever academic prize in college. Meanwhile, her dad, bored now that Cody's opportunity has vanished, grabs a few candy almonds from a bowl and tosses them into his mouth.

"And it gives me great pleasure," continues Tillman, "to present the Academic Scholar of the Year Award to someone who has devoted herself to her studies while others, shall we say, comfortably slid into the senior slide." A collective murmur of laughter ripples through the tent.

"Wait for it," Dawn whispers to her mom, unable to contain her excitement any longer. Her mother's eyebrows shoot up, surprised, as if to say, *You?*

Play it cool, Dawn coaches herself. *Like Garett.* She checks her dress, making certain the back isn't tucked into her underwear or anything, and flips her hair over her shoulder.

"And the winner is…" Mr. Tillman clears his throat. She straightens in her seat. "Rose McIntosh!"

It's as if she's been sucker punched, and Dawn actually leans over, clutching her stomach.

"Honey, are you okay? Did you think you were going to win?"

Dawn takes a moment to collect herself before straightening in her seat. She shrugs, tears stinging her eyes. It's like a TV game show, where she was confident that she'd selected the winning door only to discover that it had an enormous "Bankrupt!" sign waiting behind it. She can almost hear the TV audience gasp, *Oh, no!* at her bad luck.

"Of course not," she says now, but it's harder to lie to her mom than anyone else in the world, especially when she's staring at Dawn with those huge brown eyes of concern. "Well, maybe. Just a little bit. I worked really hard this year, you know?"

"Oh, honey. I'm sorry. Who knows how they decide these things?" Meredith leans in and says a bit more softly, "Besides, it feels like the end-of-year awards mostly go to the kids who haven't been recognized before."

Like me! thinks Dawn but doesn't say it.

"I mean, look at your brother. If *he* didn't get Athlete of the Year…" Her mother's voice trails off, as if confirming everyone's thoughts that the process must be rigged. "Anyway, it doesn't matter because we're so proud of you."

Dawn manages a feeble smile.

"Remember when we used to give you a dollar for every A you earned?"

"Yeah," Dawn says. "It was the only way I ever made any money."

Meredith laughs. "Well, consider those As on your last report card to be money in the bank."

Dawn rolls her eyes, embarrassed. "It's not like I need you to pay me for my grades anymore, Mom. I can handle disappointment. Really."

She reaches over to squeeze her hand. "I just want you to understand how proud we are of you."

"I know, Mom." When a waiter sets down tiny plates of cheesecake, Dawn grabs one and stabs at her dessert. Her mother means well, of course, but a part of her can't wait to be done with college and this whole weekend. Can't wait to put Bolton in her rearview mirror and arrive in Chicago, where people will appreciate her for who she really is, for what she's really worth. When she will no longer have to live in anyone else's shadow. Even that of her beloved brother, whom some days she adores and loathes in equal measure.

SEVEN

"Win some, lose some, huh, buddy?" Roger nudges Cody. Her ex-husband doesn't seem to notice that their daughter has fled to be with her friends, that she might have been expecting a prize, as well. To be honest, the thought never occurred to Meredith, either, which makes her feel a tad guilty and ashamed. Why *didn't* she assume Dawn might win something in recognition for all her hard work? What does it say about her as a mother that her thoughts automatically gravitate toward her son whenever the matter of achievement arises? Or that she so proudly told that Penelope woman that she was Cody's mom, not even mentioning Dawn once?

Probably because Cody has always been her easy child, the one who lends himself to bragging rights. Rarely does she have to worry about him, except for those times when he's out on the football field and she recites fervent prayers to keep him safe. But Dawn has kept her up plenty of nights, the daughter who ingratiated herself with the mean girls in high school only to be kicked swiftly to the curb by those same girls. The daughter who spearheaded the move up to Boston for the twins' junior year in high school and then, to be fair, back to New Haven for their senior year. Dawn's emotions screwball all over the place, and though Meredith doesn't put much stock in astrology, sometimes it does seem as if her daughter co-opted all of the trademark sensitivity genes of a Cancer, sparing none for her brother.

Cody has always been athletic, popular, a straight-A student, the kind of son other parents gush about as if he were their own. Steady and stable, he reminds Meredith a little of herself when she was a kid. But her daughter can fly into a rage over nothing at all and the next minute burst into tears, which has the disconcerting effect of Meredith's never quite knowing what Dawn is thinking. Come to think of it, her mercurial mood swings are not so unlike her father's. Roger used to easily fly off the handle at the smallest inconvenience—a broken picture frame, a watermark stain left behind by a glass on the table, call-waiting. *Things beyond his control.* It wasn't until they'd divorced that Meredith realized how much time she'd spent tiptoeing around, careful not to upset him.

Now she wonders if Dawn's past, peppered with all that untold drama, somehow factored into Meredith's own reaction to the cheating accusation last year, when she found herself doubting her daughter's honesty. Meredith had been so quick to judge! She'd assumed that if Dawn had been accused of cheating, then she was probably guilty as charged.

"Honestly, Dawn, how could you be so stupid?" she'd shouted into the phone when the call came in the middle of the night, jolting her from a deep sleep.

"I didn't do it, Mom! I told you! It's all a misunderstanding—the Board got it wrong! Beth and I studied together, but it's not like we cheated on the exam. Why don't you believe me?"

"I'd like to believe you, but right now I'm too angry to even think straight. Joel and I will be up there this weekend, and we'll figure this thing out." In retrospect, Meredith's handling of the situation had been downright deplorable. Rather than reassuring her daughter that everything would be okay and that she trusted her, she'd done the opposite, basically calling her a liar.

It soon became clear, though, that Dawn was perfectly innocent. She and Beth had studied together for essay questions that the professor had handed out in advance. And how was that cheating when the professor more or less condoned it? The whole incident had sparked a campus-wide debate, one that eventually led to a ban on professors giving take-home exams and handing out possible essay questions in advance of finals. Meredith knows she let her daughter down, failed her during one of the most important tests of parenthood. What worries her more, though, is the other question: if it were Cody who'd been accused, would she have come to his defense immediately?

Meredith shakes her arms out, as if to set the memory loose. The self-judging of earlier tonight with Penelope in her dress (and wearing it *so much better*!) has dipped into something even more sinister, like the ways in which she has let her daughter down—and damn it, she does *not* want to go there tonight. Tonight is about celebrating, about being proud and toasting her kids.

"Ready for drink number three?" Cody and Roger have

wandered off somewhere, and now Joel stands beside her, holding out a fluorescent pink cocktail.

"Oh, honey, thank you. How did you know?" She takes the glass from him. "This looks potent. Maybe I shouldn't have it since I'm already feeling a bit wobbly?"

"Hey, you're the one who said no more than three drinks per night, right? So, you're still easily within your self-imposed parameters."

She laughs. "Thanks for the reminder." Despite her initial reluctance, the drink goes down smoothly when she takes a sip. "Do you think I should try to find Dawn? She seemed a little upset. I think maybe she was expecting to get one of those awards."

"Dawn?" The surprise in his voice is evident, which Meredith both recognizes and is embarrassed by all over again. Neither one of them thought of Dawn during tonight's awards ceremony. Only Cody.

"Yeah, well, she did get straight As this year." As if to say, *Of course, Dawn.*

"That's right," says Joel. "Nah, why not leave her be? I'm sure she wants to hang out with her friends anyway. Remember what that was like? The night before you graduated?"

Meredith understands he's asking hypothetically, but she tries to think back to that long-ago day. The campus wasn't nearly as grand then. Over the past twenty years or so, Bolton has added a dance studio, a theater hall, and a brand-new track-and-field alongside a new freshman quadrangle of dorms. These additions come in large part thanks to a few alumni who struck it rich in dot-com dollars and have turned philanthropic in their middle age. What remains the same: the steep climb up the hill to campus. A preponderance of tan brick and ivy. The quadrangle of classroom buildings that crowns the hill. The gray-stoned church with its majestic spire towering above campus.

Even though she was born too late for the free-love revolution of the sixties, she remembers Bolton's priding itself on its liberal leanings. There were a handful of marches and civil rights protests, a sit-in on the classroom quadrangle to protest apartheid, another rally to hire more female faculty. Weed could be easily had as well as some of the hallucinogenic drugs. Not that Meredith tried any of the stronger stuff—she was always too afraid she'd end up in an alternate universe, never to return. Marijuana, on the other hand, was marginally tolerated on campus, like cigarettes and alcohol.

During her junior and senior years, she'd worked as a tour guide for the admissions office, leading prospective students and their families around the green-leafed campus while chattering on about the benefits of a Bolton education. The sales pitch was simple: Bolton possessed all the rigor of an Ivy League college with the charm of a smaller New England school. Back then, the school's tagline had been The Little Harvard of New England. The thought of it makes her cringe now. She doesn't suppose anyone at Harvard ever considered Bolton to be a miniature replica of itself.

Nevertheless, she'd been proud to graduate a Bullfrog. Even prouder when both Cody and Dawn decided they wanted to call Bolton their alma mater, too. But the night before her graduation day? No, that's too far back for her to remember. A Stone Age ago. A blur that most likely included alcohol, perhaps a pinch of Mary J. She certainly doesn't recall an awards ceremony like this. If anything, prizes were handed out on graduation day, but even this memory is conjured through a hazy scrim of recollection.

"It's weird, I can't remember really. I think maybe I went out to dinner with my parents and some friends?" Meredith shakes her head, as if to bring the recollection into better focus, but nothing manifests itself. "Pathetic how much I've forgotten, isn't it?"

"But you've proven my point exactly. You had such a good time that you don't remember, and by that I mean, you probably got drunk enough that the night is forever blurred in your hippocampus."

"Right, that must be it." She loves that Joel can pull words like *hippocampus* from his therapist's vocabulary. Meredith knows all about the tiny organ that collects long-term memories from her nursing school days, but it's the rare guy, she imagines, who can bandy around such words as if they're a common vegetable, like *carrots* or *broccoli*. "Now that you mention it, I do remember being pretty hungover the morning of graduation." An image of herself and her girlfriends hunched over in their church pew for the man-datory morning meditation floats through her mind.

"See. There you go," Joel says, as if that further confirms his theory. "Let her be, honey. She'll be fine. And so will Cody." Meredith, in her concern for Dawn, has completely lost sight of Cody. She scans the room, searching for her son's seersucker blazer.

"Speaking of which, where did our boy go?"

Joel shrugs. "Off to have fun?"

"But I wanted to talk to him before we left. Make a plan for tomorrow."

Joel's face crinkles in amusement. "Honey, what more do

you need to know than to show up at one o'clock tomorrow for the ceremony?"

"But what if he needs something? Something only I can get for him? Like a tie because he spilled something on his graduation tie? Or a gift for Melissa because he forgot to get her a present, which would be typical." She realizes it probably sounds silly, helicopter-parenting at its height, but she doesn't care. She *wants* her children to need her. At least for a few more days.

Joel bends to kiss the top of her head. "My sweet worry-wart. Cody's a big boy now. Remember? You're supposed to practice letting him do things by himself."

"Mmm-hmm." The subject has become a tiny point of contention between them this past year, Joel urging her to let the kids spread their wings when Meredith isn't quite ready to set them free. As steady as Cody is, it's the little stuff that seems to slip his imagination, and she harbors doubts about whether her son is up to the challenge of handling graduation and its attendant requirements without some coaxing and prodding. But she's willing to let it slide for the moment. Joel is probably right, anyway. *Baby steps away from the nest*, she reminds herself. "Where's Mom?"

"She seems to have found some new friends." Joel points to a nearby table where Carol chats with a few other grandmotherly types, then adds, "Be right back." He sets off for the outhouses that have been set up on the lawn's perimeter for tonight's event, leaving Meredith to debate whether she should join her mother or play wallflower for the time being. Which is when Roger strides over, a big, goofy grin on his face.

"Those are some pretty amazing kids we have, huh?"

His gold necklaces have knotted around each other so that the *L*, flipped backward, resembles a *J*.

Really, Meredith thinks, *the man is too old to have monogrammed jewelry.* He's also wearing glasses, probably nonprescription, with hipster frames that don't suit him. Another Lily touch, she assumes.

"They're pretty spectacular," Meredith agrees now. A spray of crumbs dots his collar, and she reaches over to brush them off. She can't help it—the move comes to her instinctively. Just as she tidied up their table earlier, whisking away plates and glasses. Joel would call it OCD, but Meredith disagrees. Twenty-one years of mothering instills certain mantras in a person, such as *clean up after yourself—and others.*

"You're pretty spectacular yourself, you know, Meredith. You've done a fantastic job with them. You get all the credit."

She arches an eyebrow, uncertain where to file her ex-husband's unexpected praise. Roger must have downed his scotch awfully quickly if he's complimenting her. Ordinarily, she would reply, *Oh, no, it was a team effort! You contributed, too.* For once, though, he's acknowledging the hours *(indeed, years!)* of hard work and love she has poured into their children, and she's not about to correct him.

Because he's right. It's Meredith who has been there for the kids every step of the way, even when it felt like stepping off a cliff (Cody's near DUI charge one summer and Dawn's being cast out by her friends are two examples that jump to mind). Maybe the wine emboldens her to say a simple *thanks*, but she doesn't think so.

Roger grins and grips her arm, as if to better get her attention, as if she isn't standing directly in front of him. "Remember when we were first married?" *Uh-oh. Maybe he had a few scotches* before *he arrived? And where* is *Lily?*

"I try to forget." She laughs when she says it, but she's only half kidding. If it weren't for the kids, she would gladly forget most of it.

"And we used to leave little notes for each other?" It's just like Roger to get maudlin on her here at the kids' graduation when his new wife is AWOL.

"No entourage tonight?" Meredith asks, trying to steer the conversation back to more neutral territory.

"Not tonight, I'm afraid."

"Usually you travel with a throng of admirers. Let's see, where did I see you last? In the *Herald*? No, that wasn't it. *The Boston Globe*." Meredith remembers now. "You were surrounded by all sorts of young people at a New Kids on the Block concert." She pauses. "I never knew you were a fan."

"Oh, that." He waves a free hand in the air. "That was Lily's idea. She was a huge fan of theirs back in the day, and some good tickets came up. So..." His voice trails off.

"So," Meredith resumes. "And where *is* Lily tonight?"

"Home. Getting ready for the big party."

"Ah." Meredith nods. Her Spanx are digging into her waist. Another strike against Lily. She should've guessed from Lily's earlier Instagram post. Roger's new wife is too busy planning an extravagant party for their kids that she can't possibly get away for a few hours. On the other hand, Meredith is grateful for Lily's sparing her uncomfortable chitchat tonight when there's bound to be plenty ahead tomorrow, when everyone will go out for a celebratory dinner.

Were Meredith to be honest, the note-leaving was one of a handful of memories that she recalls fondly about her marriage to Roger. Would he be surprised if she told him she'd even saved a few? Not all, of course, only a couple that were particularly clever, little sayings that would appear, as if by magic, under a pillow, in an empty coffee cup, beneath her toothbrush. Paper talismans that portended the unspooling of a day. Once she discovered a note curled up in her Hunter rain boot with a line from an Emily Dickinson poem. Musings about love and whispering robins. Sure, there were some good times together—how else to explain staying married for fifteen years?

"And your hand?" She drains the remainder of her drink with her cocktail straw, grateful that the college hasn't jumped on the no-straws bandwagon yet. "All healed up, I hope?" It's been nearly three months since the accident, but the recovery process, she knows, has been slow.

Roger splays the fingers of his left hand out in front of him, the pinkie bent slightly inward. "Pretty much. Still a little stiff, but my physical therapist tells me that should resolve itself in a couple more weeks. Good thing I'm not a surgeon." He drops his hand by his side.

"I'm really sorry about—"

But he cuts her off. "Nope. Not going to talk about it anymore, remember? Not your fault. I was an idiot for looking down at my phone when you were coming up the driveway. Serves me right."

Meredith won't argue with this, and, in fact, at times, when she replays the incident in her mind, she wonders if somewhere in her subconscious when she saw Roger staring at his phone—as he did so often and frustratingly in their marriage—a switch clicked. One that shouted, "You are no longer allowed to ignore me!" and that prodded her foot to press on the gas pedal instead of the brake as the car inched its way forward.

But the thought is interrupted by Joel, returning from the bathroom. "Well, hello, again. I see you've found my wife," he says, joining their circle and prompting Roger to take a step back. She shoots her husband an amused look. Is Meredith mistaken, or did Joel just try to lay a claim, mark his territory like a pissing dog?

"Yes, I have," says Roger. "I was just telling her what a great job she's done with our kids." Now Meredith senses the metaphorical ball bouncing back into Roger's court. *Our kids. They're Joel's kids, too*, she wants to amend, but for some reason she stays quiet.

"Hasn't she? They're fantastic. I've loved watching them grow up," replies Joel.

Score 2, Joel, she thinks now. How ridiculous that they find themselves in this volley of retorts, and yet somehow it also feels inevitable, given the circumstances. Just then, an attractive woman with auburn hair passes by and gives Joel a half smile and a wave before glancing quickly in Meredith's direction. Joel's face turns bright red—the man has never been able to keep a secret. *Old girlfriend?* Meredith tries to ask with her eyes, but he won't even meet her gaze.

"Great kids," Roger repeats and then suddenly clears his throat. "Well, hello there, Carol."

As if sensing imminent discord in the air, her mother has left her table to come to Meredith's side. "I think I'm ready to head back to the hotel, honey," she announces, ignoring Roger completely. "Whenever you are."

"Oh." Meredith wasn't expecting to cut out quite so soon, but then she's not almost eighty years old, either. She eyes Joel, trying to get a read on his mood, and concludes from his nod that leaving would be perfectly fine by him, too. "Okay, sure, Mom. Let me find the kids to say good-bye before we go."

"So nice to see you, Roger," Carol states now, as if in afterthought. "How lovely that you could make it for this special night for your children." It's an insult masquerading as a polite compliment, a gesture at which her mother excels.

"And nice to see you!" He lets a small burp escape. "S'cuse me."

Carol visibly recoils, as if someone has farted out loud. "You always were such a gentleman, Roger. Now if you'll excuse *me*, I'll be waiting just beyond the tent." She adds, "Whenever you're ready, honey. Don't rush on my account."

"I'll go with you." Abruptly, Joel sets down his half-finished beer on a side tray, leaving Meredith and Roger to themselves.

"Well." Roger clucks his tongue. "Glad to see your mom still has a soft spot for me." Meredith laughs.

"Honestly? I think it gives her a reason to live, giving you a hard time whenever she bumps into you."

"Happy to oblige. Whatever I can do to ensure she lives a long, vindictive life."

Meredith smiles. "C'mon. She doesn't really hate you. She's protecting us."

"Whatever you say."

Meredith suspects her mother will forever remain the mama grizzly bear, guarding her young at the lip of the cave. In her rheumy eyes, Roger may be less threatening today than he was, perhaps, a decade ago, but he's still worthy of her vigilance. Meredith gets it, is even appreciative.

"Well, I better find the kids before we go. See you tomorrow?"

"Yeah, till tomorrow," he says and hoists his glass in her

direction while she walks away. But if she's not mistaken, she thinks she can feel his eyes still following her when she hands off her glass and slips out of the tent.

EIGHT

Back at the hotel, Joel practically leaps into their king-size bed. Apparently, a fairy entered the room while they were away because the sheets are turned down and the sea of throw pillows has been transferred to a chair. It feels good to be back in air-conditioning, where he can feel his body returning to its normal temperature instead of hovering around a hundred degrees. Also good to be freed from having to make chitchat with parents he didn't know and being ambushed by those he did. Like Roger and Kat. Meredith didn't bring up Kat in the car, but he knows she caught her wave on the way out.

"You smell minty," he says when she finally crawls into bed after her third shower of the day.

"I mistook my toothpaste for eye cream." She laughs softly. "Those tiny travel tubes look exactly the same, and I didn't have my glasses on. Maybe I'll look younger in the morning thanks to Colgate, the miracle cream. You know, it does kind of tingle." She nestles in closer, her skin cool against his chest. "Hey, who was that woman who waved at you right before we left?"

And there it is. Joel performs a ten-second internal debate about how much detail to go into. "Oh, she's just an old friend from high school. Turns out she has a daughter graduating this weekend, too. Crazy, huh? What are the odds of bumping into someone from that long ago?"

He can feel Meredith shrug in his arms. "Don't know. Probably not such long odds." She yawns, rests her head on his chest, then lifts it up again.

"Wait a sec. Old friend as in old *girlfriend*? Was that *Kat*?"

Joel runs his fingers through her hair before answering. He's told Meredith how Kat was his first love, how she jilted him over the phone years ago and more or less broke his heart. She knows the fuzzy details in the way that new lovers come to know about past lovers when you first start dating, like the abbreviated highlights of a tennis match that didn't end well. "Yep, that was Kat."

"*The* Kat?" Meredith presses.

"The one and only."

"Uh-oh. Should I feel threatened?"

He laughs. "C'mon, honey. That was what? Thirty years ago? We're talking high school."

"But she was the one that got away, right?"

"In a manner of speaking, I suppose, but trust me, you have nothing to worry about."

"Is that right?" With her finger, she traces the dark coil of hair running down his chest to his waist.

"Yes." He can't help but grin now. "Turns out she's gay."

That gets Meredith's attention. "Whoa. Didn't see that coming."

"Me, either. But apparently she's happily married to a woman."

"Wow. So many questions!" Meredith snuggles in closer. "But I'm too tired right now. I hope you'll introduce us tomorrow. Does she have a son or daughter graduating?"

"Daughter. Cassandra, I think?"

"Mmm… That's a pretty name."

Joel doesn't say anything for a minute. He can sense Meredith's drifting off to sleep. "How about Roger showing up? Did you know he was coming?"

It's quiet for a moment. "Not a clue," she says, stifling a yawn. "Typical Roger, last-minute change of plans. But I'm glad for the kids. I think it meant a lot to them, especially Dawn." He decides not to bring up the fact that, to his eye, Roger seemed to be getting pretty cozy with Meredith tonight. Not that Joel is jealous exactly, *but, come on! There was no need for the guy to stand so close.* Or, to keep resting a hand on her arm as if they were old pals.

"Thank goodness he didn't bring Lily along," Meredith says now.

"Yes, thank goodness." Joel's voice carries a whiff of teasing. He knows his wife nurses a nutty inferiority complex around Lily, who so obviously represents Roger's midlife crisis, his trophy wife, that Joel finds it almost comical and most certainly, cliché. Meredith is in an entirely different league, much classier.

"You're not still worrying about her, are you?"

"Not in the least," Meredith says, but they both know she's lying.

It doesn't matter, though, because before long, it appears

that Meredith has decided to wave off sleep for some fooling around. She's climbing on top of him, her hair flowing over her shoulders, and all Joel can think about is how incredibly sexy his wife is and how much she still turns him on. He could spend all night making love to her, trying out new positions on this bed that feels as wide and rollicking as a bouncy house. Before this afternoon, they hadn't had sex in seventeen days. Talk about a dry spell. Seventeen days! Meredith seemed surprised when he'd mentioned it.

"Huh? That long, really?"

"That long." During the last few weeks, he'd started feeling like a horny teenager, pointing out virtually any opportunity that presented itself for hopping into the sack together. He knows Meredith keeps complaining about the extra pounds she's put on since the kids, but Joel honestly doesn't see it. He thinks she looks great and catches the way other guys watch her when she walks into a room. Aside from some lip gloss and face powder ("to minimize the shine," she says), she's never been one to wear makeup—and she doesn't need to. Joel loves everything about the face that greets him each morning: the cute spray of freckles across her nose, her warm, brown eyes, the thick auburn hair. The way she bites her bottom lip sometimes when they make love, like she's doing right now.

Several minutes later, when she rolls off him, he waits for Meredith to break down the night, a favorite hobby of hers—analyzing the party's players and their various transgressions, like that mother dressed in teal or how they all thought Cody was going to win the award. Often, Joel finds himself amazed by the slights and innuendoes she will have picked up on, stuff that slid right past him when he was pretty sure everyone was talking about the Red Sox. What has she gleaned from tonight's banquet? But after softly kissing him goodnight, she rolls over, and within minutes her snores drift over from the other side.

So. That leaves Joel to perform his own analysis. All in all, if someone were to ask him, he thinks the evening unfolded as well as could be expected. There were only a few times when he had to exchange pleasantries with strangers, guys whose self-deprecating humor quickly wore thin. But those constitute minor details. And even though no one predicted Roger would show up, Joel actually admires the guy for making the right call. He *should* have been there tonight to celebrate the kids. They have only so many more milestones left to revel in as parents, all of them. Meredith ribbed Joel afterward about trying to mark his territory when he snuck up on her and Roger. And maybe he was being overly protective, a bit possessive. But can she fault Joel for wanting to make sure she was all right? Plus, what if she did something she might regret later? Like, he thinks with a small smile, break Roger's other hand.

Something else pricks at his conscience, though. While he can't exactly say what, something felt off with the kids tonight. Maybe they had a falling-out before they came downstairs from their dorm to meet them? It stays with him, that uneasy feeling he sometimes picks up from his kids at school. A feeling not so dissimilar from the one he gets when the weight shifts in bed at night and he realizes that Meredith has gotten up to fetch a drink of water. Subtle but unsettling nonetheless, an imbalance that keeps him awake until she returns. He's pretty certain Cody was smoking tonight (he reeked of cigarettes) and files it away to raise with him another time. It's more than that, though. He tried to pry it from Dawn earlier, asked her what was going on between her and her brother. But no amount of gentle questioning could dislodge the slightest information.

Tonight Cody had seemed super jazzed, as if he'd downed ten Red Bulls before the banquet. It's a popular party trick among kids, Joel knows: counter all the alcohol you consume with an energy booster to keep you awake. Red Bull and vodka make for a potent mix, and maybe that's what the kids were doing when they'd disappeared from the tent. He wonders if he should have called them on it, then scolds himself for being a hypocrite. Wasn't he just telling Meredith to go easy on them, let them have a little fun? There's no worse buzzkill than your stepdad telling you to lay off the sauce on the night before graduation. Besides, Joel knows as well as anyone—the kids were headed off to more parties after the parents left. The night, as they say, was still young.

He rummages around for his glasses on the bedside table to check the clock across the room. *12:32 a.m.* If he has any hope of functioning tomorrow, sleep is critical. Tomorrow is the real deal, the big day. All his antennae need to be tuned to high alert to run any potential interference between Roger, Lily, and the rest of the outlaws, as he and Meredith occasionally refer to them.

Within minutes, sleep blissfully overtakes him.

Lily and Alison have been drinking. Heavily. Lily hasn't the faintest idea when Roger will return home. And why would she? He hasn't bothered to text or call. She and Alison are having themselves a fine old time without him. They've moved from the pool to the lounge chairs by the pool, and now they're sitting in the family room, where Lily lies on their exceedingly comfortable leather sofa. Around nine o'clock, when the mosquitoes had started siphoning off their blood, they'd piled up their plates and moved the party inside. *Party for two*, Lily thinks smugly. *Who needs Roger?*

"Hey, just get through this weekend, and everything will be fine." Alison scratches at a swollen red bite above her ankle and licks her finger to apply some saliva, an old trick. "Family events can be stressful, and you've been a member of this one for only a few months."

"Six and a half," Lily corrects. "Seven months if you round up, though I don't know that it makes any difference." She languidly pulls a tortilla chip through a bowl of salsa. The lime chips are her favorite, even though Roger hates them. Whenever she's feeling especially indulgent or mopey, she'll buy a family-sized bag just for herself. And, if she has been drinking, it's especially easy to forget every calorie that passes her lips. "I keep thinking it takes time for everyone to get adjusted, but I didn't assume I'd still feel like a third wheel."

Alison sets her glass down on the table. "You're not! A third wheel, I mean. I've seen the way Roger looks at you. Head over heels, my friend. Definitely."

Lily lies back on the sofa. Her head hurts, and the wine and tequila of earlier are mixing in her stomach in an ugly stew. Moses pads over, licks up a few crumbs littering the floor, and settles at her feet. "I just wish the kids would give me a chance. I mean, I don't expect to be best friends, but do they have to hate me so much?" She drags the back of her hand across her eyes, which unexpectedly begin to brim with tears.

"Wait a sec. Oh, hon. Are you *crying*?" Alison comes over to sit beside her and squeezes her arm consolingly. "Look, no one hates you. If anything, the kids don't know how to react around you, and can you blame them? You're practically the same age."

"Okay. Not helping?" Lily counters. "I'm nine years older to be exact."

"Same decade." Alison pulls a hand through the air. "Big whoop. At least to them." She circles back around to her side of the table and flops down on the adjacent sofa. "Think of it this way. What if your mom remarried some hot dude who was only a few years older than you when you were in college? Wouldn't you be a tiny bit resentful? Or jealous? Or something?"

Lily sniffs and reaches for a glass of ice water, which prompts Moses to lift his head, sensing he might be needed, before settling back down. She knows herself well enough that if she doesn't switch to ice water now, there's zero chance of her being fabulous tomorrow. "Hard to say. It's difficult to imagine my mom ever holding on to any guy long enough to marry him."

Alison slings back another tequila shot, says, "Bottoms up," and Lily watches as her friend's face grimaces before biting into a wedge of lime. It's a visceral reaction, one that Lily imagines having duplicated herself when she'd downed her shots earlier. It's been that kind of a night. Alison slaps her hand on the table, clears her throat. "Point taken." She is familiar with Lily's complicated family history, which Lily has divulged in various installments over dinners, trips to the spa, and coffees shared post-yoga. "But think of poor Cody. He's one big walking hormone. When he sees you…" Alison's voice trails off and she shrugs.

"When he sees me, what?" Lily leans forward, really hoping her friend isn't suggesting what Lily thinks she is.

"C'mon, Lily. Don't be stupid. You're hot. Of course he

must think it's weird that his dad married a chick that he'd prefer to be dating."

Lily falls back on the couch. "You've just taken the women's movement back two decades. That's gross. Cody doesn't think about me that way. He has a girlfriend!"

"Whatever you say." Alison grabs the remote and switches on the television, flipping through the stations. She has visited enough times that she acts as if this is her house, too. Which Lily doesn't mind; in fact, she kind of loves it. Because she can offer this spacious, beautiful home to her friends, it somehow feels more like her house and not just Roger's "place" that she has moved into. Whenever Alison helps herself to food in the fridge or sleeps over in the guest room, Lily has a vague sense of paying her good fortune forward. She always wanted a pretty home where she could host family and friends. Of course, never in her wildest dreams could she have imagined a place set on the ocean with its own swimming pool and lawn crew.

"Anyway, it's really Dawn I'm worried about. She's the tough nut to crack."

"Give her time," Alison counsels. "Besides, in three short months, she'll be in Chicago. It's not like you're expected to help raise these kids."

Huh. But isn't that precisely what Lily has been hoping for all along? To join a family in all its iterations? Dawn and Cody, she's beginning to realize, though, are more or less grown-ups already, fully bloomed. There's little she can do to mother them or guide them down the right path now. Meredith would probably behead her, anyway. (Lily has caught her sideways glances at Roger, the judgmental looks that suggest she thinks her ex-husband has married beneath him.) And with a college degree and prospective jobs awaiting them both, the twins have already zipped light-years ahead of where Lily was at their age. What advice can she possibly offer them?

"I kind of want to, though," she says softly.

"What?" Alison has paused on a movie channel that's replaying *Ghost*. "Oh, I love this movie!" she exclaims and flops down on the poufy pillows that dot the floor.

"Raise them. Raise a family," Lily repeats.

She and Roger have talked about having their own baby a few times, but only hypothetically, in broad, imprecise strokes. One evening, in particular, sticks in her mind, a balmy spring night when they were dining alfresco in the North End next to a couple with a little girl, probably around three. Every so often, the little girl would climb down from her booster seat and wheel around the patio, off to investigate the pots of begonias or the water gushing from a small fountain. At one point, something possessed the girl to bring Lily a red flower she'd picked, and Lily had cooed with thanks.

"See? Everyone finds you enchanting," said Roger.

Lily smiled. "Do you ever think about having another?"

"Another? As in another kid, you mean?" His pointer finger circled the edge of his wineglass.

"Yeah."

"I haven't given it much thought, I guess. They're a lot of work!" He laughed. "As I think you're beginning to see with Dawn and Cody."

"Oh, they're not so terrible," Lily had lied. In truth, she'd met the kids only a few times by that point, and they'd been horrible each time. Cody mostly didn't say anything, but Dawn threw Lily the stink eye whenever she got the chance. And how about the time, only a few months ago, when Lily lent Dawn her Jeep to run errands, only to have Dawn call saying she'd gotten into a little fender bender? *I'm fine*, she reassured Lily. *But your car might need a little work.* Lily had rushed to meet her (Roger was out golfing) and reassured Dawn it was no big deal, only a dented fender where Dawn had backed into a Dumpster. On the sly, Lily took the car to the repair shop—Dawn had made her promise not to tell her dad and Lily had foolishly agreed, thinking maybe it would foster a bond between them. If anything, though, it had accomplished the opposite.

"Why? Are kids something you'd want?" Roger asked that night.

Lily dipped her bread in the olive oil pooling on a plate between them. "Not sure. Maybe. I still have plenty of time to decide, right?" She'd brushed it off as if they were discussing a possible trip to Greece next year, a weekend getaway to the Berkshires. "I'm only thirty, after all."

And he'd taken her hands into his, softly kissing each fingertip. "The world is your oyster. And I, for one, feel like my world is complete with you in it."

Now Alison stares over at her as if Lily has shot off a .22 rifle in the room. "Well, girlfriend, if that's what you got into this marriage for, then I suggest you and Roger get busy creating some mini-Lilies or Rogers." She launches a pillow across the room at her. "And here I thought you were all about the money and extravagant lifestyle," she teases. "When really you're a softy. All you need to be happy are some cute little baby toes and fingers."

Lily whips the pillow back. "Stop it!" she cries. "So what if I do?"

"Oh, nothing." Alison flops down on her pillow. "Just

prepare for your life to pivot about a hundred and eighty degrees."

"I wouldn't mind. I think it might actually be nice. You know, a chance to raise a daughter like she should be raised, with tons of love." Memories of waiting up late for her mom to arrive home from her shift at the bar still haunt Lily. She would never, ever do that to her own child. Of course, she'll need to stop popping the little pills, but she's fairly confident she can do so as soon as she has a real purpose. Surely, if her baby's health depends on it, Lily will cut out all bad substances, eat only healthy foods, and devour prenatal vitamins like the Smarties she adores.

Looking back, it's funny how easily she slid into Roger's life, as if she were a missing piece. At the time, she'd hardly even noticed that she was leaving behind most everything that defined *her*—her waitressing job, her apartment, her friends on Beacon Hill—to better fit into his life. And what had Roger done to fit into hers? She honestly can't point to any adjustments on his part, aside from having to share his bed with her every night and opening his house, *their* house now, to her friends.

When he proposed, she'd instantly said yes. Unlike some women she knew, Lily didn't need to make a list of pros and cons about whether this was the man she should marry, whether he would make her happy. Because the answer was: *of course*. When she'd first met him, working as a waitress at the Sevens on Charles Street, she'd served his table a round of beers, and Roger had glanced up, caught her eye, and asked what time she got off work. A physical reaction had surged through her body then, suddenly giving new meaning to the phrase "makes you go weak in the knees."

She'd retreated to the back room to sit down for a minute and steady her nerves before agreeing to go out with him.

Around Roger, she feels like the most important person in the room, which, to be honest, seems to be the effect he has on pretty much everyone. Well, except for Meredith, that is. Only later in their relationship did he paint a picture of his former marriage (Lily had been too afraid to ask). He confided that Meredith had been—and was still—a terrific mom but an "unenthusiastic" wife. As soon as the kids were born, it was as if he no longer existed, he said. It became less and less appealing to go straight home from work, and he'd started hanging out in the bars with his friends, crawling into bed later and later each night, until finally he'd given up on ever making love to his wife again and had started looking elsewhere. It was a long time ago (nearly a decade!), but when Roger recounted the disintegration of his marriage, Lily felt a stab of pity for him. Her friends who'd split with their exes had shared similar tales of a flame that had dwindled, of a relationship taken for granted once kids entered the picture.

Lily can't imagine a day when she'll ever be less in love with Roger Landau. But will he be open to the idea of a new baby? Truly? Or does he assume that chapter in his life is closed? Alison has unwittingly hit the nail on the head: Lily can never be a true mom to Dawn and Cody. They won't let her. But her very own baby? She has so much love to give. Maybe it's time for her and Roger to create their very own family. There's also a deep, almost subterranean stirring that's risen in her consciousness over the last few months, one that she wasn't even aware existed: she has discovered that she's weirdly jealous of the one bond that Roger and Meredith still share: their children. Because no matter how much Roger loves Lily, no matter how much Roger and Meredith may seem estranged, they will always, *always* be the twins' parents. It's a permanent rope twinning them together till death do they part.

Nothing Lily does can change that.

She waits for Alison to say more, but at that moment Demi Moore sits down at her spinning wheel to mold a clay pot.

"Oh, this is my favorite part," her friend exclaims, and together they watch Demi rain tears all over her beautifully spun creation while Patrick Swayze attempts to reach out to her from another world, desperate to make a connection. Lily thinks she can relate.

NINE

Friday morning

"Was that a raindrop?" Meredith holds out her hand, surprised. "No one said anything about rain today. Tropical temperatures, maybe, but rain? Absolutely not." She frowns up at the sky, still sunny and blue, but turning gray at the edges, like an abstract painting.

"Nope. Definitely not rain." Joel is so determined that the day go smoothly, Meredith suspects he'd probably deny it if a thundercloud were to open up directly over his head.

"No rain," confirms her mother. "Only the humidity."

It doesn't seem fair that, with everything else going on today, they should have to contend with inclement weather. Maybe it's just her imagination playing tricks on her. They're retracing their steps from last night, ascending the hilltop that leads to the main quadrangle on campus, where the ceremony will take place later this afternoon. Despite the swig of antacid medicine she swallowed back at the hotel, Meredith's stomach still feels queasy from last night's cocktails.

She undoes the button of her blue blazer and allows herself some extra breathing room. Underneath is an ivory silk sheath, which she hopes strikes the right note of classy and elegant. Beside her strolls her mother, who is wearing her second Talbots dress of the weekend, a kelly-green tea-length dress, and her strand of pearls. Meanwhile, Joel, dressed in a navy blue sports coat and pants, definitely looks the part of a proud father.

To glance at the three of them, people might assume they're just another well-to-do family, come to witness the long-anticipated graduation of a namesake, a Conrad III or a Thelonious, Junior. No one would guess at the real story. The more time Meredith spends in the NICU, however, the more she realizes that most families are not as pulled-together as they might appear. She has watched the most sophisticated, elegant couples dissolve into pieces while cradling their babies in the NICU. Others, who seem inseparable and bonded by their love for their child, divorce only a few years later (she knows this because she keeps in touch with many of them through a hospital website for NICU parents). Sometimes the mothers who appear the worst off—unshowered, without a spouse, occasionally high on some unknown substance—are the ones who intuit almost immediately what their babies need. The NICU tests people like no other setting, and Meredith has watched parents struggle at their absolute nadir. It is both humbling and astonishing to bear witness to such profound heartbreak, such deep-seated love. Nursing has given her a richer appreciation for the Byzantine layers that create a person, a marriage, a family.

"Allergies," she says now, as she sniffles and pulls a tissue from her purse to dot her eyes. But she guesses she's fooling no one. A mess since this morning, she can't stop tearing up, thinking about her own babies. Waterproof mascara would have come in handy, had it occurred to her. And Visine. Perhaps some thoughtful proctor at Bolton will have left miniature fanny packs filled with such items on the parents' graduation seats.

When they reach the quadrangle at last, Joel lets out a whistle. "Well, well. Who invited the queen?" Spread out before them is row upon row of white chairs set on a bright green lawn, pretty enough for the Princess of Wales to host a tea party. Overnight, the entire courtyard has been transformed. Large pots bursting with white tulips and lavender hyacinth dot the lawn, and the air is thick with their sweet scent. "Looks like a royal wedding."

"It's lovely," agrees Carol. "Very distinguished."

"And look, Mom, they even got the lawn to match the color of your dress," teases Joel.

Carol eyes the field and then her dress. "So they did. Well, that was good planning on my part, wasn't it?"

On a wide stage up front a blue banner proclaims, *Congratulations Class of 2020!* Flags with *Class of 1990* or *Class of 1965* delineate sections where alumni are supposed to sit. Meredith experiences a pinch of relief that her class isn't celebrating a milestone anniversary this year, so there's no pressure to sit with her classmates. Not that she's kept in touch with any of them, anyway.

"I'll say this," her mother quips. "Bolton knows how to do commencement right. Though they've stepped it up a few notches since your day, honey." She fingers her pearls into a loose knot. "I don't remember such fancy chairs, do you?"

"No, I think we had bleachers." Meredith is only partly kidding. It's very possible they had bleachers; she doesn't recall.

The only drawback about the entire setup, as far as she can see, is that most of the chairs sit out exposed in the open, which means they'll either be subjected to punishing sunlight or intermittent rain showers during the ceremony. Already a few families comb through the aisles, deliberating over which seats are the best. "Looks like first come, first served," says Joel.

"Yeah, it's pretty much a free-for-all." Meredith removes her jacket, suddenly feeling warm. "That's why the kids suggested we get here early." Right now the clock tower reads five past noon. They have nearly an hour to kill before the seats fill up. "Where should we sit, Mom? You choose."

"Me? Oh, I don't know, honey. Somewhere near the front, I suppose. Preferably out of the sun."

"Maybe up on the right?" Meredith points to a section partly shaded by a giant oak.

"Suits me." Joel trots over and throws his blazer across two chairs and sets his coffee tumbler down on a third before another family can grab it. Their seats are positioned a few rows back from the cordoned-off area for graduates, and Meredith flops down in one, double-checking their sight line to the podium.

"Perfect," she declares.

"Should we save some chairs for Roger and his gang, too?" Joel eyes the empty row behind them.

"Oh, um, I don't know. We haven't talked about it." Meredith thinks back to their conversation about today, but neither of them mentioned anything about sitting together for the ceremony. "I think they're on their own. That's okay, right? I mean, we're going out to dinner with them afterward."

"That's *plenty*." Carol crosses her arms over her chest, as if to say, *Why would you even consider such a thing? There's no need to sit with your ex-husband's family!*

Meredith and Joel exchange amused looks. "Why don't we leave our things here to save the chairs, and then we can walk around campus, if you'd like, Mom. I know you said you wanted to poke your head into a few of the classrooms?"

"Yes, let's do that. Good idea."

They're about to set off exploring when Meredith's cell phone chimes in her purse. "Probably the kids," she says, rummaging through her bag. "Wondering where to meet up." It's astonishing how often her phone gets lost in her purse when it holds so few items—her wallet, hand sanitizer, a pack of tissues, some granola bars, a few pens and some old CVS receipts. (Unfortunately, she's not one of those women who think to swap out their purse for a fancier handbag on special occasions.) But when she finally does land on her cell, she sees it's the hospital calling. *Uh-oh.* "Excuse me, I better get this." Pressing a finger to her ear, she steps off to the side for a sliver of privacy.

"Hello?"

"Meredith? Hi, it's Jill. So sorry to bother you on graduation weekend. Do have a sec?"

"Sure, what's going on?" A slight panic rises in Meredith's chest.

"Well, our friend Mason here doesn't want to settle down, and I was wondering if you have any tricks you might want to share before I give up?"

Meredith offers a silent prayer of gratitude that this is the reason Jill is calling. While many of the babies she works with are preemies—some with veins so fragile it's almost impossible to prick them with an IV—their NICU has recently experienced an uptick in infants born to moms with addiction. Meredith knows that every twenty-five minutes a NAS (Neonatal Abstinence Syndrome) baby enters the world, yet doctors have come up with few ways to comfort these children beyond the obvious. Mason was born at thirty-eight weeks to a mom high as a kite on heroin, and Meredith is his primary nurse.

Mason's adorable face pops into her mind—dark curly hair, huge brown eyes—and, apparently, screaming his head off. Every baby in the NICU requires inordinate amounts of care and love, but there's nothing quite as wrenching as watching a newborn struggle to wean himself off a drug he never asked to be addicted to in the first place. Unlike their moms, who can immediately start methadone treatments to get clean, infants have few options to ease withdrawal other than some morphine drops and as much one-on-one contact as possible. The "drug babies," as they've dubbed them in the NICU, are the ones who require the most hands-on attention, who crave human touch or a lullaby. Around day three, when the drug begins to truly work its way out of their system, the hard work of getting clean commences. Mason is on day five.

"Oh, poor Mason. Poor you," Meredith commiserates. "You've tried dipping his paci in sugar water?" Meredith knows from experience that Jill will have already done this, but she's ticking through her own mental checklist as she talks.

"Yep."

"And all his vitals are fine?"

"Everything looks good on his monitor, but he won't stop crying." And as if on cue, Mason's screams ratchet up a notch on the other end. She can picture Jill calling from just outside the NICU room, where cell phones are banned. When Meredith was with him on Wednesday, Mason seemed to calm best when she gave him a sponge bath. It's a little thing, but maybe it will help.

"Did you try bathing him? He seemed to like the water when I had him on Wednesday."

"Oh, okay. I'll try that. Anything else?"

Meredith wishes she were there for Mason right now. What if he's grown so accustomed to her scent over the last few days that only she can calm him? "Oh, that grandpa who volunteers on Mondays?" Meredith scours her brain for a name. "Jonathan? I think that's his name. He seemed to work miracles with Mason when he was admitted on Monday. Sang him some kind of lullaby. What was it, again?" She stares up into the big oak, whose green leaves form a lattice-work overhead, and tries to call up the melody. "Oh, I know. 'Mockingbird.' Maybe try that? Or, even better, see if you can get Jonathan to come in today?" Jonathan is one of several elderly volunteers who visit weekly to hold the NICU babies, ensuring that they get plenty of one-on-one contact. Meredith knows the benefits of skin-to-skin contact. She has witnessed it firsthand, a stressed baby's heart rate calming as soon as it's held close to its mother's chest. Conversely, she has seen new moms, tense and uptight, who send their baby's heart rate soaring.

"Poor Mason. Can the doctor give him any more morphine?"

"Not likely," Jill says. "Okay, thanks, I'll try the bath,

then Jonathan. Gotta go." And with that, the line goes dead in Meredith's hand.

Joel and Carol are waiting for her at the edge of the green. "Everything okay?"

Meredith shakes her head. "That was the hospital. One of our heroin babies is going through a difficult withdrawal."

Her mother lifts a hand to her chest, as if this is the worst news possible. "How awful! Do you need to go back?"

"No, Jill's handling it. She wanted to know if I had any special tricks for soothing him since she started caring for him today."

"I hate to judge," says Carol, which fetches a laugh from Joel.

"Who, *you*, Mom? Judge?"

"But, honestly," Carol continues unfazed, "How can a pregnant woman do that to her child? Doesn't she know that if she's addicted, her baby will be, too?"

Meredith has had this conversation with enough people over the years to know better than to take offense. "It's why they call it an addiction, Mom. These are women who often can't afford to get help, who come in having never received any prenatal care. I'm sure if they could stop, they would, for the sake of their baby."

What she neglects to also say is that, in recent years, this type of drug-addicted baby has become more prevalent in their unit. New Haven prides itself on being a cultural hub with Yale University, but the seedy side of the city, which no one likes to talk about, exists, as well. New Haven holds the dubious distinction of having made the national news a few summers ago, when more than a hundred people were treated within thirty-six hours for overdosing on K2, a synthetic type of marijuana. The city's homelessness problem only compounds the drug problem.

In any case, Meredith's argument clearly falls on deaf ears. As open-minded as her mother pretends to be, Carol's opinions about mothering remain fast and true. No one should endanger a baby, which is precisely what addicted mothers do. When her cell phone rings again, Meredith remembers that Mason has a special blanket with his mother's scent that might also help. But it's Cody, calling to check in before he showers and heads over to Melon Hall. The graduates will be lining up for the processional, now only forty-five minutes away. Meredith drops into an empty chair on the green.

"Good luck, honey," she says. "We'll be watching."

Her own babies are minutes away from striding across the stage, their diplomas in hand. It's something she has envisioned only a thousand times.

"The kids?" Joel asks when she clicks off, and she nods. "You okay?"

She nods again. "I think so." But that sick feeling in her stomach won't go away.

"Come on," he says softly. "Your mom wants to check out the classrooms." And, indeed, Meredith can see Carol already striding ahead, her gray hair bobbing across the lawn. Her heart in her throat, Meredith reaches for her husband's steady hand.

Dawn half walks, half crawls to the shower, the only way to describe her clumsy trek to the bathroom. It's much too early to be awake for anyone who had as much to drink as she did last night. And yet, a quick glance at the clock reveals it's already eleven thirty. She has precious little time to get ready.

"Claire?" she calls out. But no one answers. Probably at her boyfriend's. Even Matt didn't want to sleep over last night for some reason. She bangs her knee on a box blocking the middle of the hallway. *Ouch! Crap!* Maybe that's why. Their room is a fortress, practically impossible to navigate with all the packed boxes lining the hallway.

After the party, she and her friends met up with Matt and his buddies at the Burren. An Irish band was playing, and they'd stayed till closing time, throwing back beer after beer. Somewhere in the evening, right around the time Cody arrived with Brad and Toby, she remembers holding up her hand, signaling *no more*, but right about now, she's pretty sure it didn't make any difference.

Oh, no! Her stomach lurches, and she barely makes it to the toilet in time. A moan escapes from somewhere deep inside her. *Great.* She's done what she promised herself she wouldn't do: given herself a fabulous hangover for graduation day. She grabs a towel and wipes down the seat. When she turns on the shower, she has to whack the handle a couple of times until a full spray shoots out. (It's been this way the last two months, but neither she nor Claire has bothered to tell anyone because what's the point since they're leaving anyway?) She steps into the warm spray and steadies herself, gripping the walls for a moment.

When she dips her head under the water and flips her hair up, a spell of dizziness slams her, and Dawn has to gently lower herself in the tub, closing her eyes until it passes. When she opens them again, a spider is dawdling in the corner. She watches it lazily make its way up the wall. If it were her roommate, Claire would scream. But Dawn doesn't mind cohabiting with arachnids, who serve an important role in the life cycle. In her post-alcoholic haze, she wonders if spiders need water. Everything needs water, doesn't it? But can they swim? She laments the fact that she never took biology, which might have put such details easily within her grasp. As it is, vague facts, such as female spiders will sometimes eat their mates, stay with her from a long-ago watched National Geographic show. Beyond that, the spider presents a mystery to her fuzzy brain.

She hefts herself to a standing position again, reaches up to wash her hair, and is shocked by how incredibly heavy her arms feel, as if they're weighed down by a set of dumb-bells. Her head also seems improbably far away from her hands this morning. She opens her mouth wide, letting the warm water stream in, and gargles, which sends a little down her throat by mistake, triggering her gag reflex—but eventually, mercifully, the feeling subsides. Bread, carbs of some kind, will be mandatory if Dawn has any hope of surviving the day.

It occurs to her that if she's in this bad of shape, then her brother must be even worse off. When Cody showed up last night with his friends, he was clearly hammered, unsteady on his feet, his eyes rimmed in red. Dawn fought her way over to him through the throng of people crowding the bar.

"Where have you guys been? I thought you said you were coming to the Burren after the banquet." She hated the querulous note to her voice, as if she were their mom, but she'd been looking forward to everyone's hanging out to-gether on their last night as seniors. Plus, a small piece of her had been worrying about where he was, what her brother had been up to. Had they snuck off to smoke some weed, maybe, or something worse? She'd searched his eyes for tell-tale signs, like enormous dilated pupils. Dawn doesn't re-member much from her antidrug workshops in high school, but the photos of kids high on coke stay with her: pupils so wide it looked like you could almost jump through them.

"Just hanging. We went back to Casey's room to have a few. His parents left him all this extra booze."

"Lucky you." She gave him a glass of ice water, which, on reflection, she probably should have kept for herself. "Hey, Melissa was here earlier. Not sure if she's still around." It seemed only fair to give her brother a heads-up.

"Oh, yeah?" Was it alarm that registered on his face? Or heartbreak? It would be just like her brother to break up with Melissa because he'd heard she was about to dump *him*. But Melissa would never do that to Cody, would she? Melissa loved Cody with a capital *L*, the kind that inspired her to get a secret tattoo with their initials inked into the yin-yang symbol. Dawn has never seen it, but Cody told her about it. "Fucking beautiful" is how he'd described it.

Before she could get a read on her brother, though, Brad and Toby were dragging him onto the dance floor. "C'mon, Cody. Dance with us," they pleaded in their best imitation of fangirl voices. Already a group of seniors from the girls' lacrosse team—the preppy, popular crowd from whom Dawn had always kept her distance—was circling her brother like hawks.

"Cody!" Dawn shouted over the din of the music, vying for his attention before she lost him entirely. "I have something to show you!" She'd almost forgotten. She grabbed her cell phone from the table and waved it in the air. Another text had arrived shortly after she'd stepped into the bar. Tell your brother not to party too hard tonight. Like the last one, the sender was blocked. Not a threat exactly, but still, a red flag that Cody's stalker had no intention of going away anytime soon. Dawn was beginning to suspect it might be love-jilted Melissa, after all. But Cody just shot her his signature grin and shrugged, as if helpless to defend himself against the cohort of young women pulling him onto the dance floor.

When Matt got back from the bathroom, he asked her if everything was all right.

"Yeah, sure." Dawn slipped the phone into her pocketbook. "Seems Cody has a new fan club. Word must have traveled fast that he and Melissa broke up."

"Well, if I were Cody, I wouldn't be too worried."

"Whaddya mean?"

Matt nodded in the direction of a shadowy corner of the bar, where some guy was making out with a girl, her long blond hair trailing down her back. *Melissa.*

"I passed them on the way to the john. Doesn't look like she's taking it too hard."

"Wow, I guess not."

Dawn finishes rinsing her hair and twists the shower knob off before climbing out and toweling off. Maybe her phone, dead this morning, has recharged by now. What if there's another text about her brother? She hurries back to her room, doing an awkward kind of crab crawl through the boxes, and grabs the phone off its charging port. Insistently, she taps at the button, trying to coax the screen back to life.

But when the screen pops up, there's nothing. *Nada.* No new texts about anything stupid that Cody might have done in the past twelve hours, like, making out with some random girl or stealing street signs (another offense he never got caught for sophomore year). And now Dawn has to wonder whether the shudder that just climbed through her body was due to relief—or disappointment—that no new text was waiting. She doesn't want her brother to get in trouble, honestly. But the thought that someone else might see through Cody's clean-cut exterior is a tiny bit seductive. Maybe not everyone in the world has been hoodwinked by her charming, suave twin.

The green glow of the time against the backdrop of her phone (a picture of her and Matt) stares back at her. *11:55 a.m.* She really needs to get moving. Her mom will kill her with a capital *K* if she's late for graduation.

It's here. Graduation day. Lily wears her Ralph Lauren sundress, the one that's strapless with big splashes of blue and white and that reminds her of a Kandinsky painting, but prettier. When she'd described it this way to Roger, he'd acted surprised, as if he didn't think Lily would be familiar with Kandinsky's work. "I'm sure you'll look stunning in whatever you wear," he said.

"What? You think I don't know anything about art? You're not the only one who can read, you know," she scolded, half teasing. This whole weekend, she decides, is making her crazy defensive. But honestly, why do people with college educations always assume that no one else can possibly learn anything outside the classroom? Lily is a voracious reader, eating up everything from thrillers to self-help to art history. On her bedside table sits a stack of library books waiting to be cracked open: Stephen McCauley's *My Ex-Life*, Tayari Jones's *An American Marriage*, and Tara Westover's *Educated*. Lily could be the poster girl for the self-educated American.

When she was young and the library only a few blocks from her house, she'd plant herself in the beanbag chairs of the children's section every Saturday, lapping up as many books as she could. It's where she met some of her best childhood friends, like Laura Ingalls Wilder and Harriet the Spy. Lily felt as if she *knew* those girls, and they knew her. Her first real mentor, Miss Durgin, used to have a pile waiting for her to sift through each Saturday, as if she could sense the trouble at home and understood books were Lily's lifeline. Some days Lily thinks about trying to find Miss Durgin again, or at the very least, making a generous donation to the library as a way of signaling her thanks. Were it not for Miss Durgin, she's fairly certain she would have befriended the bottle, like her mom.

Lily brushes loose powder across her neck and her freckled upper chest. Yesterday's sun has turned her skin a shade of honey brown. Her long dark hair is pulled up in a bun atop her head, with a few loose strays wisping at the sides. Dangly silver earrings, tipped with blue topaz gems, sparkle back at her in the mirror. She dabs a touch of Calvin Klein's Secret Obsession behind her ears and onto the pulse points of her wrists, and smiles into the mirror, double-checking her teeth for lipstick. She doesn't care what Meredith might think. Lily feels happy to be young and pretty and in shape. If other moms want to snicker at her and call her a trophy wife, so be it.

Remarkably, her head barely hurts after the copious amounts of alcohol consumed yesterday. Alison stayed over and will probably sleep in until later this afternoon, which is fine. It's not as if anyone's planning to return to the house after graduation, and if Alison wants to hang out all day, she's more than welcome. Lily has left a stack of fresh towels outside the guest room door along with a note encouraging her friend to take advantage of the pool. Since Roger didn't stumble into bed until almost midnight last night, she didn't even bother mentioning that Alison was sleeping over. "Did you drive home?" Lily asked him, the smell of booze radiating from his body like sound waves. "Yeah," he said. "I'm fine." And he'd patted her leg, muttering something about how proud he was of the kids, before promptly falling asleep. At the time, Lily was too drunk herself to be angry with him, though whether she is upset with him now for getting home so late or for not calling an Uber, she isn't sure. Probably both.

All she needs to do is get through today and tomorrow, and her life can return to normal. She opens the medicine cabinet, takes out the bottle, and untwists the lid. A pile of tablets spills out onto the counter. One last check to make sure that she has enough to get her through the weekend. Minus the ones Roger took for his hand, there are thirty-two pills left, which should be plenty. Though the bottle recommends taking no more than six pills in a twenty-four-hour period, Lily has pushed that number to seven, sometimes eight, in the course of a day. Since she started taking them a few weeks ago, just to dull the edges, she finds the amount of time she can go between pills has shrunk to a smaller window. Now by the third hour, the calming effects begin to wear off and she can feel herself tensing up again, her skin beginning to itch. Her body hungers for the instant ease, and she no longer has any desire to plow through that last hour or tough it out.

Once she is through the weekend, she will stop cold turkey with the painkillers. In the back of her mind lurks the realization that this might not be as easy to pull off as it might have been, say, a few weeks ago or even a few days ago. She has read the literature and understands that the body's tolerance level for oxycodone increases the more you take, the longer you take it. This only means that stopping it gets increasingly difficult with each passing day. Still,

Lily is prepared. In a silly sort of logic, she figures that if she misses that happy-go-lucky feeling too much, she will allow herself to drink a glass of wine every few hours. Swap out one vice for another. Perhaps not the ideal plan, but it's the only one she's got at the moment.

To be fair, also on the edges of her mind is the slip of paper in her top bureau drawer on which a cell phone number is written, a direct dial to someone whom her friend Haley recommended should Lily ever need a refill. When Roger was being a bit of a baby with his broken hand, Lily confided to Haley that she'd snuck a few of his painkillers for herself, which had the happy result of making his injury more tolerable for them both (and it was weeks before she'd thought of the pills again). Haley had laughed in sympathy (her own husband had just weathered back surgery), then pressed the paper into Lily's hand. When Lily saw what it was, she exclaimed, "As if I'll ever need this!" But Haley just shrugged and smiled, as if she knew better and could already anticipate the need in Lily's voice for eventual replenishments. "Don't worry about it. Everyone does it," she'd said.

Lily won't call, of course. It's not as if she's some low-level drug addict desperate for a fix (even though she suspects Haley only deigns to recommend the classiest oxycodone dealers). But it's nice to know she has a safety net in case it's not as easy to quit as she hopes. Just in case it turns out she needs a few more pills before she weans herself off. Totally. She pulls a few tablets out for today, slips them into her compact, and pours the rest back into the bottle before replacing it on the shelf. Moses pads in and tilts his head, as if to say, *What do you think you're doing?*

"What? You want one?" she asks. "Sorry, buddy. Not for dogs. Your life is happy enough as it is." She throws a pill back for herself and swallows. That should keep her calm till they're through the actual ceremony, she figures. The rest of the day she'll have to play by ear.

Moses pads back into the bedroom and circles the rug three times before flopping down. Thanks to her Instagram account, her dog has become somewhat famous. Not many influencers have a hundred-and-fifty pound Saint Bernard to feature in their photo shoots. Which reminds her: before she heads downstairs to find Roger, she should shoot a quick photo for her followers. The dress, the earrings, the whole getup has been comped to her by her generous vendors. Hashtags: #ralphlaurendress; #lizclaiborneearrings; #graduationday; #gobullfrogs! Then she takes a shot of sleeping Moses and posts it with the hashtag: #someoneisexcitedforgraduation. If only she could lay herself down next to him.

TEN

Friday afternoon

Summer is hands down Meredith's favorite season. If she were asked to name her most-loved holiday, it wouldn't be Christmas or even Thanksgiving, but the Fourth of July. She enjoys watching all that bold patriotism on display, especially when the Boston Pops pound out the "1812 Overture." But, really, she loves the holiday most because it encapsulates everything wonderful about the season. The languid sunny days capped by sultry nights, the perpetual scent of sunblock, the shouts from the kids as they dive into the water, the icy nip of cherry Popsicles during the day and the smoky taste of s'mores at night. On the Fourth, everyone converges on Carol's house on Long Island Sound, better known as "the summer house" for the fireworks. No matter what. Even when the kids worked their summer jobs, they'd shown up for the Fourth, tossing their jumble of bags into the bunk room. And every year, Meredith takes the week off from the hospital, a gap that appears like an open smile in her calendar each July. It's a time when, as a family, they can allow themselves to relax.

The last Fourth—when graduation still seemed so far away—Dawn invited Matt out to the summer house, and Meredith was surprised by how much she actually enjoyed Matt's company. A mellow kid, he'd eased into the rhythm of their days as if he'd been coming every summer. He knew how to grill a steak to a perfect medium rare, hung up his wet towel on the deck railing without reminding, and could easily pitch a tent whenever the house overflowed with guests. Most important, the boy appeared to be completely enchanted with her daughter. Knowing this should somehow ease the way for Meredith when Dawn heads off to Chicago in the fall. And yet.

"Are you okay with them living together?" her friends have asked, which strikes Meredith as a surprisingly archaic question in this day and age.

The truth is that the thought of the kids' living together—and for all intents and purposes, sleeping together—doesn't bother her nearly as much as the fact that her daughter will be a thousand miles away. *A thousand miles!* Besides, she's beyond worrying about Dawn's getting pregnant. They had "the talk" back in high school when Dawn started seriously dating a guy, who, in Meredith's humble opinion, was a bit of a slacker. It was right after she'd quit ballet and was casting around for a way to fill all her newly idle hours. As awkward as the conversation had been for them both—Dawn sitting in the passenger seat and Meredith's eyes trained on the road—Meredith had conveyed in no uncertain terms that getting pregnant as a teenager was not an option.

"Understood?" she'd asked.

"Yes, Mom, I got it. You don't want to be a grandma until I'm like forty."

"Not forty, necessarily. Just no babies till you're done with school, and that includes college."

"Yes, ma'am." Beyond that, she'd trusted Dawn to have the conversation with her doctor about what kind of birth control to use. During vacations or over the summer, the compact of tiny pink pills would occasionally get left out on the bathroom counter, and Meredith would check it each time to make sure Dawn was holding up her end of the bargain. *Insurance, not snooping,* she reasoned. As for Cody, she'd gladly passed the "sex talk" baton to Joel.

So many memories come flooding back now, insistent little recollections that lap at her mind while they wait for the ceremony to commence. The afternoon air has grown thick with humidity so that it *feels* like summer, and even in the parcel of shade they've co-opted for the ceremony, the heat verges on the oppressive. If it were any other day, Meredith would indulge in a long, lazy nap in the hammock.

A few rows down someone waves to her, and she realizes that it's Penelope from last night. Somehow, despite the fact that she was slurring her words at the dinner, Penelope looks spectacular today. Her outfit is a halter red-and-white striped jumpsuit that hugs her toned body, leaving very little to the imagination. Meredith smiles and reciprocates with a wave, though she has to laugh. There's no chance their outfits would overlap today because there's zero chance Meredith would be caught wearing a jumpsuit. She doubts she could even fit into it. *Thank goodness she won't have to play the comparison game today,* she thinks.

Then she remembers: *oh yeah, I have Lily for that.*

A handful of other parents wanders around the courtyard shooting photos with their expensive cameras—Canon Digital SLRs and Nikons with zoom lenses. It *is* picturesque, pretty enough for a postcard, with giant bins of potted tulips positioned on the lawn and endless rows of white chairs contrasting with the bright green grass. Meredith double-checks her phone to make sure it's fully charged and gets up to shoot a few photos herself.

She bumps into Matt's parents briefly (who reassure her that they'll keep a close eye on Dawn while she's in their hometown of Chicago), and then rejoins Joel and Carol. Several rows of chairs up front have been cordoned off for the graduating class. There's the constant flutter of commencement programs fanning the air, which creates an odd humming sensation, as if hundreds of bees flap their wings in anticipation. A fair number of women in the audience sport summer hats. Had it occurred to her, Meredith would have packed her own straw fedora.

Just then, her mother reaches over and digs her bony fingers into her knee. "Don't look now, but if it's not the Prince of Narnia and his princess," she whispers. "Along with His and Her Royal Highness."

Meredith turns slightly to see Roger and Lily making their way to their seats, a few rows up to the left. Harry and Edith follow behind them and then Georgie, Roger's brother. Roger caters to enough wealthy clients in Boston to be recognized, but the hushed whispers still unnerve Meredith. No one ever batted an eye when they were married! It seems impossible that in ten short years her ex-husband has built himself into a franchise, a household name representing some of Boston's favorite sports icons. She wonders how he managed to secure such coveted seats, in the "reserved" section, but then realizes she's being an idiot—

Roger has probably already promised Bolton a new science lab, a spanking new football stadium.

"Oh, honey," Carol says. "I'm so sorry you have to endure this."

"Endure what, Mom? I'm here to enjoy my children's graduation, just like you. Though you're right it could be a little cooler."

"Not the heat, her!" Carol practically hisses in Lily's direction. "As if she belongs here." Her mother rolls her eyes aggressively.

"Oh, come on, Mom, that's old news. Roger can do whatever he pleases." Meredith is trying her level best to downplay the awkwardness of the day. Of course, she's not thrilled that Lily is here! But she certainly doesn't need her mother reminding her every few minutes.

Carol grunts. "You hit the nail on the head, sweetie. Lily is sure to be old news in a few years." She waves a hand in the air. "She's fungible, just like the rest of them. Soon enough he'll be chasing some other young skirt."

Meredith has to stop and think what fungible means before correcting her mother. "I'm pretty sure we say 'woman' now instead of 'skirt.'" *Exchangeable*, she thinks. That's what fungible means. Last night, she admittedly lost her balance for a minute. When Roger strode into the banquet unexpected—unrehearsed!—her vision of how the evening would unfurl vanished in a *poof*! But she'd recovered, channeled her inner calm, and managed to act pleased by the fact that he'd made it to the twins' banquet after all. *What a pleasant surprise!* she'd said while a host of other emotions went skating through her mind. But then she had another glass of wine, watched Roger fumbling for an empty seat, and felt herself softening. He was the kids' dad after all. He had every right to join their table.

The only thing wrong with his being there was that he hadn't intended to come in the first place.

Before she has a chance to reapply her sunscreen, Roger and Lily are heading over to say hello, and Meredith braces herself for the impact. *Will it be an impact of asteroid proportions or only meteoric?* she wonders. Summoning all her strength and grace, Meredith stands to greet her ex-husband and his new wife, who, it must be said, looks as if she could be his daughter.

"Hi, Roger. Hello, Lily." *Kiss-kiss.* She tries not to smoosh the well-endowed breasts wedged between herself and Lily when they lean in for an embrace. "You look lovely, Lily." Meredith doubts that Lily's generation invokes descriptors like *lovely.* Probably *hot* or *dynamite* would be more appropriate, but Meredith wants the upper hand here. They have met only a handful of times, and under different circumstances, Meredith would be impressed by Lily's chutzpah, her youthful ambition and the fact that she has built a substantial following for herself on Instagram and Twitter. Not bad for a little girl from a tiny town in Kentucky. But since she is Meredith's replacement, Meredith is reluctant to admire anything about her.

"Thank you, you too," gushes Lily. "Congratulations. You must be so proud of the twins."

Okay, thinks Meredith. *Not bad. At least you're acknowledging I'm the one who should be proud here, not you.* Still, seeing Lily here is a bit like spotting a snow leopard in the Australian outback—she's both exotic and misplaced, her heels as sharp and narrow as a paring knife. She'd blend in much better up onstage with the graduates. Her dress resembles a summer sky, blue with bold splashes of white along the waistline, and her skin radiates a maddening dewy glow. Meredith does a quick mental calculation of how much Botox must be tucked into Lily's wrinkles until it dawns on her: *Lily is thirty.* It's not fillers that lend her perfect skin its luminosity. *It's youth.*

So what if Lily is almost young enough to be Meredith's own daughter or Dawn and Cody's sister? This is the new modern family, Meredith understands. But she'd be lying if she didn't admit that standing next to Lily has the instant effect of making her feel frumpy and matronly, as if she's the person everyone is counting on to provide water bottles and snacks. Because, bless her heart, there's no way Lily can fit anything practical into that cute little straw clutch of hers. Her hair is pulled up in an elegant bun while Meredith can feel hers corkscrewing in the humidity, and her topaz earrings dangle seductively (Meredith's pearl studs probably look like the imposters they are, purchased at Marshalls on clearance). And then there's Lily's exquisitely tanned bare shoulders, which seem to cry out for a jacket, a shawl, *something* to cover them. Roger must catch Meredith staring because he drapes an arm around Lily's shoulders protectively.

Georgie comes over to pump Joel's hand, though neither of Roger's parents makes an effort to say hello. *Not surprising*, Meredith thinks. *But how rude!* She struggles to recall when they were last all together, probably at the kids' high school graduation in New Haven. Everyone went out to dinner at Zinc downtown, and she can still hear Roger's dad complaining about the food, which was, by the way, out-of-this-world delicious: shrimp Cobb salad, fresh seared salmon, farm-raised chicken marsala. "If I'd wanted 'farm-to-table' food," Harry said haughtily after they'd tried to explain the guiding principle behind the restaurant, the freshness of its local ingredients, "I would have stopped at a farm." Afterward Roger had quietly packed himself, his parents, and Georgie into the car and headed back up to Boston.

And Meredith's relationship with her former mother-in-law can only be described as chilly, verging on frozen. In Edith's eyes, Roger can do no wrong. Though Meredith has never put the question to her, she harbors a suspicion that Edith partly blames her for the dissolution of their marriage. Maybe if Meredith had done more to keep Roger engaged, more interested in their marriage, she can hear Edith saying, then his eye would have been less likely to wander in the first place. Edith heralds from the 1950s martini-at-the-door, lipstick-wearing generation. Meredith knows this, but it doesn't make her former mother-in-law's condemning stares any less piercing. *Maybe*, Meredith sometimes imagines her retort, *if you'd done a better job of teaching your son about loyalty and respecting women, things would have turned out differently.*

"Georgie, how nice to see you." Carol takes his hand now. "Good of you to fly out all the way from London. Are you enjoying it over there?"

"Absolutely!" His enthusiasm, like his voice, fills up space. "It's a good living. I've got a little place where I can wake up in the morning and see Big Ben out my window. Nothing like it." Ever since his hedge fund needed a new London manager a few years ago, Georgie has worked across the pond. Meredith suspects there's nothing "little" about Georgie's place, but his modesty is a nice contrast to the typical Landau family bravado.

She leans in for a hug. "Georgie, it's so good to see you. Thank you for coming. The kids are over-the-moon excited to see you."

Suddenly a trumpet call cuts through the air, and the

rest of the crowd disperses to settle into their seats as a vast sea of blue, the graduates in their caps and gowns, gathers at the back of the courtyard. *Finally.* Meredith's stomach does a small flip, and Georgie quickly excuses himself to rejoin the family. As the graduation march of "Pomp and Circumstance" commences, Joel grips her hand. "Ready?"

She nods. *Ready.*

Already the graduates are beginning to make their way toward their seats in slow, deliberate steps, as if they've been instructed not to rush upon penalty of death. Cody and Dawn, she knows, will fall somewhere in the middle of the pack. She digs her phone out of her purse, toggles over to the photography icon, and waits until at last she spies them in the upper right-hand corner of the screen. When the twins pass by, she snaps photo after photo, while Joel and her mom shout out *Congratulations!*, the kids beaming back at them. *They look so happy,* Meredith thinks. *So proud.* And, ouch. *So grown-up.*

After the entire class is seated, the assembled families settle into their chairs again, and Dean Halberstam takes the podium to offer welcoming remarks. Meredith's mind wanders to a faraway place, a summer when they hosted an exchange student, Mateo, a sixteen-year-old from Barcelona. Cody, only fourteen at the time, spent the entire summer in Mateo's thrall, shadowing him and wanting nothing to do with her or Dawn or Joel. The farther away, the better. This is a bit how it feels today. Bittersweet. And, even though she understood it was just a stage for Cody back then—like thumb-sucking or the first day of kindergarten—it stung a little more than those early passages, felt less like an occasion to celebrate and more like an event to lament. Even then, she could feel her hold on her boy slipping away.

Dawn and Cody sit about five rows up. Like their class-mates, they've personalized the tops of their caps: Dawn's has rainbow fingers spread in a peace sign and Cody's sports the Bolton football mascot, a bullfrog. Meredith works to focus on the class valedictorian, who's introducing this year's commencement speaker, a bespectacled Boston philanthro-pist and businessman. The unassuming, slight man takes the stage, and Meredith is momentarily relieved that it's not her ex-husband up there, also a local philanthropist and businessman.

"Graduating class of 2020!" their speaker bellows, and cheers float out over the air. Meredith wonders if the rest of the audience is as surprised as she is by the delightful bari-tone that pours out from this diminutive man. "You might think I'm here today to talk about success as you go forward in life." More cheering. "You might think I'm here to give you tips on how to get ahead in the real world. The grown-up world? Am I right?" Shouts of "Yes," and even "Amen" rise up. It's true, Meredith realizes now: his delivery resem-bles that of a Sunday morning preacher. His soft laughter carries over the microphone, as he pushes up his glasses and stares out over the crowd. "Well." He pauses. "You would be mistaken." And there's a smattering of laughter. He knows he has their full attention now.

"Because I am not here today to talk to you about success, about getting ahead. No sir, no ma'am." Meredith catches Joel's glance, his eyebrows elevated on his forehead. "To the contrary, I'm here today so I can tell you how to fail." A hushed silence is punctuated by a few twitters. "In fact, that's what I'm calling my speech today—*How to Succeed in the World by Failing.* That's a little unusual, coming from a commencement speaker who's supposed to inspire you. But let me tell you something. There is more than one way to learn. And I'm not talking about books—although, parents, let me assure you that your children have learned *plenty* from all those books you've bought them over the last four years, and they *thank* you." Applause from parents and kids alike.

"But in real life, folks, I'm here to tell you—you're going to fail. And I don't mean getting an F on your history test or losing the championship football game. I mean *real life* failures. Some of them are going to be so small you'll hardly notice them, and others are going to be so gigantic, you'll question whether your head is still screwed on straight. Every one of you will be confronted with different challenges. And every one of you will fail at different things, at different times.

"But you know what? That's okay. Because you're going to get through it, whatever *it* might be. And you know what else? Those failures are *necessary*. Just like your successes, just like the love your parents shower on you, just like three square meals a day—those failures are the very things that make you *who you are*."

Meredith is enthralled by the slightly unorthodox message and hopes the kids are listening, Cody especially. A raindrop freckles her arm, and she scans the sky. A few more drops ping on her program, expanding circles of dampness, and she waits—but there's nothing more. Mercifully, the rain holds off while their speaker carries on for maybe fifteen more minutes, his voice crescendoing over the crowd, and then, as the audience begins to shift in their seats, he starts to wrap up, as if on cue.

"I'd like to close by sharing two quotes with you. One is from Thomas Edison." It's so quiet she can hear the thrum of crickets, the croak of a frog. "When he was busy inventing his light bulb, Thomas Edison said, and I quote, 'I have not failed. I've just found ten thousand ways that won't work.'" Laughter and applause ripple through the crowd. "The last quote I'll share with you is from the great Winston Churchill, who once said, 'Success is stumbling from failure to failure with no loss of enthusiasm.' Now I want you to think about that and remember it as you go forward in the world. Remember that. 'Success is stumbling from failure to failure *with no loss of enthusiasm.*' There are going to be plenty of failures in your life. Expect them. Count on them. Understand that they are a way to figuring out what works—and what doesn't. And Class of 2020? Don't ever lose your enthusiasm. Because you are surrounded by love, you are surrounded by people who want to help you succeed. Even if it means you have to fail ten thousand times. Congratulations, Class of 2020. You've made us proud!"

The audience leaps to its feet for a standing ovation. He has managed to pull off a rousing speech in scorching temperatures. There are fist pumps from the students, and more than a few parents share knowing nods. The man has a point, Meredith thinks as they sit back down, and better he deliver this particular message than they do.

Despite the threat of an occasional rain cloud, the sun has continued to blaze overhead, and she notices now that the back of Joel's shirt sports a sweaty imprint in the shape of a butterfly. The poor guy must be dying. But Joel cuts a glance her way, rubbing his hands together excitedly. "Diploma time!"

Meredith laughs and takes a swig of warm water from her bottle. When she goes to set it down on the ground, though, she spies something moving out of the corner of her eye. Since her chair sits right on the aisle for easy picture-taking, it's only natural that she would notice it first. A tiny frog. At least she thinks that's what it is. She watches it hop its way across the manicured grass where the students paraded earlier and holds her breath, waiting to see if it will continue up to the podium or into one of the rows where the families sit. She's about to point it out to Joel when suddenly, there's another one, about a foot away. Or maybe it's a toad? Its skin, a fluorescent green, is flecked with miniature black spots. Beady eyes dot each side of its head. "Uh-oh." Joel sees it, too. It's only a matter of time before—

And that's when a woman a few rows ahead shoots straight up, shrieking, "Frog!" As soon as she says it, dozens— perhaps hundreds—of frogs are suddenly leaping all around them, between people's feet, over chairs, a few even hurtling through the air above their heads. "It's an infestation!" cries Carol. "Of *frogs!*"

Meredith and Joel glance at each other with the same instant realization. These aren't just frogs. They're bullfrogs, of course. Bolton bullfrogs. In fact, a few even seem to be painted in the school colors of blue and white. Meredith tries to avoid being attacked while also providing a body shield for her mother. Dean Halberstam, attempting for calm, intones into the microphone, "Everyone, it seems we have a bit of a situation on our hands. I'd encourage you all to stay calm while we take a short intermission and, um, deal with these frogs."

"Hideous!" Carol cries and shakes one from her foot. Meredith is trying her best to help, but somewhere in the midst of the pandemonium, it hits her: how absolutely funny this is. Who would have thought they'd be deluged with frogs? It's a great prank, no, *the perfect prank*. She flops onto her chair, which is blessedly frog-free, and breaks out laughing. Before long, Joel joins her. Her mother stares at them as if they've both lost their minds. "What is wrong with you two? This isn't funny!" Which only makes them laugh harder.

The senior class, who apparently has orchestrated the entire ruse, darts around trying to catch the slippery creatures while congratulating one another. Meredith has no idea how the kids managed to sneak all the frogs into the ceremony at the last minute, but if their desired result was complete chaos, they've certainly achieved it. Even the parade leaders, in their floppy Bolton hats, have joined the audience's amphibious pursuit. It's pretty clear, though, that catching dozens of frogs will be impossible, and so people begin chasing them out of the courtyard entirely. "Shoo! Shoo!" yells a young woman in the row ahead.

Finally, after several more minutes, Halberstam resumes the podium and encourages everyone to take their seats. While there still may be a few frogs afoot or "ahop"—he attempts to joke—he hopes for the sake of the Class of 2020 that the remainder of the ceremony, namely, the awarding of the diplomas, may go on. If there's an errant frog or two hopping around, *please*, he urges, *do your best to ignore it. I assure you they're harmless.*

Joel leans over and whispers "ribbit" in Meredith's ear, and she has to cover her mouth with a hand to suppress the giggles. Then, *shhh*. He points to the stage, as if she needs reminding that Cody's and Dawn's moment is almost upon them, and she works to pull herself together. Until finally, she hears the names she's been waiting for.

"Cody William Landau, Phi Beta Kappa," announces Dean Halberstam, and Meredith inhales sharply while her only son strides across the stage, shakes hands with the dean, accepts his diploma, and poses for a photo before heading off the stage. The audience is clapping so hard that she can barely hear Dawn's name when it's announced next. Before she knows it, Cody has descended the platform, and Dawn glides up for her turn.

"Dawn McKenzie Landau, cum laude." Meredith claps and claps for her little girl who walks across the stage, her posture erect after all those years of ballet, to collect her diploma. She poses with the dean for a photo and then appears to float off the stage. Meredith's hands sting but she doesn't care. She keeps clapping as a cavalcade of images flashes before her. The countless battles over homework. The years of ballet lessons, broken pointe shoes, and football games. The visits to the emergency room when Cody got a concussion on the field, and another when Dawn broke her arm after flying over her bike's handlebars. The time when six-year-old Cody asked if she "painted her face on," or when nine-year-old Dawn told her that she "looked skinny for her age." The dozens of teachers' conferences, the SAT prep, the college essay, the phone calls home late at night because one kid needed help on a paper or a lift home for the weekend. The bold dash of Cody into the end zone in this year's championship game. Dawn's turning her grades around senior year. After a whole raft of emotions, both joyous and despairing over the past twenty-one years, today Meredith feels only gratitude and pride.

And joy. Her kids have done it. They are graduates, free to go out into the world and make their name or, as their speaker said today, fail until they get it right, whatever "it" might turn out to be.

She looks to Joel and is surprised to see that his eyes are edged with tears. "You're such a softy." She gives his forearm a squeeze. "And here I thought I'd be the one with all the Kleenexes."

Joel lifts a hand to swipe at his eyes. "Allergies," he says jokingly. "I'm just so ridiculously proud of them." And that's when Meredith realizes it—Lily or no Lily, frogs or no frogs, blistering temperatures or not—this may well be the best day of her life.

ELEVEN

The release of the frogs surpassed even Cody's wildest expectations. Earlier, he and Brad had worked it out so that, after the commencement speech, Brad's younger brother, Josh, and his friend would sneak off to the bathroom in the main hall, where two boxes of frogs awaited in a locked stall (Cody and Brad had placed them there right before falling into line for the graduation processional). From there, Josh and his buddy would return to the courtyard, and from the shelter of a clump of azalea bushes, set the frogs free. The plan, which could have gone awry in so many different ways, had gone off without a hitch. Hundreds of tiny frogs hopping around the courtyard and croaking their lungs out! It was the *sauce*. The ultimate senior prank, and they'd pulled it off.

But now he has to remind himself to play it cool, as if he knows nothing about its provenance or who might be involved. It's tough, though, because he's sweating bullets under his cap and gown in this heat, and he probably looks guilty as hell. A couple of buddies trot over to high-five him.

"Cody, man, that was ahh-mazing."

Cody shrugs, looks around to make sure no one official is within hearing range, and says, "Yeah, well, it was a team effort, as you know." He's referring to the fact that about two weeks ago, he and Brad collected money from seniors interested in contributing to the senior prank. It had been surprisingly easy to locate frogs for sale online, which were also relatively inexpensive (apparently, frogs were a popular feeding source for pet snakes). For ten to twenty measly bucks, a senior could purchase their "own" frog. Sixty percent of the senior class had participated, which Cody thought was pretty damn impressive. Of course, Dawn couldn't be bothered, so he didn't even ask her. Sometimes it surprised him how out of the loop his sister was. All she cared about anymore was hanging out with Matt and her cross-country friends. And avoiding the Admin Board at all costs.

"Dude, that was awesome. We hit the ball out of the park!" Brad is so euphoric, you'd think he'd just scored the winning run in the World Series, but even Cody has to agree. His face breaks into a wide grin.

"I know. It was sick. Totally worth it just to see Halberstam running around trying to catch them all." He pulls Brad aside. "Hey, make sure your brother and his pal know how much we appreciate it."

"Already taken care of." Brad assures him. "They've been duly compensated for their efforts, no worries."

"Cool." As he says it, a frog hops by them, and Brad

breaks out laughing. "Man, the Class of 2020 is going to go down in infamy."

"And I suppose we have you guys to thank for that?" His sister has snuck up beside them.

Cody feigns innocence. "I'm sure I have no idea what you're talking about."

"Yeah, right. Anyway, we should really find Mom. She's probably freaking out, wondering where we are."

Cody can't disagree with that. "Later, dude," he tells Brad and follows his sister's cap with the dorky peace sign on top while keeping an eye out for Melissa. At the beginning of the ceremonies, he'd spotted Melissa in line, but she'd pulled her gaze away as soon as she saw him. He doesn't know what to think. Maybe they really *are* broken up? He told his sister they were, but his conversation with Melissa yesterday plays through his mind. He's not quite sure how to reconcile what was said with what's in his heart. They'd been lounging on the quad, Cody enjoying the tickle of a blade of grass that Melissa was trailing across his face, his eyes closed. Their talk was about the summer, about how lame it was going to be and how much they'd miss each other. She still didn't know what she wanted to do next year and was calling it her "gap year" (though technically Cody is pretty sure that applies to the year between high school and college). But whatever. Whatever she decided to do was cool with him, he told her. Which was when, somehow, the conversation had gone south.

"You know, we could make a plan," she'd suggested, playfully pulling the grass across his cheek and down to his earlobe.

"Yeah?" The tease in her voice sounded promising.

"For next year, I mean."

"Oh?" He cracked one eye open. "What do you mean?"

"I mean you and me. Maybe we could, you know, be together."

"You're going to come visit me, right?"

"Of course, silly." She kissed him softly, and her lips were sticky and sweet with gloss that tasted like watermelon. "But I wouldn't need to visit you if we were together." He tried to parse her words for their true meaning. Was she suggesting they move in together? Not that it would be so bad, but they'd never even discussed her coming out to North Dakota. That was big, as in she'd be hooking herself to him without any plans of her own. He wasn't sure he could handle the pressure. What if things didn't work out between them?

"Whoa." He bolted upright. "Are you saying you want to move to North Dakota with me?"

She rolled her eyes. "Duh. Yes, Cody Landau, that's what I'm driving at."

"But I thought you were going to hang around LA, see if you could land an internship with a movie producer or something? You know, your gap year."

She tossed the blade of grass away and shrugged. "The more I think about it, the dumber it sounds. I think it would be a lot more fun to hang with you on the reservation."

"Huh." He'd lain back down, wondering what had sparked the change of heart. The thing was, Cody was looking forward to striking out on his own for a year, no attachments whatsoever. He'd worked hard to land this job and was already drawing up lesson plans in his head for his students. He was going to change lives, make a difference. If Melissa came out, that would throw a whole wrench into his first year. He'd be worrying about *her* all the time, making sure she was happy.

"What? You don't think it's a good idea?"

"I don't know," he said. "I'm thinking."

"Well, maybe you shouldn't think so hard."

"What would you do out there?"

He could almost hear her shrug. "I don't know. I'm sure I could find something. Maybe I could be your assistant in the classroom?" She inched closer and rested her head on his shoulder.

But that struck him as a horrible idea. He didn't want Melissa in the classroom with him! He'd be totally distracted, as would his students. She was way too cute to hang out in the back of the room and help with passing out papers.

He sat up again, trying to figure out a generous way to say this, but then she'd pulled herself up so that her face was level with his and the blue of her eyes seemed to have shifted a shade darker. "What? What's wrong?"

"Nothing." He slipped his flip-flops back on. "We never really talked about it before, though. You're kind of springing it on me."

At which point, it was as if pointy knives had sprung from her head. "I thought you'd be excited about it! Happy to know you'd have some company." She jumped to her feet, hands on her hips, and shot him a familiar look—righteous and wronged.

"Geez, don't go all postal on me, okay?" he said.

"Postal?" Her cheeks flooded with color, which had the effect of making her look even cuter. "We've been dating for almost *four* years, Cody. Four years." She held up four fingers as if to underscore the point. "Don't you think this

might be a logical next step? Putting down some roots together?"

Logical next step? Roots? What the hell were they talking
about? "First of all," he began, trying to keep his voice on
an even keel. "I don't know if they'll renew my contract
beyond one year. And second of all, how is it that we've
gone from having a perfectly nice afternoon to you yelling
at me because I don't think it's a great idea for you to pack
up and move to North Dakota all of a sudden? You know
how messed up that is, right?"

Melissa spun away from him. "My bad. Never mind. My
mistake. I thought we were in love. No, let me correct that.
I thought we loved each other as in I'll-follow-you-to-the-
ends-of-the-earth love. Apparently I was wrong."

"Hey, I never said we wouldn't be together some day."

She twisted her lips in disgust. "You just did! If you can't
commit now, Cody, when will you?"

He was dumbfounded into silence. "I thought I was already committed," he tried, but his voice wavered, sounding
unconvincing even to him.

"Not if you can't even entertain the idea of spending a
whole year with me."

"Mel, that's not what I meant—" But she'd stormed off.

"Call me in a few years when you're a grown-up," she
huffed over her shoulder.

Cody assumed it was a short-lived drama—they'd gotten
into some crazy fights before and they always made up, usually with some pretty amazing sex. Pretty soon, he figured,
she'd text him a sad emoji, saying she was sorry for freaking
out on him. But when she didn't, he'd grudgingly folded,
texting her one word, *sorry*, followed by a string of hearts.
That should have done the trick.

But then his text had gone unanswered (which really ticked him off), and the next time he saw her was at the Burren, with some other guy's hands buried in her hair, his tongue halfway down her throat. Melissa knew she'd find him at the Burren last night. It was a revenge make-out session, pure and simple, and Cody refused to take the bait. Instead, he'd allowed his drunken self to be pulled out onto the dance floor with some of the lacrosse girls. *You want to play that game? Fine. I can screw around, too*, he thought.

But now that their blowout is twenty-four hours behind him, he's missing her like his thumb has been lopped off. It literally *hurts*. How things got messed up so quickly makes his head spin. He's pondering all of this while he tries to keep up with his sister's screwball path through the crowd to their parents. The courtyard air is tinged with a ripe smell, the aroma of sweat, cologne, perfume, and excitement all blending together in a kind of funky, primal fragrance. There are so many families milling about that they almost stride right past their mom and Joel.

"There you are!" His mom exclaims and pulls them both into a fierce hug. "Congratulations! I'm so proud of you two."

"Bring it in, kids." Joel joins the group hug, and while it feels good to be on the receiving end of all this adulation, Cody finds himself pulling away before everyone gets too misty-eyed. "Way to go," Joel says. "Congratulations. You're officially adults now. Good luck to you." He slaps Cody on the shoulder in half jest. "And how about those frogs? They pretty much stole the show."

"Yeah, totally nuts," Cody agrees, playing it cool. He can tell his stepdad is searching for clues, asking in code if he's somehow behind the frog invasion. But Cody's not about to fess up to pulling off one of the coolest pranks in Bolton's history. He's not that stupid.

"Does anyone have some water?" Dawn gathers her hair up in a loose ponytail and dramatically fans the back of her neck with her program. "I'm dying in this heat." In typical mom fashion, Meredith hands over what's left of her water bottle and then fumbles through her purse for something else. *Granola bars.* Cody, suddenly realizing how ravenous he is, wolfs one down in about a minute.

"So, let me see, let me see," his nana insists. "I want to lay my eyes on the actual diploma." From the envelope, Dawn slides out the creamy stationery with *Bolton College* embossed on the top, her name scrawled in calligraphy along the bottom. "Oh, honey, that's fantastic." His nana takes the diploma and admires it before handing it back. "Congratulations."

"And, Cody, let's see yours now." He appreciates that his nana is trying to include him, but honestly it feels like overkill to show off both of their diplomas. Still, no one says no to Nana, so he unfastens the envelope and reaches in for the certificate.

Except it's not there. The envelope is empty.

His heart does a tiny flip. Does this have something to do with the frogs? Has he been found out? Or is it something more sinister, like the photo that Dawn flaunted at him yesterday?

"Um, there's nothing in here," he says.

His mom shoots Joel a confused look. "Huh, that's weird."

He pulls the envelope open wider just to be certain he's not missing it when his eye lands on a small, rectangular piece of white paper stuck at the bottom, which he retrieves and reads out loud. "Unfortunately, there appears to be a slight issue with your diploma. Please report to Dean Halberstam's office promptly after graduation ceremonies to resolve said issue." When he glances up, his eyes meet Dawn's. *Shit.* He's been caught—for something.

"How strange!" His mom looks from Joel to him and back to Joel. "We're all paid up on tuition, right?"

"Should be," says Joel.

"There must be some misunderstanding." She waves a hand in the air. "Maybe the note was meant for someone else who hasn't paid? I mean, how many kids do they have graduating today? Over a thousand? It would be easy to confuse things. Your diploma probably got mixed up with someone else's. Someone who hasn't paid in full. It's only a matter of time before they figure it out."

Cody is grateful when Joel nods and says, "Yeah, that must be it. The dean announced it and all, so it's official. Now we just have to find the piece of paper so you can show it off." He's kidding around, trying to keep things light, which Cody appreciates. But his stomach isn't cooperating, and he knows he's got to find Brad, see if he has the same notice in his envelope. Because then he'll know. That this has to do with the frogs.

"Dawn, honey, double-check yours," their mom instructs. "Maybe Cody's got slipped into your envelope by accident."

They all watch while his sister shakes her envelope as if his might be hiding somewhere inside. "No, it's not here." She eyes Cody, and he wishes she would go away because his sister is so transparent and everyone can tell she assumes there's a very good explanation for why his diploma has gone missing.

He really needs to find Brad.

"Uncle Georgie! You made it!" Dawn suddenly races over

to throw her arms around their uncle, whom they haven't seen in forever. And then, next thing he knows, the entire Landau clan has engulfed them—Georgie, his dad and Lily, his grandparents. His dad pumps his hand, says, "I'm proud of you, son," and Lily leans in to hug him, though Cody tries to keep his body from touching hers.

His dad won't stop talking about the frogs, either. "Pretty genius senior prank, if you ask me. Did you kids know anything about it?" Both Dawn and Cody shake their heads.

"Not really," lies Cody. "We knew something was up."

Dawn kicks his foot, and he shoots arrows back at her with his eyes. *Shut up*, he attempts to convey telepathically.

"What? Why do you all look like you're headed to a funeral instead of a graduation party?" His dad scans their group and his mom smiles thinly, as if she can't decide whether to say something or not. It's quite possible his dad will fly off the handle and storm the dean's office, and yet Cody can't figure out a way *not* to tell him about his missing diploma. Roger checks his watch, a gold Rolex with a clock face as big as a walnut. "We only have a couple more hours before we're due at Artu. Should we grab a quick drink somewhere in Davis Square before heading into town?"

His father's query is met with silence, and all Cody can think is *well, this is awkward*. Until his mom speaks up. "It seems that Cody's diploma is, um, missing." She pauses. "And that he might have to pay a visit to Dean Halberstam's office first."

"What do you mean? Cody?" His dad spins around to him for clarification. "Is that true?"

He tries to meet his dad's eyes, but it's no use. Cody will always cry *Uncle!* first when confronted with a face-off against the famous Roger Landau, Esquire. "Yeah. My diploma must have gotten mixed up with someone else's."

"Well, that's outrageous," his dad huffs. "How much have I paid this school and they can't even get your diploma right?" He glares at Meredith with a look that's at once questioning and accusatory. Cody is tempted to point out that it's not just his dad, but his mom and Joel, too, who have footed the bill for college, but decides now is not the moment.

"Oh, I'm sure it happens from time to time," his nana chimes in. "Maybe we should proceed to the dean's office and get it sorted out?"

"Sure," Cody says. "Just one sec, though." Out of the corner of his eye, he has spotted Brad, and Cody sidles over to Brad's family, accepting their congratulations as graciously as he can. His heart, though, is full-out racing.

"Brad, man, did you get your diploma?" he asks, pulling him aside.

"Yeah. Why? What do you mean?"

"Mine wasn't in my envelope. Just a note saying that I should check in with the dean's office."

"Oh, shit." Brad's eyes widen in alarm. "The frogs? Do you think they're gonna nail us?"

Cody shrugs. He so badly wants to play it cool, but if he's screwed things up with the frog incursion, he doesn't know if he'll ever forgive himself. The diploma should be his for the taking! He's given Bolton College their best years of football in recent memory, not to mention graduating at the top of his class. "Apparently, not you," he tells Brad.

"Hey, let me know what happens, okay? I'm your wing-man, if you need me."

"Thanks, dude." Cody isn't sure if he means he'll cover

for him, take the blame or at least partial blame, if it comes to that, but frankly he'd rather not test his friend's loyalty right now. He trots back to his own family, who waits expectantly, his dad's arms crossed and his mother's mouth pulled into a tight, uncertain smile.

"Okay, ready," he says. "Let's go."

TWELVE

Maybe it is something trivial, Cody thinks as they start walking, like the college never logged his final tuition payment into the computer. Maybe this has nothing to do with the frogs. Or that other thing. On their way to the dean's office, some random woman stops his stepdad to say hello, as if they're best buddies.

"Joel! Hi, again. I wanted to introduce you to my daughter, Cassie. And my partner, Ruby."

"Oh, Kat! I was wondering if I'd bump into you again. Nice to meet you, Cassie. Congratulations." Cody watches his stepdad shake hands with a slightly plump girl with a head of thick red curls, her diploma clasped in her hand. "And you, Ruby." It dawns on him that this Kat person and Ruby are a couple, as in married. He glances at their ring fingers, and sure enough, they're both sporting plain gold wedding bands. Ruby's dark hair is cut in a pixie, and a stud diamond earring sparkles in her nose. She's pretty in a harsh way, Cody thinks, with sharp cheekbones, deeply set hazel eyes. Weirdly, she seems to be sizing up his stepdad.

"And I should introduce you to my family. Kat, this is my wife, Meredith, and my stepkids, Dawn and Cody. And my mother-in-law, Carol." It's pretty obvious that Joel has no intention of introducing Roger or anyone in his family, even though they hover awkwardly on the sidelines of the conversation.

"So nice to meet you," his mom says, laying it on thick, like she's not at all surprised by this chance encounter with a woman who appears to be good pals with Joel. "And congratulations to you, Cassie."

"Thanks."

"Hey, do you guys know each other?" Joel gestures between the red-haired girl and Dawn and himself, but they all shake their heads. Cassie says softly, almost so quietly that Cody can't hear her, "I think I might have seen you around campus." He's not sure if she means him or Dawn, but he lets it slide because mainly he's wondering what the heck the girl's mom is doing talking to Joel? How do they know each other?

"Kat and I used to go to high school together," says Joel. *There it is.* "We're from the same town, same neighborhood even."

"Oh, I see," says his nana, as if this explains everything.

"How nice," Meredith says. "What a small world."

"I know, right?" Kat braids her fingers through Ruby's. "How awesome is it that we both get to see our kids graduate from the same college now? If that isn't life coming full circle, I don't know what is."

Silence falls over them for a moment until his mom intervenes. "Well, it's nice meeting you all. If you'll excuse us, we've got an appointment to keep."

"Of course. See you around." Kat proffers a little wave with her free hand.

"Sure thing. Nice meeting you, Cassie," Joel says. "And Ruby."

As they walk away, his mom turns to Joel. "How did I do? Did I do okay?"

He grips her hand and kisses it. "You were perfect."

Dawn casts Cody a sideways glance, as if to say, *How bizarre was* that? but at the moment he's got bigger fish to fry. His dad and Lily are walking a safe distance behind them when Joel comes up beside him.

"Cody, man," he says softly. "I don't know what's going on with your diploma, but whatever's behind it—if it's not missing—you'd be smart to come clean. Tell the truth, you know?"

Cody nods his head, pretending to listen intently, but his stepdad has no idea about the depth—or range—of his sins. There's a lot he could get nailed for beyond the frogs, pranks dating back to freshman year even, like the weekend when he and his buddies cracked the glass door in Theton Hall on a drunken bender or when they'd broken into the dorm's canteen and stolen an entire box of Milky Ways, high as a cloud.

"I haven't read the bylaws of Bolton," Joel continues, "But something tells me if you get caught in a lie, it'll be bad news. And if, I'm just saying, *if* you had anything to do with the frogs—" he hesitates before continuing. "If you had anything to do with them, just admit it. Okay? That's my humble opinion. You can always negotiate a fair punishment that won't include taking your diploma away. You *earned* that diploma."

"Got it," Cody says. "Thanks." He appreciates the advice, but it's also making him feel like a loser. How did the school find out about the prank before it even happened? Someone must have ratted him out. Maybe the same kid who sent Dawn the photo. *Maybe it's Melissa*, he thinks for a millisecond. But, no, she wouldn't be that cruel. He wonders if the dean can actually take his diploma away for a silly prank? Wouldn't that be ironic? As if the sting of not winning last night's award for Athlete of the Year wasn't enough and now this? The excitement of the day has quickly shifted to full-on panic, and his stomach roils all over again.

Joel holds the door for everyone as they step inside the cool office building and wind their way down a long marbled hallway toward the dean's office. After checking in with the assistant, Cody flops down in a brown leather chair to wait, and his nana and Dawn excuse themselves for the ladies' room. Lily announces she's going to sit on the front steps outside, which is a relief. Cody doesn't need her here to witness his downfall, if that's what's coming. Just then, the office door swings open.

"Cody, hello. Mr. and Mrs. Landau, nice to see you," says the dean. "Come in, come in, please." There follows an awkward moment when Dean Halberstam, clearly familiar with his dad, assumes that his dad and mom are still a couple. Meredith quickly corrects the misunderstanding, though. "I actually go by Mrs. Parker these days. And this is my husband, Joel, Cody's stepdad."

"Oh, hello. Right. Sorry about that. Come in." They file into his office, an oak-paneled room layered with oriental rugs of reds and blues. Several framed certificates dot the walls, a baccalaureate from the University of Virginia and a master's from Harvard. He circles behind his desk, sits down and gestures for everyone to do the same.

"Please, have a seat." His reading glasses, propped up on his head, lend him a professorial air, and Cody thinks he might vomit.

"I helped plan the frog prank," Cody blurts out suddenly, surprising even himself. *Might as well rip the Band-Aid off now,* he thinks. *Get it over with.* The dean glances up from the manila folder in his hands, his eyes crinkling in amusement.

"I see." Then he does something that surprises Cody—he laughs softly, just a little, but enough for everyone to hear. "Well, thank you for telling me. That was a good one. Not overly original, perhaps, but a difficult prank to pull off, I'd imagine."

Cody falls back in his chair, an enormous weight lifted off his chest.

"I should have known you were behind it," the dean continues. "It does have your signature cleverness all over it, doesn't it? Where on earth did you find all the frogs?" He sounds genuinely curious.

Cody leans forward to answer, but the dean holds up his hand. "No, wait. Don't tell me. On second thought, I'd rather not know.

"Look, here's why I've summoned you to my office," he continues. "I'm going to cut to the chase because I know you folks are eager to be on your way. Yesterday afternoon I received a disturbing email with a photo attached to it. From an anonymous sender." Cody stiffens in his chair.

From the folder, the dean retrieves a printout of the photograph of Cody and Eddie Rudolph, who holds out a small backpack to Cody. Cody hands Eddie a paper. For a brief moment, relief actually washes over him: it's the exact same photo that Dawn showed him yesterday. He'd been worried there might be more incriminating shots floating around somewhere. The dean holds the photo aloft, rotating it around their group, giving everyone ample opportunity to review it.

"Does this look familiar to you?" he asks.

"Um, I think so. That's me. And that's—"

"Hold on a second." Roger pushes up out of his chair. "I'd like to have a moment with my son before this meeting goes any further."

The dean appears momentarily surprised but recovers quickly. "Of course, Mr. Landau. Take your time. I hope you'll understand I'm just doing due diligence here. We all know Cody's track record and that he's an outstanding student. Still, when something like this arrives, it behooves me to ask a few questions."

Roger says, "I still don't understand why we're here. That photo's hardly incriminating."

"I'd agree. At first glance, it looks like Cody is handing a paper to this other boy who gives him a backpack. But I'd like to better understand the nature of the exchange, given what was said in the email." He pauses. "Perhaps you'd like to know what it said?"

His dad searches Cody, but he just shrugs. "Sure. Why not?"

Halberstam slides down his glasses, glances at another piece of paper in the folder, and reads. "I quote, 'Drugs for papers? What do *you* think it could be, Dean Halberstam?'"

His mom gasps, but his dad rolls his eyes. "Thanks for sharing it with us, but we all know that photo proves absolutely nothing. Even with the tagline. Sounds to me like sour grapes. Maybe a jealous teammate or a jilted girlfriend. Who knows? It could be anyone who's unhappy with Cody's success. It certainly doesn't give you a reason to withhold my son's diploma." His dad settles back into his chair.

"I tend to agree." The dean temples his fingers. "Cody, have you received any threatening emails recently? Can you think of anyone who might send me this photo? Do you think you might be in danger?"

Cody shakes his head, his foot bouncing. He's not about to get his sister involved. It hadn't occurred to him, though, that he might be in danger, that the dean would be concerned for his safety. It's almost creepy when he puts it that way. "No, no one I can think of."

"I hope you understand that school protocol demands that I investigate the allegation."

"Allegation?" his dad counters. "This isn't an allegation. If the person who sent you this photo was certain of his convictions, then he should have had the balls to own up to it personally. *That's* the person you should be questioning, not our son."

"Roger." His mom rests a hand on his knee.

"Maybe Cody can enlighten us?" Joel suggests, and suddenly Cody feels everyone's eyes on him. *Tread carefully*, he thinks.

"Are you comfortable with that, Mr. Landau, or would you still like to speak with Cody privately?"

His dad and mom exchange looks. "I'm certainly comfortable with it," she says. "I can't imagine Cody would have anything to hide, and if he does, he's better off coming clean with us now." Her voice is freighted with a muted threat, which Cody receives loud and clear.

As if his dad thinks better of it, he waves a hand in the air. "Sure, why not? Go ahead, son."

Cody takes a breath. "Um, I'm not sure what you want me to say. That's me and this guy Eddie Rudolph. He's a junior. We were at the gym last week. He's returning a backpack I left behind."

"And?" The dean presses. "I was hoping you could explain what the paper is. Why you might be handing Mr. Rudolph a paper?"

"My son isn't obligated to tell you anything more than he wants to," says his dad, but his mom intercedes again.

"Roger, please. Cody isn't on trial here. Let him tell his story. I'm sure there's a reasonable explanation. Which we'd all like to get to the bottom of so he can get his diploma." Dean Halberstam nods, as if in complete agreement.

"Um, it's just a paper," Cody continues. "Eddie asked me to look it over and make some suggestions. You know, like edit it. It was for psych and I'm pretty good at psych."

"And how do you know Eddie, exactly?" The dean shifts in his chair.

Cody shrugs. "We met at the gym. We both like to work out on the rowing machines. I told him once that I was thinking about switching my major from history to psychology. Guess he thought that meant I was good at it."

"And do you know what grade Mr. Rudolph received on this paper?"

Cody shakes his head. "No?"

"Well, I do," says the dean, his chin jutting forward. "He got an A."

"Good for him." Cody is unsure where the dean is headed with this. There's no way he can prove that Cody wrote the paper. He'd been sure to delete it from his hard drive the moment he'd handed it off, an easy four-pager for Introductory Psychology. The paper had been a breeze to write. And he's already given Eddie a heads-up about the photo. Shortly after Dawn showed him the picture, he'd tracked Eddie down to say he might want to lay low for a couple of days. They'd rehearsed the details of their story: Eddie asked him to look over his paper, and Cody obliged with comments. Eddie was returning a backpack that Cody had left behind on a bench at the gym. Plain and simple as that.

"And did Mr. Rudolph give you anything in exchange for your so-called edits?"

"Whoa, there." Roger holds up a hand. "I'm not sure I like the direction this is headed in. If Cody says they're edits, why are you saying 'so-called?'"

"No, Dad. It's all right." He leans forward in his chair. "I've got this. They were *edits*," Cody says between clenched teeth, barely having to fake his irritation. "If you're trying to accuse me of what I think you are, I did not write Eddie's paper for him. He wanted help, suggestions. There's a big difference."

"So, are we done here?" his stepdad pipes up.

"Almost." Dean Halberstam shuffles some papers. "If you'll bear with me for one more minute. I just need to hear from you that there was nothing in the backpack that might be of interest."

"Cody, you don't have to answer that if you don't want to," his dad counsels, but Cody shakes his head.

"No, I want to answer. There was nothing in the backpack aside from maybe some old socks and a smelly T-shirt. I forgot it on a bench at the gym and Eddie grabbed it for me. And, you know what? I'm starting to get my feelings hurt here." Cody can feel himself gaining steam in his convictions, no matter how false they might be. They've already robbed him of the award for best athlete. "I've given everything to this school—I've worked my butt off on the football field for you guys. For four years. And *this* is the thanks I get?"

"If I may, I think I'd like to step outside with the dean before this conversation goes any further," his dad interjects smoothly. "Dean Halberstam, a word, please?"

Uh-oh. Cody's not sure what he said. Did he just incriminate himself somehow? A cool sweat rises on the back of his neck.

The dean appears surprised again, but says, "Of course, Mr. Landau."

As they exit the room, Cody stares at his mom, whose expression registers alarm and then settles into something else. It takes him a minute to recognize it but then he sees it: it's her angry, I'm-disappointed-in-you look.

He just can't tell if it's meant for him or his dad.

Joel can feel himself seething. This is *not* how these meetings are supposed to go. If a kid is culpable, you question him directly, not step outside with a parent and give the kid time to collect his thoughts. What if he and Meredith weren't there? When Cody reaches for his phone, Joel shakes his head.

"Um, probably not a good idea right now," he says and watches Cody slide it back into his pocket with a shrug.

No way is he going to let Cody text this Eddie guy, make sure his alibi is rock solid. His own students wouldn't get the chance, so why should his son? This behind-the-doors meeting strikes Joel as highly unorthodox. Is this truly how the world operates for folks like Roger Landau? People who, because of their wealth or stature, are accustomed to getting their way? Joel can't recall ever being a witness to such preferential treatment, but at the moment, he's got a bad taste in his mouth, like he licked a metal flagpole.

At the forefront of his mind are the "side-door" admission scandals that have paved the newspapers of late, stories of wealthy, privileged parents who've bought their children's admission into elite colleges and who are now paying the price. Joel had experienced a sense of smug satisfaction when word broke that those same parents would be prosecuted for their hubris, but not in a million years would he have guessed that one day soon, he might find himself on the other side of the fence, party to a quid pro quo exchange where his own kid's possible wrongdoing would get swept under the rug. Of course, who knows if that's what's really going on here. Maybe Cody *is* innocent. Maybe the dean doesn't have enough on him to withhold his diploma, and Roger is kindly reminding him of this fact? Both of these remain possibilities.

His eyes shoot from Meredith to Cody and then back to Meredith, who meets his gaze briefly before looking away. Since Joel has already said his piece on the way over, he's biting his tongue now. But it's not easy. Especially when Roger keeps acting as if he's the guy holding the reins to this meeting, which strikes Joel as presumptuous and also, quite possibly, reckless. What if Roger offends the dean? There's one guidance counselor in this room, and nobody seems to care what he might think, not even Meredith. In fact, Joel is beginning to feel as if she's counting on Roger with his elaborate lawyering tricks to get Cody out of this mess. Maybe it's his own ego that's making it difficult for him to see the situation clearly, but Joel doesn't think so.

He's fairly confident that of the three men present here, he knows Cody the best. And if anyone can get Cody to talk, to tell them the *real* truth, it might just be him.

Then again, no one has bothered to ask him.

Meredith doesn't know what's going on, but the fact that Roger has asked to talk to the dean in private does little to reassure her. Maybe her ex-husband knows more than they do? Or is this typical Roger Landau, aka hotshot lawyer, who's going to bully the dean into submission with fancy words and perhaps an even fancier check? She certainly hopes not. Meredith wants her son to be exonerated, of course, but not in a back-alley sort of way. If he has, in fact, done something wrong, then they need to deal with it. Not teach him that he can get away with anything because his dad happens to yield influence about town and has deep pockets that the college would surely like to pick further.

Joel stares at her, looking a bit nonplussed himself by what's just transpired. She doesn't imagine that as a high school guidance counselor, he gets many requests for one-on-one talks with parents in the middle of a meeting about their child's questionable behavior. But she knows him well enough that he'd never say this in front of Cody. Always, Joel has been careful to be respectful when it comes to the kids' dad. Still, there's a certain unseemliness about the private meeting that's being held out of earshot that doesn't escape the three of them.

If there's something truly going on, maybe she can help. Maybe she and Joel can somehow make this better. She knows her son well enough to recognize that, even if he's not trading papers for drugs as the photo might suggest, something is off, haywire. In a last-ditch effort, she tries to ask him.

"Cody, what is it? What's wrong. Something's going on. You can tell us, honey, whatever it is. We'll figure it out."

She probably sounds as if she's speaking in tongues, using euphemisms so as to avoid what they're actually talking about. Drugs? Heroin? Is Cody using? Dealing? She doesn't know if she can handle the answer. If he has been using, then he's been putting on one heck of a good show. *Phi Beta Kappa. Varsity football team.*

She stares a long moment into her son's eyes. Her little boy is in there somewhere, and she resists the impulse to shake him free. A flicker of something—indecision? Guilt? Fear?—darts across his face. For a second, she believes he's going to spill. Tell her the truth.

But then, as if thinking better of it, he shakes his head and rearranges his expression into something like steely resolve. Or perhaps it's indignation. "It's nothing, Mom. Seriously. No big deal. They're trying to make a mountain out of a molehill." And just as quickly as the moon passes between the Earth and sun during a solar eclipse, the moment vanishes. Whatever version of the truth they might have seized upon is gone.

She glances at the clock on the wall. They've been in this meeting for twenty minutes already, and Meredith can feel herself growing impatient with her ex-husband for whatever cockamamie deal he might be trying to cut. She knows she should be grateful they have a lawyer at their behest if Cody really does need protecting, but aren't they getting ahead of themselves? Her ex-husband's words echo in her head from years ago. *It's called a preemptive strike, Meredith.*

*You take the prosecution down before they can even lob a complaint
in the defendant's direction.*

And, suddenly, it all comes flooding back to her—the
way Roger would condescend to her with his slick lawyer-
speak whenever it came to the kids. As if his courtroom
strategies could be applied equally and as winningly at home
with four-year-olds. *Yeah?* She'd felt like shouting at him
sometimes. *You want to spend twelve hours a day at home with
them? Go ahead. Give them your most persuasive argument for
why Dawn deserves the blue sippy cup, and not Cody. See how
it works out. I guarantee you they'll be pulling each other's hair
out, and you'll be ready to head for the hills in about five minutes.*

When Joel's hand reaches out to her, Meredith practically
jumps. She's almost forgotten where she is.

"What do you think they're doing out there?" she asks.

"Hard to say. I'd imagine the dean doesn't want to miss
out on a chance for the new Landau library or gymnasium.
He's probably got to tread carefully himself. He certainly
doesn't want the school to get slapped with a lawsuit from
Roger Landau."

Cody guffaws and Meredith shoots him her best death-
stare. "The situation you're in is not to be taken lightly. I
hope you understand that. Truly."

His gaze falls to the ground. "I know."

Joel has echoed her thoughts to some extent as well,
though. The dean probably wants to be sitting in this room
with them as much as they do, which is to say, not at all.
The *swoosh* of Roger Landau's money flying out the window has no doubt crossed his mind. But because of school
protocols, he must at least inquire. Meredith understands,
but it doesn't stop her from wishing the whole thing would
disappear so they could get on with the business of celebrat-

ing. She vacillates between worry and indignation on Cody's behalf. *Honestly, my son graduated Phi Beta Kappa,* a distinct honor bestowed on only a handful of students. How could they possibly think that he's involved in drugs! Or cheating!

At that moment, the door swings open, and the two men return, rearranging themselves in their respective seats. Meredith tries to read the mood of the room and isn't sure if she should be encouraged or concerned that her ex-husband appears to be all smiles.

"So, Cody." The dean resumes. "Your dad and I have agreed that there's nothing here worthy of keeping you any longer. Thank you for answering my questions to my satisfaction." He rolls open his top desk drawer and pulls out the coveted diploma. "I apologize to you all for any inconvenience this may have caused."

Though she didn't realize she was holding her breath, Meredith's lungs expand.

"Under full disclosure, I should also say, as I told your dad, that we invited Eddie in to tell his side of the story this morning." He pauses. "And I think you'll be happy to know that he corroborated your version of the facts. Which leads me to agree with your dad. That this whole thing has been plotted by a jealous kid. Watch your back out there, though, okay?"

"Will do, sir." Cody jumps up to take his diploma. "Thank you."

Meredith smiles and stands to shake hands with the dean. "Thank you," she says, relieved and admittedly slightly suspicious about this turn of events. When they gather up their things to leave, she can't help but notice that Joel is frowning, as if he can't condone a single thing that has happened here.

THIRTEEN

Friday evening

"Do you want me to grab the kids' gifts out of the trunk?" Joel asks when they pull into an off-street parking lot that's so small it could double as someone's driveway.

They're only a few blocks from the restaurant, but Meredith says, "No, let's leave them till after dinner. I don't want to upstage Roger and Lily in case they didn't bring a present."

"Fat chance of that, but all right," he agrees.

On the ride over, they'd talked in code about the meeting with the dean. Meredith didn't want to upset her mother unnecessarily. No need for her to know how close Cody might have come to being expelled. *There was a slight misunderstanding, some confusion over another boy,* they'd explained. To which her mother had nodded resolutely, as if she'd foreseen this very outcome all along. But Meredith can tell Joel still thinks something's amiss. Does he really suspect drugs?

She'd almost asked Cody point-blank, on their walk back to the car from the dean's office, if there had been drugs in that backpack (he could tell her now that they were alone!), but then she'd thought better of it. He'd denied it twice already—once to her (in that vague way when he'd said they were making mountains of molehills) and once to the dean. What was the point in rubbing salt in the wound? She tells herself that it would be completely out of character for their son to be involved in drugs of any kind. Then again, she would have said the same thing about several mothers in her NICU ward, who turned out to be heroin addicts.

Meredith values Joel's opinion, not only as Cody's step-dad but also as a counselor. Does he think Roger paid off the dean? She wouldn't put it past her ex-husband, who's accustomed to throwing money at problems to make them disappear. Her thoughts hearken back to the recent scandal of celebrities paying huge bucks to ease the way for their kids' acceptance into college. Has their family just stuck a toe into this cesspool? She sincerely hopes not, for Cody's sake, more than anyone else's. Still, as slick as Roger can be, he *is* a lawyer with a sterling reputation. Surely, he wouldn't sink that low, would he? As far as she could tell, the dean lacked any hard evidence, save for a photo with a suggestive tagline from an anonymous finger-pointer.

It *could* have all been an innocent exchange, as Cody described. It's possible, she thinks. Maybe unlikely, but possible that there are several layers to this story, one overlapping the other in a kind of intricate web that would exonerate him completely. Which would, furthermore, mean that nothing transpired other than a heart-to-heart chat between her ex-husband and the dean, a conversation where she can imagine Roger saying, "You've got no case here. Let's call it a day and move on."

Yes, she thinks, that's the explanation she's going with. At least for tonight. There was no cheating involved, no drugs, no money exchanging hands, no threats made. She nearly laughs at herself—honestly, does she think they're all starring in a true-crime movie? The stress of the day has gone to her head. As taxing as the last few hours have been, they were, she tells herself, based on a colossal, unfortunate misunderstanding. *Moving on*, she thinks.

Outside, the evening has turned, if not exactly cool, at least milder. Up ahead, the kids, who opted to drive over with Roger's family (the twins can never get enough of Uncle Georgie), make their way along the uneven brick sidewalk, and Meredith hurries to catch up with them. During the weeks leading up to graduation, she and Roger had discussed at length where to go for a celebratory dinner (Joel had been indifferent, happy to travel wherever), and eventually, they'd all agreed on Artu, a cozy Italian restaurant on Charles Street. It strikes her now as the perfect choice, mainly because they could all use some comfort food, preferably with heaps of olive oil and cheese.

The last time she was on Charles Street was probably four years ago, when they'd driven up for Thanksgiving weekend during the twins' freshman year. They'd splurged and checked into the Fairmont Copley Plaza so that they could spend the weekend Christmas shopping, ducking into the posh shops of Faneuil Hall and then winding their way over to Charles Street, where old-fashioned gaslights with bright red bows looped around their necks lit the walkways. Is it possible that she and the kids walked arm in arm while snowflakes drifted down around them? Well, that's how she remembers it, anyway. The day had been enchanting, like being caught inside her own snow globe.

It's May now, but the historic street remains as charming as ever, with its scattering of subterranean restaurants, boutiques, art galleries, and the occasional nail salon. They pass NRO Kids (stuffed with preppy pint-size clothing), Moxie (its storefront sparkling with gorgeous shoes), and The Paper Company, where Meredith once found the most exquisite stationery. She'd consider tucking into the store now, were it not for her ex-husband, who already strides half a block ahead of everyone else.

She has almost forgotten this annoying trait of Roger's, but a *zing!* of familiarity pierces her now. Traveling with Roger always felt like more of a chore than an escape. His fastidious attention to schedules, his endless quest to pack in the maximum amount of sightseeing, lent every family outing a rushed feeling, as if they were competing on *The Amazing Race* instead of enjoying a relaxing vacation. "Just think of him as your own private scout," a friend advised her once, when she'd confided this irritating peccadillo. "He wants to make sure you don't get lost."

But Meredith remained skeptical. Something about Roger seemed to demand that he be first, slightly ahead of the rest of the group. Maybe it was genetic? Yes, that was it, she'd concluded back then—Roger hailed from a long line of "doers" and "seekers." Harry and Edith, Georgie, they all sought out nonstop adventure, and when there was none to be had, they'd fashion their own. Meredith remembers finding it all so exhausting, especially on vacation. Given the choice, she would much rather collapse in a lounge chair and escape in a good book than pack her day with endless activities.

Roger has almost reached the restaurant now, where she

knows he'll double-check their reservation and table, ensuring that everything is as it should be. Meredith glances over at Lily to see if she's at all perturbed, but Lily is busy talking with Dawn about the New Kids concert. Why does it still irk Meredith then? Why does *she* feel the urge to call out to Roger and tell him to slow down, for goodness sake, and wait for the rest of them? He's not even her husband anymore! *Enjoy the ride*, she used to tell him. It seems that with the divorce there should also be a passing of the torch for the things that used to drive her nuts. *Lily* ought to be annoyed right now, not her. Then again, that's probably why she and Roger divorced: they were never compatible in the first place.

Entering Artu requires descending a few steps below street level before passing through a doorway that opens onto a cool, cavern-like space, and she's reassured to glimpse Cody giving his nana a hand. Inside, thick wooden beams crisscross the low ceiling, small candles flicker on square tables, and a brick fireplace doubles as a wine cellar. Meredith feels herself relaxing before they even sit down. There's the delicious aroma of sauce, the soft murmur of conversation, and the reassuring clatter of pans coming from the kitchen, as if the chefs are already hard at work prepping their meal. Best of all, there's dim lighting. Which means the difference in her age and Lily's may not be as pronounced as it was in this afternoon's sun.

Roger stands beside a long table at the back of the room and waves to them. Their party of ten nearly fills up half of the floor, and Meredith experiences a moment of dread as she realizes she hasn't done the appropriate prep work to position herself where she'd like to sit, which is to say, next to Joel and as far away from Harry as possible. But as it turns out, the seating arrangement—five small square tables pushed together—works in her favor. On either side of her, Joel and Dawn take a seat, and her mother and Georgie bookend both of them. Directly across from her, Cody slides into a chair, and Roger and Lily sit to his left. That leaves Edith on Cody's right and Harry down in the corner, a suitable distance away. Not that she doesn't like Harry, but now she won't have to listen to him complain about the bread's not being warm enough or the wine's not being properly chilled.

Shortly, menus are in hand, Roger requests ice waters for the entire table, and Meredith fishes out her reading glasses to better peruse the menu. *Seared sea scallops. Linguine scampi. Penne puttanenesca. Lasagna. Pollo marsala.*

"It's hard to decide," she says, thinking out loud. "Everything looks so good, doesn't it?"

"Oh, I know. It really is." Lily reaches for Roger's hand. "Roger and I used to eat here all the time when I lived on Beacon Hill. It's one of the best restaurants in the neighborhood. Probably my favorite."

Oh. Meredith welcomes this news like a sock to the stomach. Is that why Roger suggested Artu? Because he assumed Lily would be comfortable? Because it's her favorite? Roger and Lily probably shared romantic candlelit meals here, perhaps in this very corner of the restaurant. *It's their place*, Meredith thinks. She feigns a smile, says, "Isn't that nice? I had no idea," and shoots Roger a pointed look.

When their waiter returns, he rattles off a list of specials, but Meredith can't help but notice that he squares his body with Lily's, as if he's speaking directly to her. This sense of being invisible, which overcomes her whenever she lunches with her younger mom friends, isn't so surprising as it is exhausting. Not to mention, humiliating. A pinch of anger

grabs her. Even though she understands that Lily represents
Roger's new family, Meredith considers it verging on the
insensitive for him to have included her tonight. Lily is an
interloper, an intruder, on this, one of their most precious
nights with their children.

After they've ordered, Meredith reminds herself: *grace*.
Her motto for this evening. She can make lemonade out of
lemons with the best of them. She will kill Lily with kindness, this woman who has charmed her ex-husband with her
perky breasts and her pert little nose, who has invaded her
children's graduation dinner, their lives. She turns to Lily.

"So, Lily, I see you've got quite the fan club on Instagram.
I don't know how you do it."

Lily sets down her ice water. "Thank you. It's fun. I enjoy
it, and it keeps me busy."

"What is it that you do again, dear?" pipes up Edith from
the other end of the table.

"I'm an enhancer," Lily says loudly, using her hands.
"Kind of like an influencer, but not nearly as important."
Meredith can tell she's trying to sound humble, but poor
Edith has no idea what either an influencer or an enhancer is.

"What did she say?" Edith leans in front of Cody. "She's
influencing someone in the next election?"

"No, Mom." Roger tries to explain. "Lily works in computers. She helps people decide what kinds of products they
should buy." Which, Meredith thinks, is putting it generously.

Edith breaks off a hunk of crusty bread and slathers it with
butter, her enormous diamond ring winking in the candle-
light. "Oh," she says, as if she's giving this explanation considerable thought. "I'll never understand computers. Good
for you, dear."

Roger and Meredith exchange glances. They both know Edith has no idea what Lily does, but that's okay.

"But really, I'm curious," Meredith presses. "What exactly *is* an enhancer? I mean I have a general idea—you endorse products online, right?—but I always thought that was what an influencer does?"

"It is." Lily helps herself to the bread, and Meredith experiences mild surprise that the woman allows herself any carbs at all. She would have expected Lily to consume only fish and water tonight. "I'm more like the backup, the person they call in when a product is languishing. I'm there to remind people that it's still in style. Kind of like the understudy to the lead in a play."

"Mmm. Interesting analogy." Meredith dribbles olive oil onto her plate and pulls a breadstick through it. "An understudy," Meredith says. "Kind of like you have to memorize all the lines, know all the material, and hope that you'll get your big break someday?"

Lily's expression dims faintly across the table, as if she senses that she's been insulted but can't quite identify how.

"Sort of, I guess." Her eyes fix on Roger. "Anyway, it's a good way to boost my number of followers so that if I ever want to write a book about fashion someday, I'll already have a built-in audience."

"Really?" Meredith senses astonishment blooming on her face. Roger's little ingenue is considering writing a book? Lily's implication that becoming an author is as easy as establishing an online fan club irks Meredith further. Maybe it's because everything seems to come *so easily* for women like Lily and that these days even beautiful, not-so-smart women can write books that will sell a gazillion copies. Simply because they have a following on Instagram or Twitter. "Sort of like the Kardashians, then?"

Roger coughs into his napkin. She's struck a nerve. He knows precisely what Meredith thinks of the Kardashians, ever since she forbade Dawn from watching the show. Not even he can miss the jab that's been leveled at his newly minted wife. Lily leans back in her seat and eyes Meredith warily.

"So, anyway," Roger says in an obvious attempt to change the subject. "How about those frogs today? Weren't they something?"

And as easily as that, the conversation turns to leaping frogs, the commencement speech, the heat, any number of topics related to the day. All except one, which is the window of time when no one was certain if Cody would receive his diploma. Meredith takes the opportunity to excuse herself to the ladies' room, where she locks the door and decides to remove her Spanx that have been cutting off circulation to her entire midsection. She's about to stuff them into her handbag before reconsidering, and they hit the trash barrel with a satisfying thud.

Back at the table, their food has arrived, and Joel lifts a glass as Meredith reclaims her seat.

"To the very brilliant Dawn and Cody," he proposes. "May you go on to find great success, make lots of money, and share it generously with your parents." It inspires a few chuckles and *Hear, hears* around the table. Meredith sips her wine and recites her mantra for the weekend again: *I will be the Jacqueline Onassis of graduations*. Except Jackie O. would never treat anyone as shabbily as Meredith treated Lily earlier, and for a brief moment she's ashamed of own bad behavior. She hoists her own glass in the air.

"To Dawn and Cody. You've made us proud, kiddos. We love you—regardless of whether you make lots of money or not! Congratulations." She winks and clinks glasses with her children and the rest of the table.

A few moments of silence ensue while everyone digs into their respective meals. Meredith's shrimp scampi steams before her, reams of homemade spaghetti topped by giant pink shrimp lined up like pretty semicolons. She pops one in her mouth, glances around the table, and is struck by all the generations represented here—grandparents and parents, stepparents and kids. It's impressive. And Dawn and Cody still have so much to look forward to: that sweet, magical time in their early twenties when they get to crack open the world and discover what matters most to them. Soon enough, they'll be thinking about marriage, maybe even having their own children.

And that's when it hits her: *What's to stop Roger from having another child? With Lily?* What if the marriage actually lasts (even though Meredith would be willing to bet against it)? What if Lily gets pregnant? And Dawn and Cody have stepbrothers and stepsisters?

The whole thought is so unsettling, so *unpleasant*, that she devours her meal as if she were stress-eating an entire gallon of ice cream on their fluffy sofa back home. With the *ping* of a glass (Roger's) her meandering thoughts are interrupted. "Please, keep enjoying your meals," he says, "but I'd like to make a small announcement while we have everyone's attention." Lily's doting gaze lingers on him as he speaks. *Oh, please*, thinks Meredith. *Spare me the love fest.* Maybe the vodka tonics have gone straight to Lily's head.

And then, she thinks: *Small announcement? Oh, no. He wouldn't dare!*

Meredith grabs Joel's hand. Is her ex-husband truly about to announce that he's expecting a baby on the night of his oldest kids' college graduation? There's so much that's wrong about that, or maybe *anachronistic* would be a better word, that Meredith finds herself sputtering nonsense.

"Oh, huh. Really? Right now? You're going to tell us? I mean, a *small* announcement?"

Roger reaches for Lily's hand, twinning his fingers with hers. "So, Lily and I were hoping to share some news and this seems like the perfect time.

"Dawn, Cody." Both of her children's faces have turned pale. "Lily and I would like to..." He pauses for effect, a move that the man has perfected after so many years in the courtroom. "Invite you on a trip to Bora-Bora with us this summer!"

The clatter of a fork onto the table startles everyone. Cody's.

"What?" Dawn asks wide-eyed, as if her brain is still struggling to process what has been said—and what hasn't.

"What?" Meredith repeats.

"Bora-Bora!" He claps his hands together. "Wouldn't you kids love to see French Polynesia? It's supposed to be beautiful. I thought it could be one last hurrah with your old man—and Lily, too—before you head off to your jobs."

"Oh, how marvelous!" Edith pats her mouth with her napkin, leaving behind little pockmarks of pink lipstick.

"I hear Bora-Bora is boring, boring," says Harry, laughing at his own bad joke. "Just kidding. Sounds terrific!"

"Well," Carol says. "Isn't *that* a surprise?"

Joel's fingers are pressing into Meredith's thigh, tethering her to reality, to some sense of sanity. Or maybe he's trying to make sure she doesn't say something she'll instantly regret. She swallows, breathes. *Okay, so, it's not what I thought Roger was going to say. But still, does the man not know the meaning of tact?* The fact that she'd been so concerned earlier that her gifts might upstage Roger and Lily in any way is comical, and a flash of indignation strikes her. It's typical Roger, trying to buy his kids' affection with outrageous gifts. The kids have summer jobs—they can't just pick up and leave on a whim! Did Roger even consider checking with her first? They've always granted each other this courtesy in the past, whenever one of them was planning to take the kids out of state. When did that understanding change? Now that Lily is in the picture, all bets are off?

"And when exactly is this vacation supposed to happen?" Meredith asks icily.

"Oh, right. The second week in August. We figured that would still give the kids some downtime before they head off to Chicago and North Dakota."

"I see." Meredith drains the rest of her water. "Um, I hate to state the obvious, but the kids have jobs this summer. Back at home. In New Haven." What goes unspoken is that Roger will be ripping them away from her during their last summer at home, before they head off into the world. This summer is supposed to be *her* time with them! He's had them up in Boston for four years.

"Yeah, I know." He winks. "But I figured I can pay them for whatever wages they might miss that week."

Meredith makes a clucking sound. "That's hardly the point."

"Chill, Mom," Cody says now. "It'll be fine. I need to head to school the last week in August, anyway, to get ready for my students."

"Yeah, I think it will be fine, too," Dawn says brightly.

"Bora-Bora? Really, Daddy?" She throws her big, saucer eyes his way, clearly delighted.

"Of course, we won't take them if you'd rather we didn't," Lily interjects, her tone conciliatory. But Lily knows full well that they've got Meredith trapped. She signals her best SOS to Joel, who strokes his beard thoughtfully.

"Well, it does sound like a pretty amazing trip," he says. "I'm sure we can figure something out, right, honey?" Meredith, rendered mute, nods.

"I'm so excited!" Dawn, whose sangfroid around Lily appears to have melted instantly at the thought of coconut drinks in a stilted hut above the South Pacific, leaps up and goes over to Roger. "Thank you, Daddy!" Then to Lily. "You, too, Lily. Thanks."

"Yeah, thanks," repeats Cody. "That's like, out of this world, awesome. I'm stoked. Totally."

When the waiter returns for dessert orders, Meredith says, "Um, Roger, can I have a word with you for a minute?"

"Sure thing." He pushes back his seat, clearly pleased with the reaction to his surprise, and tosses his napkin onto the table.

As soon as they step outside, Meredith lays in. "Really? You went ahead and booked this extravagant trip for the kids without even checking with me first? They're supposed to be with me and Joel for the entire summer."

His face scrunches up in confusion. "Oh, no. Did you have plans for that week, too?"

"No!" She gives him a little shove on the lapel of his blazer. "But that's not the point." Roger waits, leans back against the stair rail.

"Okay. So tell me. What *is* the point?"

"The point is that this is the kids' last summer at home

and you're taking them away from me. You should have asked first. It would have been the polite thing to do."

"I apologize." He holds up a hand. "It didn't occur to me. I thought everyone would be happy."

"They'll have to get their passports renewed," Meredith snips. These are the kinds of details that she always handled for the family, things that would never occur to Roger in a million years.

"Good point. I'll make sure they're on it."

"Also, I'm not entirely convinced that Cody deserves such a generous gift after what we just endured this afternoon, are you?"

Roger's shoulders hunch up around his neck, like a turtle. "That was nothing. The dean was making it into a big deal, but they didn't have anything on Cody."

"Did you pay him off?" Meredith regrets the question instantly, but she needs to know.

Roger folds his arms across his chest. "Of course not! What kind of a father do you think I am? I'd never do that. Give me some credit, Meredith. I am a good lawyer, however, and once I was able to talk with the dean in private, it became clear that it wasn't really Cody they were after. It was that other kid, Eddie."

This is news to Meredith. "Really? Why?"

"Apparently, he's got quite a reputation for himself on campus as a dealer."

"For drugs?" Her stomach dips.

"Yeah, I'm not sure for what exactly, but they were hoping to nail him."

"And so, did you ask Cody?"

"Ask Cody what?"

"Jesus, Roger! Stop playing me!" She can't believe how,

for someone so smart, her ex-husband can be so incredibly dense sometimes. "Did you ask Cody if there were drugs in that backpack?"

"No, I did not. The number one rule in criminal law—don't ask your client a question you think you might not like the answer to."

"Oh, that's great. Really wonderful parenting." She walks little circles around the small square of bricks that fronts the restaurant. "We're talking about our son here, not some reprobate you're representing."

"Look, what do you want me to do? Cody's a smart kid. I don't think he would have been able to accomplish all that he did at that school if he were high on drugs half the time, do you?"

She ponders this for a moment and shakes her head. "No, not really. It doesn't *feel* like something he'd be into, either. He cares too much about his body, you know, lifting weights, keeping fit for football."

"I agree." Roger reaches out and attempts to grab her hand but lets his arm fall when she takes a step back. "Look, if it's any comfort, I think our son was scared out of his mind. If something serious was going on, I have to believe he would have told us in private." He pauses. "Maybe someday we can ask him, but why not tonight try to enjoy the fact that we have two exceptional kids who just graduated from college with honors? How about it?"

Meredith nods, waiting for the punch line. Is there more to come? But maybe Roger really means it. Maybe she needs to calm down and enjoy this moment as opposed to blowing it up.

She's about to agree and take the high road, until she remembers: *Bora-Bora.* And all her indignation comes charging back. Her kids will be in a tropical paradise with their dad and his gorgeous new wife for a week. Maybe that's what's really driving her crazy.

"You know…" she begins and then hesitates. For a moment, she considers telling him the truth about Lily, that the kids don't like her and that she's an embarrassment to the whole family. It's *so* tempting. Nearly half his age! Someone needs to tell Roger how inappropriate the marriage is because clearly he can't see it himself.

But, for some reason, she says nothing.

Maybe it's because Meredith hasn't had enough wine or maybe it's the hopeful, expectant look on her ex-husband's face that makes her tamp down the urge to hurl arrows his way. She marches up the stairs to the sidewalk and glances down the street, with nowhere to go. Random couples stroll along in the fading summer light, and Meredith inhales the air that's scented with freshly blooming lilacs. Eventually, her racing heart begins to settle. What good would it do to get into all that now? *Channel your inner grace*, she coaches herself and takes another breath.

"You're right," she says finally, quietly, coming back down the stairs and sensing Roger's relief. No, she won't tell him how silly he looks sitting next to a woman half his age, how his life has turned into one monstrous cliché. Not tonight at least. Tonight is about the kids.

Instead she says, "Let's go celebrate our wonderful children," her olive branch waving as they step back into Artu.

Later, after they part ways with the Landaus, Meredith tells the kids, "Joel and I have a little present for you two in the car. Come with us and we'll drop you back at school?"

Dawn and Cody exchange brief glances. "Sure."

On the walk back to the car, Carol hands each of them an envelope. "A little something from your nana to help you celebrate." Inside is a thick stack of green bills.

"Oh, my goodness," exclaims Dawn. "Thank you, Nana!"

"Holy cow, how much is in here?" Cody demands none too delicately.

"A thousand for you each. Consider it an advance on your future inheritance."

"Mom, you shouldn't have," scolds Meredith, but they both know nothing she says will change her mother's mind. Still, she's alarmed to realize that Carol has been walking around with two thousand dollars in her purse all day. "Don't you dare lose that, kids."

Back at the car, Joel has already opened the trunk and passes two packages to Meredith to present to the twins. "Happy graduation," she says. "I know it's not much, but I hope you'll like it."

Dawn rips back the wrapping paper, only to squeal when she sees *Dawn Landau's Greatest Hits, 1999–2020*. "A photo book? Oh, Mom, this is amazing." She starts flipping through the pages in the dim light of the parking lot. "It must have taken you weeks to pull this together." There are yellowed photos from when Dawn was a baby, on to her toddler shots and first steps, all the way up to her very last cross-country race. Throughout the pages Meredith has interspersed funny sayings from the kids that she has kept in a journal over the years. Her own personal keepsake.

"Oh, wait. I almost forgot." She searches in her purse and grabs the photo, sliding it into the last cellophane page. It's a picture of Dawn, striding across the stage in her cap and gown. Meredith made Joel duck into a CVS to print out a copy on the way to Artu. "There, now it's complete."

Dawn hugs the book to her chest. "I love it. It's the best present ever."

"Yeah, pretty cool." Cody pages through his own photo album, to which Meredith adds his graduation photo, as well.

"Wasn't sure we were going to be able to include this one," she teases. "Glad we got to in the end."

"Ha ha," he deadpans. "Very funny."

"Anyway, I know it's no trip to Bora-Bora—"

"It's perfect, Mom. Really." Cody drapes an arm around her. "I love it."

Meredith manages a smile. "I'm so glad," she says. After the roller coaster of emotions of the last twenty-four hours, she is completely and totally bereft. She has nothing left to give her children today.

Nothing, that is, but her own unwavering, unconditional love.

FOURTEEN

After they drop Roger's parents and Georgie at the hotel, Roger and Lily pull into the driveway, the house lit up like a jack-o'-lantern with two lights glowing upstairs and a row of windows illuminating the first floor. Timed lights flicker on at exactly seven o'clock and shut off at eleven. When Roger started traveling for weeks at a time for work, Lily wanted to make sure that the house always looked as if someone were home. There probably aren't many criminals in well-to-do Manchester-by-the-Sea, but the lights (plus a recently installed alarm system) help her to sleep soundly at night.

Lily has dozed off on the short ride back from Boston, whether because of her second vodka tonic or sheer exhaustion, she's not sure. One thing she is certain about: the tremendous amount of relief she feels now that they're home. It leaves only tomorrow to endure. She shifts in her seat and unbuckles her seat belt. "Mmm…home, finally," she murmurs.

Roger reaches across the car and squeezes her knee. "You made it. You were a rock star tonight, by the way. Thank you."

"Ha! Hardly." She stretches her arms out in front of her. The dashboard clock insists that it's ten thirty, even though it feels more like two in the morning. "I think Meredith officially hates me."

"Meredith? No, she can be icy but it's a tough weekend for her. Her babies are graduating. Don't take it personally."

Lily cranes her neck from side to side. "No, I'm pretty sure it's personal. She doesn't like me."

"Baby, how can anyone not like you? You're the sweetest, prettiest thing out there."

Typically such words would reassure her, but tonight, with the fresh memory of Meredith's underhanded insults about her work as an enhancer, they sound condescending. She's confident that Meredith would never allow Roger to call her a "pretty thing." Lily releases her hair from the bun that's been holding it hostage all day. Despite the fact that she slipped a pill back in the ladies' room at the restaurant, probably around six, her head is pounding and her arms itch like crazy. It's time for another.

"It's funny you say that," she says now. Roger has come around to open the car door for her. "I kind of felt like the odd woman out tonight, like no one really wanted me there."

He reaches for her hand and pulls her to standing. "Oh, honey. You're overanalyzing. No one thought that. And I, for one, was thrilled to have you there. I don't enjoy sitting anywhere near Meredith's mom. Talk about *hate*. Now, there's someone who really knows how to lay it on thick."

Lily manages a small laugh. Carol clearly doesn't like Roger, which strikes Lily as so strange after all this time has passed. It's possible she may dislike Roger even more than Roger's mom, Edith, dislikes Lily. Although *dislike* might not be the right word. Edith acts as if Lily is a pungent cheese that she's pulled out of the fridge by mistake.

"You're right. She despises you. Anyone can see that. But how weird is that? Wouldn't you think she'd have moved on after all this time? It's not like you divorced *Carol*."

"Bingo," he says.

They enter the house through the adjoining door to the garage, and he tosses his car keys into the ceramic dish sitting on the hall table. There's a note from Alison, tucked underneath the dish. "Thanks for letting me hang out! Hope graduation was great! Xo, Ali." Moses pads over, and Lily leans down to accept his kisses. Let him lick her face clean, she thinks. She no longer needs to impress anyone tonight.

Roger strolls over to the kitchen cabinet and pulls out two glasses. "Oh, honey." She shakes her head. "I don't think I can have any more. I really want to get some rest before the party tomorrow."

"Come on. Come sit with me on the deck. One tiny drink," he calls out as he ducks into the wine cellar for a fresh bottle. Lily sighs. Does the man ever get tired? He was out till late last night for the kids' banquet—something they've yet to discuss—although in light of this evening's dinner, Lily feels more magnanimous toward her husband. She sees how he struggles to be included in his own children's lives, how Carol abhors him and Meredith abides him because he is Dawn and Cody's dad. Even the kids seem to gravitate toward their mom.

Well, now that Dawn and Cody are officially grown-ups, Lily suspects these kinds of family gatherings will become even less frequent. At least they have Bora-Bora to look forward to. Or, she hopes they do, assuming Meredith doesn't put a last-minute veto on it. Assuming the kids won't object to Lily's tagging along. She heads upstairs to change, pulling her dress off along the way.

If memory serves, one pill should remain in the tiny makeup bag that she packed this morning for graduation. In the bathroom, she pulls out the zippered tote, fishes out the pill from her compact, and swallows, wishing she could hurry along the serene feeling that will eventually envelop her. *Thank goodness for these*, she thinks. *The only thing that will get me through tomorrow.* She slips into her pajamas and brushes out her hair.

Back downstairs, Roger already sits on the deck, staring out at the ocean. Wide swaths of light from an almost-full moon brighten the backyard. "Come join me." He beckons to her through the screen door and holds out a glass of wine. He has shucked his jacket and tie, unbuttoned his shirt and rolled up the sleeves. Her husband is undeniably handsome with his dark hair and bright blue eyes. Tall and lanky, he radiates a self-assurance that would probably come across as cocky in most men. But it's not just because he's a local celebrity that gets people's attention, she thinks. Even if her husband were a garbage collector, he would still turn heads. Lily goes over, settles into his lap, and takes the wine.

She knows that Meredith thinks her ex-husband is a jerk, that he can't be trusted. And as much as Lily is convinced that Meredith despises her, she has also noticed Meredith staring at her occasionally, as if she longs to entrust Lily with a deep, dark secret. Perhaps warn her about Roger? Tell her how he cheated on Meredith and the kids? List the alarming number of girlfriends he has courted over the years? Maybe even convince Lily to pack her bags and leave before Roger beats her to it?

But Lily has heard it all. Roger already confided in her about his playboy days, and it's not as if she was a nun before they met. She has her own share of skeletons in the closet, one-night stands best forgotten. She pushes up her husband's glasses and begins to plant soft kisses along his cheekbone before he takes her wineglass and gently sets it down on the table. Within minutes, he has managed to shimmy her pajama top and bottoms off and next, her panties, down around her ankles. They slide onto the deck floor, and, not for the first time, she finds herself grateful that the closest neighbor lives a mile away.

"You're crazy beautiful," he whispers. "Do you know that?"

"*Hmm*...you're not so bad yourself," she gets out between kisses.

She'd wanted Roger to look through the slides for tomorrow. She'd meant to review her trusty checklist to ensure that everything is set for the party. But right now, while they make love, it hardly seems to matter. The party will be better than fine, she reassures herself. The effects of the pill are beginning to wind their way through her body with a sweet, tingly feeling, and she pushes away any uneasiness the night has stirred in her. Frankly, at the moment, she'd be content to drift off to sleep right here in her husband's arms until the morning sun warms their naked bodies.

Honestly, what else could she possibly need?

Nothing, she tells herself. And then, from somewhere deep inside her: *everything*.

As soon as they get dropped off at their dorm, Matt's text pops up on Dawn's phone. Hi. You back yet? Wanna meet up? Head to the Square?

Cody reads it over her shoulder. "Sounds like fun. Party time. Can I come?"

Amazingly, Matt and Cody are friends. Not best friends, but cool enough to hang out together. So, the fact that her brother is inviting himself along doesn't strike Dawn as all that unusual. What does surprise her is how Cody can possibly consider going out after the day they've just had.

"Are you kidding me? I'm completely wiped out. I'm going to bed."

"Aw, Donny, you're no fun," he says, invoking her nickname from when they were kids.

Sorry, but I'm beat, she texts Matt. Wanna come over here?

Sorry, but I already promised the boys I'd meet them. See you tomorrow?

Dawn experiences a prick of irritation that her boyfriend has already made plans without her, but the sheer exhaustion she feels trumps any desire to get together.

Kay, she types back. See you tomorrow then. Have fun. Xo

To which Matt responds with a heart-eyed emoji.

"You should text Matt yourself, if you want to go," she tells Cody, hesitating before heading into her dorm. "Hey, do you think Mom's going to be okay? She seemed kind of upset tonight."

Her brother grins as if it's a stupid question. "You know Mom. She doesn't do well with change."

Dawn considers this. "I suppose you're right. But it's not like we're never going to see her again after this summer. She really didn't like the fact that Dad is taking us to Bora-Bora."

"Yeah, well, she'll get over it." Sometimes her brother can be a real jerk, but Dawn chooses to ignore it for now. She's too tired to pick a fight. "So, are you going to tell me what really happened with the dean today?" She's been dying to get the details. The only thing Cody said on the ride over to Artu was that it was "no biggie," just "a little misunderstanding" and then he'd shoved his diploma into her hands, as if to prove the point.

Dawn was relieved. *Of course, she was relieved!* She didn't want Cody to get kicked out of school. But a little voice inside her head had protested. *How come that was so easy for you? How come you and Dad can make every problem disappear with a wave of your hand? And, oh, by the way, where were Mom and Dad when I needed them?* Because neither one of her parents had even bothered to show up on the day of her meeting with the Admin Board. "Just tell the truth," they'd advised, as if they were reluctant to get involved. Her very fate had been left in the hands of a few gray-haired professors. While Cody, *only Cody*, waited for her outside the conference room door, Dawn had worked diligently to defend herself.

Her brother shrugs now in typical fashion. "Well, you were right about the photo. That's what they were hung up on, not the frogs. I even told the dean that I was behind the frog prank and he didn't seem to care."

"Really?" She can't mask her surprise. She'd been hoping it was the frogs, which somehow strikes her as a more forgivable infraction, and not the photo that had put her brother in the hot seat.

"So, what did they say?"

"They wanted to know if I was trading a paper for drugs, just like the email said."

"Cody! *Were* you?" Maybe now that they're alone her brother will finally confide in her.

"What does it matter? They couldn't prove anything. I told you that photo meant nothing." He weaves his fingers together and cracks his knuckles, making her wince. "It also helps to have your dad around when he happens to be Roger Landau."

"Yeah, I'll bet," she says a tad sarcastically. *Not that she would know.* "Did Dad pay him off or something to make your little problem go away?"

"Nope, didn't even need to stoop that low. Like I told you, they had nothing on me. It was Eddie they were trying to nail. At least that's what Dad told me later. Everyone knows Eddie's selling drugs on campus. They just haven't been able to prove it."

"Huh. And what about the paper. Did you really edit it for him?"

"Gotta plead the Fifth on that one, sis. It's for the best."

"I'll take that as a *no* then," she says, which is fine. If her brother wrote Eddie's paper, she doesn't really care. It's not like she's the morality warden or anything. It's more the drugs that she's worried about. "But, Cody, you're not messing around with drugs for real, are you? I mean, you'd tell me, right? You'd tell me if you needed to get help, right?"

He reaches out and tousles her hair. "Aw, little sis," he says. "I love how you worry about me. But don't. You're wasting your time. Seriously."

And what is she supposed to say to *that*? She hugs her photo book to her chest. "I'm going to pretend you just said, 'No, Dawn, I'm not using drugs. That would be so stupid of me, especially considering I have my whole life ahead of me!'"

He cocks his head to one side. "Hey, that was well put. Thanks." And with that, he turns to leave, but not before softly saying, "Hey, Donny, ever hear of Adderall for late nights?"

And that's when Dawn realizes what was in the backpack. The last piece of the puzzle clicks into place.

Cody can admit now that he was a little worried—actually, more like petrified—while he sweated it out in the dean's office. He didn't want to lose his diploma. Not when he'd worked his ass off! He didn't know if his dad was hoping to hatch some kind of deal with the dean when they stepped outside, but frankly, by that point, he didn't care. He would have cut a deal with the devil. If he'd left there *without* a diploma, his life would have been totally ruined, as in over. He could kiss his future goodbye. The high school would retract his job offer, and he'd never be able to get into graduate school, let alone land another job.

When his mom looked at him with those searching, concerned eyes, he'd almost cracked. *Maybe it would be better to tell the truth if the dean was going to stumble onto it anyway?* He could cop to the Adderall but not the paper, maybe. But then he'd performed a quick calculation in his head: he'd covered his tracks as best he could; his dad was talking to the dean; and Cody didn't *think* the school had anything to pin on him. The odds seemed to lean in his favor. So, he'd shut down, told his mom there was nothing to worry about, and took maybe the biggest risk of his college career.

Cody had only been trying to help in the first place. Eddie was a nice enough guy, and though Cody knew he had a reputation for dealing drugs, it never came up between them. Then one day, Eddie mentioned he was freaking out about a paper due for Introductory Psychology, and Cody told him that the class had been a breeze when he took it freshman year. Which was when things got interesting.

"Yeah, if it's so easy, how about *you* write my paper?" Eddie joked. Or so Cody had thought.

"Yeah, right." He continued to pull out miles on the rowing machine while Eddie rowed next to him.

"No, man, I'm serious," Eddie continued.

"Dude, I hardly have time to study for my own finals let alone write a paper for you."

"It's only four pages. Easy for you to do. I'll make it worth your while."

Cody had been vaguely intrigued. He'd assumed Eddie was referring to a little weed, maybe something stronger. Maybe straight-up cash. "Yeah, like how?"

"Let's just say you'll be nicely compensated for your efforts."

Cody had never written anyone's paper before, but he was confident he could dash off a four-pager in about an hour. No sweat.

"Surely, there's something you could use to help you through finals week?" Eddie had hinted.

Cody hesitated for maybe a millisecond. He should have hesitated longer. "Come to think of it, I hear Adderall can be helpful for late-night cramming."

Eddie had nodded, looking straight ahead while the whir of the rowing machines drowned out their voices. "Funny, I've heard that, too." They'd set up a date to meet the next day at the gym, and that had been that. When Cody opened the backpack in his room, he'd discovered a bottle of Adderall, ten tiny pills to be taken every six hours or so. He'd popped the first one immediately and soon after felt as if he'd downed five Red Bulls in quick succession. The stuff was amazing! He was up all night studying for his economics final, a class that he was practically failing. He needed to pull off an A on the final, 75 percent of his grade, to pass. But he'd done it—gotten the A and lifted his grade up to a B+. To be honest, he hadn't given another thought to Eddie or the paper or the pills until Dawn had flashed that photo at him yesterday.

Oh, shit, he'd thought, even though he'd done his best to play it cool in front of his sister. Right before the awards ceremony under the tent, he'd run up to his room to flush the last few pills down the toilet and stuffed the bottle in some random Dumpster behind the dorm. Later that night, he'd tracked down Eddie so they could get their story straight. Taking Adderall wasn't technically illegal—he knew kids who took it all the time and some who had actual legit prescriptions for their diagnoses of ADHD. But writing someone else's paper was grounds for expulsion.

What had he been thinking?

He knows he's lucky to have gotten a hall pass this time. He'd nearly texted Eddie to give him an update tonight, tell him that everything was copacetic and not to worry. But then he'd remembered they'd agreed not to be in touch for the next week, so as not to raise suspicion or create a text trail. If he doesn't bump into Eddie randomly tonight, Cody will catch up with him in a few days.

He trots down the hill from campus, across the rotary, and lands on the sidewalk headed into Davis Square. It feels good to be free, away from the tension between his mom and dad and Lily that's so thick it's almost claustrophobic. On his trip in to meet his buddies, he checks his phone for the hundredth time for a text from Melissa. *Nothing.* It feels weird that she has no idea about what's happened to him over the last twelve hours. Usually their phones are blowing up with texts to each other all day long. He really needs to talk to her, get things straight between them.

He pulls up her name on his phone and begins to type. Hiya, can we talk?

Well, that was an interesting day. Joel steers the car back to the hotel while the soft hum of NPR on the radio fills the air. Meredith's eyes are closed, though he can't tell if she's actually asleep or merely lost in thought. If he had to make a list of the top ten most memorable moments from today, there are some he would have expected, and a few others that he couldn't have dreamed up. In no particular order of importance, he formulates the list as they shoot along the highway:

1. The invasion of the frogs. (One for the record books, for sure.)
2. The ungodly heat. (Also for the record books. It must have been one of the hottest graduations in Bolton history. Joel thinks he probably lost five pounds.)
3. The kids receiving their diplomas. (As amazing as he'd dreamed it would be, even if Cody's was delayed.)
4. Running into Kat, her wife, and her daughter. (Not as weird as he'd expected.)
5. The meeting with the dean. (Weirder than he'd expected.)

6. Roger's private meeting with the dean. (Was Cody involved in drugs and should they be worried? Apparently, Roger didn't pay off the dean, which is a relief. Meredith managed to tell him this on their walk back to the car tonight. But why must Roger be such a perennial prick?)

7. The spaghetti and meatballs at Artu. (Out-of-this-world delicious and probably helped him gain back the five pounds he'd sweated off earlier.)

8. Watching his wife poke holes into Lily's job description.

9. Getting Roger's Bora-Bora trip sprung on them over dinner and watching Meredith squirm, as if she were ready to fly over the table and strangle Roger.

10. The fact that his mother-in-law had been toting around two thousand dollars in her purse all day. (*Two thousand dollars!*)

Forty-eight more hours to go.

He'd almost felt sorry for Lily tonight while he watched her across the table, smiling at all the right moments, her eyes glazing over with an expression that suggested she was listening when, really, she wasn't—until, of course, Meredith laid into her. Joel has been there before, knows how it feels to be the odd man out. And he wonders if Lily dislikes these awkward, blended family gatherings as much as he does. If anything, she might feel even more uncomfortable—after all, he's had several years of experience with this kind of thing. The relative newbie on the block, she still has to prove herself. And Meredith was definitely not making it easy for her tonight. If only he had his guide for stepfamilies to hand to Lily. He bets she could add a few choice chapters of her own to it.

Grant me strength. Grant me patience. Grant me a sense of humor. He's had to recite his serenity prayer only a few times this weekend and feels pretty lucky with the first two, although the one about humor has faltered here and there. Tough to keep his sense of humor during the meeting with the dean. Funny how the explosions he'd been expecting—like Harry's or Edith's saying something off-color or Lily's wearing an inappropriate outfit—haven't occurred. At least not yet. But other things have rightly blindsided him.

If Cody really is involved in drugs, then Joel has missed all the signs—and he's more than a little irritated with himself. Maybe he's fallen into the trap of granting Cody golden-child status like everyone else in the family. Still, he'd kept a sharp eye on him throughout dinner, and there was nothing to indicate that his son was high or jacked up on any kind of illegal substance. To the contrary, Cody and Georgie were probably his two favorite dinner companions of the entire evening.

Well, at least everyone is still in one piece, he thinks. *And, most important, both kids have their diplomas in hand.*

Only forty-eight more hours to go, he repeats to himself.

If only he didn't fear that the worst was yet to come.

When they get back to the hotel, Meredith hugs her mom good-night and tells Joel she'll be up in a few minutes. She can't bring herself to rehash the evening with him just yet, and she wants to check in on Mason. During dinner, Jill left a voice mail with a brief update, but Meredith wants to make sure he's doing okay. A comfy, oversize chair next to the fireplace in the lobby catches her eye, and she collapses into it. Though it's much too warm for a fire tonight, she thinks it must be wonderful to sit here by a roaring hearth during the winter. Maybe they can come back for the holidays. If Roger and Lily can go to Bora-Bora, then surely she and Joel can afford another long weekend in Boston. No reason they can't start feathering their emptying nest with vacations, too!

When she dials the NICU, Jill answers right away and informs her that Mason is doing as well as can be expected. "He seems to have calmed down since this afternoon. That sponge bath really helped. Thanks. He pretty much needs nonstop cuddling, though, poor thing. As soon as I put him down, he starts crying bloody murder again."

Meredith's heart breaks for the little guy, but she knows that he's in good hands. "Okay, thanks for keeping me updated. Good luck tonight. Hope he falls asleep for you so you can get a few minutes' break."

On the other end, Jill laughs. "That would be nice, but I'm not counting on it. Hey, how was your day? How was graduation?"

"Oh, good." For a second, Meredith almost launches into the highlights but then remembers she shouldn't hold Jill up. Besides, what would she say? *Cody almost didn't graduate. He might be into drugs; we don't know for sure. My ex-husband's new wife looks like she could be his daughter. We were attacked by slimy frogs in the scorching heat. Roger is treating the kids to a trip to Bora-Bora, and I made them these lame scrapbooks for graduation gifts.*

Instead, she says, "It was fine. I'll fill you in next time I see you."

When she hangs up, a group of bridesmaids clutching bouquets of long-stemmed white roses sails through the hotel lobby. Their dresses are a tasteful shade of deep purple, almost an eggplant, a color and style pretty enough to be worn again after the wedding. Meredith thinks back to her own wedding day with Joel. They'd wanted to keep the ceremony simple and had tied the knot at a small Unitarian church in New Haven, followed by dinner with a small group of family and friends. No bridesmaids, no groomsmen. Meredith didn't even wear a traditional white gown, just a three-quarters length ivory silk dress. Funny how little she remembers about the actual day. The memories that stay with her are, instead, those tied to family. Like when they all headed up to Canobie Lake Park and Joel won an enormous stuffed giraffe for Dawn and a stuffed gorilla for Cody. Or when they rented a house on the Cape for a week and everyone would sit around the campfire at night and try to one-up each other with scary stories.

In contrast, she remembers more about her and Roger's wedding *day* and less about their years together as a family. Maybe it's because Roger, determined to log the insane hours to make partner at his firm, was so seldom around when the kids were young. Or maybe it's simply because when she'd married him, she was young enough to care about the details of her wedding day. Naively, she'd assumed that a beautiful wedding ensured a beautiful life together. Theirs had been a huge fete at a country club with ocean views and more than two hundred guests. An eight-piece band played, and the guests had danced until the band flicked the lights and shooed everyone home. It had been the kind of wedding a girl dreams about, followed by a romantic honeymoon in Bali.

Quite a contrast to how they'd first met, back when she was working as a nurse in the ER. Roger had presented with a broken nose, cracked by a teammate's elbow in a pickup game of basketball, and he'd been holding a blood-soaked T-shirt. The shirt caught her eye: Green Bay Packers. Meredith, who'd grown up in Wisconsin, struck up a conversation.

"So, you're a Packers fan, I see."

"Oh, no, it's my buddy Brian's. He lent it to me. Or, I guess gave it to me is more like it. Can't imagine he's going to want it back." And he'd cracked a half smile before wincing. Meredith could see that the nose was askew, the crack up high. "Anyway, he's from Wisconsin. A diehard Packer fan."

"Must be a good guy," she said. Had she been flirting? "Aside from the fact that he broke your nose, of course."

Roger grinned. "That's all right. I won't take it personally. He *is* a good guy, but I'm nicer. Want to go out to dinner with me sometime?"

Surprised, Meredith paused in her cleanup efforts. Roger looked so forsaken, but the deep-set blue eyes, the five o'clock shadow and his smile were enough to make her see past his crooked nose.

"Okay," she said, as if accepting a dare. "Sure. Why not?"

"Sure?" he'd asked, sounding dubious. "I can promise you that I'm much better-looking than I'm presenting myself at the moment." Which had made her laugh. And after that first date a few days later, which had evolved into an entire week traveling back and forth between each other's apartments, they were more or less inseparable until Roger proposed on the beach, the waves eddying around their bare feet.

Until, of course, the day he told her he was leaving her for someone else.

Meredith sighs at the memory. She used to be fun. What happened? A few weeks ago, an old high school friend posted a photo of her and some pals on Facebook. Meredith was looking off to the side, but she seemed so happy, so young, so carefree in the picture that she almost didn't recognize herself. What was she thinking in that photo when she was sixteen or seventeen? The years (and motherhood!) have surely aged her, but have they aged her so much that she's forgotten what it feels like to have a good time?

Things used to be different (she knows they were), but the details of how, exactly, remain hazy. Once upon a time, she and her girlfriends would go out to dinner and a movie and gossip about the guys they were dating. Once upon a time, Meredith would shop for real, actual clothes, and not just a fresh pair of scrubs or new clogs for her swollen feet. Yes, once upon a time, a long time ago, it dawns on her with a jolt—she was young and carefree—and not so unlike Lily.

Maybe, she thinks as she takes the elevator upstairs, she's not supposed to be the Jackie O. of graduations. Maybe she has been going about this weekend all wrong. Maybe a cross between Meryl Streep and Sarah Jessica Parker is more like it. Or, how about, Tina Fey and Reese Witherspoon? Now, *that* would be a winning combination. She'll never be as gracious as Jackie O. (she pretty much proved that at dinner tonight), but funny, quirky, sexy? Meredith can be all those things. She *is* all those things, she thinks, at least on a good day, and she takes a moment to pause outside their suite door before going in, channeling her best movie star vibes and realigning herself with the parts that she knows to be true.

FIFTEEN

Saturday morning

Lily is having trouble remembering what day it is. Which is ridiculous because, of course, it's Saturday, the day of the party. Somehow, though, it seems as if it should be Sunday, as if she has already lived through and survived the party and should now be permitted to relax. She slides her sleep mask up and kneads her forehead. She vaguely remembers Roger's helping her up to the bedroom last night after their romantic interlude on the deck. Beyond that, it's all a blur, although something clearly woke her. *Bang! Oh, right.* The clanging of pans downstairs in the kitchen. The bedside clock reads 8:07 a.m. Donna must already be up and at them. Lily can't imagine what else could possibly need doing this morning, aside from some last-minute tweaks she wants to make to the slideshow. All the food and decorations are set, save for the pink-and-white peonies, which will be delivered at eleven. Then she hears it: a crackle of lightning followed by a rumble of thunder.

She reaches out for Roger and shakes his arm gently. "Honey, listen." She groans. "It's raining." On the ceiling the soft thrum of raindrops plays. The forecast predicted a slight chance of rain overnight and perhaps into early morning, but every weather station promised the sun would poke through by nine o'clock, the morning ripening into a perfect afternoon. And that was the part Lily had focused on: *a perfect afternoon*. There's another rumble of thunder, and she flops onto her back. "Great," she says. "Just what the doctor ordered. A thunderstorm for our party."

Roger stirs slowly, rolls over, and drapes an arm over her. "Oh, honey," he says, his early-morning breath sour. "Don't worry. It's early. It's supposed to clear. Have faith."

She slides his arm off and swings her feet over the side of the bed. *Have faith?* Have faith when she's devoted the last few weeks of her life to ensuring that this party goes perfectly? *No, thank you.* If she'd counted on faith alone, she'd still be stuck in Kentucky. Lily has learned the hard way that if you want anything done in this world, you have to take responsibility. Well, she's taken responsibility for this party. Whether or not it succeeds will be a reflection squarely on her.

It needs to be fantastic. There is no other option. Although, given how poorly Meredith treated her last night, Lily is surprised by how much she still cares that the party go off without a hitch. Unless Meredith thinks she's a complete idiot (which, Lily grants, is a distinct possibility), she must have known Lily would pick up on her underhanded insults about her not having a "real" job. About Lily's being just a hop and skip away from Kim Kardashian in her self-absorption. It was all Lily could do not to shout across the table at her, *Who do you think is organizing this huge graduation party for* your *children? Certainly not yourself!* But she knew how important it was to Roger that the whole evening unspool amicably, so she'd kept her mouth closed. Besides, Meredith would have probably played her holier-than-thou nursing card—how could Meredith possibly plan a graduation party when she's charged with saving the lives of tiny infants in the NICU three days a week?

Oddly enough, Lily actually admires the work that Meredith does. On occasion, she thinks about a nursing profession for herself. She suspects she'd be good at it. She knows how to take care of others, doesn't flinch at the sight of blood. For eighteen years she more or less took care of herself, anyway. Lily likes the idea of doing some good in the world, beyond suggesting what sweater or handbag people should buy. Maybe, if Meredith has calmed down today, Lily will ask her how she broke into nursing.

She stumbles into the bathroom, brushes her teeth, and smooths her hair. This morning requires two things if she's going to survive: coffee and a pill. Already, the scent of hazelnut New England coffee, her favorite, floats up the stairs, so Donna will have taken care of that part. She opens the medicine cabinet for the bottle of oxycodone, feeling a palpable craving in her fingertips.

Except something's wrong.

The bottle isn't in its usual spot, wedged in between the Tylenol and Pepto-Bismol on the top shelf. Her eyes quickly scan the shelves below, but there's only the typical stuff: cough syrup, Advil, nail polish remover, a box of Band-Aids, a bottle of leftover antibiotic pills from when she contracted bronchitis last winter. She takes out the amoxicillin, shakes it, peers inside. There are only a few pills left, and she tosses them into the toilet and flushes.

A stab of panic grips her next. There was a bottle with at least thirty pills on the shelf yesterday, she's sure of it. She shook them out and counted them! Did she put the bottle back somewhere else? She yanks open the top drawer of the vanity. Toothpaste and extra toothbrushes. The drawer below holds all of her straightening irons and hair products, and the last drawer brims with stuff she's forgotten about. Expired teeth-whitening strips, some fancy face cream she bought online, abandoned combs and barrettes. It's disgusting—she should clean it out after this weekend. But where did she put the pill bottle? She thinks back to when she transferred the painkillers into her zippered makeup bag for graduation yesterday. Maybe she left the bottle out by accident? She scans the bathroom, then slides the door open, and walks into the bedroom, where Roger has rolled over and fallen back asleep. She checks her bedside table, the top of her bureau, her walk-in closet, in case she misplaced the bottle somehow. But it's not there.

She spins around, her eyes scouring the bedroom. Has she left it downstairs somehow? But no, she knows that's crazy. Lily never took the pill bottle out of the bathroom for fear Roger would notice it missing. Nevertheless, in a last flicker of hope, she searches her pocketbook. Maybe she dropped the bottle in after she filled her straw clutch? Her fingers rummage through but find nothing except a tin of mints, money, and lip gloss.

Then it occurs to her: maybe Roger moved them. It's his prescription, after all. Maybe his hand was acting up and he needed to slip a pill into his drink to ease the soreness, the stiffness that settles in from time to time when he misses a physical therapy session. And didn't he skip his appointment yesterday for graduation? *Yes, that must be it.* Lily's heart settles—she's so relieved by this easy, sensible explanation. But how to ask Roger where he has left it without inviting suspicion? She scans his side of the room, his bedside table and bureau, but it's nowhere obvious. She'll have to ask him directly.

She sits down on the bed next to him, gently shakes him awake. "What time is it?" he asks, slightly panicked. "Did I sleep through the whole party?"

Lily laughs lightly. "Of course not. I wouldn't let you do that." She hesitates for a moment. "Hey, did you take one of your painkillers yesterday for your hand?"

Roger is still half-asleep but manages to answer. "You mean my oxycodone?"

"Yeah," she says, reluctant to offer more.

"Oh, no. I threw them out. Tossed them down the toilet. I don't need them anymore. Didn't want any of the kids sneaking around our medicine cabinet during the party. It seemed smarter to get rid of the stuff."

All of a sudden, Lily finds it difficult to breathe. She needs a pill as soon as possible. There's no way in the world she can survive today without the placid river those pills send her down.

"Why?" he asks.

For a split second, a ridiculous thought races through her mind: maybe Cody really is doing drugs (even though Roger told her he'd denied it) and, if so, maybe she can ask him if he has any extra oxy lying around? But that's nuts! She can't ask her stepson for drugs. Roger would never forgive her, and even Lily will admit it's not exactly a stellar example to be setting for her stepson.

"Oh, it's nothing. No big deal. My back was hurting a little. Too much heavy lifting, I guess, before the party. I'll manage. I'll pop an Advil or something."

She hops off the bed, suddenly focused on only one thing: finding more oxycodone. No way can she be expected to be the life of the party, the hostess with the mostess, without a magical pill to point the way. She grabs her phone and heads downstairs to greet Donna and pour herself a generous cup of coffee.

"Good morning!" Donna is dressed in a crisp white shirt, black pants, and a black apron, and radiates pure enthusiasm. She hands Lily a cup of coffee, which she gratefully accepts. "Splash of milk and two sugars, right?"

"Yes, thank you."

"So, are you ready for the big day?" Donna busily arranges dainty quiches on a tray. "It stinks that it's raining right now, but I checked the forecast and this whole front is supposed to move out by ten thirty or so. That should give us plenty of time to finish setting up. Fortunately, the tent kept the tables and chairs dry. That was a good idea by you."

Lily nods and sips her coffee, gazing out on the dreary, rain-sodden backyard. Even the white tent stands abjectly in what can only be described as a downpour at the moment. Lily appreciates Donna's optimism, especially when she can barely muster the energy for anything beyond drinking her coffee. She has to figure out a way to get a few more painkillers.

"If you'll excuse me for a minute?"

"Go, go," urges Donna. "I'll handle everything. That's what you're paying me for!"

In the family room Lily flops onto the couch and waits for her phone to come to life. She texts Haley. Hiya pal!

Sorry to bug you but I'm fresh out of you know what. Happen
to have any more on you? It's an emergency. Graduation party
at our house today!!

Seconds later, Haley has typed back. Oh, no! Wish I could
help, but we're out of town this weekend. Have you tried Antonio?

She reads the message twice. *Has she tried Antonio?* No,
she hasn't tried Antonio because to do so would be to join
the ranks of the addicts who seek him out regularly for
a fix. Lily is decidedly not one of those people. But then
again, if Haley recommends him, he can't be all that bad,
can he? What harm can it do for one little weekend? Maybe
housewives all over town are hitting him up for a little extra
something to take the edge off, just like housewives of the
1950s used to pump themselves full of amphetamines. Is
this the big, dark secret that no one talks about at book
club or in line at the grocery store? The thought hits her
like a sledgehammer. Maybe Lily's valiant efforts to keep
this all a secret is for naught. Maybe there's no shame asso-
ciated with a little pop of oxy these days. *If it's what everyone else is doing…*

She climbs back upstairs to her bedroom and pulls out
the slip of paper buried beneath her socks in her top bureau
drawer. Roger's voice floats out from the shower, singing.
She goes into her closet, flips on the light, and punches in
the number on her cell. After two rings, she hears a voice.
"Hello?"

"Hi, um, is this Antonio?" she asks and takes the leap.

Minutes later, she is grabbing her car keys from the ceramic bowl and heading out the door. "I'll be right back,"
she calls out to Donna. Roger is still upstairs in the shower.

She'll be home before he even notices she's missing. "Forgot one little thing." Donna waves. She's too busy counting how many canapés will fit on a silver tray to notice.

The route Lily takes to the parking lot behind the elementary school winds through town. The hypocrisy of getting drugs anywhere near a school occurs to her, but she honestly doesn't care at the moment. If she can just get her hands on a few more pills, she'll be fine. She double-checks her wallet at the stoplight. Five hundred dollars. Ordinarily, her wallet isn't nearly so flush with cash, but she dropped by the ATM yesterday in order to be prepared for the long weekend. Is five hundred enough? Lily has no idea how much it will cost. She's never paid for drugs on the street before! Will Antonio want fifty dollars? A hundred dollars? More than she can afford? She realizes she should have asked him before she hung up the phone but she was so nervous, all she could say was that Haley told her to call.

"Yeah? Okay, well anyone who's good with my lady Haley is good with me. How many do you want?"

"Um," Lily hesitated. "Maybe fifteen pills?"

"Lady, are you sure that's gonna be enough?"

Lily had already done the quick math in her head. If she figured on up to six pills per day, that would get her through the remainder of the weekend easily. "Yeah, that's more than enough," she said. She'd forgotten to ask if they were talking about oxycodone, but what else could it be? That's why Haley had given her Antonio's number in the first place, wasn't it?

"See you behind Memorial in twenty minutes."

"Memorial? As in the school? The elementary school?" She felt like such a neophyte but she had to be clear.

"Yeah, where else? Later." And the line went dead.

So now Lily travels along back roads to the school in case someone might be following her. She's acting a little paranoid, she knows, but she's never done this before. It takes her fifteen minutes to get there when it should only take five. She circles the Jeep in front of the building and then heads around back, where the playground and the tennis courts are. On the drive over, the sky has begun to clear so that it looks curtained, one side dark and gloomy, the other brightening and blue. Maybe it's a sign that her luck is changing.

When she pulls up, a gray Mini Cooper waits in the lot. Is she supposed to park next to it or hover a safe distance away? She decides to park a few spaces over in case it's not Antonio. When she turns off the car, she glances over at the Mini Cooper and spies a young woman sitting behind the wheel. Not Antonio. Lily slumps in her seat, hiding behind her largest sunglasses. Within minutes, the girl, probably around seventeen with ombré-tinted hair, climbs out of the car and heads toward her. Lily panics. This isn't Antonio. Could this woman be an undercover cop about to bust her? Her palms are sweating, the back of her neck prickling. The girl gestures for her to roll down her window.

"Can I help you?" Lily asks innocently.

"That depends. Are you Alicia?"

Lily nods. It's the name she gave Antonio.

"You called Antonio?"

She nods again, still unable to speak. What if this girl is wearing a wire? Lily has been watching too many television shows.

"Okay, good. Well, I've got something for you, if you've got something for me."

"Where's Antonio?" Her voice sounds like a horse's whinny. She's so nervous she thinks she might throw up.

The girl throws her head back and laughs. "You thought you were going to meet Antonio? My papi?" She's amused by this for some reason. "No one gets to meet Antonio. He takes the calls. I do the deliveries. So do you have something for me or not?"

Lily lets this information settle for a minute. This Antonio guy pimps out his daughter to sell drugs? This is where Haley has sent her? She's equally horrified and desperate, but desperation wins out in the end. "Um, yeah, how much?"

"Antonio said you wanted fifteen pills. So, that's four hundred."

"Oh, wow. I didn't realize it was that much. Maybe I don't need so many? It's just for a little back pain I'm having." She finds herself spinning a web of lies for this complete stranger.

"Like I said, my papi's expecting four hundred dollars. It's a good deal, lady. I'd take it, if I were you."

Lily hesitates. Does she really want to negotiate with this girl and, by extension, with Antonio? Torture scenes dart across her mind—fingernails being ripped out, eyeteeth removed with a set of pliers. She's probably better off accepting whatever is offered and getting the heck out of here. "Of course," she says finally and counts out four hundred dollars from the bills in her wallet and hands them over.

The girl takes the money, stuffs it in her coat pocket, then reaches into her other pocket for a brown paper bag, which she passes through the window to Lily.

"Thanks." Lily doesn't know what else to say.

"Thank *you*. Have a nice day." Lily watches the girl return to her car, get in, and drive away, as if she has performed this little ritual dozens of times—and she probably has. Her hands shake when she opens the bag and pulls out the bottle.

In place of a prescription label, there's a white sticker with the words *oxy, 15 tablets* scribbled across it. Otherwise, it looks like a regular bottle she'd pick up at the pharmacy. She unscrews the lid, examines the pill (which happily resembles the ones she's been taking, except these are pink, not yellow) and throws it back with a swig from her water bottle. She allows herself a moment to breathe and waits until her hands cease shaking. Then she starts the car and heads home.

SIXTEEN

Saturday afternoon, 12:30 p.m.

Sometimes when Dawn feels worried or depressed, she'll play the *At Least* game. Joel got them started on it years ago whenever they would complain about something trivial, like their ten o'clock curfew or the lack of sugarcoated cereals in the cupboard. *Well, at least you're not homeless*, he'd say. *At least you're not a starving child in Africa. At least you're loved.* It always struck her as trite, a dumb distraction, but the older she gets, the more she finds herself playing the game, like a reassuring smooth rock she can rub her finger over on tougher days.

Ironically, today is one of those days. They're on their way to her dad's house, and while the car should be filled with mindless chatter, everyone is silent. She wishes her family would relax, but she imagines her mom is bracing herself for more upstaging by her dad. And her dad's house is probably the last place on earth that her nana would willingly visit. Cody, meanwhile, slouches against her shoulder while trying to sleep on the drive up, because, as he's already confided in her, he's "wicked hungover" after meeting up with Matt last night. Dawn is wedged in between her nana and her brother. She shoves her brother's head off her shoulder and watches it flop against the back seat, his mouth agape. To make matters worse, the radio station is tuned to a country western channel (at her nana's request) that's annoyingly partial to Hank Williams.

Yes, Dawn is living in her own private hell at the moment. And because Matt's family is forcing him to hang out at his cousin's house in Lexington all day for his own graduation party, Dawn won't even get to see him until dinnertime.

So. Back to the *At Least* game. *At least my whole family can come together to celebrate graduation (even if some would rather not). At least I have a boyfriend. At least I have a nana who loves me and parents who seem to care about me on most days. At least I'm healthy. At least I'm not homeless. At least I'm not living in a Serbian war zone waiting for the next bomb to drop. At least I'm not alone, without a job, sitting in front of the television with my hand deep inside a bag of potato chips. At least I'm not pregnant and alone. At least I'm not a drug addict or an alcoholic. Or a serial killer or a wife beater. Or a Republican.*

The last one makes her smile because she's pretty certain her nana is a Republican, though Carol is too discreet and old-school to ever say so. Her nana doesn't believe people should tout their political views but rather keep their opinions to themselves until revealing them in the voting booth, much like sins should be kept secret until confession. That Dawn includes being a Republican on her *At Least* list would no doubt enrage her nana. *Oh well*, she thinks. It's a new generation, the #metoo generation, and she's proud to be a part of it.

Half an hour later, they're pulling up to her dad's house, where already ten to fifteen cars edge the circular driveway. Joel parks behind a red Mercedes convertible. *Probably one of her dad's friends.* Her nana, she realizes, has never set foot here, and Dawn senses her astonishment at the mansion that greets them.

As she climbs out of the car, her nana clucks her tongue. "Honestly, hasn't Roger ever heard of ostentatious wealth?"

"What do you mean, Nana?" Cody's eyes are still bleary with sleep.

"This," she says, gesturing toward the house. "Some people don't understand that it's not polite to show off how much money you have. That if you're lucky enough to *have* money, then you should put it in the bank for a rainy day or save it for when you really need it. This house," she pronounces, "is show-offy."

"Now, Mom, be nice," warns Joel. "We're not here to stir up any fires."

"Oh, is that right?" her nana asks archly. "I'll be very well behaved. Watch me." She winks as if to suggest she'll be anything but.

It's funny, but Dawn has been here enough times that the house, while impressive, no longer strikes her as insanely big. It used to, when she was younger. She remembers wondering if there were servants inside when she first laid eyes on it (she was twelve). The white clapboard house is fronted by a wide portico with columns stretching up like tree trunks, and to her child's eyes, it resembled the White House, the only other home Dawn had ever seen with columns. Gradually, though, over the summers when she and

Cody came to visit, it began to feel like their home, too. And on the odd weekend in college, they'd sometimes rent a car to drive up, say hello, beg a free meal, and throw in a few loads of laundry. Still, if her nana is stunned by the outside, wait until she sees the inside, thinks Dawn. And the backyard that winds down to the beach.

Above the portico hangs a sign that reads, *Congratulations, Dawn & Cody! Class of 2020!*

"How nice," her mom volunteers, but Dawn can tell she's struggling to be nice herself. "Should we ring the doorbell?"

"Mom, it's our house, too. I don't think we need to ring the doorbell." Dawn pushes open the heavy front door and ushers everyone into the foyer. A bouquet of pink-and-white peonies sits on a cherry credenza with a gigantic mirror above it. Aside from the mirror and an oil painting of the sea, the walls remain bare, pristine. The heady scent of barbecue drifts through the air.

"Well, isn't this something?" says Carol, scanning the foyer. "I'd say Roger has done quite well for himself."

Before anyone can respond, Lily rounds the corner from the kitchen and calls out, "Hello, everyone! Welcome! Come in, come in." Lily is wearing a pink-and-green polka-dot Lilly Pulitzer apron (*how fitting*, Dawn thinks) over a green sundress. Her hair is pulled back in a loose ponytail, bringing to mind a preppy Audrey Hepburn. She casts a brilliant smile their way. She's acting happy, *too happy*, really, as if she's a flight attendant welcoming passengers into her own home. Maybe she's just being a good hostess. Or, maybe she's already been drinking.

After last night, Dawn assumes all bets are off for good behavior. She doubts Lily missed her mom's veiled comments about her job as an enhancer. Typically, Dawn has a tough time feeling sorry for her stepmom, but last night a shudder of dismay rippled over her as her mom drilled Lily, as if she were slowly dissecting a frog and enjoying every minute of it. She'd almost told her mom to lay off but then reconsidered. Lily was a grown-up. *Let her save herself*, she'd thought.

Now, after an exchange of obligatory hugs, she casts around for her dad.

"Your dad's out grilling," says Lily, as if reading her thoughts. "He couldn't wait to get the party started." *There's that smile again.*

"I'll bet. What a lovely home you have, dear," her nana says. "Absolutely stunning."

"Thank you!" Lily's voice hits one decibel too high. "Come in. Let me show you around. The party is out back. Hope you brought your bathing suits!"

Her brother shoots Dawn an alarmed *what's-wrong-with-her* glance as they follow their stepmom down the hall, through the sparkling, well-appointed kitchen, and out into the backyard. Maybe it's nerves. It hits Dawn that this may well be the first time Roger and Lily have hosted the entire family in their home. She's not even sure Joel has been inside, although he's obviously seen the house on drop-offs during summers past.

They head out back to the deck, where her dad is manning the grill with a dopey chef's hat. "It's the guests of honor!" he exclaims, setting down his spatula. Tidy rows of barbecued chicken and ribs line the grill. When he spins around, she notices the inscription on his hat: *Master Chef, Graduate's Proud Dad*. "Hi, Daddy. You look ridiculous in that hat, you know."

"Really? I thought it was kind of cool. Give your old man a hug." Dawn obliges before Cody.

"Nice hat." Cody extricates himself from his dad's embrace. "Except the apostrophe is in the wrong place."

"Ha! I was wondering who would notice first. Do you know how hard it is to find a chef's hat that acknowledges you might have *two* graduates in the family? Next to impossible." He turns to their grandmother. "Hello, Carol. Welcome to our home. Make yourself comfortable. Can I get you something to drink?" Her dad rattles off the lines as if he's been rehearsing them all week.

"Thank you. I'll have a gin and tonic, please. What a lovely home you have, Roger."

"Thank you. It's been a labor of love. I'll grab you that drink. And thank goodness the weather cleared! My mom and dad are sitting down by the pool, if you'd care to join them." He points to a patch of shade about ten yards away, where Edith and Harry wave. Her dad is acting kind of weird, too, but Dawn chalks it up to the pressure of hosting such a huge party. Even though she and Cody invited several friends from school, Roger informed them last night that close to one hundred people had RSVP'd. Dawn was stunned—she and Cody don't have that many close friends between the two of them! Then he'd explained that he'd taken the liberty of inviting a few of his own friends as well as a couple of clients. He wanted to show off his kids, as he put it. Dawn can't argue about whomever her dad wants to invite into his own home, but it still strikes her as odd that their graduation celebration has somehow morphed into a glad-handing party for him. Then again, it's her dad. *The more, the merrier* has always been his mantra.

Guests cluster by the pool, although Dawn doesn't recognize anyone except for Edith and Harry, and Georgie, of course, who seems to have already ingratiated himself with a new circle of friends. Off to the left sits an enormous white tent filled with little round tables, sending images of a future wedding reception tiptoeing through Dawn's mind. She and Matt could have an amazing time dancing to a band beneath the stars here (though she concedes her mom might not approve). Next to the tent, a competitive game of cornhole is already underway between a few of Cody's friends. When a waiter materializes at her side with a tray of barbecued wings, Dawn gratefully helps herself, heads down to the pool, and drops her bag on a lounge chair before going over to greet her grandparents.

"Hello, dear," Edith says. "So nice to see you again. You must feel like you can finally relax."

"Yes," Dawn replies politely after hugging them both. She's never been close to this set of grandparents, especially after the divorce, but she does feel a certain obligation to at least thank them for coming to the party, which she does now.

"Of course, honey. We're very proud of you and your brother. You take after your grandfather, who always did well in school."

Dawn smiles and accepts this for the crock of baloney that it is. Her dad has told her countless stories about Harry's bad behavior in college, so much so that he almost got expelled. She thinks he confided in her right before she was about to face the Administrative Board herself, in a misery-loves-company kind of way, but she refrains from mentioning this now.

"That must be it," she says instead. "Good genes. Well,

I should say hi to some other people," Dawn lies. "Thanks for coming. I really appreciate it."

Edith waves a bejeweled hand in the air. "There's a card for you and Cody from us around here somewhere. Ask your father where it is."

"I will, Grandma. Thanks." Dawn retreats to the deck, where off to the side the DJ is setting up his turntable on the patio, still wet from the downpour earlier. That her dad and Lily have hired a DJ, rented a tent, and put on such an extravagant spread both pleases and embarrasses her. Her friends will assume she's spoiled beyond belief, but, in a way, she doesn't care what they think. In a few short months, she'll be headed to Chicago with Matt, and this part of her life will become a distant memory.

As more guests start to filter in, Cody comes up beside her and hands her a Diet Coke. "I thought you might need this almost as badly as I do," he says. "What's up with Lily? Is she high or something?"

Dawn snorts. She assumes he's kidding, but what if he's right? Something is definitely off with their stepmom. She shrugs. "How should I know? You tell me."

He gives her a lopsided grin. "Touché."

"What about Melissa? Are you guys seriously broken up? She's not coming to the party?"

"Not as far as I know. I tried to talk to her last night, but she didn't seem all that interested in talking to me."

"Wow." This information still amazes Dawn. Somehow she'd assumed Cody and Melissa would be together forever. "I thought you guys were, like, made for each other."

Cody shrugs. "Jury's still out, I guess."

Someone calls out her name and she spins around to see who it is. "Is that Dad?"

"Cody, Dawn! Come over here. I want to introduce you to someone." Their dad ushers them into his circle a few steps from the grill. "Jerry here played football back in the day for Stanford and then for the Forty-Niners in the early 1990s." Jerry Tomas is a massive man who towers over even her father. He turns his broad shoulders toward her and shakes her hand so hard that Dawn has to rub it after he releases it. His chin hides a deep dimple, and he has light blue eyes that startle against his tanned skin. Dawn seems to recall hearing something scandalous about a Jerry Tomas a few years ago, though she can't recall exactly what. Something involving a young woman, maybe? In any case, it appears that her dad has represented him at some point in his career. She's a little confused as to why he's here.

"Is that right?" says Cody.

"I hear you're a superstar player, Cody. Ever consider going pro?"

Cody laughs. "Sure, it's more a question of whether the pros would ever consider me. Which they haven't. And for good reason. I'm a shrimp."

It's true that her brother is tiny by NFL standards. Only five feet ten inches but he's as fast as a bullet on the field, which should count for something, it seems. Scout after scout has counseled Cody that the big leagues won't take him seriously, despite his stunning statistics in total yardage and catches. He'd get pummeled.

"That's a shame. Well, you never know. Someone might still come knocking on your door. What are you up to next year?"

Dawn finds herself growing bored by this particular conversation and scours the patio to see if any of her friends have arrived yet.

"I'm teaching high school students. On a reservation in North Dakota starting in September."

Tomas tilts back on his heels, as if to take better measure of her brother. "You don't say? Well, good thing your dad here makes a mint representing folks like me." He slaps Roger on the back and lets loose a good-natured laugh. "Everyone knows there's no money in teaching, but it's a noble profession, for sure. Good luck, son." He shakes Cody's hand once more and nods to Dawn. "And lovely meeting you. If you'll excuse me, I'm going to help myself to some of that delicious barbecue your dad has been cooking up." And as he walks away to help himself to a plate, Dawn remembers: Jerry Tomas was accused of doing something sleazy, like assaulting a woman in a hotel room at an away game. It had been splashed across the front pages of every major newspaper, and if she recalls correctly, he'd gotten off on a technicality.

"Really, Dad? You represent *Jerry Tomas*? Isn't he the guy who—"

But he cuts her off before she can say more, holding up a hand. "Yeah, yeah. But that was a long time ago. I just represent him in some financial dealings." He gives her a wink. "Besides, he was acquitted, remember?"

Dawn rolls her eyes and marches off in search of another soda. Her throat feels parched, and the thought of being near her father or any of his clients is too much to stomach right now. The whole thing is beyond disgusting, especially when they're supposed to be celebrating their graduation. Doesn't anyone in her family have moral standards anymore? Or has morality, like stirrup pants and fidget spinners, gone out of fashion, and someone simply forgot to tell her? Just then, she spies Shauna and some other friends sneaking in through the side gate. *Thank goodness*. Dawn trots over to say hello before grabbing Shauna by the hand and dragging her classmates down to the beach. Because, as her brother likes to say, *I am so done with this scene.*

Even Meredith is surprised when she steps onto the deck and sees the white tent, the waiters flitting about like butterflies, and a DJ setting up. Terra-cotta pots filled with red geraniums edge the deck and patio down below. As if at a hotel, lounge chairs topped with pristine white cushions frame an aquamarine pool. She instantly dislikes Lily even more for upstaging her not only in the looks and youth department but also in her ability to throw a marvelous party—*for Meredith's own kids*. She should have expected as much when the formal invitation arrived in the mail (shimmery gold with elaborate script) or when she spotted Lily's earlier post on Instagram. But even Joel admits, as they avail themselves to the lemonade, that nothing could have prepared them for *this*. Roger and Lily's house resembles Camelot. All that is missing, perhaps, are regal white swans floating on the pool.

For a second, Meredith experiences a pinch of envy. If she and Roger had stayed together, this might have all been hers and the kids'. But then she stops herself. It's silly to second-guess her life, especially when she and Joel have everything they could possibly need. As nice as it might be to live in such a mansion, it would probably grow old after a while, and all at once, the movie *The War of the Roses*, starring Kathleen Turner and Michael Douglas, flashes before her. Yes, if she'd settled here, that's how her life would have undoubtedly turned out, she and Roger swinging from the chandelier, trying to kill each other.

Roger's enormous Saint Bernard, whom she hasn't seen in ages, trots over to say hello. "Hey, Moses, buddy. You've gotten so big!" She bends down to run her hand through his thick fur and is reminded how much she misses having a dog around the house. Back when the kids were young (and Meredith was still feeling guilty about the divorce), she'd relented after they'd begged for a dog for months. One of her colleagues had advertised a new litter of Goldendoodles for sale, and when they'd driven out to the house "just to see," Slippers had bounded over to them as if he'd been waiting for them his entire puppy life. With white fluff on each paw and a small patch of white on his forehead, Slippers was his name before Meredith had even agreed to take him home. Then, during the kids' junior year in high school, he'd passed away, and she couldn't bring herself to replace him. But maybe now enough time has gone by.

"He likes you. He's trying to give you kisses," says Lily, who has come over to join her.

"Is that what it is?" She laughs as Moses's wet tongue slobbers her. "I don't think I've seen him since he was a puppy. He's huge! How much does he weigh now?"

"Oh, about a hundred and fifty pounds, give or take a few."

"Wow—that's a lot of dog to love—and feed."

"Yes, it is." Lily is holding a cocktail in one hand and a canapé in the other.

"Lily." Meredith straightens. She's about to apologize for her obnoxious behavior at dinner last night, but Lily beats her to the punch.

"You know, I don't think I've ever said this to you directly, but you and Roger have done a great job with the kids. Cody and Dawn are really special. You should be proud."

Meredith feels surprise blooming on her face. "Thank you. That's very kind of you to say. They can be a little tough, sometimes, but they're good kids." She might as well be apologizing for her entire family, for her own regrettable behavior last night, but then she stops short. *Why not let bygones be bygones?* If Lily is willing to make nice, why shouldn't she? "And what an incredible party this is! Thank you so much for hosting."

Lily cocks her head and smiles, as if Meredith has said something amusing. "You're welcome. It's the least Roger and I could do. If you'll excuse me for a minute, I should really check on Edith and Harry."

"Sure." Meredith watches her head down the stairs toward Roger's parents, grateful that tending to her former in-laws no longer falls under her own umbrella of duties. She searches for Joel, who appears to have joined the group that includes Georgie. A handful of guys is laughing, back slapping, telling stories. He'll be fine, thinks Meredith. And her mother, after receiving her requested gin and tonic, has blessedly gone to sit with Harry and Edith. As more people begin to arrive, Meredith wonders exactly how many guests have been invited. A few of the kids, including Cody, have already changed into their bathing suits and launch cannonballs off the side of the pool. Meredith grabs a glass of wine from a passing tray and wanders toward the water.

Though she wouldn't be caught dead in a bathing suit next to Lily, she's already wishing she could take a quick dip. She tugs off her light linen jacket, unstraps her sandals, and goes to sit down at the pool's edge, where she can at the very least swish her bare feet through the water.

From this vantage point she spies Roger, deep in conversation with two men in polo shirts who look like business acquaintances. And then there's a woman in a crisp apron, buzzing around the lawn and swapping out old drinks for fresh ones. Maybe the designated party coordinator? Surely, even the amazing Lily hasn't pulled off this extravaganza all by herself. A slight sea breeze drifts off the water, and a Hootie and the Blowfish tune floats across the yard. *This is almost pleasant*, Meredith thinks.

"You know," Lily says, taking her by surprise again. "I'd love to talk to you about nursing sometime." She slips off her Jimmy Choo sandals and dangles her own feet in the pool, as if Meredith has just invited her to sit down. Which is confusing—wouldn't Lily prefer to keep her distance, especially after last night? "It must be so rewarding to care for newborns, especially in the NICU, where you can really make a difference."

Meredith's first thought is, *Oh, honey, if only you knew.* But then she realizes that Lily's earlier Pollyannaish cheer has been replaced by something that sounds remotely like genuine interest. Perhaps Lily wants to be Meredith's friend? The thought amuses her because, of course, this was *Meredith's* original plan at dinner last night, to kill Lily with kindness. But Lily won that round fair and square when she and Roger announced the Bora-Bora trip. Maybe that's what Lily is up to—trying to make nice since she knows Meredith is still simmering about the trip.

"I've been thinking about going into nursing myself."

Oh, really. Meredith can't imagine anyone less suited to nursing than Roger's new wife. Well, to be fair, she doesn't know Lily very well, but she can't imagine how she'll maintain her Instagram following dressed only in scrubs. *Maybe she can alternate the colors*, Meredith thinks uncharitably.

"How interesting," she says now, striving for equanimity. "What makes you think you'd like nursing?"

"Oh, I don't know. I've always loved babies."

Meredith nods and smiles tightly as she used to do when her single girlfriends would tell her how much they wanted a baby. *Easy for you to say*, she'd reason. *You have no idea of the amount of work involved!*

Lily loosens her hair from its ponytail, releasing gorgeous long locks that she combs her fingers through before pulling it back up. Her apron has disappeared, and the sundress she's chosen for today is much more subdued than yesterday's outfit. It's a pretty green sundress that manages to play up her eyes instead of her breasts. "Did you happen to see that video about the baby and his mom's beating heart? Oh, I'm sure you did. What am I asking! You're a nurse."

But Meredith shakes her head. "No, what's that?"

"It's all over the internet." Lily pauses when one of Cody's friends creates a tremendous splash with a dive. "Anyway, it's incredible. This little baby lost his mom, I'm not sure how—maybe during childbirth?—and you see him crying and crying while all these people hold him and try to comfort him. I even think his dad holds him. Nothing works. And then the most amazing thing happens."

Meredith waits for it. She's not expecting Lily to say anything that will impress her—if Lily's idea of nursing is watching baby videos on YouTube, then she's in for a brutal awakening—and yet Lily surprises her. "So the man who was given the mom's heart when she died? He holds the baby and as soon as he does, the baby startles, like he recognizes the heartbeat coming through that man's chest. And then he instantly calms down and even starts to smile. It's like he's saying, 'Oh, hi, Mama. I've been looking for you.'"

Meredith glances down at her arms that have sprouted goose pimples. The story is remarkable on so many levels. A baby recognizing his mother solely by the rhythm of her heartbeat. Intuitively, it makes sense to her. If the child has never seen his mother before, how would he know that a man wasn't his mom? Babies don't know gender affiliation, but they've been listening to their mother's heartbeat for ten months in utero.

Still, there's something else that strikes her. It's almost as if she's glimpsing Lily through fresh eyes, the way she might look past someone with frizzy curls and then see them the next day with straightened hair. Suddenly, their beauty comes into sharp focus. Not that Lily's beauty has ever been in question but the core of her certainly has, at least for Meredith.

I'll be damned, Meredith thinks. *The girl actually has a heart.* "That's a remarkable story." She squeezes Lily's forearm in some kind of unspoken solidarity before standing up to go in search of more wine. She needs to leave before she finds herself actually liking the girl. And before she feels any worse about the way she poked fun at Lily's job last night. "Thanks for sharing it with me."

Joel runs through the litany of addictions he learned about in graduate school. There are all types—the obvious, like drugs and booze and sex and food—but also the less apparent, like love or work or hoarding. He knows that addiction is not a behavior that people can control, but a chronic brain disorder, where certain areas malfunction. Sure, maybe someone could have said *no* to that first offer of vodka or heroin or painkillers, but after that, it's anyone's guess who will be able to exhibit self-control when it gets offered again. In Joel's humble opinion, everyone shares a predilection for addiction. Some more than others, but still. Whether they actually act on it is another matter.

When he stops to consider life's struggles—everything from trying to pay the mortgage to dealing with physical pain—it's no wonder that so many people are turning to the things that can furnish relief these days. *Life is so hard.* His students tell him this all the time. Everyone is dealing with something, he reassures them, though he's not sure that it helps. He suspects psychiatrists with adult patients hear this complaint even more often. Life *is* hard. Getting through can sometimes be rougher than people are equipped for, and without good support systems like a family or friends, it's easy enough to find yourself turning toward whatever vice will help to dull the pain. In Joel's case, it's usually food and beer. And though he doesn't tag them as addictions per se, these are his vices, what he "takes" when he needs to chill or decompress. Like downing an extra beer after he bumped into Kat the other night.

He watches Cody goofing around with his friends in the pool. His stepson was pretty adamant about there being no drugs in that backpack, and yet, history suggests otherwise to Joel. If he knows anything about adolescent behavior, it's that denial often presents the first path of resistance. And he's a little ticked with the kid for putting them through all that stress and drama yesterday. As far as he's concerned, Cody got extremely lucky. This time. If that Eddie kid hadn't corroborated his story, the result might have been one hundred and eighty degrees different. And even though Joel understands that the dean couldn't deny Cody his diploma without any hard evidence (and certainly not with the famed Roger Landau in his office), Joel's not willing to let Cody off the hook quite so easily.

The photo seemed pretty damning to him, particularly the caption that accompanied it. Why would someone go to all the trouble of taking a photo and then sending it to the dean? He supposes it could be sour grapes, but it smells like something else to him. What Joel wants to know is this: Does Cody have a drug problem? Because if he's doing drugs, something like oxy or heroin, then his whole college career has been one big joke. And if he's in trouble, Joel wants to get him help. Into a treatment center, probably. He knows the best in Connecticut. That means Cody's summer job as a camp counselor will be a wash—and maybe even Bora-Bora—but no matter. If he's in trouble, they need to intervene before it's too late.

He has half a mind to corner the kid and get the real story right here, right now. But he knows Meredith would kill him. The storm has passed for the moment, and she should be allowed to relax, to enjoy the party. Any confrontation with his stepson will have to wait till later. But it's coming. Joel can feel it. He's watched too many kids go down the dark path of "trying out" a drug and then finding themselves hooked. Parents, well-meaning and well-off, who are dumbfounded by their children's downward spiral into addiction and denial, who drag their children into rehab only to get a call from the center telling them that their child has run away. Again. No way is he going down that path with his own son.

For the moment, he'll keep an eye on Cody, watching what he gets up to with his friends today. This morning the kid looked positively exhausted, but Joel couldn't smell any-

thing on him, not even cigarettes. If Cody is smoking something, it's not marijuana. Which both relieves and worries
him. Because if he smelled the earthy scent of pot, at least he
could rest assured that's probably what they're dealing with.
Nothing but marijuana in that backpack. Not ideal, but not
necessarily life-destroying either. At the same time, the fact
that Cody seems clean might indicate something more serious is going on. Heroin. Cocaine. If it's one of those two,
Joel doesn't know if he can forgive himself. He's trained to
notice the very symptoms of addiction in his students—
sluggishness, weight loss, track marks on the arms, crazy
eyes—and here he may have missed it in his own kid. He's
going to get a good look at Cody's bare arms at some point
today. If he's been shooting up, Joel might have to strangle
him right here at his own goddamned graduation party.

SEVENTEEN

Saturday afternoon, 2:30 p.m.

When Meredith excuses herself from the pool, Lily grabs her chance to escape upstairs. No one will miss her for a few minutes. She hardly knows anyone here, anyway. Of the roughly one hundred guests, Lily recognizes a mere handful, including Dawn and Cody. Alison and a few other friends were invited, but since most of Lily's pals work in the restaurant industry, they weren't available today. How she wishes Alison were here to talk her through any potential land mines! Her conversation with Meredith went all right (no wineglasses hurled her way), and yet whatever information she was hoping Meredith might share with her about nursing wasn't exactly forthcoming. Maybe talking about the infants she works with is upsetting to her.

Whatever the issue, Lily will not allow herself to get worked up over it. She has reached out to Meredith twice at this party, even congratulated her on raising great kids!

It's clear that, while she might not despise Lily outright, Meredith has zero interest in getting to know her better or in becoming friends. If Alison were around, she would tell Lily that winning over her husband's ex-wife is an exercise in futility—and why does Lily even care so much in the first place? Something must be wrong with her that she wants to befriend Meredith. She knows precisely what she needs: one more little pill to get her back to Even-Steven, Steady-Freddy. Her nerves are jangling again, that ugly self-doubt licking at her thoughts. There will be no succumbing to self-doubt today. Absolutely not.

Back in the kitchen, Donna busily orders the waitstaff around and pulls out an extra tray of hors d'oeuvres from the fridge.

"Party's going great!" she sings out when Lily passes through. "Don't you think?"

"Yes, fabulous. Thank you, Donna. Everything's perfect."

She hurries up the main staircase, nearly tripping as she takes two at a time. When was the last time she popped a painkiller? Right before the party started? But was that before the prep began after the rain let up, around eleven, or when people started arriving, around twelve thirty? If it's two thirty now, she's early either way. She tries to remember. She's certain she took a pill around nine thirty, as soon as she paid for the bottle in the parking lot. Regardless of when she took her last pill—eleven o'clock or twelve thirty—she has already surpassed the prescribed dosage of one pill every four to six hours. *Oh well.*

The pesky thought gets easily swept away by the nagging craving in her mind. Rules are made to be broken anyway, she thinks. And with this party swirling all around her, she's in desperate need of a good, soul-soothing rush. No one can blame her for any of this weekend's almost catastrophes, the near misses. Lily is not the wicked stepmother here. Quite the opposite. If anyone should shoulder the blame, it's Cody or even Roger for not protecting her, for not running better interference. Lily may never measure up in Meredith's eyes, but who cares? She's the one who lives in this beautiful house. She's the one who might make another baby with Roger someday. *So. Let Meredith walk around feeling superior today*, Lily thinks. *Tomorrow the kingdom will be mine and Roger's again.*

She rummages through the top drawer of the vanity for the rogue bottle, pulls it out, and shakes a tablet free. (Regardless of what Roger thinks, she's not worried about the kids sneaking up here to steal her stash—they wouldn't dare cross that line, just like she'd never snoop through their drawers.) She fills a glass with tap water and is about to swallow the pill when it occurs to her that it usually takes a while for the oxycodone to work its magic. But she's already a nervous wreck! If she waits for the oxy to take full effect, the party might well be halfway over. Somewhere she remembers reading that if you crush it up and snort it, the drug delivers quicker relief, shooting straight into your bloodstream.

But, whoa. Hold on a minute. Does she really want to go there?

Snorting it sounds like something only an addict would do, and Lily's definitely not an addict. On the other hand, how different can it be from swallowing the pill? It's practically the same thing, only with express delivery. For a moment, she considers chewing the tablet, but she's afraid the taste might make her gag. No, mashing it up is the better way to go. With the bottom of her hair spray bottle, she smashes the pill into powdery bits on the counter. Then she rolls up a tissue blotting paper, her fingers shaking slightly—and sniffs the powder, feeling it scoot directly up to her brain.

There's a flash of white lights, and her nostrils feel as if they're on fire as she grips the countertop, light-headed and panicking for a second. *What the hell have I done?* But after another moment, the world comes back into focus, and her face stares back at her in the mirror. She still looks like herself. *No one can tell*, Lily thinks. One nostril has a dusting of powder on it, and she swipes it off with a tissue. *Wow.* She wasn't expecting such a rush. But the sense of calm beginning to envelop her right now is heavenly. She stands there another minute, luxuriating in the almost weightless sensation that's taking over her body—until gradually, the most intense sense of euphoria glides over her. It's as if someone has opened a window onto an entirely different party, beckoning her to come take a look.

And suddenly, Lily realizes how wonderful this day really is. All of Dawn and Cody's friends are so nice! And Roger is delighted with the party. Lily has been paranoid this whole time, but why? Everyone seems happy. And the weather has turned out to be glorious. Finally, Lily is part of a family, something she has longed for ever since she was a little girl. She can almost imagine their comforting arms wrapping around her in a hug.

She opens the bathroom door, feeling as if the very air lifts her as she floats down the stairs back to the party. Not once does she consider the bottle of pills that has rolled off the vanity and onto the bathroom floor.

"You wanted to talk to me?" Roger, apparently discharged from his grilling duties, hovers above her.

"Oh, hi, there." Meredith straightens in the Adirondack

chair she's commandeered for the last fifteen minutes while Roger slides into the chair next to her. "Thanks for coming over," she says. "Mostly, I wanted to apologize for attacking you last night about the trip." Above them, frothy clouds tumble lazily across a brilliant blue sky, this morning's thundershowers long forgotten.

She watches him pull a hand through his thinning hair, his eyes trained on some faraway point on the beach, and can't help but think that her ex-husband has aged. They all have, of course, but Roger's face has thinned and unfamiliar lines crease his forehead. Even his hands, always so masculine and strong, are flecked with liver spots. "Consider it forgotten," he says now. "It was a long day."

Meredith nods.

"You were right, though," he admits. "I should have run the trip by you first. It's just that when my assistant found the deal online, it seemed like I should jump on it. I wanted to do something special for the kids, you know?"

Meredith laughs softly. "And this wasn't enough?" She gestures to the party going on around them.

He smiles, his eyes focused back on her now. "You know me. I like to one-up even myself."

"Ah. As if I could forget." She plays with the metal ring tag that circles the stem of her wineglass, identifying it as her own. For whatever reason, Lily handed her the tag with a tiny metal boot, not so dissimilar from a Monopoly piece, though now the thought occurs to her that maybe it was Lily's subtle way of giving Meredith the metaphorical boot.

"Anyway, it's okay," she says. "I've had some time to adjust to the idea, and the kids seem excited to go. So long as it's all right with their summer employers, I don't see why not." She pauses. "Maybe going forward, though, we could both work at being better communicators. Open the channels, you know? When the kids got older, we started relying on them to pass along information, but too much stuff gets lost in the pipeline as a result."

"But they didn't even know about the trip," protests Roger. "It was a surprise."

"I realize that, so it's not the best example. But still. I think we could do a better job. You seemed to have no problem texting me about this party, for instance. I don't appreciate being flabbergasted by news in front of my own children."

For a moment he's silent before nodding solemnly. "Fair enough. Understood."

"And now that they're going away, like *really* away." Her voice has turned wistful, which she fights to check. "Who knows how much they'll confide in us?"

Roger cocks an eyebrow, as if it's a novel idea. "You think they confide in us now?"

She shrugs. "Probably not everything. Cody, obviously not. But Dawn usually talks to me about stuff, especially this last year. I feel like she's grown up a lot." And that's when it hits her. It's not just Dawn, her baby, she's saying goodbye to at this graduation; it's as if she's waving goodbye to a new best friend, someone whom Meredith actually enjoys talking to and spending time with now. "Anyway, I hope they'll still talk to us about the important stuff."

"Such as when they need money," Roger offers.

Meredith laughs lightly. "That's how it's supposed to work, though, right? When you let your kids go? They contact you only when they need something from you?"

"Well, that depends. I don't think *you* can ever fully let

them go. That's one of the things I've always admired about you, Meredith."

She sighs and leans back in her chair. It's true. She would be the first to admit that she's greedy when it comes to her own children. She wants the world for them, the whole kingdom. The job. The life partner. The kids. The happiness and inner serenity. If someone is going to foster world peace, why *not* Dawn or Cody? She has spent a lifetime worrying about them—at the park on the swings, at the swimming pool in the deep end, when they first walked home alone from school. And then the more nuanced kinds of worries snuck up on her, such as, were they growing up too quickly? Were they involved with the mean kids? The countless hours Meredith has devoted to fretting about her children probably exceeds the total number of hours they've been alive. If that's even possible. But somehow it feels like the right calculation.

"I just want them to be happy," she offers finally.

"I know. Me, too," Roger says. "Remember when we took that trip to Disney World and Cody said it was the best week of his life?"

Meredith smiles. "I do." That had been one of her favorite vacations. The kids were in second grade and had been humming with excitement. For three days, they'd raced around the park, packing in as many rides as they could, Cody and Dawn insisting on riding the Thunder Mountain roller coaster *Again! Again!* as soon as they got off. And when the park doors opened, they were back the next day, staying through the fireworks until both kids, so tuckered out, had to be lugged back to the hotel on piggyback. That was when things had been good between her and Roger. "Are you saying that we can never top that week? That it's all downhill from here?"

Roger throws his head back and laughs. "I hope not. But the memory makes me smile. I've been thinking about when the kids were little a lot lately."

"Mmm. I know what you mean. Me, too."

"You were so amazing with them. Still are." His hand reaches out and rests on top of hers, surprising Meredith. "I don't know that I ever told you that back then. I'm sorry about that. I was too caught up in work, but even that's no excuse. I couldn't see the forest for the trees."

It occurs to Meredith that it's the perfect metaphor for Roger's wandering eye, his desultory heart back then. He, indeed, had too many "trees" in his life, most of whom wore a size 40D cup. She places her hand back in her lap. "Thank you," she says. "I'll take a compliment anytime, and they *are* pretty spectacular kids."

"I hope we're around to celebrate a lot more occasions like this going forward." He pushes up out of his chair and leans over to plant a small peck on her cheek, so light it's almost infinitesimal. "The demands of being a host call. I'm glad we had this little chat, though. Enjoy the party. You deserve it, probably more so than the kids." When he leaves, her eyes follow him back to the barbecue and that's when she spots Joel, staring back at her from across the lawn. Meredith shrugs innocently—it was only a quick peck on the cheek. Still, her husband looks slightly annoyed.

She gets up and heads over to do damage control in the one place where she wasn't expecting to.

The oxy has kicked in, leaving Lily feeling relaxed and totally, completely, blissfully happy. Thank goodness she decided to crush it up this time—the sense of euphoria swoops in much more quickly, which is exactly what she needed. A teensy extra hit. She wanders through the party without a care in the world. Nothing and no one can upset her now. And look how happy everyone is! A few people approach her to congratulate her on a fantastic party. *See*, she thinks. *No one is whispering about me, calling me a trophy wife or a gold digger.* People like her! They're grateful for all her effort, the gazillion hours she has spent planning this gala. Maybe she should go into party planning instead of nursing? One of Roger's friends told her she has a real flair for it, and even though he delivered the compliment while staring at her chest, he seemed sincere.

She should really be getting ready for the kids' slideshow, but why interrupt a good thing when everyone seems so content? Maybe they can premiere it later tonight, when dusk begins to settle. *Yes, that's a better time for a slideshow, anyway.* She winds her way lazily over to the pool, where the boys and a few of Dawn's friends play keep-away. Lily is more than open to being a part of this whole messed-up family, if they'll let her in. In case they haven't noticed, she's been more or less killing herself on their behalf—and she has half a mind to point it out to them.

But when she spots Dawn, dangling her legs in the far end of the pool, a wave of sympathy sweeps over her. Cody and his pals are having a grand time playing keep-away. Lily imagines it can't be easy getting upstaged by your twin constantly, especially when he acts like an idiot half the time. Dawn glances in her direction and surprises Lily by offering a small wave. Maybe, Lily thinks, Dawn is her way into this family. Maybe her stepdaughter doesn't hate her quite as much as Lily imagines. Or, at least, not as much as she used to.

"Hey, there. How's it going? Mind if I sit?" she sidles up beside Dawn, who peers up at her in her sunglasses.

"Be my guest. It's your house." Not exactly the friendly invitation Lily was hoping for, but beggars can't be choosers, she thinks as she sits down.

"So, where did you disappear to?" Lily asks. "I haven't seen you much today."

"Funny, I was about to ask you the same thing." Lily's heart stops for a second. *Is it that obvious what she's been up to? Is Dawn about to blow her cover?*

"What do you mean?"

Dawn shrugs. "Nothing. I just haven't seen you around. Guess that's because my friends and I hung out on the beach for a while." She hugs herself. "The water was freezing!"

"Well, it is only May," Lily reminds her. "Give it time. You're not going in the pool?"

"Nah, I wanted to sit for a while. Anyway, Matt won't be here till later."

"Oh? I'm sorry to hear that," Lily says, her words running together ever so slightly. "Something come up?"

"His parents are making him go to a party at his cousin's house in Lexington." Dawn gives her a funny look, or maybe Lily is imagining it?

"Ah." Lily tries to focus her thoughts. "Well, you must be excited about living together in Chicago." Roger, she knows, is less excited about this idea, but she won't let on. Dawn's a big girl. She can make her own decisions, Lily assumes.

"Yeah, I can't wait."

"I'll bet." Lily thinks back to when she was Dawn's age. Did she even have a serious boyfriend at twenty-one? No, definitely not. It occurs to her that maybe there are things that Dawn can confide to Lily that she can't say to her mother. They're not so far apart in age, after all. Maybe Lily can be of use. What does she wish she knew at Dawn's age? *That guys can be real jerks, but as long as you know who you are, you'll be okay.*

The thought that maybe she's been going about this step-mom thing all wrong occurs to her. Maybe Dawn desperately wants to talk about Chicago but hasn't because her parents are both skeptical about her moving to a city to be "with a guy." But Lily can relate. Lily can listen. Maybe Lily can be someone for Dawn that no one else in this family can—if not a friend exactly, then a big sister. The thought grabs her like a fresh wind, and she stretches her arms out behind her to better lean back, eager to be of help. She feels a little wobbly, which is weird because she's only had one glass of wine. And the urge to lie down on one of the chaise lounges, maybe take a quick nap, is immense. But the opportunity before her, to actually bond with Dawn, is too tantalizing to pass up. "So," she says, "tell me more about Matt. He sounds like an amazing guy."

Dawn glances back at her, a shy grin spreading across her face.

Joel has gone for a walk on the beach, which is probably for the best. *Let him cool off*, Meredith thinks. *This party can't exactly be easy for him.* She stands off to one side of the lawn, watching the kids who are contorting their bodies into what she supposes are meant to be dance moves. One boy spins through the air in an actual backflip, and a scattering of applause dimples the air. She scissors her legs together—she needs to pee—and hands over her empty glass to a passing waiter before heading into the house.

The downstairs presents somewhat of a maze, but eventually she locates a powder room off the kitchen and then another behind the family room, both occupied. Since waiting isn't an option, she hurries past the giant wooden whale (the Nantucket ACK painted on its fin) and climbs the stairs in search of a bathroom. Theoretically, she's family. And she's more than a little curious to see what this house looks like on the second floor, where she has never set foot before.

Upstairs, there are at least five bedrooms and an office. There's a pretty bedroom, the walls painted a deep purple. *Dawn's.* Then there's Cody's room, with its Red Sox and Patriots banners strung across the walls. It hits Meredith for the first time that yes, her children really do have two bedrooms in two different homes. She wanders into what must be the master bedroom with its enormous canopy bed—and can't help but imagine what fun her ex-husband and Lily must have here.

Meredith rushes to the master bath, her bladder about to burst, and after relieving herself, washes her hands at a sink where the faucet turns off and on by motion detector. *Ridiculous*, she thinks. *It's like a hotel.* When she dries her hands, a bottle on the floor catches her eye, and she bends to pick it up. Across the front on a white sticker are scrawled the words *oxy, 15 tablets.* These are not prescription pills that Roger would be taking for his hand, not with this ad hoc sticker. No, these are off market. Probably black market. And all of a sudden, her concerns about Cody come flooding back. *Has he been up here during the party sneaking these?* She'll kill him, absolutely throttle him at his own graduation fete. She grips the bottle, then reconsiders, and tosses it into the trash. She races downstairs to find her son, to check his pupils. If they're the size of pinholes, she'll know—she'll know that he's been using.

Outside, she marches over to the pool, where he's treading water, his head bobbing up and down like a baby seal.

"Cody, I need you to get out of the pool."

"Now? Why? What's going on?"

"Get out. Right now." Her bare foot taps against the ceramic Mexican tiles that edge the pool's perimeter. The boys' game of H.O.R.S.E. comes to a halt while Cody's friends look on, curious and confused. Meredith thinks she might explode while she waits for her son to pull himself out of the water and wrap a blue towel around his waist.

"Geez, Mom, chill. What's the matter?" A small puddle forms at his feet and she grabs him by the arm, tugging him over to the shade of a Japanese maple. She doesn't care if she's making a scene. His eyes are red—probably from the chlorine. But his pupils? She stares into his eyes, seeking the awful confirmation that her son is high on oxycodone. She waits to see if his pupils will remain constricted, or if they'll expand to adjust to the shade, as they should. For a second, they seem frozen, and her stomach roils. But then, ever so slowly, Cody's pupils begin to dilate, adapting to the muted light.

When her hands drop by her side, she realizes they're trembling. His pupils are fine. *Absolutely fine.* If anything, his eyes stare back at her accusingly. Her son is not high on oxycodone, at least not at the moment.

"Nothing," she says. "Sorry. You're fine."

"What the hell, Mom?" Cody protests.

"Watch your language," she cautions. "I thought maybe you were doing something you shouldn't be."

Mild confusion flickers across his face before landing on

indignation. "Oh, so that's how it's going to be from now on? You and Dad are going to accuse me of using drugs even though I've never touched the stuff in my life?"

She takes a step back, surprised that he's calling her on it here in front of his friends. "We don't have to discuss this now," she says quietly.

"The hell we don't. I'm not going to have you and Dad doubting me for the rest of my life because of one stupid picture. That picture meant *nothing*." He spits out the word as if he can't believe the amount of time that has already been wasted on it.

"Look, I said I'm sorry." Meredith holds up her hands. "There's no need to attack me."

"Well, same goes for me," Cody sneers.

"Hey, what's going on here?" It's Roger, coming to the rescue.

"Nothing." Meredith shakes her head, acutely aware that any party conversation around them has dwindled to a soft hush, though the beat of a Bon Jovi tune still thrums through the air. "A simple misunderstanding."

"Son, is everything okay, or do we need to take this inside?"

"Everything is awesome, Dad. Frickin' spectacular."

"Hey, there's no need to use that language with me or your—"

But he doesn't get a chance to finish the sentence because just then a scream slices through the air. "Mom? Mom!" shouts Dawn. "Come quick!"

EIGHTEEN

Saturday afternoon, 3:00 p.m.

After walking along the beach, Joel loops back toward the house. Roger's "estate" is over-the-top gorgeous, as if he has strolled onto the set for *Lifestyles of the Rich and Famous*. *Whoever said "money can't buy you happiness" hasn't seen this house*, Joel thinks. He can almost imagine what it must be like coming home to this every night—dinner on the deck, magnificent sunsets, the thrum of the waves kneading the shore. *Heaven*. That people actually live like this is slightly astonishing to him, and even though he has seen the house before at summer drop-offs, until today, he's never stepped foot beyond the foyer. It's as if the gates to Xanadu have been shuttered to him all this time, while the kids have been having the time of their lives. If only he could bring a few of his students up here for a field trip! Show them what's possible when you graduate college and get a good job (no need to mention the part about Roger's being a lawyer).

Now that he's had a few minutes to cool down, he can see the recent little exchange between Meredith and Roger for what it was: two parents concerned about their kids. Roger's peck on the cheek meant nothing. Still, that doesn't mean Joel has to like it. If he had his way, Roger would stay a hundred feet back from Meredith at all times. Maybe if he writes his handbook one day, he'll include a chapter on ex-spouses, too. *Never approach your ex without first seeking approval from the new spouse.* Yeah, there should definitely be a section on exes because *they're* the ones who really need to recalibrate their behavior, deleting the tiny gestures of affection they once took for granted.

What really confuses him, though—the more he gets to see Roger in action—is how Meredith could possibly be attracted to them both. Because they're polar opposites. Couldn't pick two more different guys to fall in love with. Maybe, Joel ponders, people actually have *two* soul mates in life, not one. The first is kind of like the try-out period, with the second being the real thing. Maybe Roger's flash and dazzle were irresistible to a younger Meredith, but now she realizes that a guy like Joel suits her better for a lifelong companion. Otherwise, how else to reconcile it?

There's a wall of seagrass dividing the property from the beach, and Joel cuts through it, placing himself on the gravelly walkway that leads to the backyard. *Grant me strength. Grant me patience. Grant me a sense of humor,* he recites. Only a few more hours before they can head back to the hotel. It's oddly quiet, and he realizes that's because the DJ has stopped playing tunes. *Must be taking a well-deserved break,* Joel thinks. But then he spots Meredith and a few others darting across the yard to the far end of the pool, where a small crowd is gathering. Something's not right. Moses starts barking his head off.

Joel trots over, slightly out of breath by the time he arrives. "Excuse me, excuse me, coming through." He uses his bulk to his advantage while pushing through the circle of people that currently surround his wife. When he finally reaches the eye of the storm, Meredith, Roger, and Dawn are all bent over a young woman in a green dress, who appears to have fainted. *Lily.* Meredith's head is tilted over Lily's, which jolts Joel from his confusion, because his wife is clearly listening for breath sounds. Swiftly, she angles Lily's head back, plugs her nose, and begins administering breaths of air.

Cody grabs Moses by the collar and starts dragging him back into the house. "C'mon, boy. C'mon, let's go!"

Meredith breaks for a second, looks up and catches Joel's eye. "Call 9-1-1," she says calmly. Then she counts aloud before beginning again. *One, two, three, four. Breathe.*

And Joel starts punching numbers into his phone like crazy.

For a moment, Meredith thinks Roger might actually strike Cody in light of his fresh talk, but the thought vanishes as soon as Dawn's scream slices the air. Instinctively, she spins toward the pool, panicked that someone has cracked his head open in a diving stunt. But all eyes are focused on the far end, where Dawn is crouching over a woman in a green dress. *Lily.* People begin yelling for help, and Roger calls out Lily's name as he races to her side. Meredith's legs feel strangely immobile—until finally, her blood is pumping again and she hurries toward the small crowd forming.

"Who's a doctor here?" Roger cries out, cradling Lily's head in his hands. Meredith scans the group quickly, because surely one of Roger's guests must be a doctor. But when no one volunteers, the brief silence feels deafening. She peers down at Lily, who, were her lips not turning a pale shade of blue, might have merely fainted. But that color tells Meredith there's no time to waste, no waiting for a doctor to step forward.

"Will someone get Moses out of here?" she yells, unable to think with all the barking.

"Meredith, can you help her?" Roger stares at her with pleading, desperate eyes. "Please?" She bends down to listen for breath puffs, already suspecting what she'll hear. Nothing. *Think, Meredith, think.* Her heart is racing. She reaches for Lily's wrist and detects a faint pulse. That's good.

Meredith is fairly certain that what she's witnessing is an overdose, that the bottle of pills she assumed belonged to Cody, even Roger, in fact belongs to Lily. The blue lips, the stopped breathing are all telltale signs of an opioid overdose. She begins the steps for rescue breathing, which have become ingrained in her mind over the years, although she has to recalibrate slightly because most of the breathing she performs is on tiny babies in the NICU.

"What happened?" she demands of her daughter between breaths.

"Nothing!" cries Dawn. "We were just talking. And then she said she felt like she couldn't breathe and the next thing I know, she passed out." Meredith blows in again, watching to make sure Lily's chest rises. *Five more seconds. One more breath.*

"Roger, is Lily on any medication?" Meredith needs to

know exactly what she's dealing with here. Are there other drugs involved? "Did she take anything?"

Roger stares at her, unblinking. "Not that I can think of." Either he's hiding what he knows to protect Lily's privacy or he honestly has no idea. "Oh, she had a glass of wine, I guess."

For a brief moment, Meredith panics, thinking she's neglected to pack her naloxone kit, a lifesaver for opioid overdoses, in her beach bag for the party. But, no, some inner voice must have reminded her to transfer it from her purse to her bag today, just in case. Was it the episode with Cody yesterday that made her extra vigilant? Perhaps, but these days she rarely travels without it, this magical antidote that can reverse the effects of an overdose within minutes, mostly because she knows she would never forgive herself if someone died on her watch. In her lifetime, she has had to use it three times—twice with moms of babies admitted to the NICU and once on a woman who'd collapsed in an aisle of the grocery store. But that's three lives saved.

"Dawn, honey, grab my bag—it's by the lounge chair." Meredith continues breathing into Lily's lungs. "C'mon, Lily," she coaxes. "Give us something." Lily's lips have paled to an alarming shade of purple, and her fingertips are bluing, as well. Meredith plugs Lily's nose again and makes a tight seal with her lips.

"C'mon, back up, everyone. Give them some room." Joel is playing security guard. "Ambulance is on the way, honey," he says more softly. Within seconds, Dawn is back at her side, fat tears rolling down her cheeks.

"Dig through until you find it," Meredith instructs, ignoring her daughter's tears. She can't afford to get emotional right now. "The red Narcan kit." Her daughter's eyes widen as soon as she hears the word *Narcan*—she knows as well as any nurse that Narcan is used to treat drug overdoses—and immediately dumps the contents of Meredith's bag out onto the ground, seizing the red packet. With shaking hands, she unzips it and passes it over.

"Here, keep breathing for her," Meredith orders, and Dawn quickly moves into position, cupping her mouth over Lily's and assuming Meredith's place. Meredith has reviewed CPR with her kids enough times so that, God forbid, should they ever need to, they'll know what to do. It's a small godsend at the moment. Now she rips the nasal spray from its plastic packaging and slides it in, blasting the naloxone into Lily's right nostril. Time is of essence. Meredith can't screw this up. It's not her smoothest delivery, but it will have to do. When there's no immediate reaction from Lily, she resumes her breath puffs. "Come on, Lily. *Breathe!*"

Meredith prays she's provided the antidote in time. She prays it's the *right* antidote because if it's *not* an opioid overdose, the naloxone will do blessed nothing. It can take a few minutes to kick in, but surely it's been a minute by now? She has one more naloxone spray she can use, if needed. She's supposed to wait up to four minutes to see if Lily comes to before administering a second dose, but the wait is excruciating. In the driveway, the wail of sirens stipples the air. Finally.

"C'mon, Lily. You need to come back to us." Meredith takes another gulp of air and resumes rescue breathing while everyone waits.

Fifteen seconds. Thirty seconds. One minute. Ninety seconds…
Dawn cradles her knees and silently prays. *Oh, God. Oh, God. Oh, God. Please let her be all right. Please. Oh, please. Oh,*

please. Oh, please. Her entire body is shaking. Her dad cradles Lily's head while he rocks back and forth on his knees. While Dawn couldn't swear to it, she's pretty sure her dad, an agnostic, is reciting his own silent prayer. It's as if everyone else has slipped away and she, her parents, and Lily are all trapped inside their own private bubble where time has slowed to a crawl. Even though Dawn doesn't believe in angels, it almost feels as if she can sense their downward gaze while they silently urge Lily to join them.

"I don't know how much longer I can keep going," her mom says. "Roger, you might have to take over."

But her dad shakes his head helplessly, as if he can't possibly be asked to be a part of this, his wife's untimely demise.

"No!" Dawn shouts, unprovoked, and her parents turn to her, alarmed by her sudden outburst. But it's her own scream of frustration—at the beckoning Fates above, at her dad for being so hopeless in this moment when Lily needs him most, at her mom for saying she won't be able to go on breathing for Lily, and for Lily, who seems to be slipping further and further away from them with each breath that eludes her.

"Don't you dare die on us, Lily." Dawn leans in toward her now, as if they're having a heart-to-heart conversation. "Don't you dare. Do you hear me? We're going to have lunch together, damn it. We're going out for ice cream and cocktails and whatever else you want to do. You just have to wake up, okay? You *have* to start breathing! Please, Lily, please. Please breathe. We love you."

Dawn's head drops into her hands, and she starts crying in earnest. Somehow, some way, she has had a hand in her stepmom's death, she's sure of it. Maybe if she'd been nicer these past few weeks, Lily wouldn't have taken whatever drug it is that has caused her to overdose. Dawn is ashamed of how mean she's been to her stepmom, especially when Lily has never been anything but nice to her, lending Dawn her Jeep, not freaking out when Dawn crashed the rear fender, offering her a glass of wine on the odd weekend when she came home, treating her to lunch. Maybe if Dawn had thought about someone else *other than herself* yesterday and today, Lily wouldn't be in the mess that she's currently in. Maybe if Dawn had stopped to ask her stepmom how *she* was doing, Dawn wouldn't be by her side right now, pleading with her to breathe. *To live.*

Just then, a small army of men and women dressed in white shirts and pants spreads over the backyard like picnic ants, armed with a stretcher and an enormous red toolbox that Dawn realizes is a first aid kit. Her mom steps out of the way as a paramedic with floppy blond hair slips an oxygen mask over Lily's face, checks her pulse, and questions Meredith on what happened, what she has done up to this point. Each time she fills him in, he nods approvingly. He double-checks Lily's pulse, shines a bright light into her pupils, and confirms the Narcan dosage that Meredith has administered.

"You did well." He lifts Lily's arm and wraps a cuff around it, then prepares to give her a second dose of naloxone. The air is thick, silent. *Deafening.* Until that is, a small sputtering sound escapes from Lily's lips, and her eyes shoot wide open. She tries to rip the oxygen mask from her face, but the medic steadies her hand, puts the mask gently back in place, and explains that it's helping her to breathe right now and that she should relax. Lily gives a small nod and settles down for a moment. Dawn's dad, still cradling her head in his hands, begins weeping into Lily's hair. "You're okay. You're okay, sweetheart," he repeats again and again. "It's all right. Everything's okay now. I'm right here."

"Oh, thank God, she's all right," someone from the crowd cries out. There's hesitant, muted applause, as if people aren't sure whether it's appropriate to clap or not. Dawn watches as Lily struggles to sit up, seemingly dazed, trying to understand what has happened and why she's surrounded by strangers with stethoscopes draped around their necks.

But it's all okay, Dawn thinks. *Because Lily is alive.*

"You're alive," Dawn whispers, her voice incredulous.

"Welcome back," says the medic with the floppy hair. "You gave us quite a scare."

Nurses aren't supposed to get emotional. Meredith knows this, and yet this has been no ordinary rescue. She can't believe how close they almost came to losing Lily, this woman who has been the bane of her weekend, and who now looks so fragile and vulnerable that Meredith searches for a blanket or towel to drape over her protectively. As soon as she saw Lily's lips turning blue, her nursing instincts had kicked into full gear, the judgmental part of her brain clicking off. Nothing else mattered except making sure she survived. When she'd spotted Lily collapsed by the pool, not breathing, it was easy enough to put two and two together—the Pollyannaish attitude that Lily has managed to exude for the entire weekend, the contraband pills. Instead of being the source of her envy and anger, Lily is the one person in the family whom Meredith should have been worrying about all along. Not Dawn. Not Cody. Not even Joel.

And as a nurse, she's mortified that all the signs eluded her—the way Lily kept checking her watch at dinner last night before sneaking off to the ladies' room or the way she kept scratching her arm, another sign of a junkie in need of a fix. She'd been so eager to find fault with Roger's new wife that she'd neglected to see that some of Lily's "faults" might actually be troubling signs of something else. Meredith may have administered the naloxone, but she did precious little to ensure that Lily wouldn't need it in the first place.

As the paramedics lift her onto a stretcher, there appears to be some confusion among the guests about what exactly has transpired. Meredith will leave it to Roger if he cares to explain or not. Then she remembers: *the bottle of oxycodone!* She runs back into the house to dig it out of the trash. At the very least, Roger needs to know the truth.

Meredith and Joel accompany Roger while he trails the paramedics, who wheel Lily out to the ambulance.

"Protocol," the medic who appears to be in charge explains. "She'll be fine. She's lucky she had a nurse here to give her the naloxone."

They hoist the stretcher into the ambulance, but Lily's hand reaches out unexpectedly for Meredith's, their eyes meeting for a brief moment. "Thank you." Her voice is thin, crackly through the mask.

"You bet." Meredith squeezes her hand back. "Get better soon."

"Yes, thank you, thank you both." Roger clambers into the ambulance after her. His hair sticks out helter-skelter, his eyes swollen and red from crying.

"I'll check in with you later," Meredith tells him, and sneaks him the bottle of oxycodone. "She'll be okay now. She's in good hands. And, Roger? Look after yourself. You've had a pretty good scare yourself." He nods, but it's not clear if her words even register. Her ex-husband still appears to be in shock.

When the doors close, Joel gathers her into his arms, and Meredith lets herself collapse against the weight of him, the bulk of him. It's exactly what she needs right now, this ballast that is her husband. She's crying softly into his shirt, and he tells her everything is going to be all right, that she literally saved Lily's life. "But I froze at first!" she says through her tears. "I should have figured out what was happening before she blacked out."

"Shh," he tells her. "Don't you dare feel guilty. You're the hero here." Gradually, her tears subside, and he lets her go, takes her hand. They wander around to the backyard, where most of the guests are gathering up their belongings, heading for their cars. Donna still roams about, refilling drinks and encouraging people to stay, but it's clear that no one's heart is in the party anymore. Meredith tells her not to bother—people should head home, and the graduates would prefer to rest, anyway. She grabs a trash bag and begins tossing discarded soda cans into it, but then stops when she realizes she has absolutely no interest in cleaning up right now. If necessary, she can ask Donna and her crew to come back tomorrow.

"Joel, honey?" she asks, not entirely sure whether her husband is still within earshot. "Can we head back to the hotel?"

But it's Carol who responds. "I think that's a splendid idea." Meredith spins around, startled to discover her mom standing next to her and holding her bag.

"Mom!" In the recent chaos, she has completely forgotten about Carol, who now gives her arm a small squeeze. "Where have you been, Mom?"

Her mother smiles at her. "Watching you, honey. I'm so proud of you," she says. "Well done."

★ ★ ★

Dawn nearly forgets to call Matt to tell him not to come to the house—the party is over. *Kaput.* She promises to fill him in on the details later, but she can't bear to get into it over the phone. She goes over to hug her mom and tell her how incredible it was to watch her in action, saving a life.

"Don't sell yourself short, sweetie. You were critical, too," says Meredith, hugging her back. "I couldn't have done it without you. A lot of people panic under pressure, but you were amazing. You did everything you needed to."

"Thanks." Dawn would be lying if she didn't admit she's a little proud of herself, too. Even though she still feels like a jerk for how she's been treating Lily (and she's resolved never to be mean to her again, unless, of course, she really deserves it), it's nice to know that she can rise to the occasion, if needed. Maybe those few lifesaving breaths she blew into Lily's lungs will help to slowly redeem herself in her stepmother's eyes. It's something to hope for, anyway. "Are you, like, okay?" she asks her mother now.

Meredith's expression widens in surprise, and Dawn feels a flicker of guilt that no one has thought to ask her mom this very question the entire weekend. "Yeah, I'm okay. Thanks for asking. I'm just so relieved that Lily came back to us."

"Me, too," says Dawn, though it sounds funny to hear those words coming from her mother, seeing as for most of the weekend neither Dawn nor her mom wanted to be anywhere near Lily. "So, it was an overdose, right?" It's probably obvious, but she'd still like to hear it from an authority. Her mom nods.

"Oxycodone. And to think I never once suspected Lily could be doing drugs. Only your brother." She shakes her head.

Dawn bites her lip. "It's okay. None of us did. The important thing is she's going to be all right." She pauses. "Thanks to you."

"And you." Her mom studies her face for a minute. "How about you? You okay? That was a pretty scary thing to be a part of."

"Yeah, I'm fine." Dawn doesn't want to get into what a mess she really feels like, all the twisted-up knots inside of her. Instead, she says, "I think I'll go find Cody. See how he's doing."

"Good idea." Meredith wipes her hands on the sides of her dress, probably as relieved as Dawn that they aren't going to engage in a heart-to-heart discussion just yet. For the moment, her mom can chill.

A few minutes later, Dawn locates her brother in the hammock under the maple tree. "Scoot over," she says and hops up next to him, sending the hammock swaying.

"Well, that was real, huh?" he says.

"Yeah, that's one word for it." Her brother flicks her arm with his finger, an annoying habit he used to do when they were little.

"You did good, Donny. You almost made me proud." She grins at the half praise, which, she knows, is the most Cody's willing to offer anyone these days.

"Gee, thanks. What happened to you, by the way?"

"I was on Moses duty. He wouldn't shut up so I brought him into the house. By the time I got back to you guys, you were already breathing for Lily."

She tugs on the rope that swings the hammock from side to side and lets her eyes close, drifting off into space. There's the sound of car doors slamming out front, probably the last of the revelers to go. The thrum of the waves on the beach floats up to the house. If she works hard enough, Dawn can almost imagine herself in Bora-Bora. She wonders if Lily will still be able to join them. Dawn has only a vague idea of what's demanded of an addict to get clean, if that's what they're even talking about. Maybe Lily only tried heroin or oxy or whatever at the party and had a bad reaction, or maybe the drug was laced with something more powerful, like fentanyl. Maybe she's not an addict at all.

But the way her mom and dad were talking in hushed tones makes her think there's more going on, that this is not Lily's first foray over to the dark side.

"Hey, guys. How are you holding up?" She cracks one eye open to find Joel standing above her, peering down at them. Even her unflappable stepdad looks exhausted, as if today has robbed him of every last ounce of energy. "Your mom, Nana, and I were thinking of heading back to the hotel. Do you guys want to come along? We can drop you back at school, too. You might still have some packing to do?"

Dawn exchanges glances with her brother. "Um, I think we'll hang here, if that's all right. Make sure everyone is okay when they get home from the hospital."

Cody nods in agreement. "Yeah. We'll be fine."

Joel glances back and forth between them. "You sure? They might keep Lily overnight for observation." She can tell he's worried that they've been traumatized, scarred by what they witnessed an hour ago. He's cute when he dons his invisible counselor hat. "That was pretty scary," he continues. "Dawn, you were incredible, by the way."

"Thanks. But, yeah, we're good. We'll just chill here for tonight." She loves her stepdad, but she can't get into it right now, won't dissect her feelings about Lily's overdose the way she knows he'll want her to. Their little therapy session will have to wait till later.

He takes a few steps back, as if deliberating whether he's truly comfortable leaving them on their own. "Okay, if you say so," he offers finally.

"Oh, I want to say goodbye to Mom and Nana, though, before you go."

She tries to push herself out of the hammock, but it takes a few attempts—she's like an awkward hermit crab working to escape from its shell. "Me, too," says Cody, swinging his legs out much more gracefully.

"Right, good idea." Joel sounds relieved, happy even. As if this simple step will make the whole leave-taking that much easier for them all.

And Dawn, for one, is all too glad to play along.

NINETEEN

Saturday evening

Lily doesn't remember much—only that while she was listening to Dawn prattle on about her boyfriend, she'd started to feel terribly sleepy and short of breath. Which seemed odd, given that all she was doing was sitting there. So, she'd ignored it. But then her fingers started to tingle, and her toes. And next thing she knew, she was lying on the pavement, staring up at Roger's face.

It must have been the oxycodone. Either she took too much, or the stuff she bought off Antonio was skunked. When she opens her eyes now, Roger is sitting beside her. "Hey, there," he says softly, stroking her arm with his thumb.

"Where are we?" Her throat is croaky, and she feels as if she's surfacing from underwater, the whole world blurry and slightly out of reach.

"We're going to the hospital to make sure you're all right. You passed out. You're in an ambulance."

She nods her head, which sends a searing pain along the back of her head. Someone else, a medic, lifts her wrist to check her pulse.

"What day is it?"

"It's Saturday, honey. Remember? The party?"

The party? Oh right. They were having a party in the backyard for someone. But who? She can feel herself drifting off to sleep again but wants to ask Roger who the party was for. It seems important that she know this fact, and she tries desperately to form the words. But they're gone before she can catch them, silver minnows swimming out of reach.

When the ambulance jars with a bump, she startles awake again to find Roger turning a bottle over in his hands. It's the oxycodone. He senses her watching him and holds it up for her to read the label. "Meredith found it in our bathroom," he says. "Is this what you were taking?"

"I think so." She closes her eyes. She's so very, very tired. She could probably sleep for a week, maybe an entire month.

The next time she wakes, the world has turned dark outside the window and she's lying in what appears to be a hospital bed. The sheets are white and starchy, and an antiseptic smell permeates the air. Roger, asleep in a chair next to her, opens his eyes as soon as she stirs.

"Hi, love. You're awake. How are you feeling?"

Lily gauges her level of pain on a scale of one to ten, like doctors will ask a patient to do. She tells him that her head is definitely a ten.

"Poor honey." He offers her a cup of water with ice chips, and she sips gratefully. Apparently, she has a roommate because *Family Feud* blares from the TV on the wall. A light blue curtain divides the room, so she has no idea whether her roommate is old or young, kind or annoying. "Do you feel like talking about it?" Roger asks.

She shakes her head, which sends streaks of light shooting through her brain, and her eyes well up with tears. Does she want to talk about it? About how she slipped a few of Roger's painkillers a while back and before she knew it, the pills were the only way she could get through her tough days? No, she'd rather not. His eyes are rimmed with red. He's been crying, and Lily's heart breaks. She's responsible for this. "Can it wait?"

He nods. "Of course it can." He grasps her hand and squeezes.

"It hurts," she says now, tears streaming down her cheeks.

"What hurts?"

She turns away. How can she explain that she's not talking about one specific thing but the entirety of her? That everything hurts. Her throbbing head, her stomach, her mouth that's so dry it feels as if it's on fire. But that's not even the half of it. *Everything hurts.*

"Everything," she says now, trying to explain. She wants to make him understand so that he won't feel so bad. But a heavy cloak of exhaustion envelops her again, and her eyes begin to close.

"It's okay, honey. You're not really making sense, but you've been through a lot. Just rest now. We can talk later."

Roger probably assumes she's still high on the oxy, that she's delusional. But that's not it. How to explain the feeling of deep sadness, the loneliness that sweeps into the house when Roger heads off to work? And sometimes even when he's home. She knows how outrageous, how ridiculous it

will sound. She's married to one of the most famous law-
yers in Boston, for goodness sake! Look at the magnificent
house she lives in, look at her handsome husband. She even
has a family—of sorts. Most people would give their right
arm to emulate Lily and Roger's lifestyle; she understands
how true this is because she used to be one of them.

Lily can still recall waitressing back in Kentucky at the
Ninety-Nine and wistfully watching the families who
would drop in for dinner. She'd study the women especially, the way they swiped the milk mustaches from their
children's faces, the loving manner in which they'd lean
into their husbands, rest their head on a shoulder, as if they
were all a piece of one larger puzzle. How Lily had longed
for that life! While she scribbled down their orders on her
little white pad, she was also taking notes on how to trans-
form herself into someone better than who she was, than
who her mother was.

But now that she's living it? She thinks her own DNA
might be at odds with such a lavish existence, as if her body
is experiencing an allergic reaction to all the wealth and
good breeding that surrounds her. With the oxycodone,
though, that feeling disappears, vanishing in a blissful *poof.*
With the little pills her life becomes bearable again, the
edges muted, shades of purple and lavender coloring everything. She begins to tell her husband, to offer this explanation so that he'll understand, but he lays a finger across
her lips.

"*Shhh.* Get some rest." She feels the coolness of his lips
press against her forehead. Again, she tries to swim up from
the haze. If only she can explain this feeling of emptiness
to him, one that has insidiously snuck up on her over the
last few months, she's sure he'll understand and her actions

will make perfect sense to him. She wants to tell him it's not his fault.

"Not you," she manages to get out, and he squeezes her hand again.

"I know," he says.

"So tired." *Another time*, she thinks. Another time and she can explain how she never meant it to get to this point, that she was confident that she could stop the pills after this weekend. That she's pretty sure that she still can. She just overdid it this weekend. She needed an extra boost to take the edge off, to staunch the feeling that she wasn't good enough. Can he forgive her? Because she's so sorry. So sorry to have created such a royal mess for the kids' graduation weekend. So sorry for everything. They didn't even get a chance to see the kids' slideshow.

She thinks of the photos she posts on Instagram. It's all a mirage, of course. And if it weren't so pathetic, it would almost be laughable. Do her followers really think she can be so easily charmed by a cashmere sweater, a chic hobo bag? Perhaps a few years ago, when a part of her believed that money and happiness were intertwined. But who is she kidding? No one, as it turns out.

She can't sustain this lifestyle, this relationship. A baby, she realizes, will only prolong the inevitable.

As much as she loves Roger, it's all so exhausting, this pretending to fit in. A year and a half of it has nearly killed her. She can't keep up. It's quite possible that Roger will never understand this explanation. Maybe they can try therapy. Maybe once she puts the pills behind her and gets a real job or goes back to school, she'll feel relevant again. But she understands that her husband doesn't hail from the same universe, probably won't ever fathom how she feels. And even though she suspects he'll say he gets it—this sense of being an outsider in her own home—the distance between their two worlds is infinitely, perhaps irreparably, unbridgeable.

And because of that, she understands that one day she will, most likely, leave him. And her heart cracks yet again.

TWENTY

Sunday morning

"He didn't have any proof whatsoever. He was just trying to scare me," Cody says.

They are loading up one of maybe a hundred packing boxes into the U-Haul trailer that Joel rented earlier this morning. "Okay. Fine, so the photo didn't prove anything exactly." He shoves the box back as far as it will go, hoping to make room for the assorted lava lamps and footlockers that are headed home to New Haven with them. At least Cody has agreed to leave behind the godforsaken recliner. Dawn's boxes are already loaded into the trailer, neatly arranged and labeled, in the far back. "I'm more interested," he says, grunting as he gives the box a final push, "In what actually happened. Such as, was that a finished paper you were handing Eddie and what was in the backpack?"

Cody bends to lift another box. "Don't worry. My diploma's safe."

"Great. You worked hard for it. You deserve it." And Joel means it. He understands kids screw up from time to time, and he knows how crushing it would have been if Cody had lost his diploma in a last-minute screwup. Still, he wants the truth. Needs to understand if this was a onetime occurrence or more like an ongoing business arrangement between Cody and Eddie. "I still want to know what happened, especially given what we saw with Lily last night." He wedges another box into place. "The truth, Cody. Are you involved in drugs or not?"

He can feel Cody's eyes on his back, maybe debating if the risk of telling his stepdad outweighs the risk of not telling him. "I promise you, you do not want to lie to me." Joel climbs out of the trailer and eyes his stepson warily.

"If I tell you the truth, are you going to tell Mom?"

Joel shrugs. "I can't promise you I won't. Depends on what you have to say."

Cody glances around, but there's no one near them, unless you count the dozens of scattered cars in the parking lot where frustrated parents attempt to fit four years' worth of their children's lives into various sized trunks.

"It was dumb," Cody says finally. "But it was just that one time, I swear." *Uh-oh.* Joel braces himself for whatever's coming next. "I was super stressed. I didn't think I was going to be able to finish all my papers and study for exams. And if I didn't get an A on my econ final, I could have flunked the class. I just needed something to give me an edge. Get me through finals week. And that's it."

"Can you be more specific? What's a little something?"

Cody hesitates before hefting another box into the back of the U-Haul. "It was just some dumb Adderall. A lot of kids use it to stay focused when they have a big project due.

Eddie said he'd give me some if I'd write his Introductory Psych paper for him. It helps you stay up all night. It's even legal, so I don't know what the big deal is."

"Correction—it's legal when a doctor *prescribes* it for you," Joel clarifies. "Oh, and that part about writing a paper for someone else? Not so legal." He's disappointed in Cody's explanation, frustrated to hear that the kid really did stoop so low. Something else bugs him, though it takes a few seconds before he lands on it. "Wait a sec. You're telling me that you wrote a paper for this kid Eddie so that you could get Adderall to help you stay up and study for *your* finals? That makes no sense. You recognize the irony there, right?"

"Yeah, well, that was an easy paper to write. I could have done it in my sleep. It only took an hour."

Joel waits for the rest of the story to spill out, but just then he spies Meredith and Dawn heading their way across the quadrangle. Cody sees them, too. "Anyway, that's the basics," he says.

Joel runs through the facts as he understands them. Basically, his son cheated. For someone else. For drugs he shouldn't have taken. But, the fact that it's only Adderall they're discussing here and not something ten times worse, like crack or oxy, provides some solace. He won't need to check his stepson into rehab this summer after all, if he's being truthful.

"Please don't tell, Mom, okay? She'll freak out if she finds out about any of this."

Meredith and Dawn are drawing closer. "I don't know if I can promise you that." Joel considers how he'd handle the same situation with a student. "That was pretty stupid of you, I hope you realize. Trading a paper for prescription drugs? Idiot move, buddy. You're lucky no one could prove it." He feels as if he should say more, offer a lecture about the importance of integrity and how, when you come right down to it, integrity is all you have in life. *Your word.* But that lecture will have to wait because Meredith and Dawn are only a few feet away. "I'd suggest you start thinking about how and when might be a good time to give your mom the outline of the story. She's going to be asking, and I find that being truthful is usually the best strategy."

Meanwhile, Joel contemplates what kind of punishment he can levy that will fit Cody's crime. The house could use a new paint job. *Yes*, he thinks. *That should fit in well with Cody's job as a football camp counselor this summer.* Cody can paint the house on the weekends as his penance and reflect on his mistakes.

Dawn and her mom are walking back from the proctor's office, having just turned in her dorm key. It's official. She is no longer enrolled at Bolton College. She is free to go out into the world and make her mark, which both excites her and scares her half to death. Earlier this morning, she'd met Matt for coffee and a donut at the corner store before his family left for Chicago. Matt's dad had been eager to hit the road, not leaving much time to get emotional, which was probably for the best. Their goodbye had been swift and teary-eyed, but Dawn knows she'll see Matt again soon. Which should be enough to get her through today at least.

Her mom, though, has been acting weird all morning. Maybe the whole Lily episode has affected Meredith in ways she didn't realize. Maybe, Dawn thinks, she can atone for her sin of being oblivious to Lily's pain by doing right by her own mother.

"How are you holding up, Mom?" she asks casually.

Meredith waits a beat before answering. "Oh, you know. It's all the usual emotions. Proud and excited for you guys. And a little sad, I guess, because I'm afraid about what happens after today."

"What do you mean?" Dawn works to slide her right foot back into her flip-flop that has slipped off while walking. "Cody and I are going home with you guys for the summer."

"I know. But after that. After you go away to Chicago and Cody heads to North Dakota…" Her mother's voice trails off. "I don't know. I guess I feel like I'm losing you and your brother both at the same time. That you aren't going to need me anymore after you head off to your fancy lives halfway across the country."

Dawn takes a step back. "Wait a sec. Is that why you've been acting so crazy lately?"

Meredith stops walking and half smiles. "Well, I'm not sure about *crazy*. That seems a little harsh, don't you think?"

"Oh, Mom." Dawn steps forward and pulls her into a hug. "You know that's never going to change, right? We're always going to need you."

"I hope so," Meredith says. "But it feels strange, like I'm finally getting to know you kids as adults, and now you're about to leave."

"Well, you're still the first person I want to call whenever something good happens—or bad," Dawn tells her.

"Really?"

"Of course! No one gets as excited about my good news as you do. And no one's a better listener than you when I'm upset. And you know," she carries on, thinking out loud as they continue walking, "we'll always have a spare room in Chicago. You can come visit us anytime."

"I can't tell you how nice that is to hear." Meredith swipes at her eyes. "I'm sorry. I've been trying so hard not to get emotional this weekend. Guess I kind of dropped the ball in the final hour, huh?"

Dawn laughs softly. "Um, more like the last few months. Honestly? You've kind of been a mess, Mom. But I get it. Change is hard."

Meredith's eyes crinkle. "Now who sounds like the parent?"

Dawn smiles, then shrugs. "What can I say? You taught me well."

When they reach the boys, Meredith asks if they're all packed.

"Almost. Just a few last boxes to grab. Be right back!" Cody calls over his shoulder and trots up the hill to his dorm.

"Almost there," says Joel, shooting her mom a knowing look, which Dawn assumes means he's eager to get on the road.

"Yes," her mom agrees. "Almost there is right."

Cody checks his phone on the way back to the dorm. There's a text waiting from Melissa, saying her family is about to head out and can he meet her in the north end of the main parking lot? Sure, he texts back. Be right there.

The night that he headed into Davis Square to meet up with Matt, he'd bumped into her, again at the Burren, except this time she was with her girlfriends and not some random dude trying to make him jealous.

"Hey." He'd gone over to her. "You're not returning my texts anymore?"

She'd looked away, flipped her hair, and asked her friends to give them a second. When it was just the two of them, she said, "I suppose I could, but I'm not really sure what the point is? You made it pretty clear what your plans are for next year. That they don't include me."

"Mel, you know that's not what I meant. I'm sorry. I was an idiot. I was surprised. You've got to give me a few minutes to adjust, you know? That's pretty big news."

She'd twisted her straw wrapper around her finger in tiny knots, forming a paper ring.

"Anyway, if you want to come out to North Dakota and hang with me, that's cool. More than cool. We might have to look for our own place, though, because the school was going to give me on-campus housing. I'm not sure they allow couples." He'd thought it through, how it could work.

She nodded. "That's nice. That you've thought about it, I mean." Cody was afraid to touch her, fearful she might slap him, but he took a chance and wrapped an arm around her waist, pulling her close, smelling the familiar honeysuckle scent of her shampoo.

"I love you, Mel. You know that."

"I know." She'd pulled back and braided her hair into a loose knot, looking thoughtful. "I've been thinking about it, too. Maybe I don't have to move out right away, you know? Maybe I could visit you for a couple of weeks, once you get settled, and we could see how it goes? It's possible I could be bored out of my mind."

Cody grinned. "Yeah, I suppose it's possible. Unlikely, but possible." Leave it to his girlfriend to put him in his place.

That things are back to normal, or the "new normal" as he thinks of it, makes the world seem navigable again. For forty-eight hours, everything had turned topsy-turvy. But Lily is going to be okay (his dad called from the hospital last night to tell them so). His mom and dad have chilled out enough so that they're not fighting every second, and even though Joel drilled him on the photo (as Cody fully expected him to), that exchange didn't go nearly as badly as he'd feared. He still doesn't know who sent the photo of him and Eddie to the dean and his sister, and maybe he never will. He's all right with that, though. What's most important is that Melissa wants to see him before she leaves. Finally, it feels as if everything is turning right-side up, the way it should be. He grabs the last two boxes from his dorm room, takes one last look around the emptied-out space, and says a final goodbye. "Later, dudes."

When he reaches the parking lot, he spies Melissa right away, the sunlight glinting off her golden hair. She sees him and waves, and he sets down his boxes so he can run over to her. Because, honestly? It doesn't feel like he can get there soon enough.

Meredith smiles back at Joel when he says "Almost there" because they both understand it for the euphemism that it is. They're in the last stages of packing up. They're almost there, to the end of this, graduation weekend. They're almost there, to the end of worrying about what could go wrong (as it turns out, nothing they thought and pretty much everything they didn't). They're almost there, to the finish line of running interference between in-laws. Almost there, to the end of trying to tamp down jealousies and hostilities and tempers that might flare over the weekend. Meredith thinks back to the world map on their wall at home with its heading *Where Have You Been?* Funny, although there are only a few pins in it at the moment, if she could poke a green thumbtack through for every emotion she's weathered this weekend, the map would be flush with color.

Almost to the end of this particular chapter in the twins' lives, and, for once, Meredith is beginning to realize that maybe she doesn't need to worry quite so much. Dawn has a good head on her shoulders, as evident from her quick thinking yesterday when she helped with Lily. She'll flourish in the Windy City, with or without Matt. And Cody will be just fine, too. His path might not be as straight and narrow as Meredith would like, but then again, whose is? Without the ups and downs of the last twenty-one years, life wouldn't have been nearly as rich or as interesting.

And as much as she fears that her children might be leaving the nest for good, her rational side understands that this can't be. There will be plenty more milestones to celebrate in her kids' lives, perhaps a graduate school commencement, or a wedding, or a grandchild. Things that will bring them back together as a family time and again. She only hopes that she'll have learned to be more graceful in her dealings with her ex-husband and his family by then.

She parks herself next to Joel, who is sitting on the U-Haul's back step, awaiting Cody's last boxes. "Did you talk to Roger?"

"Yeah, he says Lily's feeling a little better this morning. Sounds like they've got their work cut out for them, though. Lily doesn't seem to think she has a drug problem."

Joel nods as if he's heard this excuse a hundred times before. And he probably has from his students. "They'll get through it," he says now.

"I think so, too." And as soon as she says it, Meredith realizes how much she wants this to be true. Lily, it turns out, has been taking painkillers for only a few months. It's not ideal, of course, but it's not as if she's been taking them for years. If anyone can beat this, Lily—who has weathered quite a lot of bad behavior from her new family—can. Lily, she admits, is a lot stronger than Meredith has given her credit for.

Several yards away she sees her mother, who's gone in search of coffee, heading back to them. Carol carries a box loaded up with foam cups and, it turns out, a bag stuffed with bagels. She passes them out and, after taking a bite, immediately declares the bagels subpar. "Not good at all. Too mushy."

Meredith glances at Joel and grins. "How is it, Mom, that you're always armed with the perfect arch comment? Don't ever change."

"And why would I?" Carol demands.

"Absolutely right," agrees Joel, letting go of a laugh. "Why would you? We wouldn't want you to be any other way, Mom."

Just then, Meredith's phone pings. It's a text from Roger, a quick thank-you. She's been emailing him articles about oxycodone and withdrawal all morning. While the paramedics had worked on Lily yesterday, she'd pulled him aside to inquire about the bottle of pills, and he'd acted completely surprised. "I had no idea Lily was even taking these," he said. "How on earth did she get them?"

"Probably a friend of a friend. That's usually how it works," Meredith said. "The important thing is to make sure she gets the help she needs." She'd held off on delivering an entire lecture because it wasn't what Roger needed to hear at the moment, but she wanted him to understand that Lily's situation wasn't so unusual. "There's no shame in it. It's an illness, just like diabetes or depression. Don't blame Lily."

He shook his head, still in shock. "I don't blame her. I blame myself. How could I have missed it?"

"Lots of people do," Meredith said gently. "It's easy to miss."

Now she allows herself a moment to unwind in the bright sunshine, cupping the warm coffee in her hands, before they start the drive back to New Haven. The heat wave has finally broken, and a cool breeze blows through campus this morning. It's been a long seventy-two hours. Meredith almost feels as if she has lived several lifetimes in the last three days. In other ways, it has gone by remarkably quickly. If someone had told her that she'd reach the end of the weekend actually caring for Lily, Meredith would have brushed it off as ridiculous. But she's surprised to discover that she *does* care, hopes Lily will be okay. As it turns out, even the gorgeous Lily Landau is vulnerable—which somehow makes her more likable. In the same vein, if someone had said Cody would come an inch away from getting kicked out of school, Meredith would have thought it outrageous, impossible. And yet, they've lived through that drama, too. Other things she would have never predicted: Joel's bumping into an old girlfriend. Joel growing jealous over Roger's peck on the cheek. The fact that her daughter informed her this morning that Matt will be flying out to New Haven to visit in a few weeks. And Dawn's flawless performance in helping her nurse Lily back to life.

But perhaps the biggest surprise is a reckoning of her own kind—Meredith's own realization that it's time to let these incredible kids who are hers, who have been her life, fly. Not so long ago she could identify with the mother in the short film, *Bao*, who's so desperate for her son to stay that she eats him up, her metaphorical dumpling, to keep him close. As soon as she watched that movie, Meredith got it instantly, understood that mother's impulse whole-heartedly. Her love for Dawn and Cody is overwhelming, all-encompassing. She would happily gobble them up to keep them close.

And yet, now, seventy-two hours later, she realizes the impossibility of this, the metaphorical devouring of her children. She knows there will always be another baby to tend to in her neonatal ward, another fragile soul in need of cradling whom she can bundle up in love. And while she may not have been the Jackie Onassis of graduations (far from it!), she will try to be more graceful when it comes to the next stage, the letting go. Her babies have grown up—they need to thrive, and no doubt stumble, on their own terms. She will be there for them, of course, only a phone call away. And she will arrive on a moment's notice, if asked. But it's time to give them the final, gentle push beyond the nest.

Letting go, she realizes, may be the most important gift of all that she can give her children.

Cody has returned with his final boxes, and Joel shoves them into the U-Haul until they barely just fit.

"Well, kids," he says, jangling his car keys, unable to hide his eagerness to get on the road any longer. "Say goodbye to the best four years of your life."

"Oh, stop it, honey," Meredith scolds him. "The best is yet to come, right, guys?" She slides her arm through his, and then Dawn does the same, slipping one arm through Meredith's and the other through her brother's. "C'mon Mom, you've got to join in now," coaxes Meredith. "Even Cody's part of the human chain." *The human chain*, she remembers, as her mother slides her arm through her grandson's. Just like they used to make when the kids were little and everyone would curl up on the couch, their feet intertwined, and watch Friday night movies. Meredith gets that precious moment back now, her babies all grown. "I love you guys, you know that, right?"

"Yes, Mom," groan Dawn and Cody in unison, placating her.

But Joel squeezes her hand and grins. "We know, honey. Boy, do we know."

A father in a Bolton Bullfrogs T-shirt walks by and stops to stare at them. "You guys want a picture?"

Meredith laughs. She supposes they *do* look as if they're posing. "Sure, why not?" She slips her phone out of her jeans pocket, sets it to photo mode, and steps out of line to hand it over to him. Then she darts back into place, linking her arms through Joel's and Dawn's again.

"Ready?" the kind stranger calls out, and Meredith's lips part into a smile.

"Ready!" everyone shouts.

Except this time, Meredith really means it.

★ ★ ★ ★ ★

ACKNOWLEDGMENTS

To the wonderful Meg Ruley and Annelise Robey at the Jane Rotrosen Agency, my heartfelt gratitude for your crackerjack advice, guidance, and soul-saving humor. To my editor extraordinaire, Michele Bidelspach, your keen editorial eye has made this book a thousand times better than it would have been otherwise. To the entire team at Graydon House, thanks for holding my book in your caring hands and giving it the attention it needs to go out into the world. To Sandra, thanks so much for the insight into the workings of the NICU, and to Officer Ken thank you for answering my questions about opioid abuse and naloxone. Any mistakes in the book are my own. To my sister-in-law Lynne, thanks for explaining the subtle differences between an "influencer" and an "enhancer" on social media. And to Trina, Sarah, and Jen, thank you for being such wonderful cheerleaders and friends.

While any number of books and articles can be found on the scourge of opioid abuse in our nation, there were three books that I found particularly helpful in making sense of the epidemic. For an especially honest and human account of the heavy toll opioid abuse can take on a family look to Maureen Cavanagh's memoir, *If You Love Me: A Mother's Journey Through Her Daughter's Opioid Addiction (Henry Holt & Co., 2018)*. Also, Sam Quinone's *Dreamland: The True Tale of America's Opioid Epidemic (Bloomsbury, 2016)* provides a harrowing and insightful overview. And Beth Macy's *Dopesick: Dealers, Doctors, and The Drug Company That Addicted America (Little, Brown and Company, 2018)* highlights the perfect storm that cleared the pathway for addiction in our country.

As ever, thank you most especially to my family—Mike, Nicholas, Katherine, and Michael—for your love and humor that see me through my writing days. And to my amazing nieces and nephews—Eva, Sophia, Aurelia, Joey, Mark, Mia, Sarah, Matt, and Sean (and, of course, my own kids)— I look forward to watching you parade proudly across the stage one day to collect your very own college diplomas. Much love to you all.

BEST BEHAVIOR

WENDY FRANCIS

Reader's Guide

GRAYDON
HOUSE

1. The twins' college graduation represents very different things for each character. For Meredith, it's the beginning of an era in which she fears she'll lose them. For Lily, it's the chance to become part of the family. For the twins, it's freedom. Why do you think the author chose a graduation to bring this family together? What memories do you have of family graduation celebrations? What does graduation represent to you?

2. How would you describe Meredith and Roger's relationship at the beginning of the novel? How has time and distance informed their relationship? And how do you think their relationship changes as the story progresses? Why do you think the author chose to tell the story from Meredith's, Joel's and Lily's points of view, but not Roger's?

3. At the beginning of the novel, Meredith ruminates that this graduation is "seventy-two hours of good behavior." To some degree, we're all on our best behavior during big family celebrations, but things do get a bit out of hand for some of these characters. Do you think that the

characters in the novel are trying too hard to behave well in front of one another, and as a result are lying about who they are and the state of their lives? Why is the facade so important for them to maintain? Or do you think this level of subterfuge is common at family gatherings like this? And if so, why do we feel the need to pretend around the people who are supposed to love us the most?

4. Throughout the story, Lily works tirelessly to put together the perfect graduation party for Dawn and Cody. Who is she trying to impress? What is she hoping to gain? And why does it matter so much to her? How does this change over the course of the novel?

5. Meredith tells herself that the reason her marriage with Roger didn't work out was because "Roger simply wasn't cut out to be committed to another human being, much less to a family." But when he marries Lily, Meredith is forced to acknowledge that this isn't true. How do you think Roger's marriage to Lily has changed the way Meredith views her own marriage to Roger, both the good parts and the bad? How do you think her perceptions change as the novel progresses? How does it affect Meredith's relationship with Lily?

6. Throughout the book, the past and present collide time and time again. For example, Joel runs into Kat, his college girlfriend, and wonders if he's been remembering things differently than how they actually happened, and Meredith is forced into close proximity with Roger, inevitably bringing memories to the surface. As a result, these characters are forced to reexamine themselves through the lens of time, and what they discover surprises them. Have you had any similar such experiences?

7. How would you characterize Roger's relationship with Dawn and Cody? Do you think the divorce colored their memories of him, if at all? And do you think their relationship will be different after graduation weekend ends?

8. Meredith and Lily are both extraordinarily different women and both fell in love with and married Roger. What do you think attracted them both to Roger in the beginning? How are their marriages to Roger similar—and different? Did Lily's revelation at the end surprise you? Why or why not?

9. Meredith thinks of Cody as "the easy child, the one who lends himself to bragging rights... Steady and stable, he reminds [Meredith] a little of herself when she was a kid." But Cody is the one who almost doesn't graduate and lands in real, serious trouble. And Meredith thinks of Dawn as someone who can "fly into a rage over nothing at all and the next minute burst into tears, which has the disconcerting effect of Meredith's never quite knowing what Dawn is thinking. Come to think of it, her mercurial mood swings are not so unlike her father's." Do you think parents naturally gravitate toward the child who's most like them? Why or why not? Has that been the case in your family? Do you think this dynamic will change in the Parker/Landau family after graduation weekend?

10. This graduation is Lily's first big family event and she takes the responsibility to heart. So much so that it almost kills her. After the shocking events of the family party take place, do you think the family sees her differently? And what do you think happens to Lily afterward? Does she stay married to Roger? Why or why not?

11. The heart of this story is coming to terms with the past, accepting your family for who they are and strengthening family ties. How does each character in the Parker/Landau family accomplish this? Which character did you feel closest to and why? Which character was the most unlike you? Did anyone surprise you at the end?

Meredith and Lily are extraordinarily different women—both successful and driven in their own way with big hearts. Which character did you relate to the most? Did your loyalties change as the story progressed?

Initially, I identified most with Meredith, who so desperately wants everything to go right for her kids and who can't imagine letting them go after graduation. Add to that the general stress of the weekend and having to deal with her ex-husband and his new wife, and all I wanted was for Meredith to survive the weekend with her dignity intact. But the more I got to know Lily (and fleshed out her past), the more I began to cheer for her, too. As the old adage goes, everyone is dealing with something, so be kind. Meredith tries to be kind, but she's not always successful. By the end of the book, I was rooting for both women. They may never be best friends, but at least I hope they have a better understanding of each other.

Throughout the course of the book, we hear from Meredith's, Joel's, Lily's, Dawn's and Cody's perspectives, but never Roger's. Why didn't you include Roger's perspective?

Well, to be honest, Roger always seemed a bit full of himself, so on some level I was probably wary of entering his mind. What if I didn't like what I found there? I do hope, though, that he becomes more appealing by the story's end, when we see that he truly cares for Lily and harbors some regrets about his bad behavior toward Meredith. Like everyone else in the book, Roger is vulnerable, but he's loath to show it.

When you began the story, did you know exactly how it would end? Were the characters' journeys solidified in your mind before you started writing? Did anything surprise you as you were writing?

I rarely know how a book will end before I begin—I wish I did! I have a vague sense of the plot, but for me, the characters and the setting always take precedence. I imagined all sorts of things going wrong over the course of the weekend but didn't know exactly what. Carol, Meredith's mother, surprised me in that she kept popping up, inserting herself into the story with an arch comment. Although she wasn't in the original cast of characters, she made sure to whisper in my ear while I was writing. Also, Lily's "issue" was always in the back of my mind because I think it's such an important, timely topic that we all need to be talking about. Colum McCann, author of the phenomenal Let the Great World Spin, once likened the process of writing to playing music—the idea being that you have to let the music take you where it may, which strikes me as a lovely and apt metaphor.

How has writing this book been different from writing your three previous novels?

I wish I could say that each novel gets easier, but I'd be lying. Every time, you have to stare down a blank page and begin anew with an entirely fresh cast of characters. I have noticed that I seem to be inadvertently truncating the time frame for each new book. My first novel, Three Good Things, took place over the course of several months; my second, The Summer of Good Intentions, over a summer; and my third, The Summer Sail, over one week. This book is set over a long weekend, so it presented new challenges in terms of packing a lot into a very short time period. Who knows, maybe the next novel will occur all in one day.

As the story progresses, the reader gets an inside perspective into three very different marriages in this book: Meredith and Roger's, Meredith and Joel's, and, of course, Lily and Roger's. Which relationship was the most fun for you to write about? Did that surprise you? Was there anyone you were rooting for—or not rooting for? And where do you see Roger and Lily in five years?

Meredith and Roger's relationship is bittersweet. There's still a kernel of love there, I think, but even after all these years, the wounds Roger inflicted haven't fully healed for Meredith or the kids. Meredith and Joel are probably my favorite couple and were the most fun to write. I love that Joel remains unflappable and amiable, especially given the circumstances, and I'm thrilled that Meredith finally found a good man. As for Roger and Lily, their relationship is more complicated, more ambiguous. Lily has a great deal to sift through before she even begins to tackle her growing sense of isolation in her marriage. It would be nice if they could stay together, but I suspect Roger and Lily have a long road ahead of them.

Best Behavior beautifully tells the story of a dysfunctional blended family who love one another but are just trying to get through graduation weekend. What inspired the story?

And why did you choose graduation weekend as the event that brought the Parkers and the Landaus together?

I wanted to explore the dynamics of a "modern family" up close, and a college graduation weekend seemed like the perfect pressure cooker to do it in. A lot of my friends also have "emptying nests," so college graduation—and all its attendant emotions—has been on my mind. And although my eleven-year-old is still very much at home, my two step-kids (not twins!) will be graduating college soon, reminding me that the question of "What's next?" isn't far away for any of us.

Before beginning your writing career, you were a book editor. How does your experience as a book editor inform your writing? What do you love most about writing? And what is your least favorite part of the process?

For me, the hardest transition from editor to author was resisting the temptation to immediately edit everything I wrote. I had to give myself permission to write clunky sentences in order to get a story down on the page. Otherwise, it would take me all day to write a paragraph! Being an editor taught me about overall pacing and character development, but it also taught me that it takes a whole team of gifted folks to make a good book. The fresh perspective that my own editor brings to each new manuscript always amazes me— and improves every story. The part I love most about writing is when the characters start to flow naturally and follow you around everywhere—to the grocery store, to the hockey rink, into the basement to do laundry. That's when I know I'm truly absorbed in my work. The hardest part is starting again, confronting a blank page.

What are your favorite books about families? Which authors capture the feeling of family for you?

There are so many! I'm just reading Mary Beth Keane's wonderful Ask Again, Yes about two families forever bound together by a tragedy. Lynda Cohen Loigman's The Two-Family House is another sweeping saga across generations that I devoured. I also love novels about, for lack of a better word, dysfunctional families, probably because they feel so real and so true. Anything by Emma Straub is on my list, as are Cynthia D'Aprix Sweeney's The Nest and Stephen McCauley's very funny My Ex-Life. I'm a huge fan of Sally Hepworth and Liane Moriarty, and then there's Elin Hilderbrand for delicious stories about summering families. Elizabeth Strout's intricately drawn worlds always feel achingly true, and her characters, vibrantly alive. As for the classics, George Eliot's Middlemarch would have to be my all-time favorite that touches on the dynamics of marriage and family ties.

What are you writing next? And can you tell us anything about it?

My new novel takes place at a tony Boston hotel on the water, where four separate guests' lives collide after a tragedy occurs on the premises. Stay tuned!